COATTAILS

Happy reading,

Margaret Lee Kiely

December, 1992

COATTAILS

Margaret Lee Kiely

Codornices Press
1991

Acknowledgments

To MY HUSBAND, John, whose fishing jacket provided the coattails for me to hang onto into adventure. I have experienced some surprising fly-fishing activities with friends in back country areas of far away places. John has checked my accounts of fishing and of its equipment meticulously, if sometimes painfully, from the point of revision.

And to Johnny, our elder son, not only my most constant supporter, but also my most thoughtful, knowledgeable critic.

To these two and to all the persons who have helped me bring these fishing stories from my mind into the reality of print, I give you my heartfelt thanks.

Margaret Lee Kiely
August 25, 1991

Contents

COATTAILS

KASHMIR

Houseboat

"RUG MERCHANTS ON RUNWAYS?" Phoebe MacLean's question stopped her husband midway through collecting his belongings. His eyes followed her glance out the window where women in brightly colored saris clustered around a rug merchant. The MacLeans and their friends were landing at Srinagar, Kashmir, after a long flight from San Francisco.

"They're not on the runway," James explained. "The Kashmiri FAA, or whatever it's called, wouldn't permit that. Too dangerous. The merchant is on the loading ramp." Her husband returned to his collecting.

But Phoebe continued, "Clever rug merchant. He isn't wasting any time. Do you think these women just came off a plane?"

"Probably from India, coming here to escape the summer heat. Maybe this is the best place for the merchant to display his wares. You'd better get ready to land."

"Just take one more look, James. The colors of the women's saris are like a rainbow of butterflies. See how everyone flutters around the merchant. He spreads his rugs before them like an array of jewels. It's a scene from *The Arabian Nights*."

Phoebe couldn't take her eyes off the exotic setting. What an exciting beginning for their Kashmiri fishing trip with their good friends from San Francisco, Ben and Susan Sergeant and Andrew and Helene Holcomb. "But James," she pointed out, "look at the heavy leather purses that the women are carrying. They don't go with their saris."

"Don't women tourists always carry heavy purses? You should know that. Hurry, Phoebe, gather up your own magic carpet, or you may miss the fishing trip."

Reluctantly, Phoebe prepared for departure, but her mind was still on the Indian women. She wondered if she'd ever be close enough to a rug merchant on this fishing trip to make a purchase herself.

At the baggage counter, a Kashmiri man, black caracul hat set on his head at a jaunty angle, came hurrying to meet them, arms outstretched in welcome. "I give you greetings! I am Mr. Tunda," he said. "I am your fishing guide and your host at my houseboat."

He pointed to a line of men waiting attentively. "These are my brothers," he boomed. "Give them your baggage tickets and follow them to the cars. They will take you to Lake Dal outside of town where my houseboat is moored."

One brother came toward the three women, bowing elaborately. "I am Jabar. My parents have fifteen children. I am the twelfth. Follow me closely." He swept them through the crowded airport to a paved area filled with automobiles that looked more like hardshelled beetles than automobiles. He stopped at a clean but ancient car.

Phoebe wished fleetingly that she could have touched base with James before being whisked away, but they were already in the car before she even spotted him.

Jabar laboriously worked his way out to the road leading from the airport. He maneuvered the automobile into a queue, made up mainly of pony-driven carts, each bulging with so many passengers that some riders were forced to stand on steps descending from the rear of the vehicles. They reminded Phoebe of tourists and schoolchildren, hanging precariously to the open-air cable cars in San Francisco.

"Look at the decorations over the windows and the back archways where the steps come down. Garlands of flowers painted everywhere," said Helene Holcomb.

"Workers coming back to town from their jobs on the farms," Jabar explained.

The Kashmiri trip had been Andrew Holcomb's idea initially. He suggested it to Ben Sergeant and James MacLean, two good friends and fishing companions. They were enthusiastic about the trip. The three men invited their wives to come along.

Andrew and James MacLean were fellow engineers in the same San Francisco construction company. Ben was a corporate lawyer whose firm had long handled the legal work for this company. Through the men, the wives had become close friends.

Andrew's wife, Helene, was a very competent person. When she found an exciting new venture and broached it to her friends, she took on the research, whether it was a local hike or a trip to theatres in London or a Shakespeare Festival in Ashland, Oregon. Her friends valued highly her helpfulness and constant loyalty to them.

Susan and Ben Sergeant were a couple that melded their diverse interests in a way that enhanced their lives and frequently that of their friends. Ben was not only a brilliant lawyer, but he was equally outstanding in any activity that he pursued. For example, he was not satisfied with being a competent skier in the nearby Sierra Nevada Mountains. He became an outstanding helicopter skier in Canada as well.

His wife, Susan, was interested and knowledgeable both in art and music. She enriched their fishing with trips to local museums and concerts, and overcame the reluctance that the men might have about taking time away from fishing. To her credit were such experiences as opera at Glynbourne, England, and festivals in Salzburg and Edinburgh.

When the two taxis drew up to a large lake, Jabar told the women that this was Lake Dal. Graciously he escorted the women from the taxi to the boat landing. He gestured them over steps of a stile set in a stone wall.

On the other side of the steps they found small boats that looked like enclosed Venetian gondolas, with upholstery and cushions made of brightly flowered cotton fabric, different for each boat.

Phoebe was relieved when she saw that the men were joining their wives in their gondolas. A boatman poled them into Lake Dal. Phoebe pulled open the cretonne curtains as wide as they would go. Trailing her hand in the limpid water, she looked around.

Along the bank of the left shore, houseboats lined up, one after the other, like floating tract homes painted in cardinal colors. The only differences were the flower boxes and gangplanks.

Mr. Tunda's gondola stayed in the lead for the entire trip. He guided his small regatta sedately around a wide bend where Phoebe saw him speak to his boatman and gesture toward the shore. The boatman guided the gondola smoothly to a gleaming houseboat anchored alone. Flower gardens, riotous in color, bloomed along both sides of the deck. The boat was larger than any others that they had passed, and it looked very new.

Mr. Tunda's eyes gleamed with excitement. "My houseboat!" he called to the guests in the other gondolas that glided near him. "It has just been finished! We will dock here. Please follow me. You will ascend the gangplank and wait on the deck."

The Americans obeyed and after they disembarked, crowded onto the small front deck. Ribbons festooned the door, the entrance to the houseboat. "This is a housewarming!" Mr. Tunda boomed. "You are the first guests to stay in my new houseboat. Its name is *The Golden Dawn*."

Then, turning to Andrew, he thrust a pair of scissors into his hand. "Cut the ribbon, please. I understand that this is the proper way to celebrate a housewarming. My home is your home while you are here."

Gallantly, Andrew accepted the scissors and stepped forward. "Thank you on behalf of my wife and my friends for this honor, Mr. Tunda. I cut the ribbon and christen this new houseboat, *The*

Golden Dawn, an appropriate beginning for our fishing adventure in Kashmir."

They all glowed with pride in Andrew. On the shore, a crowd of Kashmiris stood nearby, watching avidly. "My relatives!" said Mr. Tunda with a sweep of his arm.

The relatives sensed that they were being introduced. The women bobbed heads and the men touched their peaked calico caps. To Phoebe, the caps resembled those that she used to make for her children out of folded funny papers, except that these were made of cloth.

The housewarming completed, Mr. Tunda led them through the door into a formal salon with intricately handcarved, heavily varnished furniture. He beamed paternally at the chairs and tables, which, they learned later, were all made by members of the Tunda family.

Finally he led them to a corridor that extended the length of one side of the wide houseboat and held four bedrooms in a row. "Each with its own bath," Mr. Tunda hastened to explain, arms spread wide.

"In one hour, after you have freshened up and begun your un-packing, we will meet on the upper deck. There, I will introduce you to a very important friend of mine who is coming for dinner." Mr. Tunda bowed and began his departure. Would his out-stretched arms disappear last, like the Cheshire cat's smile?

"Just a minute," said Ben Sergeant, their lawyer, who liked things well-defined. "Before you leave us, can we talk about where we will be fishing tomorrow?"

"Later," said Mr. Tunda, a response with which they were to be-come very familiar.

The Americans met on the upper deck before Mr. Tunda and his guest arrived. The lake shimmered in the late sun and the movement of life on its waters fascinated the visitors. Work boats, pleasure boats, and water taxis attracted their gazes.

Using the glasses standing ready on a tray, James poured wine for each of them to toast the beginning of their Kashmiri fishing trip.

"This is from the Bordeaux country of France, one of the few bottles that we brought," James explained. "We intended to bring more, but in Paris when I checked the amount of Kashmiri duty on wine, I found it to be 150 per cent per bottle. We changed our minds quickly about bringing a case. We sent the rest home from France with a business friend. Sorry. To our Kashmiri fishing trip!"

Mr. Tunda, arms outstretched, arrived with his guest. Phoebe couldn't decide whom the wide arms were welcoming, his friend or them. "This is Mr. Mohammad, my great friend," he boomed.

Mr. Mohammad began systematically to circle the group, saluting each member with a vigorous handshake and a low bow. This completed, he took a stance before the visitors and began a formal speech. Phoebe expected to see him take out his notes at any minute. "Many of my colleagues visit your country for graduate work, as I did. I attended Cornell University eight years ago."

He paused to accept a Coca-Cola from Mr. Tunda. Phoebe soon discovered that Coke and Pepsi were the national drinks in this Muslim country. Stock in the soft drink companies must be soaring as a result. "Move closer," Mr. Mohammad told them.

"On my first summer holiday at Cornell, a classmate took me to the Adirondack mountains. He provided me with a fly rod to use and began to teach me to fly fish. It changed my life.

"Several years later, when I returned to Kashmir, I was unique in my knowledge of fly-fishing. Therefore, I was the logical candidate for appointment to the newly created job of Superintendent of Fishing. In this capacity my goal has been to eliminate spin-fishing from my country! Tomorrow you will see how I have accomplished this. There is now only one stream where I allow spin-fishing."

"How have you managed this heroic feat?" asked Ben directly.

"You will find out later," Mr. Tunda interrupted to explain firmly. "Dinner will now be served." He gestured toward the steps.

In the dining salon, the guests found a table set for seven, with a Tunda relative standing behind each chair. Mr. Tunda did not sit with them, but he hovered nearby during most of the meal.

The main dish was lamb curry. Mr. Tunda hastened to announce that the curry seasoning was made by his mother. "I think her curry spice is the best in our land."

"I buy my curry in a small yellow box at the grocery store," Phoebe said.

Mr. Tunda cast a glance full of sympathy toward her. "In Kashmir, each family makes its own. My mother will not even tell me her recipe."

The lamb dinner was followed by a serving of fruits so exotic that the only ones Phoebe recognized were the mangoes. These were peeled and sliced by the attentive family members, standing at alert behind each chair.

When Mr. Tunda reappeared after a brief absence, he told his guests that even though people of his faith did not drink coffee or tea, he served fine blends of both on his houseboat. "You will now return to the salon where my brothers will take care of you because Mr. Mohammad and I need to conduct some important business."

He gestured to direct his guests toward the salon and continued, "Tomorrow, after a fine sleep and an English breakfast, you will leave at nine o'clock by water taxi for fishing." Looking at Ben firmly, Mr. Tunda continued. "At that time, but not before, I will tell you about the place where Mr. Mohammad and I have decided that you will fish first."

"We will be most interested to hear," Ben answered.

"Good night, all. I shall include your fishing goals in my morning prayers at four a.m.," said their host.

Before they went to bed, Phoebe and James climbed again to the upper deck. Lake Dal was luminous in the starlight. The water lapped against the houseboat. "Can you believe where we are?" Phoebe asked, slipping her arm through James's.

"Or that tomorrow we will be fishing for brown trout in Kashmir?"

9

"We'd better get to bed fast," said his wife, turning toward the steps. Then she stopped and pointed low on the horizon. "Look, James, a sliver of a new moon. We'll have a full moon while we are in Kashmir."

"Seen from a houseboat on a lake."

"Goodnight, sweet prince. The moon will have to get along without me until tomorrow night. I'm exhausted."

Force Majeure

THE NEXT MORNING, after a large English breakfast of porridge and eggs, with goat cheese providing the local touch, they stepped from the dock into the waiting water taxis. The MacLeans found that Mr. Tunda was in their boat.

Surrounding the fishing party were other smaller native boats, each occupied by two women. While one poled, the other dredged up what looked like seaweed. Mr. Tunda explained, "The women are harvesting seaweed for fertilizer. That's what makes our vegetables and fruits healthy, very healthy," he added.

Another small boat, so burdened with vegetables that it was a marvel that it stayed afloat, drew up beside them. The boatman spoke briefly to Mr. Tunda. When he had poled away, Mr. Tunda explained, "My cousin. He grows the best produce on the lake. I buy all he can sell me for my excellent table." He nodded his head for emphasis.

As Mr. Tunda spoke, Phoebe's head nodded in unison. When Phoebe mentioned this to Helene and Susan in the taxi, they agreed that the nodding was hypnotic. "Sometimes I feel like a member of the family, at least my head does," Susan added.

"I feel that we are the only six people in the area who *aren't* related to him," Phoebe laughed. "Last night his mother's curry and now his cousin's vegetables."

The three women were put together again in Jabar's car. They melded into a queue of vehicles, mainly pony-driven public lorries driving workers to farms in the country. Each had its own distinctive, bright floral decorations. Passengers not only packed the lorries but hung precariously from the back steps.

"These people would handle our San Francisco cable cars like pros," Helene decided, "same motion, same skill at hanging on tight!"

They were surprised to see that the houses they passed in the small villages and even in the open country were all three stories high. "Why do the top floors seem to be empty? If they aren't lived in, what are they used for?" Helene asked Jabar.

"For harvesting and storing grains. When farmers don't have such large houses, they do their harvesting along the roadsides."

"I hope we get to see that," said Phoebe.

"You will," said Jabar, sounding very much like his brother, Mr. Tunda.

At each crossroad where the jitneys stopped to pick up passengers, people congregated, squatting as they talked. In the doorways of nearby houses, other people rested on their haunches as they visited and watched. "I see Kashmir has its own kind of squatters," Susan commented, "and I haven't seen a glimpse of a table."

"Aren't the rainbow-colored tufts on the pony harnesses wonderful?" Phoebe said. "How our Emily would love to see a pony-driven bus, or, better, to ride in one! I'm sure I can't take a pony or a pony-bus home to her, but at least I'm going to try to buy her a pony collar from a harness."

As they drove further from town, the farmhouses had more land between them. Each field now seemed to be a diked rice paddy. Most of them were flooded with water.

Entire families were working in the paddies, some people thinning small rice plants and tying them in bundles, others carrying these bundles to paddies that had been partially drained.

There, young children were planting the young rice shoots, followed by agile barefoot boys who watered each one. They balanced on the dike walls like Olympic acrobats, carrying the water in small, long-handled baskets in the shape of hummingbird nests. The baskets were so closely woven that they held water.

So fascinated were the women with the rice paddy operation that when their driver abruptly turned off the main road, following Mr. Tunda, Phoebe had trouble refocusing on the fact that this was a fishing trip. They stopped near an open field where a group of Kashmiri men waited. They were all dressed in khaki, the only difference being the fabric of their cocked hats. Mr. Tunda motioned everyone out of the cars.

"These are your guides," he announced. "Mr. and Mrs. Sergeant, you will fish the beat nearest here, with Jabar staying with you. I will take the Holcombs to their beat, and my brother Answar will take the MacLeans. At one o'clock we will bring you back to this spot where we will have lunch. Good fishing."

Answar motioned to the MacLeans to follow him. Two Kashmiri men joined them. One picked up the fishing rod cases, as well as James's fishing bag, watched closely by James. Phoebe brought up the rear. When they arrived at the river that meandered serenely through farmlands, Answar stopped beside an imposing sign, white with large black letters, that proclaimed, "To spin is to sin." James stood, amazed.

"Do you suppose this is the way Mr. Mohammad intends to eliminate spin-fishing, Phoebe? Nothing more? No warnings to prospective poachers? No announcement of penalties, just the sign?"

James couldn't budge from the sign. "I guess every stream except the single one that Mr. Mohammad has reserved for spin fishing has such a sign. Just think, first, the poachers need to read English and then they need to be very law-abiding to make this system work."

Answar touched James's arm to indicate that he had called the other two Kashmiris over. "This is your guide. His name is Tarak. The other man is your spotter. His name is Nath. I will return here for you in time to take you back for lunch." He bowed himself away.

James watched him hurry away and told Phoebe, "How's that for the briefest fishing instructions ever? Exit Answar. I bet these two men he's left us with don't even speak English."

"At least it's nice to know their Christian names, I mean *first* names," Phoebe laughed, remembering their Muslin religion. She looked hard at the hats of the guide and spotter, whispering out loud, "Tarak, green-checked hat. Nath, red polka dots on blue."

After Answar left them, James sat down, pulling his tackle box near. "So, after hours of planning and miles of travel, our fishing is about to begin."

Phoebe opened the two rod cases for James as he examined the river. "Even though the water's pretty high, let's try dry flies first," he decided. "Then if they don't work, we can switch later to nymphs." He opened his fishing box and Phoebe took the covers off the rods.

James began to set up his rod. Phoebe paralleled his actions, proud of her self-sufficiency. First, she connected the sections of the rod securely, then she fastened the reel on the rod and strung the line through the guides. "Now what dry fly? Can I use a Deer-haired Yellow, the one Andrew fishes with all the time and calls a goofus bug? I prefer the name, *Deer-haired Yellow*."

"Sure, it's always a good one," answered her husband, preoccupied with putting a grey fox variant on his leader. Phoebe admired his skill. She could also tie on her own flies, and did, but she always worried about whether her knots would hold, even though she threaded the line through the loop extra times before giving the final pull.

They noticed that the two guides had been joined by a collection of friends. From the moment that James took out the flies and they each began to tie them on the lines, the sounds from the Kashmiris rose from a murmur to an angry buzz. "They don't like something we're doing," James said. "Maybe it's our choice of flies."

"They probably are used to worms, or, perish the thought, spinners," Phoebe answered.

"Unless they are involved in a quandary over whether to earn money as guides and spotters or to confuse us so that we won't catch the fish that could otherwise feed their families," her husband conjectured.

James called the guides to him. They separated from their friends and stood attentively. "I fish with artificial flies. Do you speak English?"

They both nodded affirmatively and jabbered in their own tongue. They motioned James to pull off the fly. He shook his head and cradled the fly in his hand as he waved them off. They retreated, mumbling, to their friends.

The sound grew louder, almost threatening. "It doesn't sound like a quandary to me, more like the beginning of a conflict. I don't think I like it," Phoebe stated.

But James was unperturbed. He stood up, stretched, and methodically began to check his fishing vest pockets for essentials: fly box, dressing, pliers, mosquito repellent, and Polaroid glasses. As he picked up his rod, Phoebe asked, "Are all the bets settled among you men? Is it the usual, longest and most for each day and the same for the whole trip?"

James nodded, "Plus all the specials. The betting is on fish caught either on dry or on wet flies. I'll hike downstream first, then fish up to meet you. You start right out fishing upstream, and I'll join you in time to meet Answar and return to the lunch spot. Are you sure you have everything you need?"

"Yes," Phoebe told him. "You spoil me, and I love it," she said, waving him off. Half the crowd of noisy Kashmiris followed her husband and Tarak. The other half waited expectantly for Phoebe and Nath.

She fought the temptation to skip fishing, to find a comfortable rock to use as a backrest while she contemplated the river or perhaps wrote in her journal, thus neatly evading the Kashmiri followers.

But she began to lecture herself silently but firmly. "Don't be critical of people just because their customs are different. I'm sure they feel their protests to us are well-founded. After all, this is their country and we are only visitors here."

Strengthened by this brief philosophical interlude, she started walking upstream along the bank. So did the Kashmiris. When she found a likely spot where a fish might be feeding in the shadow of a rock, she stopped. So did the followers.

She let out some line and began to false cast, watching that her back cast stopped at one o'clock and stayed high enough to avoid bushes. Conscientiously she stopped the forward line at eleven o'clock, releasing it briskly as though she were throwing a ball hard across the stream, hoping that when she propelled it to the river it would stretch out in a straight line on the water.

The first casts over the water resulted in so many wiggles in the line that she couldn't possibly expect a strike. But when she finally began to straighten out her casts and the fish still didn't strike, her annoyance cut through her concentration.

She began to be conscious of a continuing sound behind her. What was it? She cast again. It was the Kashmiris. After each cast, they let out a long, loud disappointed sigh. She found that the only way to keep them quiet was to false cast.

She'd cast five times and steel herself for the Greek chorus. Then she'd false cast for a breath of quiet. Then she'd cast again. When she moved, they moved.

Her casts improved from the practice, but no fish responded. The Kashmiris continued to moan.

Time after time, her cast gave the fly a good float, right under the nose, she was convinced, of some invisible fish. "Take it, silly," she scolded. "You know I can't fish too long in one stretch of river. I'll soon need to move on. Hit it!"

That did it. A fish struck. Smartly she set the hook.

Not a moan from behind her. Carefully, she reeled in when the fish was quiet, letting line run out when he swam upstream. He made one splendid jump. Who said that browns don't jump? He

15

looked seventeen inches to her, at least. Almost a counter. In the men's contest, eighteen inches was the length required to count, but the women weren't in the contest.

The purpose now was to land the beauty, measure him and release him. The excitement of the first strike of a trip burst upon her as if it were the first strike of her life. She had always been convinced that the fish had the advantage. He could see her movements and she could only guess at his.

Suddenly, as if to prove the point, the fish jerked the line out and swam away. The battle was on. She was horrified to see her rod tip forced into a deep dip. She heard the Kashmiri chorus suck in its breath and begin to moan.

Holding the rod firm, inch by inch, she raised the tip. To her relief, the line held. Finally the rod tip was upright. Her audience exhaled in relief. But it was only momentary. The fish was off again, swimming away hard.

She held her stance and began the whole process again. She kept her grip firm, reeling in when possible, releasing when necessary. Her concentration riveted on the fish. For a fleeting moment, she yearned for an English-speaking guide at her elbow, comforting and encouraging and instructing her. Sssh. Concentrate. Eyes and thoughts only on the fish.

She risked a quick glance over her shoulder and spotted a break in the steep bank where the river had cut out a small beach. Could she make it to the beach by herself and still manage to hold the fighting fish taut?

Not yet. Halfway to the beach the fish took off again. She fought to maintain her footing and get the zinging line under control. Step by painful step she made it to the beach. The fish fought until he was as tired as she was. He couldn't run again. She brought him into the shallow water where he lay inert.

She reeled him gently up on the pebbles and held him with one hand just long enough to loosen the line in order to place the rod beside him briefly for a measurement. Next, with one hand she loosened the line to enable her to take the pliers from her fishing vest pocket and, with a quick twist, to release the fly from the mouth of the fish.

She lifted the fish firmly and, steadying him against the front of her jacket, carried him to the stream. Pointing his head upstream, she eased him into the water and stroked him gently until he caught his breath. He gave a joyous wiggle and swam away, a happier, wiser fish.

Suddenly, a chorus of angry shouts beat down upon her from the Kashmiris on the bank. A shower of stones pelted down from above her. The crowd of jabbering Kashmiris descended to the beach and formed a semicircle around her. They kept gesturing to the stream, then at her, howling in disbelief. She had released the fish! She felt threatened and very separated from James.

How could she try to explain? All she could do was keep shaking her head and keep motioning them away. After what seemed like forever, the Kashmiris climbed back up the bank, but the sound of their mutterings still buzzed around Phoebe's ears.

She washed off her fly, blew it dry, put on more dressing, and walked down the bank to another fishing pool. Wearily, she thought of other things that she might like to be doing, like shopping in Srinagar. "The Superintendent of Fishing has his work cut out for him, teaching his guides and spotters about Catch and Release fly-fishing," she thought.

The next curve brought Phoebe, and again her Kashmiri followers, to a school yard. Under the branches of a huge banyan tree, she found young Kashmiri students sitting at plank tables, pursuing their studies and writing industriously on small slates. Phoebe noted the British flavor of the scene and remembered that at one time, most tourists in Kashmir were English families living in India.

In a strong British accent, the young Kashmiri schoolmaster came up to her and inquired politely about her fishing. She answered, equally politely, and intended to request permission to observe his class. But she changed her mind when she saw the guides and their friends belligerently airing their grievances to him.

She ignored them all and walked on, continuing to fish, not always casting to a fish, but just casting. Suddenly, to her surprise, she had a strike from a cruising fish. James always said that browns didn't often strike when they were cruising, as salmon did. Here was the exception, one swimming away with her fly.

She set the hook and began to follow the fish as he swam upstream. He seemed large and very determined. She quickly glanced backward and saw that the whole class was following her, probably pursuing the study of a new subject entitled 'American Lady, Fishing.' Each student had a hand raised above his slate, poised for note-taking. A lesson in science? In sociology? She wished that all the students weren't watching her so eagerly.

Suddenly, the line went limp. She reeled and stopped, then reeled again. There was no feeling at the end of the line. It could mean only one thing, no fish. She had lost him.

Nearby, she heard the clipped British voice of the schoolmaster say, "Rotten luck. But carry on. Cheerio." He began herding his class back to their more routine lessons. At least the students didn't scream at her as the spotters did.

Instead, they formed a line and followed their schoolmaster. Now, what would he tell his class? Would she and her fishing become a major study topic? "Fishing . . . a sociological perspective." And would his clipped intellectual analysis be followed by a heated debate from some students who might be supporters of the Kashmiri guides' point of view?

At the next bend, a stone bridge crossed the river. On the other side, Phoebe found herself in a farmyard full of animals. As she progressed, the cows, horses, and sheep moved slowly away, to the cackle of chickens scattering brainlessly at her approach. Under the bridge, she saw two dark shapes that looked like large fish. Too much barnyard animal pollution around here even for Catch and Release.

Anyway, fish that large had probably learned to resist worms, spinners, and anything else offered by the farmer's children or by the farmer himself. She moved on.

She followed a straight stretch of river beyond the farmyard. In the distance, she could see sunlight flashing on James's rod. She walked toward him, casting occasionally to keep the Kashmiri chorus silent.

She kept thinking of Robert Louis Stevenson's poem, *The Shadow*:

> I have a little shadow that goes in and out with me,
> And what can be the use of him is more than I can see.

only she had half a dozen shadows!

When she and James arrived at the meeting place, they had a few minutes together before Answar arrived. "How did your morning go?" she asked.

"Fine. Isn't it a beautiful river? I caught one counter, eighteen inches and a half."

"What happened when you released it?"

James laughed. "All hell broke loose. You must have caught a fish too, to ask that question. I hope their noisy reaction wasn't too upsetting for you. By the way, don't mention my fish when we are having lunch. I will, at the right moment."

"O.K., boss."

"How long was yours, Phoebe?"

"As well as I could tell, seventeen inches or so before the motley crew descended. I couldn't make them go away. Their noisy disapproval felt pretty threatening. You're going to have to love me a lot to make up for my fishing under such conditions!"

"O.K., sweetheart."

At the lunch spot, they found their friends already seated on the ground around a picnic cloth held down at each corner by an upright brass container holding four vessels stacked in the frame. "Food stays very hot in these carriers. You will see," said Mr. Tunda.

"When we go shopping, *if* we go shopping, I must have some of these," said Helene.

"Me too," said Susan.

"I'll make it unanimous," Phoebe added. "Did you two fish?"

"I hiked," said Susan.

"I'm saving up for this afternoon," Helene replied.

"Let me tell you what to expect," Phoebe began and told them about the reaction of the Kashmiri followers. She stopped when she heard Ben ask a question.

"How'd you do, MacLean?"

"How did you do?" James reversed the question.

"I don't mind telling you," Ben answered. "Andrew beat me by a good half-inch. I accept defeat."

"But how long was the fish?" James asked.

"I smell a contest," said Andrew. "All right, mine was eighteen."

"Mine was eighteen and a half," James announced, "and fat."

"What did you take him on?" Andrew asked.

"A minnow muddler. The water was too high for a dry fly, so I switched to a wet."

"Now, just a minute, MacLean," said Ben the lawyer. "I need to mention something that Andrew and I decided just before you came in for lunch. Actually, we started discussing it on the houseboat. In light of the distance we have traveled to fish here, and, I might add, of the considerable expense that we have all gone to, plus the fact that one of our trio only fishes with dry flies—in light of these facts, we have decided that we will employ *force majeure* to change the rules of the contest. For the duration of this trip, we will fish with dry flies only."

"Well, I'll be damned," said James, "an autocratic change from the initial agreement between the three of us when I wasn't even present. I can see that I am overruled, but next time, I want representation. And at this moment, I demand that my fish, taken on a wet fly before I knew that the rules had been changed in my absence, be counted the winner this morning."

"Fair enough," said Andrew.

Ben chuckled, "You agreed too fast, James. I didn't have a chance to bring up my next argument that I think is rather clever, if I do say so myself."

"Pipe down, barrister Ben, else I might bring a challenge to your case," James said. "I accept, under these conditions: first, that my fish win this morning's contest, and, second, that you both accept an additional ten dollar bet with me, that, using a dry fly according to the new rules, I catch the biggest fish of the trip by a half-inch or better."

"Agreed," came a quick response in unison.

Phoebe turned to Susan. "I can't believe James. He sounds more legal than your Ben!"

"They both sound like little boys to me," Helene said.

"They are," Phoebe concluded.

Mr. Tunda offered to deliver the women to their husbands a little later in the afternoon. They declined, since Susan and Helene had decided also to go fishing after lunch. "We're motivated undoubtedly by curiosity to see the Kashmiris in action," Susan admitted.

"But remember, you have to catch a fish first to see the Kashmiri show!" Phoebe added.

At the place where Mr. Tunda deposited her, Phoebe was surprised to find not only Nath, the spotter, who had been with her that morning, but again all his friends, patiently waiting at the beginning of the beat assigned to her. She could see James and his guide some distance upstream. The spotter took charge immediately.

She fished for some time religiously where Nath gestured, but with no results. Wrong religion? Not a Muslim? Finally, with a flourish, he brought her to a spot obviously special to him. He pointed across the river where there was a line of willows. It was immediately apparent to her that the river was too wide for her to cast to the other side, even from midriver. He beamed emphatically, pantomiming a cast across the stream. She realized that protesting was futile. She nodded her head and entered the river.

Gingerly, she waded into the stream for as far as she felt reasonably secure. At least she had no back shrubbery to contend with. But the solid willows ahead of her, interspersed with a few small trees, were a different matter. The water line on her waders was approaching her waist. What was she doing out here?

Sounds like catcalls came from the watchers, dry and safe on the shore. In order to put off returning to face the Kashmiris' reaction, she decided to cast from that spot but not to go any deeper. She cast steadily with no strikes. She wasn't spanning enough distance.

One last cast. She dug her feet firmly into the gravel and cast wildly, with all her strength, too much strength. The fly did reach the opposite bank, but it lodged itself high on a branch of a small tree. That fly was irretrievable. Now she could retire from this impossible fishing. She began to tug to break the fly from the leader.

The friends of the Kashmiri guides began to raise a howl that was the most uninhibited yet. She glanced over her shoulder to see what was going on. They were pointing across the river where the spotter and a friend were climbing the tree. Soon they reached the fly and released it smartly. They called for her to retrieve it. This was a nightmare that she couldn't get out of.

Nath motioned strenuously for her to resume casting. He began looking for a place shallow enough to recross the stream and far enough from her not to disturb a fish. When she saw him find such a crossing place, she looked around for his helper. He had left his helper still perched in the tree! No vote of confidence in her, certainly.

In spite of herself, she began to admire the spotter's persistence. What a fly fisherman he would have made in a different culture!

The chorus on the bank behind her was beginning to tune up for action. What a fix she was in. Why wasn't her loving husband here to extricate her?

Finally, she anchored her feet securely enough again to recast. She was positive that the fly would fall safely short of the bank and the tree. And it would have, except for a playful gust of wind that carried the fly straight into the tree to the branch where the helper sat. He unfastened it deftly and firmly motioned her to cast again.

Didn't he realize that no self-respecting fish would strike after all this commotion? She motioned that she wished to move. He signaled back that she needed to carry on right there. Resigned, she began a delaying action. She took out her fly box, balanced her rod under her left arm, and began to replace her very limp fly in midstream, a feat that pleasured her soul and also gave a rest to her casting arm.

A short distance downstream, she saw James fishing upstream to meet her. At last, she had her excuse to stop this ridiculous marathon in which she had become involved because of her spotter. She needed to join her husband.

Turning toward the shore, she began to reel in as she walked. Suddenly a fish struck her trailing line. It gave a steady pull but no strong run or leap. She reeled in as smoothly as she could while she continued to walk backwards to the shore. The fish seemed strangely accommodating.

She found a small beach barely large enough to hold a fish, much less land him. She maneuvered him into the cove, only to feel the line go absolutely dead. Was the fish off? She applied pressure as hard as she could, hoping he'd break off. The line didn't reel in. The fish was applying pressure too! He was holding.

Continuing her backward walk to the beach, she touched land. She reeled in fast, lifting her rod as high as she could. Jerking hard on the rod, she landed the fish on the sand. She put a firm hand out to hold him and laid her rod beside the fish to measure its length.

In her fishing jacket pocket, she found her pliers and freed the fly from the mouth of the fish, ready to return him to the stream. As if on cue, the Kashmiris scrambled down the bank, two men in the lead. This time, each had a club in his hand. They rushed to reach the fish before James did. They were racing with him.

Phoebe dropped to her knees, covering the fish with her arms. James arrived, yelling fiercely. He jumped down the bank, pushing the men away from Phoebe and the fish. He grabbed one Kashmiri's club and brandished it like a sword, yelling, "Get away from my wife's fish. Clear out."

The men clambered up the bank on all fours and disappeared. Phoebe exhaled the breath that she didn't know she had been holding. She felt the tension in her body begin to disappear.

James picked up the fish and carried him to the water, stroking him gently and pointing his head upstream. Phoebe watched anxiously. After what seemed an endless time, the fish slowly began to move sideways back and forth, still cradled in James's hands. When sufficient strength returned to him, the fish gave a strong movement and swam away. When Phoebe looked toward the bank, there wasn't a Kashmiri in sight.

Phoebe hooked her arm in James's and kissed him gratefully. "Thank goodness you arrived when you did."

"I had to save my fishing pal," he responded simply.

She smiled at him, but her mind was still on the Kashmiris. "James, if a solicitous wife were to ask a spotter when he came home at night, what kind of day he had, do you think he would say, in Kashmiri, 'If I tell you, you wouldn't believe it?' How did you do with your fishing this afternoon?"

"Good fun, but no counters. Oh, well, tomorrow is another day."

"And another river," his wife added.

Merchants and Fishing Camp

ANDREW HOLCOMB won the day's contest, with Ben close behind. Both fish were longer than James's. On the way back to Lake Dal in the dusk, they could see cooking fires glowing inside the houses and people squatting around them. "I'd hate to eat my meals that way," Susan decided judicially.

"But think how strong their thigh and calf muscles must be," Helene, a tennis player, added.

No pony carts accompanied them on the trip home, too late for public transportation. When they arrived at their own boat landing, they found other gondolas tied up there. Mr. Tunda explained, "Friends of mine. After dinner, you will meet them."

"Good, but I'm glad dinner comes first. Right now I could eat a horse," Andrew said.

"You mean a lamb," Ben corrected.

"Can we change first?" asked a feminine voice.

"Of course," Mr. Tunda said, adding proudly, "For the present, this is your home and your country. However, as your host, it is my duty, as well as my pleasure, to show you some of its treasures. That will be after dinner tonight."

The lamb again was delicious with homemade curry from Mr. Tunda's mother, served with fresh vegetables supplied by Mr. Tunda's cousin. The chapati bread was fast becoming a great favorite with everyone. "Too much so for me," Phoebe said.

Susan held up a piece of chapati bread. "You can see where the baker slapped the dough into his open palm and transferred it, shaped like his cupped hand, right into the oven. Maybe later Mr. Tunda can let us see chapatis being prepared."

"Later," laughed Helene.

After dinner, Mr. Tunda ushered them into the salon. With a grand gesture, drawing their attention to the whole room, he told his guests, "All the furniture here was carved in our own shop on the place. We will talk about our family furniture business later."

He then directed the friends to four men who stood quietly waiting. "These are my friends, all leading jewel merchants of Srinagar, here to show you their treasures. Because you are my guests, they will give you a very good price."

"So the stores come to Lake Dal," Helene said, a little ruefully, "instead of our going to Srinagar."

"I still want to see Srinagar," Susan said.

"Me too," added Phoebe. She heard Andrew ask one of the jewel merchants, "What about the duty?"

The gentleman responded, "I will explain that to you later. But first, let me show you and your wife my jewels. Our sapphires are world renowned."

"'Step into my parlor, said the spider to the fly'," Phoebe murmured.

"What did you say?" James asked. Phoebe didn't answer. James continued, "I think you'll like this shopping trip, dear. Come try it," he continued and led her to the tray of magnificent sapphires that one of the merchants had laid open for inspection.

"*The Arabian Nights* again. I've always thought that I fancied an emerald, my birthstone," Phoebe answered, "but I suspect that preference is about to be changed!" She turned her attention to the beautiful blue gems.

At an hour much too late for fishermen, each couple possessed a beautiful Kashmiri sapphire. "How can a stone that dark have so much fire and light in it? It's as though it were alive. James, what a darling you are. I am so thrilled that I'm even feeling tender toward the Kashmiri fishing guides!"

At breakfast, their host explained that they would be away from the houseboat for two nights, staying in a government fishing cabin.

"I would like each couple to pack one small bag for night clothes and other belongings. We will have two days of fishing in the foothills before we return."

Later, while they waited for Mr. Tunda to finish supervising the packing of a basket and ice chest of foodstuffs, Susan told her friends what, besides the sunrise, she had seen early that morning from the upper deck. She noticed much activity around the Tunda family compound behind the houseboat. Then she saw that Mr. Tunda, his brothers, and other male relatives, were all kneeling, facing east, and offering their morning prayers to Allah. "Where do the women do their praying?" she asked her friends.

No one could answer. Mr. Tunda arrived with the supplies. He loaded his guests' suitcases and the fishing gear into a large gondola. On the other shore, there was an additional car joining the usual morning procession heading for the country.

Soon they began to climb into the foothills, leaving the rice paddies and planted fields behind. The farm houses became smaller. They passed sawmills along the road and glimpsed snow on the distant peaks. "The Himalayas," Mr. Tunda told them.

Often, the road followed a river. "It's running pretty full," commented Andrew, "and side streams are bringing in lots of silt."

"Nature doesn't change with geographic boundaries, does it?" added Ben.

"Same fishing conditions, same runoffs. A Royal Wulff might be in order today, easier for a fish to see if he tries to look in this kind of water," finished James.

"We will go to the cabin before we fish," Mr. Tunda told them. "This will be simple living, not like my fine houseboat. There are six places to sleep. You can choose where each of you will sleep."

The cabin had two rooms and a screened porch. In one of the rooms they found two single iron beds; two fold-out canvas camp beds and two yard chaises provided the choice for additional sleeping accomodations.

The other room was designed for cooking and eating. Meals would be prepared on an open grill, with a dome-shaped oven built above it. "I am the cook," Mr. Tunda told them, "and a very good one. After you decide on sleeping arrangements, we'll go fishing before supper."

Ben's fine legal mind picked up the challenge of choosing sleeping quarters. "This decision obviously calls for drawing straws. All in favor so signify."

"So long as we retain the option of sleeping on the floor if we deem it expedient," Andrew said.

James and Phoebe drew the chaises, which they decided to put on the porch. They set their duffel bags out there and were ready to go fishing. "From what I saw of the river coming up, the water looked too swift for waders," James decided. "Let's not bother putting them on now, Phoebe."

"Suits me. What fun to be together, James. I much prefer fishing with you than with a guide."

Small gnarled trees grew along the edge of the river. Their twisted roots were submerged in the stream while their upper branches offered good perches for dapping in case casting was too difficult, which it was.

Before long, the three men changed their strategy and returned to the cabin for their waders to give them more mobility. They jumped from rock to rock, discovering pools where small but very active fish provided them with an exciting hour.

The women's excitement came from their concern for the safety of their men. They all took to the trees. Phoebe's words of caution to James were lost in the loud, gurgling conversation of the river. She leaned against the tree trunk, saying prayers for James's safety and felt as though she were a damsel in Sherwood Forest instead of a fisherwoman in Kashmir.

When the couples returned to the cabin, Mr. Tunda was intent upon his meal preparations. Three chickens wrapped in large green leaves were baking in the oven. A pot of rice simmered on the back of the grill set above the smoldering coals. Mr. Tunda shaped chapati dough on the heel of his hand, and then put this bread in the oven with the chickens. A large bowl of tomatoes stood on a small table nearby, undoubtedly from his cousin's 'fine garden'.

"Next, I'll prepare the corn, grown on our own place," Mr. Tunda told them.

The men poured drinks from their small supply, for everyone except Mr. Tunda, whose Coca-Cola for religious reasons spurred the company's sales. The women soon joined them after changing scarves as a way of dressing for Mr. Tunda's special dinner. They found the men, using two folding camp beds pushed together as a table, playing a San Francisco style domino game, interspersed with fishing talk and conversation about the bets.

Andrew was summoned to the kitchen by Mr. Tunda. "Here's some news hot off the grill," he told everyone when he returned. "Mr. Tunda says that if the river farther up in the foothills where we will fish tomorrow is still high, we'll return to sleep at Lake Dal tomorrow!"

"You mean we'll have an extra unscheduled fishing day below?" Ben asked, a gleam in his eye. "What if we return to the *force majeure* stream?"

"I'm ahead of you, pal," Andrew responded. "I've already suggested that to our host. He told me he can phone the Superintendent of Fishing and arrange it, if we want him to."

"The *force majeure* stream suits me fine," James laughed. "The sooner the better. I intend to show you two up, and that would be a good place to do it."

"Slim chance," Ben said.

Mr. Tunda's dinner was masterful. They ate Kashmiri *haute cuisine* sitting on two folding camp beds.

Afterward, in order to avoid their makeshift beds as long as possible, the friends conversed on the cool porch until they couldn't keep their eyes open. Finally, they made up the beds with the well-worn cotton sheets and blankets that Mr. Tunda had provided and fell asleep with more ease than they thought possible.

One minor incident was reported the next morning. In the middle of the night, two husbands collided on their way to a comfort stop. "At least it was two people. That's better than one person and a large animal!" quipped Helene at breakfast.

Breakfast was hearty and hot: hot coffee, hot tea, hot porridge, hot eggs, hot chapatis, and hot sauce. The sauce also was made by Mr. Tunda's mother, with a red hot pepper content similar to the curry.

"This morning," Mr. Tunda told them as they were preparing to leave, "at the river where we will do our fishing, we may find a few other people. It is an area very popular with summer tourists from New Delhi. Also, the banks of the stream have been concreted to contain the spring runoff."

"Interesting," commented Andrew dryly.

"How is the fishing there?" James asked.

"It can be very good, but it depends on the water," Mr. Tunda responded.

A couple of hours later, the cars turned off the small road onto a larger one that continued toward the Himalayas. This road was full of traffic. "It looks too populated for our fishermen," Helene said to her car mates. "But maybe we're coming to a resort town with some shops."

Jabar, their driver, answered Helene's question about shops. "There will be a few shops, but they aren't at all like the ones in Srinagar," he told them.

"But we may never get to Srinagar!" Susan wailed.

With some difficulty, Phoebe came to a decision. "You two shop and I'll fish. Then, send word by Jabar if you think I should come join you."

"I know. You want the best of both worlds," Susan accused.

"I have accommodating friends!" Phoebe retorted with a smile.

The distant Himalayas were beautifully snow-capped. The mountain air from the open windows was intoxicating in its freshness. No wonder the Indian tourists liked to come here.

The Americans found out that the river running through the center of town was indeed caged in concrete, with a grassy area between the river and the street of shops. Families filled this park area that edged the river. Mothers in bright saris busied themselves with setting up picnics, small children ran around everywhere, with fathers lounging on blankets and grandparents sitting nearby on folding chairs. It was a mountain streamside scene different from any that they had ever experienced.

When the car deposited the fishermen with their equipment, many pairs of curious dark eyes followed every movement that the

Americans made. Susan and Helene immediately braved the stares and headed for the shops.

Mr. Tunda told the men, "Perhaps you will have more privacy if you cross to the other side by that footbridge. I have seen some large fish strike along the dike. Bringing them in is difficult because of the riprap on the face of the dike. You will need to be careful."

After advising the men, Mr. Tunda turned and saw Phoebe, waiting alone. She sensed his discomfort. Tensely, he asked, "You decided not to go shopping with your friends?"

Phoebe nodded. "I prefer to fish rather than to look at souvenirs."

He surveyed the river. "It will be better if you stay on this side. I will fish with you until I am needed on the other side. Then, perhaps, you will go shopping?"

Phoebe nodded again.

He positioned her, pointed to where she should cast, and then backed away, his eyes darting constantly to the other side of the river. Instantly, the space he vacated was filled by an Indian gentleman, ringed by his curious but timid progeny.

In a clear British accent, he introduced himself and asked where she was from. When he heard the words 'San Francisco', he launched into an enthusiastic account of a television show that he remembered seeing.

The Indian gentleman examined her choice of fly. His misgivings were more subtly expressed than were those of the Kashmiri guides, but present, nevertheless.

When she prepared to cast, he moved politely out of her way. But before she could make her second cast, another pleasant Indian gentleman took his place, showing off his own impeccable English and asking about San Francisco.

She was lucky. This time she made two casts before a polite cough announced the presence of the next observer. She was now opposite Ben Sergeant.

When she saw him get a magnificent strike she motioned, a little brusquely, to her current companion to be silent in order to try to hear the comments from across the stream. Offended, he moved away.

Ben's fish leaped above the rough water and showed himself to be a beautiful counter. Ben handled him masterfully.

She followed the adversaries upstream on her side of the river, barely avoiding several family conclaves. Jabar was with Ben, but Mr. Tunda left her abruptly to join the action on the other side, dodging expertly through family picnickers as he moved.

Ben let the fish run, reeling him in when possible. She knew he was hoping the fish would tire himself out. He worked to stay abreast of the fish and firmly managed to hold that position. Phoebe saw him motion to Jabar to run for the net. Ben's patience and strength amazed Phoebe.

She saw him switch his rod to his left hand without losing control of the line, in order to take the net from Jabar in his right hand. She knew that Ben would have only one try to land the fish. Unconsciously, she crossed her fingers and put her tongue in her left cheek, as the children used to do when they were small, their talisman to make a special wish come true.

Leaning far over the wall, Ben extended the net, keeping the line taut. In one fluid motion he swooped the net under the fish and lifted the net, with the fish in it, out from the water. Thrusting the rod into Jabar's hands, Ben lowered the net to the ground.

Immediately, both the fish and the net began to flop toward the dike. Jabar tossed the rod to safety and fell on the fish. "Twenty-one inches" she heard Ben say.

Ben extricated Jabar, the fish, and the net and lifted his prize. Phoebe saw him shake his head sadly. The magnificent fish was dead.

"At least we'll now have a fine breakfast fish," Phoebe thought, "or perhaps even a dinner fish, complete with a touch of Mrs. Tunda's curry."

She was sure that Ben would now be ahead in the contest.

Mr. Tunda motioned the fishermen to the cars. The friends congratulated Ben on his battle with the fish. The women had returned from their shopping with only an assortment of souvenir trinkets. They were ready to turn towards home. But that was not part of Mr. Tunda's plan.

His car led them farther up into the foothills to a high valley. Here, to their surprise, they found two quarter-mile pony tracks, side by side. On one, children were riding ponies, wildly galloping, little Kashmiri cowboys.

On the other track, Indian women sat astride their ponies and were being led around the ring by young boys. The women constantly urged the boys to make the ponies go faster. Their saris fluttered in the breeze as with one hand, they clutched the pommels of the saddles and with the other, their heavy leather purses.

"The sights you see on a fishing trip your mind could never conjure," Phoebe decided.

The trip back to the houseboat was long, but on the way they headed into a kaleidoscopic sunset. "Hard for the two drivers, but file it under 'M' for 'Memories, Unforgettable'", Helene said.

Jabar interrupted to point out a Gypsy encampment to the left. Dark tents were set behind open fires that matched the colors of the sunset. Outlined by firelight, women of all ages performed their evening chores while the men lounged nearby. A violin played softly.

The slanting rays of the setting orange sun burnished the brown faces and highlighted the profusion of turquoise and coral jewelry that the women wore around their necks, arms and ankles, and had braided into their dark hair. Black eyes were dusky mirrors of the sunset.

When the gondolas finally deposited the couples at the houseboat, the party found more friends of Mr. Tunda's, fur merchants, waiting for them at the gangplank. "After dinner, of course," Mr. Tunda reassured them. But that night, the travelers were tired and business was not brisk.

The next morning was Friday, and at breakfast Mr. Tunda

made an amazing announcement. "Today, my brothers, sons, and nephews go with me to the mosque. I will take you with me to Srinagar. You will shop while we go to the Mosque. First, you will go to a rug factory to browse until I finish my prayers and return for you. Then I will accompany you to other shops." He bowed himself out of the dining room before they could question him further.

"Oh, women. Oh, ye of little faith," said Andrew, "you're going shopping, after all."

"Have mercy on our poor wallets," said Ben.

"What, no fishing?" asked James.

But the men had lost their audience. The women had disappeared to change from fishing clothes to clothes more suitable for shopping.

Phoebe never forgot her first view of the ancient city of Srinagar. The buildings seemed to have been constructed by interlocking many delicate pieces of natural colored wood. Latticed windows and balconies, even latticed towers, gave the houses an airy, lacework effect. The window frames seemed to be parqueted. The effect was that each house looked like a different layer of an elaborate cake, each layer slipping slightly sideways from the weight of years.

"James," Phoebe said, "remember when our son, Malcolm, had the toothpick hobby, building amazing creations by glueing the toothpicks together? Don't these houses remind you of the things he built?"

"They do. His were slightly tipsy too, as I recall."

"And remember his outrage when the things would collapse?"

"I do indeed. That's when he'd come to Daddy to ask for structural help, usually impossible to perform."

"James," Phoebe said, "what keeps these Srinagar houses from collapsing?"

"Darned if I know. They defy all the rules of modern engineering."

By the time they arrived at the rug factory, the visitors were deeply absorbed in the personality of old Srinagar. History peeked out at them through the shutters of every window and balcony. The women were certain that from several balconies, they glimpsed exotic veiled harem women from ancient times watching them as they passed by.

They drove by citadels of the past, forts that spoke of conquerors like the incredible Greek, Alexander the Great, and of Akbar, the mightiest of the Moghul emperors.

As Phoebe stood with James outside the door of the rug factory, she gazed at the profile of the old city, punctuated by minarets and domes and the River Jhelum winding through it. "James, some day, we'll need to return here as tourists, not fishermen, and spend time learning more of the history."

James said, "I agree, but let's read up on the history first. Now, let's go see rugs."

Mr. Tunda introduced his friend, the foreman, who would show them around while he was at the mosque. "Pasang is a Buddhist from Nepal. He does not attend my mosque. I will return in time to help you with any purchases that you might want to make."

Mr. Pasang greeted them with a bow, hands together, fingertips up. "*Namaste*," he said, "my greetings."

He led them up steep stairs, explaining over his shoulder, "No women work here, only boys and men. The women work at home."

"What woman doesn't?" was Helene's aside.

Mr. Pasang continued. "My four sons are weavers here. My four daughters help their mother with rugs at home, mainly putting on fringe. Come this way."

They entered a room filled with looms, at which boys who seemed to be between twelve and sixteen years old perched on the loom benches. A caller sat on a high seat behind them and sang out numbers indicating which shuttle the boys should push through the loom. Each shuttle was filled with different colored thread. Older men were threading the idle looms with warp threads.

The boys sat with their backs to the outside windows. "We have no electricity here," Mr. Pasang explained. "We work only by natural light. The designers prefer it this way. The callers work from the design. The boys work by numbers only. Each number represents a different color thread."

When the callers took a break, the young weavers did also. They were eager to communicate with the visitors as they stretched their backs and sipped Coca-Cola. Mr. Pasang proudly introduced each of his four sons.

Too soon, he told the visitors that it was time to go downstairs to the showroom. Their eagerness to look at rugs overcame their reluctance to leave the weaving room and the friendly boys.

In the showroom, they first had to take part in a ritual ceremony, drinking hot tea in tall glasses. The friends found it awkward to drink the hot tea slowly and politely, surrounded as they were by hundreds of rugs, with eager young boys waiting to roll them out for their inspection.

Each couple staked out a corner. Two young helpers rolled out jewel-bright rugs, one after the other for the MacLeans. Soon a mountainous pile of rugs grew beside them. "James, how can we ever choose?"

James took charge. "I'll make it a little easier. Let's decide to bring home two for us and two for Emily and David, who haven't been married as long as the others. For the rest, we'll bring home one per family."

"It may take me the rest of the trip to decide," his wife said.

"Not me," James told her. "I have fishing to do."

James kept the MacLeans's discussion and decisions moving briskly. They had their choices made by the time Mr. Tunda arrived. He helped with the purchases and arranged for them to be shipped to the United States by sea mail.

When Mr. Tunda accomplished this action for them and for the others, he was eager to move the group to the shop of another friend. After all, this was a fishing trip and he was through at the mosque. "The finest *papier-mâché* work in the world is made

36

here," he told them. "I am taking you to my friend Abdul's shop. He has the very best."

"This is fun," Helene said. "I want to meet more of Mr. Tunda's friends."

The women bought lavishly at this shop: boxes, trays, bracelets, vases, as well as some elegant larger vases to make into lamps. "My Christmas list is shrinking wonderfully," Helene said.

"So is my birthday list. I'm even buying gifts for future weddings," Susan added, "and finally, gifts for myself!"

"Before we return for lunch, we have time for one more visit, to my friend, Mr. Subhana-the-Worst. His shop is filled with the very best Kashmiri embroidered scarves, bedspreads, and dress material."

"Why is he called the 'Worst' if he is the best?" asked Andrew, logically.

"That is his name," answered Mr. Tunda, matching logic with logic.

By the time they arrived at Mr. Subhana's shop, the men had become enthusiastic shoppers also. Phoebe was sure that the label, 'Subhana-the-Worst' didn't hurt the sales. "I'm fast outgrowing my 'goody' box," Ben said. "Do you have a spare chest around, Susan?"

After the purchases were paid for and wrapped, Mr. Tunda said, "Since my other friends will continue to bring their jewels and furs to my houseboat, and since I have a family shop for the finest Kashmiri furniture, I think we can now return to the houseboat."

He continued with a stern glance to Phoebe, "Then, after lunch, I would like to take the men to a stream that is not far away and has good late afternoon fishing."

The men gave a cheer, and Phoebe, like Br'er Rabbit, didn't say 'nuthin'. The shopping trip was most definitely over.

After lunch, the men changed into fishing clothes, gathered their gear, and went off, laughing like schoolboys playing hooky. Sometimes, Phoebe wondered why they made such an effort to

37

take wives along on their fishing jaunts. "It must be love," she decided.

That night, the cocktail hour on the upper deck was very special. The men had had good fishing, rather, good releasing, in spite of the antics of local guides and spotters. And for once the women had enjoyed time to bathe and dress in a leisurely manner for dinner. The moon added magic to the evening, painting a translucent ribbon across the lake.

James brought out one of the hand-carried bottles of French wine, *Château Pavie*. Amid such beauty, the quiet camaraderie made them reluctant to go down to dinner.

"It is necessary to finish dinner so that you can meet my friends, the fur merchants, who are returning," Mr. Tunda announced. "They are bringing coats for you to see. Then, perhaps, my brothers and I will show you our cabinet shop."

After dinner, they still found the furriers easy to resist, but Mr. Tunda saw to it that they didn't resist his furniture. The women would have preferred a tour of the nearby kitchen with its outside cooking fireplaces. Instead they all dutifully bought small tables carved by Tunda family members.

"Tomorrow, we return to the river that you call by that name that is hard for me to pronounce," Mr. Tunda told his guests after his family merchandising had been successful. "We shall have breakfast one-half hour earlier. Good night, all."

Preparing for bed, James broke the news to Phoebe that the next day would be their last day of fishing. "Mr. Tunda has just told me that he has been checking our connections in New Delhi. He has found that we need to leave a day earlier than we had thought necessary, in order to make our connections to Tunis. Are you sure that we want to visit Malcolm and his family in Tunis on the way home?"

"Darling, we need to. They live so far away from us. But what a rotten shame that you will miss some fishing time. How do you feel about it?"

"Of course, seeing Malcolm and his family is the important concern, but I intend to fish hard tomorrow, my last day and my last chance to catch up with Ben and Andrew, who are both ahead of me. I've thoroughly enjoyed this Kashmiri fishing trip, Phoebe, particularly with your fishing right with me. However, tomorrow may be slightly different."

"I understand. Good night, sweetheart, and good luck."

"I'll need it. Thanks, dear."

At breakfast time the next morning, Mr. Tunda was called to the telephone. When he returned, he announced solemnly that he had just been given a big piece of news by the Superintendent of Fishing. "He has done you a great honor. He is renaming the Veri-nug River in your honor. It will be called from now on by those words that I cannot pronounce, the river we go to fish today."

"You mean he is calling it the *Force Majeure River*?" Ben asked. He seemed to be choking into his napkin as he asked the question.

"Yes. The Superintendent of Fishing has spoken. It is a final decision." Mr. Tunda took off his caracul hat, the first time they had seen him without it. Was it in reverence to his friend or to the new name? "Andrew, if you will write the word down, I will give it to my friend."

"Thank goodness, we didn't need to leave yesterday!" James whispered to Phoebe. "Andrew and Ben will undoubtedly start a new contest when I leave, but today that river with the new name is calling me."

Excitement accompanied the MacLeans all the way across the lake. As she trailed her hand in the soft water on the way to the taxi landing, Phoebe already felt nostalgic for Kashmir. "I mustn't call this a gondola, James, even though it reminds me of Venice. I now know its correct name. It's a shikara. I will be sad to leave the shikara and this lake."

When they arrived at the familiar river with the new name, Jabar dropped James and Phoebe off at their beat. Tarak and Nath, guide and spotter, were there waiting for them with the same group of friends. "The internal management of this operation is very impressive," laughed James. "I'll go downriver first, then leapfrog back to where you are fishing. Together, we'll meet Jabar and return for lunch."

"James, today is too important for you to waste valuable time returning to me."

"Don't be silly. I can hike faster than you."

"I bow to the obvious. Thanks, dear. Taut line, and all that sort of thing."

History repeated itself with Phoebe's fishing. The Kashmiris did a good job of pointing out likely places where fish might be. She lost some, but she had some good strikes and brought in a couple of nice ones. She still had to beat away the thundering Kashmiri herd long enough to measure and release the fish. One fish was at least eighteen inches, as well as she could tell before the mob descended.

She walked on toward the meeting place with James, filled with the spell of Kashmir and saddened by the thought of their departure tomorrow. Here the river narrowed. The opposite bank was shaded by heavy willows. A flurry of wind parted the bushes and permitted an arrow-like shaft of sunlight to penetrate the shadows. She saw, lying close to the bank, a large dark shape.

Behind her, the Kashmiri chorus immediately came to life. They pointed, they called, they jumped up like animated exclamation points. Phoebe realized that a fish with that large a shadow was too big for her. "It would be perfect to put James back into the contest," she told herself.

She shook her head to the Kashmiris, marked the place with her red bandana, and hurried downstream to find James. When she drew near, she hated to break into the rhythm of his casting, interrupting his private world of fishing like a thoughtless intruder. But this might be important.

"James," she called, "follow me quickly. There is a huge fish upstream. I saw his shadow, and the Kashmiris are acting as though they know him by reputation. Come cast to him quickly. He's probably been evading fishermen for years."

"You cast to him," James called.

"I don't want to. He's too much fish for me. He needs a fair fight with a worthy adversary."

"You're an incurable romanticist, and I need a big fish. Lead on, do you have a scarf to give me, fair lady, for a token, when I do battle with this giant you've found?"

"My red bandana will have to do. I've already put it where I spotted him. But do hurry. I can hear the Kashmiris still yelling about the fish."

"All right. Here comes your knight."

"Don't forget to pick up your lucky red bandana," she called to him as he passed her. She followed more slowly, filled with tender thoughts for him. It was he who was the incurable romanticist, always had been, one of the reasons she had fallen in love with him.

When she caught up with him, she positioned herself on the shore where she could see the whole tableau that she hoped would develop. James's guide and spotter and a few of their friends joined her Kashmiri crowd.

Carefully, James assessed the situation and the problems that it presented. He looked over his supply of dry flies and lifted one from the box. He began to tie it on his leader. It looked to Phoebe like a Royal Wulff, a good choice for a shadowed lie, since its white fluff of feathers made it more visible. "At least, it would be to me, if I were a hungry trout," she told herself. "I hope this one is ravenous."

The Kashmiris didn't agree with the choice of fly. Their protestations were the most mournful dirge that she had heard from them yet. James moved into the stream and began to practice roll casting over the water some distance from the fish. He glanced toward her, shaking his head and shrugging his shoulders to show the difficulty of the lie.

She stood up, anxiously crossing fingers, tongue in her left cheek, and praying softly. She was so busy with the ritual that she almost missed James's first cast underneath the willows. The fish didn't rise to the fly, but James retrieved the fly so gently that there was not a ripple in the water to disturb a fish.

The Kashmiris sighed, their disappointment apparent, but did she sense a slight counterpoint of admiration mixed in with the negative chorus?

James continued casting very deliberately until he had covered every inch of the shadowy domain, dominated perhaps by a huge fish. Then he quietly reeled in enough to lift his fly out of the water. He examined it, dried it, and added more dressing. Then he went back to covering the arc completely one more time.

After this was done, he shifted position slightly and changed to a Deer-haired Yellow fly. That did not please the Kashmiri men. James's first cast from this location was too high. The fly lodged in a willow branch. Before the guide could even start toward the opposite shore, James gave a strong slow tug. The line came free, minus the fly but high enough in the air so that the fish, Phoebe hoped, had not been disturbed.

James replaced the fly. She couldn't tell what it was, but it looked like a Parachute Adams. Again, he cast to the same place, floating it by the mouth of any fish that might be waiting. Phoebe sneaked a glance at her watch, concerned that they would be late for lunch. During that moment, she heard a mass sucking sound from the watching Kashmiris.

She saw that the lower branches of the willow tree were moving, and so was James, his rod held high. The fish had struck and was swimming strongly upstream. James was leaping through the water, miraculously surefooted, keeping pace with the big fish so that his line wouldn't play out too fast.

Phoebe stumbled along the shore after the adversaries as fast as she could, trying to avoid any noise that might be a disturbance just in case James or the fish could hear anything. She would never forgive herself if she dislodged a rock or a shower of dirt that might alter the outcome.

KASHMIR

The Kashmiri men had no such concerns. They streaked ahead of her, their excited comments enveloping her like a banner of sound in a gale wind.

Ahead of James, the river widened. He plunged deeper into the water. Then Phoebe saw why. A marshy island split the river into two courses. If the fish reached the farther branch of water, that would mean sure disaster to James because, even in his waders, he couldn't follow the fish into water that deep.

Rod high, he felt for a good lodging place for his feet. Quickly, he reeled in as far as he could without too much strain on the line and made his stand there. Painstakingly, reeling in and letting out as little as possible, he fought the fish into the nearer branch of the river.

Walking backward, he maneuvered the fish toward the shore. Whenever he had a chance, James glanced toward the beach, obviously looking for a place to bring in the fish, if the line held that long.

"Maybe moments like this," Phoebe thought, "are the reason they call fishing a solitary sport. It's just the fisherman and the fish and nobody else."

The closer to shore James brought the fish, the more often the fish tried to run. "A second wind. Poor thing, he doesn't know he'll get released," Phoebe told herself.

James's rod was high, the line short. The fish was now close enough to be visible in the shallow water. Phoebe ran to the bank. "You can use my rod to measure, James," she called, "but the Kashmiris are right behind me. Tell me where your camera is so I can try to get a picture before they arrive."

"Back pocket, thanks, Toots."

He walked far enough inshore so that he wouldn't need to drag the fish very far across stones. "Get out of the way. I'm bringing him in."

He slipped the fish quickly out of the water, eased him above the rocks, and gently brought him onto the grass. Phoebe laid her

43

rod beside the beauty so that James could measure him, and then she located the camera.

She snapped a picture of James with the fish just as the Kashmiris thundered down the bank. But before they descended, James had released the hook from the mouth of the fish and taken him into the shallow water.

He pointed the fish upstream, to the howls of the Kashmiris, and stroked the stiffness out of him. The fish gained his breath and swam away quickly.

Phoebe closed her ears to the protests of the Kashmiris, her thoughts filled with James and the fish. Aloud she called, "My wonderful knight, you were marvelous. How long was he?"

"Over twenty-two inches. That satisfies me, contest or no contest. Of course, I'd like to win. But don't say anything about it when we join the others. I'll tell them myself."

Although they left the Kashmiris still howling on the beach, when they walked back to meet Jabar at the rendezvous point, the horde was already there, jabbering and gesturing to Jabar. It was obvious that they were giving him the Kashmiri point of view of the big fish story. Later, Phoebe insisted to James that she was sure that as the Kashmiris left there were small smiles on their faces, victory smiles?

At the picnic spot, everyone was gathered around the tablecloth spread under a shade tree. Brass nests of warming pots again held down the four corners. Phoebe must ask Mr. Tunda to be sure to order one set for her.

"How did you do, MacLean?" Andrew asked.

"The question is, how did you two do?" he parried.

"We've both had good mornings, nothing to beat Ben's on the concrete dike," Andrew said. "What a river this is for browns. I'll never forget it. I took three from one pool, none over twenty-one inches. But, as you know, you have to measure fast, because of the Kashmiris's protests."

"He also had two other fish," added Ben. "He must be tops for number of fish. My two this morning were beauties also. I have my work cut out for me tonight, reckoning up the contest. Now, don't hold up my bookkeeping, MacLean. How did you do?"

"Well," said James, stretching out his tired legs to prolong the moment. "It went this way. I was fishing alone in a quiet spot when Phoebe called me to a place where she had seen the shadow of a large fish. It was the world's worst location for a fisherman and the safest for the fish, a pool buried in willows too far away to cast to, even from midstream."

Phoebe broke in, though she knew how it annoyed James to have her interrupt a story. "When I first saw the shadow, the Kashmiris began to carry on wildly. They yelled and pointed and jumped up and down. That's when I ran after James. They knew that fish was special."

"What did they know?" asked Helene.

"Probably that he was one extremely ornery fish," James said and continued. "There he lay, safe in his willows. I had to roll cast to him the whole time. It went on so long that I knew he must be gone."

"Was he?" Helene asked.

"No, but when he struck, he took off upstream with me in pursuit, and darned if he didn't head for the opposite side of an island in the river that loomed up midstream. By the time I worked him back over to my side of the river, I was almost over my waders."

"Then what happened?" asked Susan, who loved a good story.

"I beached him. Phoebe handed me her rod to measure. She got my camera and managed to take a picture of him before the mob thundered down the bank, almost on top of us."

"Give us the size, man, and stop the dramatics. I'm waiting for the bad news," said Ben.

"Over twenty-two inches, and if I had had time to use a tape measure, it might have shown more."

"Nice fish, James, congratulations," Andrew said. "He'd be worth saving and mounting, if it weren't for the distance. How about lunch in a hurry, Mr. Tunda. I have to get to fishing. We still have this afternoon to beat James's twenty-two, plus."

But nobody beat it.

That night during cocktails on the deck, Ben worked on the books. James's record held. He had the largest fish so far.

The women talked quietly. "Mr. Tunda is right. This is truly our home for this trip, one surrounded by great beauty," said Susan. "I'll miss it when it's time for us to leave, though things won't be the same after tomorrow. Mind if I pop in on you, Phoebe, while you pack?"

"I'd love it. You too, Helene. The men won't finish settling the bets until long after dinner. Then, let's all come back to the deck one last time."

James won the money for the biggest, Andrew for the most, but Ben won the high total of cash. "Of course, I'm the scorekeeper," he laughed.

After dinner and packing, the friends returned to the deck, to watch moonlight on the water and to listen to the soft sounds of boats being poled along Lake Dal. "One of our best fishing trips," was Andrew's verdict.

"Very satisfactory," Ben agreed.

"On the Vale of Kashmir," James added quietly.

"Spoken like a poet," Phoebe whispered to him.

The next morning, Phoebe and James dressed in traveling clothes while the others donned the usual fishing gear. They were to cross the lake together. Mr. Tunda's relatives lined up on both sides of the pier, smiling and waving good-bye to the MacLeans.

On the other side of the lake, Phoebe and James began their goodbyes to the others. Ben interrupted them. "We're going fishing by way of the airport," he explained. "After we wave you off, we will take a final look at Srinagar."

So the MacLeans were sent away in style, with their fishing pals on the right side of the plane and the rug merchant on the left. "See, the same Indian women, looking at the same rugs," James pointed out.

"And the same butterfly saris and the same heavy purses!" Phoebe added. "James, there's so much more to fishing trips than just fishing—friends, strange places to visit, hot curry, merchants, pony carts. Let's keep adventuring, shall we?"

"Couldn't suit me more." James agreed, opening the book on Kashmir that he had brought to read on the trip down. He turned to page three.

ARGENTINA

San Martin de los Andes

MARIGOLDS AND MASS forever spelled Buenos Aires to Phoebe MacLean. Fly-fishing took her there.

When her husband, James MacLean, decided to join the first fishing trip offered by Orvis Company to fish in Argentina, she accepted an invitation to accompany him and his brother-in-law, affectionately called "Uncle Bill" by the family.

On the day they left San Francisco, James received a letter from Felipe Flora, their Argentine guide, stating that the anticipated party of twelve had dwindled to five.

In Buenos Aires, the Americans checked into the Hotel Grande and inquired about a Saturday afternoon Mass. Along with the directions, the concierge proudly pointed out that the nearby church was the finest in the city.

Colorful wooden figures of saints stood in separate niches in the high Baroque back screen of the altar. This afternoon, in the niche belonging to each saint, there rested a bouquet of orange marigolds. As the three travelers hurried down the aisle, flaming fingers of sunset streamed through the tall window opposite the altar, highlighting the vibrant color of the flowers. Full of awe, they slipped into a pew.

"It's like Moses's burning bush," Phoebe whispered to her husband, "like being present at a small miracle."

After Mass when they had returned to the hotel, Phoebe asked,

"Will we have time for a shower and then some duffeling before dinner? I hope so."

"Me too. I want to check my fishing gear," Uncle Bill responded.

"You mean you haven't checked it since we were getting ready to land in Buenos Aires?" James teased.

"You can never be too careful," Uncle Bill answered. "What would I do if I lost it?"

In the cocktail lounge before dinner, Bill was relaxed and in good form. His fishing equipment had weathered both the plane trip and the taxi trip to the hotel. He wouldn't need to make another major check until tomorrow morning after the trip to the airport.

Uncle Bill lived in Pittsburgh, a continent away from the MacLeans in California. Now over drinks, they reminisced about other fishing adventures that they had experienced together.

The trio had progressed to joyful anticipation of this Argentine jaunt when a short grey-haired man, accompanied by a slim young woman, abruptly interrupted their conversation. Apparently, he had been watching for them.

"I am George Simpson. This is my daughter, Joan. We have received a last-minute confirmation from Felipe Flora for our reservations to fish with your party. Since we will be flying with you tomorrow, may we join you now for a drink?"

Phoebe thought his question purely rhetorical. As he spoke he managed to seat himself, find a chair for his daughter, and assume the demeanor of the host of the party.

Over a hastily ordered Scotch, George Simpson recounted his life history, nonstop, from his birth in Michigan to his schooling and college in that state, and on to his university studies in Oxford, England. Then quickly, as though afraid of an interruption, he hurried into an account of his present occupation.

"Now I manufacture and promote commemorative stamps for my Oxford classmates, sheiks, kings, and potentates. It does help to keep up one's contacts, doesn't it? Joan followed me to Oxford and now that she has come down, as we call graduation in England, she is in business with me. The social aspects, of course, are very important."

"What a pity that California is no longer the Bear Republic," Phoebe interjected. She felt James's glance of disapproval at her touch of sarcasm.

Finally, James extricated Phoebe and Bill from the Simpson saga, without inviting the couple to join them. They strolled to a restaurant that the concierge had recommended to them, relieved to be just a threesome again.

The maitre d' suggested the beef grill. "The specialty of the house and of the country," he told them. Uncle Bill followed his suggestion. He ordered the grill and relished every bite.

"What were the delicious small pieces of meat that were served with the ribs and steak?" Uncle Bill asked the waiter when he returned.

"Cow teats," was the reply.

Suddenly Uncle Bill decided not to wait with them for dessert.

At the airport the next morning, the Simpsons were already waiting for them. Joan reported that she and her father could not get seats together on the flight to San Carlos de Bariloche. Phoebe assumed that it must be full. She was surprised to find quite a few vacant seats, including the one next to Bill, whose seat was right behind them.

Phoebe saw Joan Simpson talking emphatically to the stewardess and gesturing toward Uncle Bill. In a few moments, with a pleased smile, she floated down the aisle to the seat beside Bill, as though she were joining a friend at a garden party. "Oh, Bill, I do hope you don't mind if I call you that. I know we'll find that we have much in common, and I do so dislike sitting with strangers. Surely you won't mind if I join you."

"Uh . . . I thought this seat was taken, Miss er . . . a . . . Stimson."

"*Simpson*, you naughty man, *Joan Simpson*. Now don't you ever forget my name again. I want you to think as highly of me as I already do of you. Oh, by the way, the stewardess told me that this seat is now empty. Aren't we lucky? I want to hear all about you. Are you married?"

Phoebe heard Bill's brusque response that he had lost his wife a year ago. Before Phoebe resolutely turned to talk with James, she heard such sweet sounds coming from Joan that she felt that if she succumbed to the strong temptation to peek, she would see Joan cradling Uncle Bill's head on her shoulder and stroking it in sympathy over his loss. "James, dear, how long is the flight to Bariloche?" she hastened to ask her husband.

"At least a couple of hours, plenty of time for gin rummy. Here are the cards. You deal while I look up the schedule. The luggage is still being loaded on the plane. We can get the game started while we're waiting our turn for takeoff. By the way, you sound like a proper Argentinean, saying Bariloche instead of San Carlos de Bariloche."

" 'When in Rome', you know," she retorted and settled down to gin rummy instead of eavesdropping. She gave such strict attention to the game, in order to drown out Joan's bantering conversation behind them, that she beat James across the board before they arrived. Bariloche gleamed clear below them, stretching along the length of the river. Some distance away they could see the large resort hotel that they had been told about, situated on the shore of a beautiful lake.

"Another time we'll stay here. But now on to San Martin de los Andes. Let's collect our stuff. After all my correspondence with Felipe, I'm eager to meet him."

Phoebe glanced at Bill, listening politely to Joan's chatter. As Phoebe got her belongings ready to leave the plane, she kept telling herself firmly, "I am not my brother-in-law's keeper."

In the airport, a smiling man came toward James. "You must be the party expecting to meet my first cousin, Felipe Flora. I am Eduardo Flora. Felipe has had an emergency on his ranch. He has asked me to meet you and take good care of you in his absence, as I will. He sends his apologies," he added.

"When will we see Felipe?" James asked.

"Oh, very soon. Now please give me your luggage stubs and wait for me in front, by the big tan Land Rover. Then we will drive to San Martin."

Felipe did not appear during the entire trip. James decided that the situation on Felipe's ranch must be one long constant emergency.

After loading the luggage into the Land Rover, Eduardo boarded his passengers. He explained, as he did, that he ran his own insurance company in San Martin de los Andes, as well as working as a guide for his cousin. "We will take the more scenic route to your lodge in San Martin. It is longer but very beautiful. Don't worry. I have a picnic in the hamper."

Dust from the foothill road seeped through every crack in the Land Rover as they drove the long miles. However, a picnic by a waterfall revived them. George Simpson insisted it was the Scotch that he had strongly suggested to Eduardo to include with the picnic that gave them renewed vigor. Whatever gave it to them, they would find that they needed this vigor before the day was over.

"We shall enter San Martin by the high lake route," Eduardo explained. "Lago Lacar is one of the most beautiful lakes in the country. From the ski resort that is in the mountains behind it, the view is fantastic, even more beautiful than your view will be as we circle halfway around the lake to the town. Our ski season opens in two weeks. Where else can you fish and ski in the same area at the same time? Next trip, bring your skis!"

Eduardo was right about the beauty. The road curved along the top of cliffs above the lake. The water was as blue as the Mediterranean. High mountains rimmed the lake on three sides. On the open side was their destination, San Martin de los Andes, with higher mountains rising beyond it. "The mighty Andes," Eduardo announced. "I will drive you around San Martin later on. Now we will go directly to the Raclette Inn."

The owner, a young Frenchman named Henri Francois, was at the door to welcome them. Henri and a servant began to ferry in the luggage. Eduardo explained, "Henri is a carpenter and builder by trade. He is working on an addition to the inn, and at the same time he is remodeling a mountain ski chalet that he owns. His wife, a native of Buenos Aires, runs the lodge with the help of her mother, who pays frequent visits from that city."

As if on cue, the wife and the mother appeared. Hanging onto the wife's apron were two young children, and she was obviously pregnant with the third. Phoebe thought that the presence of the mother was indeed a blessing. The daughter and children re-treated into the house. "I am Mrs. Cortez," the older woman said politely. "I am helping my daughter. I will show you to your rooms."

They wound their way up a narrow spiral staircase, with fre-quent landings leading from it. This first glimpse of Henri's ar-chitectural style showed it to be adventuresome and unique. They noticed small hallways with what appeared to be bedrooms lead-ing off them, all with charming but low doorways, and each room very different.

Their progress was slow, as Mrs. Cortez stopped to escort the Simpsons into their rooms first. Phoebe noticed that the beds were recessed and the bathrooms opened off the entry halls.

In the MacLeans' quarters, there was an extra bedroom, set up as a small salon. Bill's room was off the same small hallway, with the salon between.

The men frequently bumped their heads on these low door-ways, and Phoebe often stumbled on steps that she declared hadn't been there a minute before. She was relieved to find that the bed in their room was a traditional one.

Later, the bedroom salon became the scene for their after dinner three-handed gin rummy games played on one of the built-in beds, both of which had slanty roofs above them. On the other bed, they piled empty duffel bags and fishing rods.

"Cocktails downstairs at 6:30," Mrs. Cortez told them.

James and Phoebe bathed, unpacked a few of their things, and were in the downstairs lounge at the appointed time, but they found nothing resembling a cocktail hour. Bill had already arrived and was viewing the garden through a window; Joan stood close beside him, a proprietary hand on his arm. She spoke rapidly, as though, Phoebe thought unkindly, she was afraid that if she stopped Bill would leave.

Instead of the smiling host they expected, Henri was in an alcove, phone in hand, alternately shouting frantically and then listening intently. His wife, Angelique, stood by him, wringing her hands, the two children, in tears, pulling on her apron.

A weeping Mrs. Cortez arrived from the kitchen and led them into the quiet of the empty dining room away from the phone. Moments later, George Simpson joined them there. Mrs. Cortez explained to them between sobs, "There has been a terrible accident. Thank God, Henri brought his workmen down earlier this afternoon from the ski chalet because he wanted to be here to meet you. He took the shorter road home, not the lake route."

She stopped to get herself under control, then continued, still sobbing. "But another contractor brought his workers down from the ski area, along the smoother lake road, the one that you came over less than two hours ago. They were in an old school bus. The steering wheel came off in the driver's hands and the bus plunged into the lake. Thirty-three young men were drowned, all from San Martin."

She retreated to the kitchen door but stopped to call back to them. "Now that you know why we are late, please wait 'til I return with a tray of drinks, and I will accompany you to the salon where I will serve you."

The tragedy brought them, and some other guests who had joined them, past the usual small talk into an intimacy that usually takes much longer to develop. Over their drinks, they discussed the accident as though they were friends of longstanding. Joan managed her drink while still clinging, with one hand, to Uncle Bill's arm.

In the midst of their cocktail conversation, Henri burst back into the room. "Does anyone here have Type O blood? If you have and will volunteer to donate blood, I will drive you to the hospital immediately."

James whispered briefly to Phoebe and then held up his hand.

Henri nodded to him, "Thanks, MacLean. The hospital needs Type O blood badly. I'll get the car and drive you there."

The piercing ring of the phone interrupted Henri. He hurried to answer it. When he hung up the phone, he turned to James, hand outstretched.

"Thank you for offering, but your blood is not now needed. There were seventy thousand soldiers recently assigned to an army post in the next town. Some of them are now on their way to the hospital to give blood. You have all waited long for another drink. What are your orders?"

Henri sat with them briefly before he stood up to return to the kitchen. "If you will excuse me, I shall leave to help my family."

James stopped him briefly. "I don't want to detain you long, but there's something that I would like you to explain. Why have troops recently been sent to this nearby army post?"

"Don't you know?" asked Henri in surprise. "Haven't you read in your papers that a war between Chile and Argentina may break out at any minute?"

There was no response from his guests, who sat in awkward silence. Phoebe was proud of Bill when he was the one who answered Henri. "I'm sorry to say that I don't know. I have been traveling recently and have undoubtedly missed some very important news. Please tell us."

Mollified, Henri explained. "Chile has made a ridiculous claim to three of our islands south of Tierra Del Fuego, islands potentially rich in oil. They are Isla Nueva, Isla Lennox, and Isla Picton. Even though we are sympathetic to the poverty problems that beset our neighbors, we feel that this time Chile has gone too far."

Henri paced the room before continuing. "The lowest pass in the Andes between our two countries is only a few miles from here. That's why our government stationed seventy thousand soldiers close by. The Pope has agreed to mediate the problem, and that number has been reduced to twenty thousand. Let's hope that the Pope is as wise a politician as he is a devout spiritual leader. We've had many cancellations here at the inn because of this threat."

"Perhaps the others who cancelled their fishing trip, booked through Orvis, had access to news articles that we didn't see," James conjectured.

"Undoubtedly," Henri agreed. "For years, every Argentine border town has had problems with our Chilean neighbors, and you know how long our border is. Let me give you a brief example of our problems here in San Martin. Then you will understand why we are angry over this claim that Chile has made that they own our rich islands."

He continued, "For years, poor Chilean men have managed to cross our borders illegally to find work here. Then, through devious ways, they get their families over. They become squatters and put together shanties of cardboard and tin and refuse to leave. Their children go to our schools that their parents do not help support. With false documents, they register to get the advantages of our public health programs, and they pay no taxes."

Henri turned away. "Enough of this. Now I must hurry to the kitchen. Then I will help serve you the excellent dinner that my family has managed to prepare for you, in spite of the tragedy in our town. I shall come shortly to bring you in for dinner."

Over the dinner of French cuisine, prepared by Henri's Argentine family, the guests put politics and tragedy aside for the moment. They were full of compliments for Henri when he reappeared with coffee.

After he thanked them, he said, "Later in the week, I shall prepare for you raclette, the cheese dish served with small boiled potatoes that I make on the high dining room hearth. I named my inn Raclette, after this dish.

"Now I shall leave you for sad business, helping with plans for the funeral the day after tomorrow. Mr. MacLean, Eduardo will come for your party tomorrow morning promptly at nine a.m. Good night."

The next morning Eduardo brought Tony Skelton with him, a trim, quiet young man from the Orvis Company in Manchester, Vermont. He had been sent down earlier to scout out the fishing spots. Tony was the director of the Orvis Fly Casting School.

During Eduardo's introductions, Angelique Francois waited, holding a large picnic hamper. Henri did not appear.

Bill and the Simpsons traveled in the car with Tony. George sat in the front, which left Bill and Joan in the back seat. The MacLeans and the lunch were with Eduardo.

"We shall fish the Colloncura River today, one of our finest trout streams. However, if the water is as high as Tony and I found it a week ago, we may need to fish wet. I use an Olive Matuka. If you don't have any, I can give you some. There is a time to fish dry and a time to fish wet."

"Very true," said James, "though a good friend, who hopes to fish here sometime, would not agree with you. He fishes dry, regardless."

Eduardo drove down the main street. It looked much like that of any small midwestern American town except that the large, ornate Catholic church that they passed seemed more appropriate for a much bigger city. Eduardo told them quietly, "The Mass for the victims will be held here tomorrow at one o'clock. There is much to do before that. The stores will be closed all day long in commemoration."

Phoebe was relieved to see that their route did not take them by the lake. Instead, on the other side of town, they wound up a steep road that rose abruptly above the town. At the top, ranch lands spread before their eyes as far as the distant horizon. Miles of fencing on both sides of them followed the curve of the land.

"The San Martin area seems to be in a bowl," Phoebe said, "with the lake and the ski slopes behind it on one side, the Andes on the other, and now all these ranches to complete the circle."

After driving ten miles or so with ranches on both sides, Eduardo took a road heading east through more ranch lands. In the distance ahead of them, they saw a bluff that looked like a high mesa. They continued to pass mile after mile of fence posts, on many of which small brown hawks perched, looking like birds in an Audubon painting.

On the left, Eduardo pointed out a dome-like stone mountain some distance from the road. "On top, notice that there is one cross. The family that owns this ranch had three sons. When World War II began, the three brothers enlisted in the Argentine army. Before they left for Europe, they made a pact to place a memorial cross on top of the mountain for anyone who did not survive. That's why there is one white cross."

They were very quiet as they passed by the mountain.

Further along the road, the MacLeans saw a row of trees leading to a distant ranch house. "Is this the home of the brothers?" James asked.

"Yes. It's called the French ranch because the first members of this pioneer family came from France. It's the best-run ranch in the area. A spinster sister has set up a shop in the house to help the local Indians market their weavings. Perhaps we'll have time to visit her workshop later."

Eduardo turned hard left off the road just before it ascended to the high mesa. He stopped the car at a rickety gate, which sagged so much that he had to lift it up in order to push it open.

Chickens scattered around him as he climbed back into the van. "This is called the German ranch. It used to be a fine *estacion*, but the grandson of the German man who started it married an Indian woman. Their sons have let things go to pieces. The river is to the left and runs through their property."

Eduardo drove along the faint outline of a road that led them through three more dilapidated gates. The road ended at the river. "The Colloncura River. There are three good beats here—the gravel bar in the center, the upper stretch of river, and the downstream water. Then the river winds around the toe of the high mesa. Find your gear and suit up while I talk to Tony about the beats."

Tony pulled his car next to theirs just as Eduardo was explaining, "If we hadn't expected so many people to arrive from Orvis, I'm sure the company would not have sent Tony down ahead of time to explore the fishing. He's a great fisherman and has enjoyed our rivers immensely. We've taught him how to fish our rivers, and he's taught us some new fishing techniques!"

Uncle Bill stopped midway through pulling on his waders. "What a treat to have him with us. This Argentine fishing trip gets more unbelievable every minute."

Eduardo and Tony stood beside the river and studied it carefully. Eduardo finally announced, "James, you go downstream. Bill, you fish the gravel bar in front of us. I'll stay somewhere between. The Simpsons and Phoebe will go upstream with Tony."

Opposite the spot that Tony chose, curious cattle grazed on a high bank. George Simpson announced emphatically that he needed to talk over some business with Joan but then he planned to take a snooze before lunch. "Never good to rush into things, is it?" asked George Simpson.

"Where shall I fish, Tony?" Phoebe asked.

"It's all great water. I'll put a wet fly on your line first, an Olive Matuka. So choose your own spot. Just don't get out too deep."

Phoebe cast timidly, a quarter downstream, then she retrieved with small jerks to tease the interest of a fish. After a few casts, she remembered to move down three paces, the magic number. But fishing under Tony's watchful eye drained her of what confidence she had. "Please, Tony," she begged, "show me how you would do it."

"You're doing fine. Just keep it up," he answered. "I don't have my rod with me."

"Use mine."

"That's kind of you, but no thanks. Keep fishing until something strikes. Your casts should bring results."

"But I want to learn from you."

"I'll tell you when you do something wrong. Now, you fish and I'll guide," he answered, studying the water.

She returned to the river for another half-hour. It was the same.

"I think I'll go check on James," she told Tony and fled. As she was leaving, she saw Joan Simpson pick up her rod and move into Phoebe's place.

"Good luck," Phoebe thought.

She didn't get as far as James. On the way she passed Uncle Bill, his rod upright and taut. He had a fish on the line! She settled against a bank to watch, but she didn't experience her usual contentment in this role. "It's that Tony. I'm going to catch a fish next time right in front of him," she thought, "without any of his help. But right now it's Bill's show."

Bill put on a good one, a broad grin on his face the entire time. He must have had the fish on his line for some time before she arrived. He began to move toward the shore, but the fish broke water in a high jump. "Magnificent. Must be a rainbow trout," she called.

He nodded to show he heard, letting out line slightly. Was the fish running? Yes, getting ready for another jump.

Over and over the trout jumped, trying to rid himself of the fly in his mouth and Bill in his life. Phoebe knew the small hook would do no damage and that Bill would soon release the fish gently. But the fish didn't know this.

She saw Bill begin to work the trout toward shore, trying to bring him close enough to a gravel bank to land him. The jumps became smaller and less frequent. Bill tugged at his net to loosen it from the snap catch on the back of his fishing jacket and slipped it over his wrist, never stopping his steady pace to the shore.

She stood up to see better, just as Bill dipped the net into the water. With one smooth movement, he landed his catch, laid him gently on the shore, and measured him against his rod. From the look on his face, he was very pleased. He thrust his camera into her hand and held up the trout. She snapped several pictures, hoping at least one would be good for Bill's record.

He took the fish to a shallow pool, pointed his head upstream, and massaged him with small strokes until, revived, the trout swam back into his home waters. "Congratulations," she called and walked with the happy warrior to join the others for lunch.

George Simpson had arrived before them. He sat near Eduardo and talked constantly as he watched Eduardo set out the picnic. "It's just a matter of promotion. I could design and produce a commemorative stamp for your business and this town that would increase your sales and your income by fifty percent. I'll draw up a proposal that you can show your cousin. I could have the rough layout ready by tomorrow."

Phoebe wondered what the Simpsons were fishing for. She was certain that it wasn't for trout. She accepted the beer James handed her. Joan arrived, talking steadily to a silent Tony. Bill's voice interrupted her thoughts as he began to recite his pursuit in detail.

"This may be the world's most renowned brown trout area, but I've had the most active, the most beautiful rainbow trout that I've ever seen, much less caught. Ask Phoebe. She saw it. Boy, am I a happy man. Imagine, fishing in Argentina. As afraid as I am of getting my camera wet, I had it with me today, and Phoebe took a picture for me. From now on, my camera goes with me, even though I may be the only one around to snap a picture of me. Someone give me a victory drink," Bill said, with a big smile.

Phoebe tried, but Eduardo was faster than she. He handed Bill a drink and motioned to the portable table he had set up. "Come and get it."

James arrived and heaped his plate with food. "Where do we fish this afternoon?" he asked.

After Eduardo and Tony conferred, Tony answered. "You take the beat that Phoebe and the Simpsons had. Bill can take yours with Eduardo. George and the women will fish here on the gravel bank with me," Tony decided. Then with his plate of lunch, he strolled to the river to study it more.

Joan sat down by Phoebe. "I found Tony hard to talk with. Did you?"

Phoebe nodded. "I wanted him to show me how he casts, but he wouldn't. He said he is here to guide. What a waste for us."

"I've just decided that I will tell my father that I want to fish again this afternoon," Joan responded.

George Simpson managed to insinuate himself between Bill and James, plate in hand. "Say, I was telling Eduardo that he is missing a golden opportunity to promote his fishing guide service in this part of Argentina. I could handle it for him, with one hand tied behind my back. He says he's not interested, but I plan to keep in touch. How was your fishing, MacLean?"

"Some nice strikes, but no catch. I was experimenting with dry flies. Maybe with this high water, wet flies are in order."

"I used a minnow muddler," Bill reminded him.

After lunch, James went downstream. Bill hurried upstream as fast as he could in his cumbersome waders. Joan went up to Tony. "Won't you please show me where to fish?"

"All right. Phoebe, you go to the right about a hundred yards above the gravel bar. Joan and I will fish in front of camp. I'll keep an eye on you also."

Phoebe started walking away quickly, but Joan's voice followed her. "Tony, I've forgotten how my fingers go around the rod. Please show me."

"First, I'll show you where to stand in the water," Tony answered.

"Oh, I'm afraid. Please stand by me."

Quickly, Phoebe moved out of earshot. At least Tony was inadvertently helping Bill out by keeping Joan occupied. Phoebe checked the wet fly on her line and found it still usable. Carefully, she walked into the stream, feeling ahead with her toes before she stepped.

She positioned herself securely and looked over the water. Around her, the clouds billowed in profusion, white and puffy as whipped cream. Were clouds more beautiful on fishing trips, or was it that she had more time to appreciate them?

She must concentrate on her fishing, on keeping the arc high to avoid bushes and then stopping the rod above her at one o'clock. Now came the hardest part for Phoebe, bringing the rod forward strongly and releasing it at eleven o'clock, no lower. The line should lie quietly on the water, but hers seldom did. How did men get their line out so straight? "Like hammering hard and then stopping fast," was what James had told her on a previous trip.

"Like trying to throw the line like a baseball across the stream and then stopping it gently," Bill, who was with them also on that trip, had added.

"How could you hammer and throw a baseball simultaneously, and both quietly?" she had wondered for years. She mustn't get discouraged. She had set herself a job to do this afternoon, alone.

She knew that Tony would come to check on her soon. She hoped that her mistakes wouldn't show up as much with this wet fly as they had with a dry fly. She continued to cast three-quarters downstream, remembering to wait for the line to swing around the whole arc, during which she twitched it to entice a fish.

After covering each portion of water in front of her thoroughly, she moved three paces downstream and began over. No action. Time started to drag and her book to call. She saw Tony and Joan move toward shore. The only thing left was to start her counting routine. "I will not stop until I have moved at least four more times," she resolved.

She was on her third series when she noticed that Joan and Tony had moved toward her instead of progressing toward the shore. She changed her plan and cast only two more times before she came out of the river. Any fish in the vicinity had had a good fair chance. Perhaps Tony would tell her where to go next. At least, she'd rest her legs.

Slowly, half-turned, she began to reel in. A cruising fish struck. The rod tip jerked down almost to the water before she could secure her footing enough to work to raise the tip. Could she do it? Could she keep the fish on?

Tony began to bring Joan back to shore the moment he saw Phoebe's strike and then moved toward her. She forgot for a second that she didn't want anyone to be a part of this moment, even Tony. This was between Phoebe and the fish. She had something to prove to herself.

Phoebe dug her feet more securely into the river bottom and began a steady pull, reeling in an inch at a time. The fish ran. Phoebe let the line run with him but kept the slack out. When the fish rested, Phoebe reeled in until he started another run. Several times she had to follow him upstream in order not to get the line too taut. How long could she last?

She heard Tony's voice at her elbow. In spite of her resolve, it was a welcome sound. "At the end of his next run when he is resting, start walking backward toward the beach, shortening the line as you progress. You're doing well."

Phoebe obeyed and moved closer to the shore. "Will the line hold?" she asked Tony.

"If it's an Orvis line and leader, it will," Tony laughed.

She was filled with pleasure. A new friend and a fish on the line! Whatever the outcome, she was having a good time. When the fish gathered strength for another strong run, her pride in him grew. "What a fighter," she said aloud.

"I agree, but don't overstrain the leader, even an Orvis one."

Phoebe kept reeling until the fish was close enough for her to see him. A beautiful brown. But he must also have seen her. He ran out again immediately.

"Follow him but keep reeling. I'll steady you if you stumble."

Phoebe plunged after the fish, reeling as fast as she could. She felt Tony's hand on her elbow. "Now, start walking backward again," he instructed.

This time when she saw the fish in the shallow water, he was so quiet that Phoebe thought he might be injured. But she wiggled the rod tip, and he gave a tired wiggle on the end of the leader.

"Bring him into the pool to your left. I think it's deep enough for me to net him. He's a fine fish."

Phoebe carefully guided the fish to the shallow pool. Quietly, Tony netted him and held him up for her inspection. Then he laid the brown on some grass and placed a firm hand on him while he reached for his pliers with the other. Phoebe kept her line taut.

Tony got the pliers around the fly and released it from the fish's mouth with a deft twist. Stroking the fish, Tony asked, "Shall I measure him?"

She nodded, so impressed by his expertise that she forgot about wanting to do the whole complicated procedure alone.

"He's almost twenty inches, a beauty. James will be proud of you. I am proud of you."

The rest of the day, Phoebe felt tall enough to touch one of the puffy clouds. She scarcely minded when Joan called to Tony, "Now I want to catch a fish too. Come help me."

"Where will you be fishing when I help her?" Tony asked Phoebe.

"No place right now. Thank you for asking. I think I'll go find James."

Phoebe turned upstream, following a long bend of the river. Willow trees hung over the water, making her progress slow. When she could no longer penetrate them, she retreated up a steep bank to a high pasture, where she climbed several sagging fences in order to find James. She peered through the willows whenever possible, hoping to get a glimpse of him.

The willows ended abruptly, but across the river she saw a line of willows. It often seemed to her that the same willow trees somehow managed to cross the stream.

She hurried to descend the bank. At the river's edge, she spotted James. He was fishing from a large boulder not far from the shore. She waited, hoping that he would glance her way. When James finally did, he reeled in and leapt from the rock to the beach to join her.

"You shouldn't have stopped," she scolded.

"It is time to move anyway. Phoebe, what a pleasant surprise. Isn't this perfect fishing water, with good feed, good pools, and enough strikes for excitement. I'm having a great time. How about you?"

"I am too, partly because you're so happy fishing. Where is Eduardo?"

"I think he's in the van. He told me that last night he was too troubled about the accident to sleep. So instead, he began to look up the policies belonging to the young victims or their families. I suspect he is asleep now. Tell me about your fishing," James asked.

"I caught a nice brown," she told him. "Tony netted and released him for me, with Orvis expertise. Now, I'll watch while you fish. I'll be your guide."

James gave her an affectionate kiss and returned to more important matters. With admiration, she saw him choose a spot, cast several times to cover an arc of water, and then move a few paces ahead to start again. Conscientiously, he tended his fly, false casting to dry it, and, when necessary, changing to a different one. The result was such a realistic float that Phoebe felt sure that no fish could resist it. One didn't.

The minute she saw James's rod jerk down, she jumped up and ran closer, but not too close. To her surprise, she saw that James couldn't raise the rod tip. He stood tense, in only about eighteen inches of water. What was it, a monster, as the grandchildren said? A snag? A tree branch? Something had to give. She hoped it wouldn't be James. Something did, his footing!

He fell to his knees, catching himself by plunging his free arm to the bottom while keeping the line tense with the other arm. "Toots," he yelled, "my camera's getting wet. Can you come get it? It's in the back pocket of my jacket. For God's sake, hurry."

Adrenaline, or love, or both, propelled her quickly through the water to James's side. She extricated the camera and carried it to shore.

"Dry it fast," James called and took off after the fish.

By the time she followed his instructions and caught up with him again, he was making his way to the beach, rod still bent unnaturally. When his feet touched the shore, he called, "Watch out. I'm bringing him in!"

He pulled with all his strength and was barely able to swing the fish onto the grass. Phoebe spotted something dangling from its back.

"Well. I'll be," exclaimed James, on his knees by the fish. "My fly is in his mouth, but the line is snagged on something caught on his back."

With one hand holding down the fish, James jerked at his line and freed a tangle of heavy metal spinners and weights, that he held up for Phoebe to see. "Not all Argentineans, or, possibly, not all their visitors, are fly fishermen," he said curtly. "No wonder his actions were strange. His back is bleeding. I'll need to kill the fish to end his misery."

"Couldn't you still release him and not kill him?" Phoebe asked.

"No. He'd bleed to death. He was a brave fish, living with all that tackle. He must be almost twenty-one inches. I'm sorry, dear, but he *will* make a good breakfast fish for you."

"I'm not sure I can eat him. I've had enough fishing for now. I think I'll go back to the car. Shall I take your camera?"

"Yes, thanks. I'll put the fish in the shade and try a few more casts for better luck. I'll come in soon."

No one was in sight when she arrived, until Eduardo, looking bewildered, emerged from the car. "Where's your husband?"

"He'll be here shortly, with a breakfast fish. I hope we can start home soon. It's almost four and it's been a very full day."

"Fine with me. I'll tell the others. Tomorrow, because of the funeral, you'll have time for a leisurely trout breakfast."

That night, they enjoyed cocktails and French cuisine, this time without tragic interruptions. But it was bedtime that Phoebe enjoyed the most.

The next morning, after a leisurely breakfast of trout, beautifully prepared by Mrs. Cortez, Eduardo arrived, dressed in a suit. "I have chosen a tributary of the Chimehuin River because it is closer to San Martin. I'll leave you there and return for the funeral, coming back to you as soon as I can."

They found that the tributary river ran wide and shallow. Tony assigned Phoebe the middle beat. James and Bill were both upstream, and the Simpsons were out of sight. "I'll come check on you soon," Tony told her.

Before long, she couldn't see the others. This part of the river reminded her of a California High Sierra mountain stream. The sun shone on tawny stones that were the same color as the small trout that darted past.

These must have been too young or too playful to be cautious. For an hour at least, she walked upstream in the shallow river, casting her dry fly happily. It was a pleasure to catch the small trout, one after the other, and just as much pleasure to stroke breath back into them until they had revived enough to swim joyously away. This was the kind of fishing that she loved.

She finally stopped casting and stood quietly, hearing sounds that she realized were creating dissonant notes behind the pleasant babble of the water. It sounded like voices, but she couldn't tell where they were coming from, nor did she see anyone nearby.

After some intense listening and looking, she decided that they came from a high cliff above the river. She saw a half dozen men silhouetted against the sun. Ready for a rest from fishing, she went to investigate.

She glimpsed a deep pool beneath the cliff. She found that the men were busy casting large objects in an underhanded motion into the pool. But she couldn't understand the retrieving motion that followed each throw.

Under the cover of convenient shrubbery, she crept closer and watched carefully. Finally, she figured out that the men had fishing line wound around large cans, with glittery spinners tied to the ends.

She saw one man catch a fish and reel the poor creature rapidly up the face of the cliff, bumping the fish continuously against the rocks as he hauled it up. Thoughtfully, she returned to her friends.

On the way home, Phoebe described the scene to Eduardo who explained, "The airport is near the river. The men who work there are very poor and have large families. They are fishing for food. They have no fishing licenses and, as you see, no fishing rods. The wardens chase them off regularly, but they don't arrest them because they know the men have no money to pay a fee."

71

Phoebe couldn't get the cliff fishermen out of her mind that night. She kept thinking of what James often said about travel, "It gives you hooks to hang your knowledge on."

What kind of knowledge would she hang on these hooks?

Malleo River

"How would you like to plan an adventure tomorrow?" Eduardo asked the MacLeans and Bill, a few afternoons later, as they were driving back to the lodge from fishing. George Simpson had motioned his daughter to ride in the back seat of Tony's car with him, telling her brusquely that they needed to talk plans. Phoebe saw Joan cast a wistful glance toward Bill who was walking to Eduardo's car, but, almost simultaneously, she leaned over to pat Tony's shoulder as she climbed into his car with her father.

"Every day is an adventure," Phoebe answered Eduardo before the men could.

"She's right," Bill agreed. "This is certainly a class A adventure, beautiful country and amiable fish. What are you suggesting?"

"—and where?" James added.

"The Malleo River."

"Unbelievable," James practically shouted, "For years I've read of that river, but I didn't know it was close enough to reach from here. You may have saved me a whole return trip to Argentina."

"In that case, I won't take you," Eduardo laughed. "We need fishermen, the economy, you know. What about you, Bill?"

"It is on the top of my list of Argentine fishing streams to try to see. But I don't pronounce it the way you do. It's not spelled like that."

"The double l's are pronounced like soft j's, not like the ll's in 'llamas.' Incidentally, we may see some of those animals near there."

"It sounds wonderful. How long before we arrive at the inn?" Bill asked. "I need to recheck my fishing bag before cocktails, in case Joan snags me later."

"Soon enough for that. Don't worry, Bill. Incidentally, Joan's father told me before we left to drive home that they are leaving tomorrow morning. I'll arrange for their departure to the airport before we leave for the Malleo."

"That's a surprise. Where are they going?" Bill asked. Phoebe thought she detected a note of relief in his response.

"No definite destination," Eduardo replied. "I hope my cousin, Felipe, won't be upset by this change. George Simpson said it was just time to move on. Personally, I think he came on a promotional trip, and when I didn't fall for his scheme about commemorative stamps, he decided to leave."

"Such a quick change of plans must be a little hard on Joan," Bill commented.

"But after all, he's her boss," James added.

"Now let's talk plans," Eduardo suggested. "We'll leave early tomorrow, eight o'clock, with enough picnic both for lunch and supper because we will get back very late. Also, the twilight fishing is apt to be the best of the day."

"Sounds great. We'll be ready at eight, sharp," James spoke for them all.

"I'll check my fishing bag right away," Bill said.

"Right on, Bill," Eduardo agreed. "I'll talk with Angelique about the lunch before I leave this afternoon. Too bad that the Simpsons will miss the Malleo."

Uncle Bill spoke quietly, "I'm glad they won't be here to mess around when we are fishing the Malleo. The Simpsons come on a bit strong."

Phoebe saw the other men nod heads in agreement. She didn't follow suit. She was looking forward instead to a little private exaltation with James later on that night. Bill deserved better than Joan.

Eduardo arrived the next morning in a station wagon, which

meant they could all ride together. The Andes loomed to their left as they drove north. Strange remnants of the volcanic action that had formed these mountains rose from the fields, rocky remains of hard cores that wind and rain had sculptured into odd shapes. One, Eduardo told them, was called *muela*, which means 'molar'.

At lunchtime, Eduardo turned off the main road onto a smaller one that led to a red-tiled sprawling home with a wide covered terrace. "A friend of ours recently converted their home into a country inn. His parents brought up their large family here. My friend's married daughter runs it, but his hacienda is nearby. Enter, please."

The cream adobe walls, red-tiled roof, and wide tiled verandas, whose tables for six were tastefully set with colorful flowered pottery and blue glass, presented a stage for the smiling young señora who greeted them hospitably and beckoned them to enter.

However, Phoebe saw something outside the large fenced lawn, with its edging of flower beds of riotous colors, that tempted her more. It was two Argentine cowboys saddling their horses in a pasture near the house. She excused herself and hurried over to observe.

Beside each man was a pile of saddle blankets that looked like enough for six horses. One at a time, the men threw the blankets on the backs of their horses, smoothing them carefully. When half of the pile was on his horse, the younger cowboy stopped a minute, stretched his back, and turned to Phoebe. He smiled broadly in an attempt to bridge the communication gap between them. Pointing to himself, he said, "*Vaquero*."

Pleased with his efforts, he picked up a wooden frame from which hung two wooden stirrups, slung it on top of the blankets, fastened a strap hanging from it around the belly of the horse, and waited for her answer.

Phoebe didn't see any saddle. The wooden frame, with the four boards shaped to fit the horse's side and back, held the stirrups, but did the *vaqueros* only sit on blankets?

The young man coughed to catch her attention. She smiled at him and answered, "I am from California, San Francisco." Phoebe

74

pronounced the words slowly, too slowly. The older cowboy interrupted to speak curtly to the younger one, obviously telling him to
get back to work, but while he piled more blankets on top of the
frame, Phoebe heard him repeating the words, 'San Francisco'.
That name worked its magic. He cast smiles and nods and gestures
to her as he continued.

Last, the *vaqueros* tossed soft thick sheepskins on top of all the
blankets and tied their saddlebags to the wooden stirrup frame.
They mounted their horses, waved briskly, and rode away. Not until she could no longer see their full black britches tucked into their
boots, their red sashes tied around the wide-sleeved white shirts,
and, finally, their flat, wide-brimmed black hats, did she return for
lunch.

When they left the hacienda after lunch, Eduardo returned only
briefly to the main highway before he turned off on a narrow hilly
road which had many gates that the men took turns opening and
closing. Beyond a steep curve, they saw the reason for the gates—
llamas.

The herd was silhouetted on a high knoll against a deep blue
sky. With their long necks and small heads all turned in the same
direction, they looked like an Egyptian frieze. From then on, the
fishermen passed other llamas, grazing like contented cattle.

A few miles ahead, Eduardo pulled off the road into a grassy
field. "The Malleo flows on the other side of that wall of rock to
the left. Some splendid pools are there, but the footing is rough.
It's no place for you, Phoebe, but we will fish an area later that you
will like. Would you mind waiting alone?"

"Not at all. I have my book, always an agreeable friend to take
along on a fishing trip."

"Thanks," James told her, hurrying to get ready. Phoebe stayed
out of the way until she waved the men off. Talking and joking,
they disappeared around the toe of the cliff. She was alone.

She decided that a walk before she began to read would be
pleasant. But then she remembered one of the rules that James had
drilled into the family on their many mountain trips, "Never go

75

off alone in the wilderness." Was this wilderness? She decided that, in spite of fenced fields, it was.

She had just opened her book when she noticed that some llamas were grazing quietly beyond a gate, in sight of the car, and definitely more in a rural area than in a wilderness.

Slowly and cautiously, Phoebe left the car and began to walk toward the animals behind the gate. They raised their heads but did not move. How close could she come to them? It made a good game. She chose each step carefully. Closer, closer. She saw that there were several does with their fawns. The hair on the fawns looked feather-soft, particularly under their stomachs, or should she say "bellies."

A little beyond them, a larger animal kept watch. Would that be the buck? She didn't even know if that was the proper name for the male. She must look up more about llamas when she returned home.

Moving quietly, Phoebe found herself only about ten feet from the herd. The animals seemed to be as curious about her as she was about them. They stood quietly staring at her until, suddenly, one doe, head still twisted toward Phoebe, turned and bounded uphill, her two fawns following her. Halfway up, she stopped and with a toss of her head beckoned to the other animals to follow. It was only after the whole group disappeared that the buck, with great dignity, brought up the rear.

Phoebe returned to the car and her book, but even though her eyes followed the words on the page, her mind was still with the llamas.

A slow hour passed before the men returned, Bill in the lead, a smile on his face that split his countenance like a Halloween pumpkin. "How large?" she called.

"Over twenty-two inches. Tony measured it, the biggest brown I have ever seen, much less caught. James took some pictures. I'm personally going to guard his camera with my life until we get the film out of it."

In the car James told her, "Eduardo was wise not to let you

come. The boulders were killers. Bill fell twice, once with his fish on the line, and I darned near got my camera wet."

Bill overheard James and repeated, "From now on, you leave your camera on the beach, James, until the film of my fish is *in* my hands, unless you want to have a fight on your hands," he teased.

"Agreed," James answered. "All kidding aside, Bill, you fished that brown magnificently."

"Indeed you did," smiled Tony. "He cast to the fish several times so quietly that his fly looked more natural than a real one. Well done, Bill."

Phoebe turned to the other two. "How did you do?"

Tony said, "I violated one of my main principles as a guide. I couldn't resist the Malleo River. I fished also and released two beautiful browns. It would have taken three trout from the Batten Kill River at home to match each one. What a country."

James nodded. "I couldn't agree more. Even without bringing in a fish, I found every strike on this river a great experience."

Eduardo drove a short way along the road beyond the canyon until he came to a sandy beach beside a beautiful stretch of quiet water. He unloaded the station wagon in a grove of trees behind the beach that reminded Phoebe of California Monterey cypresses. Then he spread out a three-star lunch. Bill's continuing smile of contented victory provided the decoration.

After the lunch that did not seem to make a dent in the contents of the picnic hamper, Eduardo sent the eager men downstream with Tony, to fish back up. "You come with me, Phoebe," he told her. "It's your turn to fish the Malleo."

Standing where Eduardo indicated, and moving when he suggested, she cast in the beauty that surrounded her, but the fish seemed unresponsive. "They're taking their siesta. Come back to the car with me," Eduardo said, "I have some paperwork to do. We'll give the water a rest and then fish upriver again, with a different fly. The late fishing is apt to be the best, and we don't need to hurry to leave. Let's start again in half an hour."

But in half an hour, Eduardo was asleep over his papers. Phoebe reached for her book. She had read only a few pages when she saw James walking downstream in the river, stopping occasionally to cast upstream. She slipped quietly away from the car to join him. "What a pleasant surprise," he exclaimed. "Where's Eduardo?"

"Sleeping. The fish were taking a siesta, and I guess he thought a siesta was a good idea. He said we'd start again after we had let the water rest. He told me that he was up late last night, working on the insurance policies held by the families of the victims in the bus accident. How did you do?"

"Three small ones. But there are large ones in the Malleo, waiting, as we know. Isn't it beautiful?"

"Breathtaking. Eduardo said we'd fish upstream again, with a different fly."

"You've given the river enough rest. May I be your guide right now?"

"I'd love it."

"What fly were you using?" James asked.

"A Deer-haired Yellow."

"Let's change to this greenish dry fly of Tony's. He says these Argentine fish seem to like this color. I don't know its name."

"Fine. It looks like a dry fly version of the wet fly that Eduardo calls an Olive Matuka. How wonderful not to feel hurried to get back for dinner."

James put an iridescent green fly on Phoebe's hook. Its wings were as gossamer as those of a dragon fly in flight. "Tony ties some beauties," Phoebe observed.

"He told me that the whole time he was in high school, he tied flies for Orvis. That's the reason he got a job with the company after he finished college."

"He's certainly done well with them, to be in charge of Orvis's fly-fishing school," Phoebe added.

James continued, "He told me that he and his wife and young son live right on the Batten Kill River. He says he is living in the best place in the world and working at the best job he could possibly have. He's a contented man, if ever I saw one."

78

"Do you envy him, James?" Phoebe asked.

"In some ways, yes. He told me he knows the Batten Kill the way he knows the palm of his hand, fishes it almost every evening. Enough of Tony; you and I are together, fishing on the Malleo River in Argentina. I wouldn't be any place in the world right now, except here. You fish first and I'll guide. Then, when I start fishing again, we'll leapfrog each other. I'll bet you that you catch a fish before I do."

"What do you bet?"

"This fly of Tony's."

"It's a deal. Fish, here I come," Phoebe answered, "and please cooperate."

She cast Tony's fly lightly. She moved after every three casts. Her casts had improved, but the fish didn't seem to know that. She knew it would soon be time to give James his turn. Just one more cast before her turn was up. After all, this was a contest.

An obliging fish struck! Phoebe murmured, "Thank you, Guardian Angel of Fishing. Now help me fish him wisely."

She set the hook. James made suggestions when necessary, calling out the pertinent things that he had taught her during their fishing years together. She loved having him near her. The fish gave several spectacular jumps. Carefully, tip up, she kept him under control. She followed him when necessary and reeled in when possible. Finally, she brought the fish into a pool near the beach where James netted him competently, a beautiful rainbow. James measured him and returned him to the stream. If she were Tony fishing the Batten Kill, she couldn't have been happier. The new fly was hers.

James began his turn. He had one strike after the other. He landed and released fish regularly and then moved on. She was too busy keeping up with him to fish again. James certainly didn't need any help from her, but she liked to be part of his fishing and enjoyed marveling in his expert performance, learning something new each time he cast. Would she ever be able to fish that smoothly?

Supper was to be a moveable feast because no one wanted to be away from the Malleo very long. Phoebe returned to the picnic hamper to be the anchor person, helping the fishermen with their choice of food for supper.

When the last low rays of the sun were reflecting off the river, Eduardo collected his passengers for the return to San Martin. Tired as they were, they talked the whole way home, excitedly interrupting one another to recapture a moment of the day's glory.

"I know it has been a fantastic day for you all, but how many fish?" Phoebe asked, interrupting the recitals. No one seemed to find the amounts as important as the excitement of strikes on a fantastic river. Tony kindly stopped long enough to give her his statistics, "I netted at least eight fish, each, for James and Bill."

"I've had the most fantastic day of my life," echoed Uncle Bill, finally focusing on her. "I'll never forget the Malleo."

"Nor I. It was worth the whole trip," James stated.

"The unforgettable part is that each fish was a challenge, not a single easy catch among them, almost as challenging as the Batten Kill," Tony concluded.

After this final accolade, there seemed little left for anyone else to say.

San Carlos de Bariloche

FAINT FINGERS OF SUNSET lingered on the dark river in front of Phoebe MacLean and Laddie Buchanan, the Argentine fishing guide. This was several years after the San Martin de los Andes and the Malleo adventure. The MacLeans and three other couples, all fishing friends from the San Francisco area, had just arrived in a part of Argentina near Bariloche that was new to the MacLeans. But their plans had not called for a delay at the border as well as a late, chilly roadside barbecue picnic on the way to the hotel. And

Phoebe had certainly not expected an impromptu fishing lesson with Laddie Buchanan in the dark after the picnic.

The friends had been fishing in Chile for a week. The beauty of the high lake country with its sparkling streams near their friend Adrian duFloque's handsome lodge had not compensated for the very poor fishing. After a rough taxi ride on an unpaved road through a huge Indian reservation, the San Franciscans had arrived at the Chilean-Argentine border. The Indian taxi drivers dumped their bags and fishing gear in the customs house, took their wages, and left.

When the Chilean customs officials finished with them, the friends hauled their stuff outside where they expected to find their Argentine fishing guides. Instead, they found a no-man's-land strip of concrete, with a roadway on one side. In the distance, they saw the Argentine customs house.

The women huddled with their possessions like immigrants, eyes fixed across the border, while the men discussed the situation. Two men emerged from the Argentine customs house and began to shout and gesture, pantomiming to them to carry their stuff over to the Argentine side.

They hauled everything over to the Argentine side. The larger, older man grabbed a bag from two of the ladies. "I'm Laddie Buchanan. This is my brother, Donald. Just follow me. The Chileans wouldn't permit Donald and me to cross the border, even briefly, to greet you and help you with your luggage."

He led them to two sedans, one with a rowboat attached behind it. "Just toss your gear into the boat. It makes a great luggage carrier, and jump in the cars, men in one, ladies in the other, I'm afraid we'll miss supper at the hotel, but we'll figure something out."

His solution was a picnic along the way to San Carlos de Bariloche, on the bank of a small stream that flowed, they were told, into the western end of Lago Nahuel Huapi. The brothers had evidently loaded their two picnic hampers while they waited on the border. At the picnic spot, they expertly put on a welcome barbecue. Were emergencies part of their regular schedule?

Another couple had joined the MacLeans, Holcombs, and Sergeants on this trip. They were Elizabeth and Robert Anthony, good fishing buddies, also from the San Francisco area.

After the barbecue, everyone was eager to get on to the hotel after what had been a long hard day. But Laddie, as they were to learn during the rest of their trip, was an indomitable fisherman. To the consternation of the Americans, the brothers began to set up rods for some evening fishing on the small stream. Darkness, weariness, and the cold wind that swept down from the pass in the Andes soon sent the friends back to the cars for warmth.

Phoebe was bringing up the rear when Laddie waylaid her. He grasped her firmly by the arm and began to talk. Politely, she let him finish, which was her mistake. "There's a huge fish out there, waiting for you. I see him every year when we pass by. Cast a few times to him before you go in."

He pulled her back to the shore. She made a token cast into the sunset. "Shorten your line. Why do women, particularly Americans, use so much line? The fish hug the bank right under your feet. Cast again." Laddie's voice was so stern that she cast once more. Shivering in the wind, she retrieved with determination and turned toward the cars. "It's too late for legal fishing," she stated.

Laddie only shook his grey lionlike head and grasped her elbow. "Cast again."

Reluctantly, she cast one last time. On the retrieve, the line stuck. Good. Now she could leave.

"You're snagged," Laddie scolded. "Hold the line taut while I climb down the bank and release the line. Reel in when you can," he instructed and disappeared, leaving her holding the line. She peered through the dark and could scarcely make out that he was awkwardly scrambling down, favoring a gimpy right leg.

"Laddie, be careful with that leg," she called.

"My leg and I are used to climbing. There, your fly is free. Reel in."

When he finished climbing up the bank, he lowered himself stiffly on a log. "Hold this flashlight while I tie on a new fly."

"But I'm cold, and I'm worried about your leg."

"I'll get your jacket from the car. You keep casting while I'm gone. Don't worry about my leg. It's an old polo injury."

"Polo?" Curiosity kept her there a minute too long.

"Our national sport. I'll explain later. Keep fishing until I get back. We'll show your friends a thing or two."

"I'd rather be warm in the car," she said, but he had already left to get her jacket. How had she ever gotten herself into such a fix? A distant country, a strange man who was obviously an overzealous fisherman, and no James to come to her rescue. Her next cast was a protest, too strong and too long, right into the remains of the sunset.

Instantly, the rod almost jerked from her hand. The tip disappeared in the shadow of the black water. What was a fish doing out at this hour?

Laddie's excited voice came from behind her. "He's struck! You won't need this jacket now. Keep him in the sunset with the rod tip up. Reel in as steadily as you can. When the fish is close to the bank, I'll climb down. We're in this together."

"You can say that again," Phoebe muttered.

"Don't stop reeling," was the only answer from Laddie. Prematurely, he began to climb down the bank again.

She reeled in for so long that her arms felt as though they would drop off. The only way she could rest them was to let the fish run, but then Laddie bellowed up to her to keep reeling. Finally, the fish stopped running. He just held and pulled.

"Try to bring the fish toward me. When I get him in the net, pick up the flashlight by that big rock and shine it down on me."

Blindly she followed directions. She maneuvered the fish to where she hoped the bank was. Below her, she heard a splash and then a chuckle.

"Light!" Laddie's voice sang out.

She put her rod down and groped for the flashlight. The beam showed Laddie holding up a fish that was both big and ugly. "Good work, Phoebe," Laddie called.

She saw him give the fly a twist and lower the fish into the water. Lovingly, he stroked the fish back to freedom. She retrieved her rod and reeled in the line.

Laddie struggled up the bank and said breathlessly. "I could recognize him by the talon mark of an eagle on his back. I knew I would. I netted him for a customer last year, but I think he's grown since. He's longer and fatter. He's at least twenty-two inches. Now we can return to your friends, victorious!"

Near the cars, Donald Buchanan had made a fire. The men were grouped around it, talking. When James came to meet her, Laddie boomed, "She caught the monster of the river. Same fish I saw a year ago. She's earned a drink, we both have."

"I prefer some hot coffee if there's any left." Phoebe's voice quavered from the cold.

Immediately, Donald appeared out of the shadows with a thermos. He poured her a cup of coffee. "Always at the service of a lady. Come to my car. The women are driving to the hotel with me." He helped her into the front seat.

Helene Holcomb greeted her. "I gather congratulations are in order. It's about time. We want to go to bed."

"Past time," seconded Susan Sergeant. "You must be exhausted."

"I am, but Laddie Buchanan is a very determined man."

"Donald seems different and gentler," Helene Holcomb mentioned. "He's been telling us a lot about Laddie and the family and about polo."

"About polo? Laddie told me he hurt his leg playing polo."

Elizabeth Anthony answered, "So far, I've learned more about Argentine polo than I have about Argentine fishing."

Phoebe was happy to let Donald settle her in the front seat. Carefully, he followed his brother down the road. Ahead of them, a patch of twinkling lights punctuated the darkness. Phoebe roused herself enough to say, "Donald, Helene tells me that you were talking about polo. I'd love to hear about it too."

Donald answered, "It's our national pastime. You might call it our culture. I don't want to bore you. Fortunately, Bariloche isn't too far away. You can see the lights in the valley."

"Do you play polo?" Phoebe asked.

"Of course. Everyone plays. Most ranch owners have their own polo fields, and that makes for many clubs. We have great matches all the time. The women put on smashing teas afterward. Laddie's wife, Tessie, prepares outstanding ones."

"Phoebe said Laddie had a polo injury. How did that happen?" Susan asked.

"It's a dangerous sport, but what sport isn't in this life? Phoebe, you may have already noticed that Laddie can be very determined. That's the way he plays polo, particularly when he and I were younger and members of our Argentine team."

"What happened?" Elizabeth asked, fascinated.

"No one thing. Whenever he was injured, he just kept on playing. Many times I've seen his leg so swollen that the only way a doctor could get his boot off his leg was to cut it off."

"No wonder he has a gimpy leg. How did polo become such a big sport here? In our country, not many people can afford to play," mentioned Helene.

"I know, but riding horses here is our way of life, particularly on the large ranches. The English introduced polo to Argentina. It was a natural for us. Next, they talked us into entering the Olympics. We always brought home the gold medals."

"Do you still?" asked Susan.

"We did until the Olympic Committee dropped polo as an event because the same country always won, Argentina!"

"That doesn't seem quite fair," commented Helene.

"We feel the same way," Donald agreed. "Of course, we still play internationally, but it's not the same as playing in the Olympics."

Donald drove silently for some miles. When he began to talk again, his serious tone commanded their attention. "We feel very grateful to the English for having introduced polo to our country. After World War II, Argentina had a chance to repay Britain.

Many of the finest English polo players were lost in the war. The coach of the British team asked men from Argentina to come to England and instruct their new young players."

"Did you Buchanan brothers go?"

"Yes, both Laddie and I went for two years. It was hard on married men like Laddie, being separated from their families that long."

"Aren't you married?" Susan asked.

"No, I never had time to court. I live on the ranch with my ninety-year-old mother. She and I share the original big family home. She enjoys bridge, as I do. Often we invite family members in for bridge from their homes on the ranch, but we don't have to live with them!"

Again, Donald grew silent but for another reason. He was preoccupied trying to follow his brother's rather erratic progress down the road to Bariloche. Phoebe sensed that Laddie was talking fishing. Through the gloom the faint glow from the city lights illuminated Laddie's arms waving to illustrate a pertinent point.

"Ladies," Donald announced. "We have talked ourselves almost to San Carlos de Bariloche. Here is the turnoff. We go right. The road to the left leads to our finest resort hotel. Laddie says scornfully that it's for tourists, not for fishermen. Our hotel is more modest, but it is adequate for our needs. I've talked Laddie into a later start tomorrow, for the sake of you ladies."

The hotel manager had a tray of sandwiches and tea set out for their late arrival. Refreshed, Phoebe climbed the stairs to their room.

"No duffeling tonight," she told James firmly. "Tomorrow is time enough to figure where we'll put all the stuff in this small room, probably on top of the wardrobe and under the beds. With all our gear you'd think we were on a big game safari instead of a fly-fishing trip."

James had his tackle bag already open. "You go on to bed. I'll just tie up some leaders for tomorrow. Big day tomorrow. I'm sure glad you're here with me. Good night, sweet."

86

The next morning when Phoebe woke up, there was no sign of James. She wondered how long he had been up. She pushed the heavy curtains open to see Bariloche by daylight.

All the shops were open. Many proprietors were sweeping the sidewalks in front of their stores that seemed mainly sweater shops. Sweaters seemed to be the big tourist item.

She saw several chocolate shops, most with Italian names. The bakeries had German names, very international. She pulled back into the room to start enough duffeling to dress for fishing, making a mental list, as she did, of family members for whom she wanted to purchase sweaters.

Downstairs, she found Laddie in the small lobby, a list in his hand. "Good morning. I'm ordering supplies for lunch. Donald has gone after fishing licenses. The men are in the back room having breakfast. You are the first lady to appear. That's because you are my fishing pal."

"You are very gallant. Now point me to the coffee."

Phoebe found a long table set up as a sideboard. On it were cereals, juices and a toaster near a stack of dark rye bread. A collection of jams and a generous platter of cheeses completed the assortment. The coffee was excellent.

She told her friends when they arrived, "Based on the breakfast I bet the hotel is owned by Germans." It was.

Donald collected signatures on fishing licenses, while Laddie explained that the ladies would ride with him this morning. "Donald is the ladies man, but I am the one who knows this district best. It took me years to persuade the family to excuse me from the cattle business. I didn't like it and wasn't good at it. Then I persuaded them to buy the Coca-Cola distributing franchise in Bariloche as a business venture and to let me run it. The territory has many good fishing streams running through it, and, in addition, is a profitable business. Ladies, just toss your gear in the boot."

They had to fit their stuff in among paper sacks and a carton of groceries. Laddie's waders and rods were thrown on top. In contrast, they saw that Donald's trunk showed careful organization. It held a folding table, a pile of camp stools, two picnic hampers, and Donald's neatly folded boots. Donald had left ample room in the center for the men's fishing satchels.

Phoebe took a back seat in Laddie's car. "Let's rotate sitting in the front," she suggested. Laddie headed the sedan out of town and then seemed to turn the driving over to the car, as he waved with both hands to point out landmarks.

"Our ski lift is not very high, but the kids like coming down and the tourists like going up. They get a view of the Andes from the top."

They passed small, neat houses. Several people waved to Laddie. "Through the Coca-Cola distributing business, I became acquainted with quite a few people. That helped me learn all about the best fishing streams around here. Now I guide almost full-time.

"We'll turn east soon to get to a good spot I know. To the west is the posh hotel for tourists on beautiful Lago Nahyel Huapi, but it's no place for fishermen. You have to keep changing clothes, dine for many hours, and go to bed too late."

Most of the farmhouses and their barns, no matter how small the operation, were surrounded by planted fields and pastures, usually with a few head of cattle. "Best beef in the world comes from Argentina," Laddie told them proudly. "The big *estancios* like ours run thousands of head of cattle, which means miles of fencing that need to be maintained. Our *vaqueros*, cowboys, ride the fences constantly and are often gone checking them for weeks at a time. Donald rides many miles every month to make spot sweeps on our *vaqueros*. Good man, Donald."

"How many people on your ranch?" asked Elizabeth.

"Not counting the *vaqueros* who live in their own quarters with their families, we have perhaps fifty or so. It varies. We have about eight houses. My mother and Donald live in the original house built many years ago by the first Buchanan from Ireland. My family and I live in the house where we were all brought up. Two brothers and their families have houses on the ranch, and then, there are two spare houses for any married sons or nephews who happen to be working on the ranch. We also have a school, a commissary, and a dispensary."

"Does everyone play polo?" Helene asked.

"Of course. A nephew or two, sons of some brothers of mine, are now members of our National Polo Team."

"Tell us about them," Helene asked.

"Later. Now I need to watch for the red schoolhouse. That's where we turn down the road to the river. Keep an eye behind for Donald, will you?"

"We'll be the Donald patrol," Susan answered. "In fact, I think I'll make myself the Chairman of the Donald Patrol for the whole trip. While you ladies fish, I'll keep an eye out for Donald, as he comes and goes."

The schoolhouse appeared on the right. The children were out on the playground, probably for recess. "Laddie," chorused the women, "Red schoolhouse ahead and Donald behind."

"Laddie," chorused the children, running to line up along the fence, "Coca-Cola, *por favor*!"

"Not this time," Laddie called. "I'm busy working. I'll be back in a few weeks with Coca-Cola for everyone, if your teacher gives permission." Then Laddie repeated this in Spanish.

" *Espere, espere, espere*, wait," shrieked the children and ran to the schoolhouse.

They returned in a minute, followed by a smiling teacher. Shouting and dancing with glee, the students called, "*Si, si, si!* Coca-Cola, *la próxima vez. Gracias* Laddie."

"I'll never forget the schoolhouse," Helene announced.

"I hope that our men have such good fishing today that they never will either," Phoebe said, supportively.

The Buchanan brothers drove through several gates. The fishermen took turns opening and closing them. Laddie pulled up to a pebble beach where a half-mile of river ran straight before them.

Across the stream was a bank. The brothers unloaded people, gear, and picnic baskets on the beach.

The fishermen found that the bank on the opposite side of the river was at eye level. Between the fields of planted grain and the farmyard were fenced passages that let the cows get to the river to drink. Cows on their way to the river stood quietly on the bank, watching every movement that the people on the beach made. Phoebe found their steady scrutiny somewhat disconcerting.

Donald set up the table under a shady tree. It had two benches attached to it. He placed some canvas chairs nearby. "Now, sit here in comfort, ladies," he announced.

"The table will be great for 'Spite and Malice,'" Helene decided, a favorite game that she had introduced to her friends on past fishing trips.

"Fishing first, though," Elizabeth said. "I've come a long way to do this fishing."

Phoebe heard Susan remind Donald that she was going to stay nearby to watch his coming and going.

Laddie set up canvas chairs for the men near the yawning trunks of the cars. James laid Phoebe's waders and the socks that went over them on one chair and escorted her to it.

"Donald is setting up your rod. Let's get ready."

"We'll fish by couples until lunch time," Laddie announced, "the Anthonys and Holcombs with me, the other two with my brother."

"Andrew's already gone," Helene pointed out to Elizabeth, "and Robert is about to take off. May I stick with you?"

"Of course, delighted," Elizabeth told her.

Laddie set the two women up to fish in front of camp.

Phoebe followed behind James and Ben, fishing alone because Susan stayed in camp, waiting to do her patrolling of Donald. Soon Ben hurried upstream, alone. Donald waited until Ben was around a big bend in the river and then led Phoebe about halfway up.

"Here's a pool for you," Donald told her. "After we see you well started with your fishing, James and I will go on. Follow us at your leisure, but I'll come back to check on you often," he said and started after James who had already gone.

She spent more time keeping a constant distance from James, moving when he moved, than she did fishing. Would she be fishing more strenuously if she were in the contest? Probably.

Ahead of her, she saw a man on horseback ride along the beach near James, who came out of the river to talk with him. Curiosity guided her to catch up with James, but the man had ridden off before she arrived. "Who was that whose presence enticed you away from fishing?" she asked her husband.

"The owner of this land, a polo playing friend of the Buchanans. He wished me good fishing." James moved back to the river.

Phoebe found a soft tussock to sit on and pulled out her book, forgetting for the moment to keep James in view.

"Are you bored?" Donald asked, coming to check on her.

"Not when I have my book. But I am going to fish again soon."

"But first, come with me, 'Patient Griselda.' I've alerted James about a pool that I think is the best on this part of the river. He's fishing up to it now. Your reward may be seeing your husband in the midst of some exciting action."

She hurried to keep up with Donald. They arrived just as James cautiously approached a wide pool. On the upper side, a series of riffles spread almost across the river. Phoebe was heartened to glimpse shadows from some submerged boulders where a feeding fish might lie and rise to a fly. Otherwise, it looked like difficult casting on sunny waters.

James cast a little above the riffle and let his fly float down past the boulders. On only the second cast, Phoebe saw James's rod tip jerk down. It looked like a good strike. She settled herself on a fallen tree trunk to watch, putting a finger in the book to keep her place, while a refrain from a nursery song kept running through her head, 'You never can tell about fish.'

James carefully worked his rod tip up and began to follow the fish with minimum splashing, quite a feat with such a strong fish, reeling in when he rested. Donald, net in hand, kept pace behind him on the shore.

The fish broke into several spectacular leaps before his long runs, showing his size and beauty. Both men, one in the water and one on the shore, followed closely. But the fish moved too fast for Phoebe. A bend of the river took them out of her vision; however, she could still hear their voices as she followed rapidly. Donald called firmly, "Steady now and not too fast. You have all day."

A few minutes later, she heard James give a joyous laugh, then silence. Had the joy been premature? She must see. When she rounded the bend, she saw with relief that James's arm was still upright, line taut. The fish was still on.

She moved behind James, who was reeling firmly. In a moment she glimpsed the fat grey body that he had manipulated into a shallow pool in front of him. He had the fish ready to land. Donald's crouched body, net in hand, cut off her view. When he straightened up, he had the fish in the net. She heard him exclaim, "A beauty. We'll measure him carefully. Congratulations."

Phoebe ran to see the fish. James stood, arrow proud. His joy warmed her like an embrace. James pulled out his measuring tape while Donald held the fish on the grass, pressing him down with both hands.

"Well, I'll be damned," James exclaimed. "I make it over twenty-two inches. Donald, recheck for me, please, while I hold the fish."

Donald's measurement agreed. Happily, the MacLeans watched Donald release the fly, take the fish to the stream, and stroke him under water until he had enough breath to swim away. "I know a man who's having a good time!" Phoebe laughed.

"You can say that again. Now back to work," her husband instructed her, "both of us."

James's fish handily won that day's contest.

Later in the week, Laddie suggested that they return to the

schoolhouse stretch of river. James's enthusiasm led the chorus of acceptances.

At the schoolhouse, Laddie left a case of Coca-Cola with the children. Afterward, they stopped the cars on the same stretch of beach, unloaded, and got ready to fish. Laddie motioned Robert Anthony to follow him downstream. The other two men disappeared in the opposite direction.

James suggested that Robert go beyond him to some beautiful water that they had not fished the other day. Soon, James found himself very happily alone in front of 'his' hole. Every inch of his body spelled anticipation. Phoebe left the hole to him and slipped back to the pebble beach. The four women set up a 'Spite and Malice' game. But each time Phoebe could manage, she slipped off to check on James.

He was always in the same place. "I've changed flies often," he told her, "but I can't raise a fish." His patience amazed her, as it so often did.

"Why don't you move?" Phoebe finally asked.

"I know the fish are still here," was the reply.

She didn't pursue her suggestion, remembering the times that she had seen James pick up fish through sheer persistence, good ones too, when she would have moved on.

But by lunchtime, James had caught nothing. "I can't figure out what is different," he told Ben and Andrew when they gathered at the cars. Robert Anthony had not arrived yet. "It was a perfect spot the other day. Why is it different now?"

Robert arrived, breathless from running along the beach, taking giant strides in spite of his waders. "Slow down, man," James told him. "Don't break your neck. Whatever you have, you've skunked me. I didn't raise a fish all morning, and I was fishing in the pool where I caught my big one last time."

"Nothing for Ben and me either," Andrew told him.

"Listen to me," Robert exclaimed, still breathless. "You won't believe it!"

"How many?"

"Four big ones, huge, one right after the other. Ask Laddie."

"Where?"

Before he could answer, Laddie arrived, a big grin on his face. He picked out a beer from the portable 'fridge,' dropped down on a stool, and answered before Robert could. "Right around the bend below the pool where James caught his big one last time."

"Well, I'll be. What happened? I fished there all morning without a nibble."

Robert laughed, "Darned if I know, but, boy, have I had a good time." Robert's smile was as wide as the painted smile on a circus clown's face.

Laddie pulled up and raised an arm for attention, like a professor calling his class to order. "I figure it this way." He tossed the other arm around Robert's shoulder, who had moved close. "The river level has gone down, and so have the fish! MacLean, I wouldn't be surprised if Robert's biggest one wasn't the same one that gave you the honors the other day. It's a great sport, fishing."

The congratulations and discussion went on all during lunch. Helene confessed to her friends privately, "I'm glad I'm not a fish, but if I were, I know I wouldn't get caught twice!"

"You never can tell," laughed Susan. "These fish figured they'd be safe, going downstream, instead of upstream, as fish usually do. But Laddie and Robert outsmarted them."

"Success comes to our men when they think like a fish," Helene decided.

"'I think you've got it, by George, I think you've got it,'" Phoebe agreed, paraphrasing *My Fair Lady*.

Elizabeth laughed. "You've just bestowed a noble compliment upon them. On Robert's part, I accept it gratefully."

"Spoken like a true fishing spouse," Sue told her. "Your next step is to try Robert's hole yourself."

"Not on your life," Elizabeth answered. "I'll find my own."

Since this was the last day of the trip, after dinner Ben tallied the standings. Andrew won the money for the most days with the largest fish. Ben won for the most fish caught on the whole trip, James got the money for the biggest single fish, but Robert won the pot for the most fish taken out of one hole at one time at, of course, the red schoolhouse stream!

"I still think that one of those fish of Anthony's should have been counted as mine," James insisted.

"Except that he went walkabout down to my hole," Robert pointed out, pocketing the money.

Rio Grande

THE NEXT MORNING, the group flew to Buenos Aires where the MacLeans regretfully said goodbye to their San Francisco friends, who were heading home, and to Donald as well, who was returning to the ranch.

James MacLean's schedule permitted him a few extra days' fishing with Laddie. He and Phoebe were flying with him to Rio Grande, south of the Strait of Magellan. Unfortunately the MacLeans found that their seats were not on the same flight as Laddie's.

Phoebe confided to her departing friends, "From what I remember about my geography of that part of the world, I didn't think anything could be south of the Strait of Magellan."

"If it's a strait, there has to be something on the other side," Helene decided.

"For goodness sake, come back and tell us," Elizabeth said.

"I can't wait that long," Susan added. "I'm going to look up the Strait of Magellan in the atlas the minute we get home."

"I wish you were all going too," Phoebe said fervently.

"Looking in the atlas at home will be easier," Helene said. "You can tell us about it later."

"This is another example of what you learn on a fishing trip besides fishing," Phoebe said ruefully. "Phone my family when you get home and tell them that all is well, so far."

Shortly after their friends departed, James and Laddie left her guarding the MacLean gear, to check on the flights. James came back alone. "Where's Laddie?" she asked.

"He's already gone. He found that his flight leaves in a few minutes. It's lucky he travels light. He was carrying his bag and his fishing rods with him when we went to check flight times."

"But we don't leave until ten p.m. What time do we arrive?"

"Two a.m., but Laddie will meet our plane."

"I've felt all along that there was something ominous about the Strait of Magellan," Phoebe said.

"I'm sorry, dear, but here's some good news. Tessie, Laddie's wife, came to the gate to meet him and collect the fish he brought to her. She has insisted upon returning to the airport after she takes Laddie's fish to her daughter's freezer. She lives nearby. Tessie will stay with us until we leave."

"That's very kind of her, but I wish I'd gone home with the others," Phoebe couldn't keep from saying.

"Now, sweetheart, just think where you're going!"

"I am. That's the trouble."

"At least you'll get to meet Laddie's wife and the mother of his ten children. Won't that be pleasant?"

"Yes," Phoebe said faintly.

Tessie arrived, her hand extended in welcome. She was as slight as Laddie was large. "Let me help you check your luggage. Then we'll have a nice cup of tea together."

In the restaurant, she took over as graciously as if she were presiding at her own tea table. The MacLeans learned much about the Buchanan children and grandchildren. "I always enjoy meeting Laddie in Buenos Aires because I get to see two children and their families. And now on this trip I have had the additional pleasure of meeting you two."

"Do you have anyone at home with you?" Phoebe asked.

"Yes, one son. He was injured playing polo and has never married. He's well enough, though, to keep all the records for the ranch. He's a great comfort to me, what with Laddie's being gone so much."

Tessie stayed until they boarded the crowded plane. As they embraced in farewell, Phoebe felt that she had made a new friend.

The plane was crowded and stuffy. Phoebe was wedged into a narrow seat between James and a young man who was so large that he filled his seat and overflowed onto hers.

She kept waiting for the stewardess to come by to offer beverages. When she didn't arrive, Phoebe managed to free her arm enough to look at her wrist watch. It was past eleven o'clock. "Excuse me," she said to the young man beside her and struggled past him to the aisle.

"I'm going for a drink of water or something stronger," she told her husband.

In the galley, the stewardess sat on a jump seat, reading. "May I have a drink of water, please?"

"We don't serve anything to drink or to eat on this flight. That's because it's an economy flight."

"Why is there a stewardess, then?" Phoebe couldn't resist asking.

"In case of emergency," the young woman replied.

"This is an emergency," Phoebe croaked.

The young woman smiled, looking slightly embarrassed, and pointed to a tray containing a pitcher of water and some paper cups. "You may pour yourself a glass of water, if you want to."

Phoebe drank three cups of water. No desert traveler ever relished water more. She carried two full cups back to her seat mates. On the way there, she noticed that a number of the predominantly young people on the flight, many with children, were busy with the sandwiches, fruit, and juices that they had brought aboard. Wistfully, Phoebe wished that they had had more than a cup of tea with Tessie Buchanan.

The night stretched long ahead of them. The two things that

sustained Phoebe were knowing that Laddie would meet them in Rio Grande and that she could get something to eat at the airport.

As the plane approached the town, Phoebe pointed out apprehensively to James that the town didn't seem to have many lights. When they landed, the young man next to her moved into the aisle. Phoebe followed. She was almost run down by the stampede to the door. She retreated.

"Good. We're not in any hurry, Toots," James commented.

"My stomach is," she retorted.

After the hordes left, the MacLeans stepped off the plane into magic. Light diffused the southern sky, light that shouldn't be there at two-thirty in the morning. But then how did she know what should be there?

Just then, she spotted Laddie, waiting. Dear Laddie. It was late for him also.

"Welcome," Laddie greeted them. "Was the flight too bad? Give me your luggage stubs. I know how tired you must be. We'll take a cab to the hotel because I can't pick up the car I've engaged until tomorrow morning. Are you all right, Phoebe?"

"I'm not quite sure. I know I have two questions to ask you."

"Fine. One at a time would be better."

"All right, first, what are those fantastic lights that fill the southern horizon? It looks like a Hollywood light display."

"It comes from something even bigger than Hollywood. It's the summer sun from the South Pole shining below the horizon."

"You mean like the Northern lights?"

"Not precisely. Now, your second question?"

"It should have been my first, except that I was so intrigued with the lights. Can you get us something to eat, right away, even if it's just a bowl of soup? There was nothing to eat on the plane."

"It is not possible. I'm terribly sorry. Everything is closed at the airport, also in the town, and, I am sure, at the hotel. At least we have rooms. That's lucky because the hotel is filled with petroleum engineers, returning from the southern part of the island of Tierra del Fuego where they are checking out recent oil discoveries. Why wasn't there something on the plane?"

"It was an economy flight, the stewardess said. You even had to pour your own water."

"We'll make it up to you, won't we, James. How about a big fish tomorrow?"

"I want it now—and to eat, not to catch!"

James put his arm around her in the taxi as they drove through the sleeping town. "Toots, concentrate on the South Pole. That's what you'll always remember about this night."

She wasn't a bit sure about that, but she appreciated his effort. He must be just as hungry as she was.

At the hotel, they found one large linoleum-covered room that served as lobby, dining room, and bar. A man snoozed at a table that served as a desk. One naked light bulb hung from the ceiling.

James and Laddie hauled their stuff up two flights of stairs. "Good night," Laddie told them. "I don't have to wish you a good sleep. I'll meet you at eight for breakfast, hopefully with a car. My room is right down the hall."

The MacLeans cast practiced eyes on likely places to stash their gear. They created enough free space in the small room to get into the bed. There was a strange odor coming from the bathroom. "I'll investigate tomorrow," James said, pulling the bedcovers over his nose.

"It doesn't smell like oil!" Phoebe answered, following suit.

At breakfast, the downstairs room was bustling with khaki clad engineers. Many nodded politely. "I feel as though we've gotten into the wrong club," commented James. "I spoke to the manager about the smell in our bathroom. He said that there's nothing he can do about it. It comes through an air duct built too close to the bathroom. Maybe we can find two clothespins!"

Phoebe ate the biggest breakfast of her life.

Laddie explained that they would make one stop in town for lunch supplies, and then they would head for the *estancia* of a polo

99

playing friend where they would fish. "My friend wants to meet you two, so we'll stop by his office on our way to the river, which meanders through much of his land."

"What's the name of the river?" Phoebe asked.

"The Rio Grande. It doubles back and forth through the whole island. We'll fish different parts of it, but it's always the same river."

Phoebe stayed in the car while the men shopped. She couldn't have moved if she had wanted to. All the stuff that Laddie couldn't get in the small trunk had been jammed around her. When they came out of the store, Laddie slid into the driver's seat and perched a large grocery carton on her lap. They started off with a bump and a jerk.

Phoebe managed to slide the carton to one side of the car in order to look out, but by the time she could look out the window, they had left the small town.

Now miles of empty land stretched on both sides of the narrow road. At a sturdy gate, Laddie explained, "We are now entering my friend's sheep ranch. We will be on his ranch for the rest of the day. We will be fishing the Rio Grande as it flows through his property."

"I haven't seen a single tree," Phoebe commented.

"You won't. Oh, I forgot. There is a tree on one fishing beat, which is called 'The Lone Tree Hole.' Do you see all these small scrub bushes?"

"Yes. What about them?" James asked.

"There is an ordinance against cutting them down or clearing the land where they grow."

"Well, I'll be—they don't look important enough to be saved."

"But they are. The ewes lamb under them. It's the only shelter they have from the wind that blows here constantly. The sharp thorn branches of the scrub bushes help protect the lambs both from the wind and from the native predatory birds that are their enemies."

Their progress was stopped by one gate after the other. James opened them while Laddie drove through. They were now on an unpaved road. At each stop, a blast of cold wind seemed to encircle the car and shake it in its grip.

On the other side of a gate that was larger than the others that they had passed, they found themselves on a paved road that ran between neat buildings. Some were framed houses with gardens, obviously small residences. Others were buildings with signs on them which read, *Office*, *Dining Hall*, *School*, *Smithy*, *Machine Shop*. Behind the main street, they saw several very large enclosed sheds.

At the end of the village street, on a hill, stood a fine Victorian home, white with light blue trim and a wide veranda around it. "My friend lives there. He will be at the office now. We will stop there before we drive to the fishing beats," Laddie explained.

Laddie parked the car and went to find his friend. The Mac-Leans decided to remain discreetly in the car, even though they yearned to explore.

Laddie soon reappeared with a tall, slender middle-aged man. He was wearing riding britches, highly polished brown boots, and a full soft, open-necked white silk shirt. James and Phoebe got out to meet him.

"This is my friend, Señor Hernandez FitzWilliam," Laddie said in introduction. "These are my friends from San Francisco, Mr. and Mrs. James MacLean."

"Laddie tells us that you have given your permission for us to fish the Rio Grande on your ranch. We appreciate that very much," James said.

Señor FitzWilliam nodded with a smile. "Laddie and I share a mutual enthusiasm, polo. I'm happy to have his friends fish our stream. Perhaps another day you would like to look around. Today, unfortunately, I have a staff business meeting in the dining hall during lunch. I am the manager as well as the owner. That keeps my nose to the grindstone, with little time left for fishing."

"Would you like a fish, if I am fortunate enough to catch one?" James asked.

"Delighted. Perhaps later in the week, you might be interested in visiting our sheepshearing shed to watch the shearing operation. I have been told that it is one of the largest of this kind in the Western world."

"We'll look forward to that very much. Now, we'll go after the fish that I have promised you," James responded, "and let you get on to your meeting."

The manager waved them off.

The road became a mere track through fields of the protected prickly shrubs. James needed to pick his way to the gates carefully as he unlocked one after the other for Laddie.

"Where are the sheep?" Phoebe wondered out loud.

"They've been gathered into sheds, waiting to be shorn. Then before they are turned out again, some get dipped."

"Poor things. At least they are out of this wind for a little while."

The road took a sharp turn up a steep hill. They were on a high bluff beside a channel cut many years ago by the flow of the river. The Rio Grande loomed black at the bottom of the slope, its surface pocked by whitecaps as the wind funnelled down the river. The car bumped along the bank. When Laddie stopped, the men climbed out.

Phoebe slipped low in the back seat to be as invisible as possible when James returned to the car to get his waders. The wind whirled into the car as he sat on the seat pulling them on. With difficulty, he set up his rod. Laddie moved the lunch to the front seat.

"Phoebe, we'll try a cast or two before lunch. Are you comfortable?"

"Very," she lied, shifting a cramped leg.

It had begun to rain. She strained to see James through the spattered windows as he cast from the bank. It looked as though his line came right back and wrapped around his shoulders. In a few minutes that felt like a few hours, Laddie fought his way to the car. "We're going around the bend to try to find a quieter place where the river widens out. Perhaps there will be less wind. We'll be back soon for lunch."

Phoebe settled down to her book, occasionally spelling her reading with needlepoint. "It does seem a long way to come to read and sew," she mused, even though she knew the real reason she was there was James.

When the men blew in for lunch, James's face was red from the wind and from his excitement. "Toots, this is great, the most challenging fishing I've ever experienced. Two caught and two released so far, but none as yet worthy to present to our host. You must come out after lunch."

"Must I?" Phoebe murmured, but James didn't hear her.

Laddie's lunch was simple but ample, hunks of what must be Argentine beef, sliced tomatoes, and homemade bread, laced with lots of mayonnaise.

"Now, Phoebe, it's your turn," James stated, after lunch.

"Are you sure?"

"I am. You're that kind of gal."

"Really?" She had her doubts as she suited herself up and struggled outside. As well as waders, outer socks and boots, she pulled on half-finger gloves and everything else she had brought, sweater, rain jacket, fishing vest. She tied her hat on with a scarf.

"One very essential item, your glasses. Do you have them?" Laddie checked.

She nodded yes.

With a man on each side, she was propelled for what felt like a mile. They stopped on the river where there was a stony beach and the wind was somewhat less sharp, but still strong.

"I'll station you in the river where the footing is good and then go fish with James. But I'll come back to check on you regularly."

Laddie set up her rod and pulled the leader through the eyelets. "Here, hold your rod upright while I tie on this wet fly."

He propelled her across the rocky beach and into the black cold water. "Get your feet secured firmly and do not move until I come back. The ground drops off suddenly in front of you. If you get a strike, don't follow the fish. Just hang tough 'til I get back. Good luck," Laddie said and was gone.

Why hadn't she brought her wading stick? First, she dug her feet into the pebble river bottom, so deep that she felt as though they had taken root. Then she wiggled her feet just free enough to be able to swing her rod partly overhead. She finally managed to make a lopsided cast. And to her shock a fish struck! She'd had a strike in the Rio Grande!

But what to do with him? Since she was forbidden to follow him, she must get him off. She shook the line, she moved it from side to side, she gave the fish his head to get him to break the line and swim off. But the stubborn fish stayed on.

She regularly shifted her weight from one foot to the other each time she gave the fish slack to get away, always holding firmly to her beautiful rod, but the fish held equally firm.

Finally, she risked turning her body as she cradled the rod in both arms, just long enough to look around.

She located a moderately high bank behind her, safely away from the treacherous water that Laddie had warned her about. To her right was the bend of the river where the whitecapped river whirled out of the canyon. She looked to the left, praying for a beach. Instead the bank rose solidly.

Above the bank, she saw a lone tree, the one Laddie told them about? It's an omen, she thought, but for what? She couldn't wait in the river forever. She'd freeze. She decided to believe that the tree meant for her to return to the beach. If the fish wanted to go also, that was his affair.

She turned back to the grey river and unhinged her cold hands briefly from the rod. The fish was still hanging on. Cautiously, she wriggled one foot free and then the other, never stepping forward. She began to force her frozen feet, one small step at a time, sideways, toward the beach below the tree.

She was halfway to the shore when she saw Laddie returning.

She'd never thought that a guardian angel would look like Laddie. She dug her feet in again and waited.

Laddie reached her. He pried the rod from her icy grip and began to reel in. Phoebe cautiously slapped her arms against her shoulders for warmth. "Now I won't have to be a tragic Argentine statistic," she said out loud.

Finally, Laddie and the fish and Phoebe, hanging on to Laddie's fishing jacket, made it to the narrow beach beneath the tree. Laddie reeled in and dangled before her eyes a very limp fish. "I'm afraid he's drowned, poor fellow," Laddie pronounced sadly. He sounded as though there had been a death in the family. "My guess is he's a good eighteen inches. He'll make a fine breakfast fish. Congratulations. I don't have many women who fish the Rio Grande successfully."

"I bet you don't have many who fish it, period," she retorted.

"Let's go back together to check on James," Laddie decided, just as if he weren't talking to a walking corpse.

She nodded and began laboring down the beach, feeling like a moonwalking astronaut.

At first James was only a black speck in the distance, but as they moved closer, the speck became a miniature fisherman. By the time they were opposite him, he was life-size. "Come into the stream," Laddie suggested. "We'll find out how your husband is doing and you can make a few casts yourself. Then I'll help you back to shore."

"No, thank you," she told him firmly, sinking down behind a prickly bush, like a lamb seeking shelter. "You tell James to come to me later."

Laddie gave her an awkward pat and hurried into the river. She hunched down out of the wind and kept her eye fondly on her omen, the lone tree on the upper bank.

The men finally came in, laughing and joking as though they had been on a picnic in a park. "How did it go?" she asked between shivers.

"Famously. Wait 'til our fishing pals hear of this place. I can't believe it. I caught several fish, all over twenty-two inches. Imagine what it would be like without the wind."

"But the wind always blows," Phoebe pointed out. "If it's not from the Pacific, it's from the Atlantic."

"On Tierra del Fuego, I like the wind!" James announced. "Now, let's go home. We fished right through lunch time, but who needs food when you can fish? Laddie says that we'll come back here another day before we leave and fish the Lone Tree Hole. Did you see the tree?"

"See the tree? I know it by heart. I had a strike near there, but when Laddie brought the fish in, it was dead," Phoebe answered, reaching out for James to give her a hand up.

"How great. I'm sorry that I was too far away to see that. You'll have to tell me all about it, my fishing wife."

A fishing trip brought out more conversation from her husband than she heard from him the rest of the year. She knew she'd tell her fish story better when she was a little removed from the event. She'd save it for a special conversation.

In the car between opening gates, James continued to talk. "Laddie told me how *Tierra del Fuego*, *Land of Fires*, got its name. In the early days, when local Indians spotted sailing ships, they always lighted bonfires to guide them safely through all the channels and islands to the harbor. You can see that there would not have been trees or shrubbery to hide the bonfires from the mariners, who called this area Tierra del Fuego. It's a fascinating country, don't you think, dear?"

"Absolutely fascinating," his wife agreed. She was getting warmed up enough almost to mean it.

How good it felt to be back at the hotel, smells and all. Laddie went off to his room, via the kitchen to ask someone to cook the fish for breakfast.

After a shower and a change, the MacLeans came downstairs. Most of the engineers were through with dinner and seemed much more relaxed at the end of the day.

In a friendly manner, two or three at a time drifted by the

MacLeans' table to ask about fishing. Word that the purpose of their trip was only fishing, not oil spying, had spread among them. The Americans were no longer suspect. But no matter how tactfully James phrased his remarks, if the engineers felt that they dealt even remotely with oil discoveries, they changed the subject politely but firmly.

The next morning, Phoebe asserted her role as part of the trio. She went into the store with them, buying tea bags and fruit, which she washed in a back room behind the store. Then she insisted that they stop at a hardware store, where she purchased a thermos, using her own money—'mad' money, her sisters and she had called it when they were young girls going on occasional blind dates.

Finally, she reorganized the back seat of the car and the trunk. One complication in the trunk was trying to organize things around a shovel and two large thick planks of wood. When she was through, she faced the coming days in a much better frame of mind.

"Today, we go to a place on the river closer to the ranch headquarters, because at three o'clock we have a date at the sheepshearing shed," Laddie announced. "We'll go to the Lone Tree Hole later in the week."

On the road to the river before they had gotten very close to the ranch headquarters, their car became engulfed in hundreds of bleating sheep. Laddie turned off the motor, calmly picked up his fishing box, and began to sort flies.

Phoebe climbed to her knees at the back window, not wanting to miss any of the drama around them. Five sheep dogs, all of a different color, were herding the flock, keeping the sheep in tight control, one in the center, two on either side, and one in the rear. "The leader, I think," she told James, "is the brown and white one in the center. I know he is directing the others. Look at him barking directions to that dog on the right. He's sending him after that straggler, lagging behind. I could stay here all day."

"I couldn't, not with the Rio Grande waiting for us," James answered. "Laddie, can't you do something to get us moving?" He was trying unsuccessfully to pass the time by putting his fishing leaders in order.

"It's Phoebe who needs to speak to her friend, the head dog," Laddie mentioned. "Tell him to hurry the flock." He was sorting flies. "Let me show you a beauty, James."

Her husband examined it. "I've read about it, but I don't have any."

"I can let you have some," Laddie told him.

"The flock is thinning out!" Phoebe called.

Laddie started edging the car slowly through the bleating sheep. "We may see these sheep later on, being sheared. But right now, James, I agree with you. Let's go fishing."

The track they followed became very faint, even for Laddie, who stopped often to get his bearings. On the right horizon, there seemed to be a smudge of higher ground. "It's hard to figure where the river is, in this light. I think we should be heading in that direction."

It began to rain. The wind blew the water against the windshield in sheets. Phoebe felt the car nose down a small slope, then slide crazily to the bottom.

"We're at the river," Laddie announced triumphantly, braking to bring the car to a halt. "I was afraid for a minute that I'd lost it. Let's get ready to go fishing. If the rain hasn't slackened by lunch time, we'll eat in the car."

Phoebe dressed as well as she could in the car. Out in the storm, the men helped her pull on waders and over them the heavy socks and clumsy shoes that reminded her of giant Adidas.

When she straightened up, she found that her effort to get dressed had made her feel quite warm. But it looked cold and the wind felt wicked, like the breath of an evil witch.

A blast of wind yanked at her hat, which stretched above her head as far as the elastic would give. She tightened her scarf over her hat and began searching for her glasses. They weren't in her pockets.

She checked the car and the bag that held her book and needle-point. She must have forgotten her glasses. Now she'd need to burden the men with her problem and own up to her stupidity. James had instructed her that you never forget your glasses. "Without them, too many people end up with fly hooks in their eyes."

She confessed her omission, thinking that now she wouldn't need to go out in the wind. But she had not taken into account Laddie's efficiency in things related to fishing. "I have an extra pair. After I show James where to fish, I'll come back and find them for you. They will be too large, but I can tie them on so that you can still fish."

What comic book character always said, 'Foiled again'?

Laddie returned and threaded her rod, fastened on a fly, tied his glasses on her, and stationed her on a bank near the car. He cautioned her, "Don't move from this spot until I get back, hear? Don't move. I'll follow James and go investigate upstream. Just cast from the bank, good practice. I'll find a path to take you down closer to the river when I come back."

Laddie hastily thrust the rod into her hand. "It has a Wooly Worm on it. This is definitely wet fly weather," he announced and left.

"You can say that again," she laughed, but he was already gone.

The water was so far below her and the wind so strong that she knew that she would never get a cast into the river. She turned away from the wind and found herself facing down towards the bank on her left. She made out a faint path leading to the river where there was a narrow beach at the end of the path.

She was sure that she had a better chance of casting down there where the wind was less violent. It would certainly make the time go by faster, in case Laddie was slow getting back to the car. She'd have plenty of time to return to meet him there.

Carefully, Phoebe made her way down the bank. She unfastened the Wooly Worm and checked that Laddie's glasses were tied on tight. She stripped out a modest amount of line and cast across the stream, or tried to. The line wrapped around her neck and under her nose. Oh, well, what did she expect in this wind?

She reeled in and cast again, trying to roll cast across the stream. The wind gusted at the right moment and gave momentum to the roll cast. She laughed out loud. It might just work.

She kept casting. With the help of the wind, each roll cast was getting better. She began to hope Laddie didn't come too soon. This odd fishing down below was getting to be fun. At least it was different. She experimented, trying to make her casts fit into the pattern of the gusts of wind.

She had a strike! The wind and the fish had cooperated, but Phoebe had forgotten her role. Busy trying to get a rise, she hadn't taken the time to pick out a safe route to the small beach she had spotted where she hoped she could land a fish.

All she could do now, with a fish on her line, was to try to keep him on the reel and find the path to the gravel beach with her feet. The fish jumped out of the water and showed himself a very respectable fish. Phoebe kept progressing to the beach as she reeled the fish in.

She couldn't believe it. The fish stayed on and jumped again. She couldn't get a good enough footing to land him. All she could do was reel in some line.

She reached the beach and brought the poor fish in. Why hadn't he pulled off? She found the answer. The fly was embedded deep in his throat. He was bleeding and would soon be dead. If she could have released him earlier, instead of trying to make the beach, he wouldn't have needed to die. She felt terrible. What would James say?

She'd have to do something before he came back, to make up for this bungle. She knew the answer, but she hated to face it—to catch another fish, a live one.

She twisted the fly from his mouth and hit the poor creature on the head. If she ate him for breakfast, she would do so, with reverence. They had been fellow warriors in a storm.

Instead of climbing back up the bank, she remained on the

beach, with the dead fish. She had no time now to obey Laddie's instructions. She had to catch a fish, alive. Laddie should have come back sooner, anyway.

She cast as she had before, and the wind helped the roll cast. She kept casting, and finally she had a strike. The fish ran repeatedly, but each time Phoebe brought him firmly back to the water in front of her. The line held, and the fish finally gave up, a nice trout. She measured and released him. She found she was no longer conscious of the pesky wind.

It had not been elegant fishing, but it was her own. She turned and struggled back up the path to the upper bank. She placed the dead fish tenderly in the car next to the one that Laddie had killed for her and settled in the car to wait.

When the men came hurrying toward her, James was in the lead, propelled, no doubt, by a guilty conscience. "Toots, are you all right? It took us a long time to work our way into the shore. I caught two nice big ones. What a river. I'm starved."

"I released all but the first one of mine," Phoebe said. Her modesty was false, but her satisfaction was not. She'd tell her fish tales later.

Laddie decided, "We'd better start back to the sheep shearing shed. Driving will be a little slower in this rain. We'll eat lunch as we drive."

The men climbed in the car and Laddie turned it round. He drove to the slippery bank and pressed the gas pedal to the floor to make the top. He got only halfway up when the car stopped, stuck in the mud.

He gunned the motor. The car didn't budge. Phoebe felt the rear wheels settle deeper and deeper into the mire. "No problem," Laddie told them. "Laddie Buchanan is always prepared. James, move behind the wheel. I have a shovel and two planks in the trunk."

James obeyed. Time and again, when Laddie signaled, James tried to move the car forward. Nothing happened. Phoebe knew he wouldn't stand not being outside, helping, much longer. She was right. "Toots, you move into my place. I'm going outside to help Laddie."

Through the rain and the wind she managed to get the door open and switch to the front seat. She heard the men digging and shifting the planks. She kept her feet on the pedal, ready to speed forward upon command.

But she didn't have to. Laddie pulled open the door and motioned her to move over. With a jerk, he floored the gas pedal and the car jumped forward. Laddie didn't stop until he reached the top of the incline.

They waited a long time for James to make it back to them through the mud. He arrived, dragging the planks and the shovel behind him. "Good Lord, man," Laddie said, "You should have left those things alone. I was going to pick them up next time I got stuck here. Just toss them in the trunk and climb in out of the rain."

"In this weather, *next time* might be just around the bend. We might need them before we get home. Boy, am I a mess to go to the shearing." James began mopping up his face with everything available, including Phoebe's scarf.

The rain continued as they drove to the shed. "Now you see why they corral the sheep ahead of time," Laddie commented. "You can't shear a wet sheep." Laddie pulled up beside the longest shed. "I hope we've arrived before they stop shearing for the day."

Inside, a man greeted them. "I'm Pedro. Senor FitzWilliam is sorry to miss you. He needed to leave at four for an appointment. Did the storm give you trouble?"

"Some. Are we too late?" asked Laddie.

"No, the shearers work until five. Come this way."

They entered a huge room full of wooden pens and chutes. The noise of baaing sheep and the whirring of machinery filled the air. Pedro pointed ahead to a line of men, "Shearers, ten of them. They work here twice a year for a month, more if necessary. They shear all over the world and are paid per sheep. They are given food and housing by each *estancio*."

It took Phoebe a while to unravel the scene before her. On the right, men prodded sheep out of a big pen and propelled them into small pens behind the shearers. The pens were kept full. Each shearer stood by an electric outlet, with his private shears at hand.

Bare to the waist, the shearers grabbed a sheep from the small pens, hunkered him on his haunches, and began first to shear the head and then the belly. In fast fluid motions they sheared the whole body, turning the animal often from side to side, and managing to keep most of the wool, particularly that from the back, in one piece. Then, they tossed the wool on the floor, like a discarded garment.

Men called sorters collected the wool, separating it and rolling it into bundles. They put the choice part, the large hunks from the backs, into special bins beside a tall press. They tossed the dirtier rump shearings and other small bits, considered second grade wool, into different bins.

When the shearer was through, he shoved the sheep to a helper who propelled him, bleating and shivering and marked by occasional bloody nicks, into an outside run. "What happens next?" Phoebe asked Pedro.

"The wool is pressed into bales, wrapped, labeled, and taken to docks on the south end of the island, where they are loaded onto a ship."

Pedro nodded toward wide sliding doors. "The one in port now is from the Soviet Union. We sell a great deal of wool to the Russians."

They thanked Pedro for the tour and sent messages to the manager. "Tell him that I haven't forgotten his fish," James told him. "I'm waiting to bring him an outstanding one."

For the first time, Phoebe welcomed the wind and the rain. They cleared her nostrils of wool lint and cooled her face from the heat of the warehouse. "From thorn bushes to Soviet ships in one afternoon—unforgettable."

The next morning as they were finishing a breakfast that included Phoebe's fish, Laddie told them, "We're going to the Lone

Tree Hole. James can find the big fish he's promised the owner of the *estancia* there, I am sure."

"I've been calling it just 'Big Tree,'" Phoebe mentioned.

"All the same."

"The sheep station is beginning to feel like home," she added.

Laddie drove past the stretch of river they had fished the first day and parked under the lone tree, a gnarled specimen whose survival was a local miracle. This was the Lone Tree Hole. "Go a third of the way out in the river, MacLean, no more," Laddie instructed James when they were ready for fishing. "It gets deep quickly and the current runs fast. Quarter your line downstream. I suggest you try the Green Matuka first and then switch to a black Wooly Worm. What about you, Phoebe?"

"I'll wait a while and watch James catch the fish for the manager. It's the best day we've had so far. I might even get a picture of it and of James. He left the camera in the car."

"I certainly have my work cut out for me," her husband told her and went off, happy as a school boy on a Saturday morning.

Phoebe found a slanted part of the bank to use as a back rest and alternated between reading and watching. Nothing seemed to be happening in James's direction. She stood up to stretch and decided to go fishing herself. After all, it was their last day. "Just stay out of James's way," she cautioned herself.

She felt like an old hand, bucking the wind. She was able to get the line out far enough so that it made a good sweep before she slowly began to retrieve, twitching the line enough, she hoped, to entice a fish.

She hesitated several times between casts, to enjoy having no fishing problems at the moment. It was a fine sport, one that took its devotees to beautiful and varied countryside. She had time to begin to feel tender toward James for introducing her to Tierra del Fuego.

She was getting too close to James and a little too far out. Carefully, she turned, keeping her steps small so her feet wouldn't be too widespread, and began making her way into shallower water. She sensed, more than heard, something happening near James.

Back on the shore, she settled herself in a position to give her a view of James. She saw that he was holding his rod upright and high. An arc like that was the most exciting position of all for a fisherman.

On the beach, like a shadow, Laddie followed James. Phoebe glanced at her watch, one-thirty. Where had the morning gone? That was another thing about fishing. It wasn't the slow sport that most people thought it was. She suddenly realized that she hadn't gotten the camera.

She hurried to the car. When she returned, she found that James and Laddie were out of sight. She hastened after them, hoping she wasn't too late to be in on whatever would happen.

Around a bend, she found the men, James still with the fish high and taut on his line. He was reeling in. Wasn't he out pretty far?

Laddie must have thought so too. She saw him beckoning constantly. Finally, he attracted James's attention, who then cautiously began to walk backward, paying much more attention to the fish, Phoebe was sure, than to his feet.

She glanced at her watch, almost two. How strong the fish seemed to be! She hoped the hook held. She was a worrywart about James's fishing. She reminded herself that James was enjoying every bit of it, every drama, every trauma.

Laddie moved closer to her husband. It looked as though James were reeling in. "Slow does it," she kept repeating, even though James was better at the 'slow' bit than she was.

Her watch showed five after two. With amusement, she realized that she wanted some time left this afternoon for her own fishing. She must mention this reaction to James. He would be pleased.

Closer, closer, James maneuvered the fish to the shore. Suddenly his rod dipped. The fish was running again. James moved with it, trying to regain the upright position of his rod.

When he succeeded, the fish jumped again. Phoebe saw how far downstream he had swum. "Same song, second verse," Phoebe murmured, "or was it the third jump?"

Was that slack in the line? She saw that James was reeling furiously. The fish must be swimming toward him, either that, or he was gone.

Laddie jerked the net from the hook on the back of his fishing jacket. Like a magnet, the act pulled Phoebe to the water's edge.

The three met in the shallows, James still reeling furiously. Phoebe took a picture of a huge dark shadow that James now had next to the beach. Laddie quietly slid the net under the shadow and the fish exploded in one last valiant effort toward freedom and escaped the net.

When James finally got him back into the pool, Laddie was there with the net and scooped it under him again. The fish lay quiet. Laddie tried to lift him, but he couldn't budge the net.

James placed his free hand on the handle of the net to help, and together the two men lifted the fish. Laddie tried to get the fish out of the net, but he was entwined in the heavy mesh. Phoebe snapped the camera madly.

James straightened up and pulled out a tape measure. He measured the fish through the net. "Twenty-four or twenty-five inches, I make it. Can you get him out for a better measurement?"

"And for a picture?" Phoebe asked.

"It's a good thing we're going to kill the fish anyway, as sad as it is. He's been out too long from the water right now," Laddie answered as he slowly worked the mesh off the fish and handed him to James.

Quickly Phoebe took a picture of James and the fish.

"Hold him while I get the scale from my satchel," Laddie ordered. He bolted up the bank and slid back down.

He thrust the scale into Phoebe's hand. "Move away from the water and use both hands when James attaches the fish to the scale. I'll do the weighing."

"This is one of the greatest moments of my fishing life," James said solemnly. "What a fine gift for the manager!"

"Over six pounds," Laddie announced. "Man, what a fish. I wish we could have saved his life. Here, I'll take the fish from you, Phoebe, and will you take another picture of all three of us, James, the fish and me, before I kill him? I want one for my wall."

Phoebe snapped the picture and thrust the camera into James's hand. She fled away from the killing, brushing tears away as she ran. It was all the manager's fault, she decided, for saying he wanted a fish. Suddenly, she wasn't as fond of fishing as she had been earlier.

During their late lunch, James's exuberance helped bring back her perspective. When he invited her to go fishing with him before they left the hole, she accepted with only a brief hesitation. "The best kind of fishing is fishing together," she told her husband.

"But you do like it for its own sake?" James persisted.

"Definitely *yes*, but, at the same time, occasionally, *no*", she answered.

She felt it was fitting that no fish rose to their flies that afternoon.

On the way to the ranch office, the fish shared the back seat with Phoebe. "No trunk for this beauty," Laddie decided.

They found the manager still at the office, working late. He was delighted with the fish and invited them in. They declined, since they were leaving early the next morning.

Phoebe took pictures of all three men with the fish. "I'll send you a copy," James promised.

"Come back anytime, even if you don't catch another trophy fish like this," the manager told them. "I thank you very much for this beauty. It's one of the finest I've seen taken from our river in recent years."

He continued, "My wife and I will serve this at a special dinner party, with a special toast in honor of James MacLean, the donor. I'm only sorry that you will not be here to attend. There will always be a welcome for you and your wife in my home," he added gallantly.

On the way out from the *estancia*, one gate was difficult for James to open. While he worked at it, the wind whipped off his deerstalker fishing hat just as he was pushing the gate open. They all three watched it tumble through the open gate and sail off into the distance. James closed the gate quickly and jumped into the car. Laddie drove over the whole field and along the surrounding fences in search of the hat. Not a sign of it.

"Shall we go back and tell the manager?" Laddie asked.

"No," James decided. "Some perfect things need to be undisturbed. I'll donate my hat to an unforgettable country. Part of me now belongs to Tierra del Fuego."

ICELAND

Grimsa

PHOEBE MACLEAN was separated from her husband by the surge of summer economy tourists rushing off Icelandic Airlines to push their way into the small airport that served Reykjavik. The airline not only served this capital city, but the rest of the island as well. She kept James's bulging fly rod case, carried upright for safety, within view. "Hang on to me," she gasped when she finally managed to reach him and grab his arm. "I remember this mass confusion, but these people shove harder, and there are more of them."

"You wait for me at baggage claim. Here are the stubs for two duffel bags and our suitcase. I'll go after the Certificate of Fumigation papers. When I show that we had our rods and reels fumigated at home, I should be able to get through much faster than the people who didn't do that before they left."

But the MacLeans' desire for an early departure from the airport didn't work out. They had forgotten that the vans and cars going in to Reykjavik waited until all fishermen-guests were aboard before leaving. The fishing lodges required that everyone spend Saturday night in Reykjavik, before leaving for the different lodges on Sunday.

On the way into town, they passed through miles of the most desolate land that Phoebe had ever seen. The earth, covered with a bumpy grey surface, was broken only occasionally by a few intrepid green weeds that had managed to push through the hard covering.

"Tell me again about that grey stuff?" Phoebe asked James, her 'walking encyclopedia,' particularly when it came to geology and science.

"Lava flows," James explained. "Some Icelandic volcanos are still active. One recent volcano created a new island just off the south coast of Iceland. I'd like to see that some day, wouldn't you?"

"If the stores continue to stay closed on Saturday afternoons and Sundays, I'll settle for going to the new island with you," Phoebe laughed. The driver/guide started his official spiel. "In the winter months, there are only a few daylight hours. That makes the nights very long. As a result, we have the highest circulation of library books in the world. Also, we are 100 per cent literate, but our people don't seem to read all the time, because we also have the highest number of illegitimate babies in the world."

After these statistics, the passengers found so much to talk about that the driver had trouble making himself heard, even with a microphone.

James brought out one of his ever-present maps and pointed to a huge bay. "I've read some fascinating stories about this bay. Our route takes us by it. The Allies during World War II hid their ships there for repairs and refueling."

Phoebe could understand why. She placed her finger on the map and traced around the huge hidden bay. "You've told me about it. I'm pleased that we will see it. Listen, our driver, the historian, is talking again."

"The Icelandic people are proud of their role in World War II. We will be traveling around a large bay for the next few minutes. Our government offered this bay, usually shrouded in fog, mist, or low clouds, as a secret repair site for the Allied ships. The Germans never discovered this bay."

The guide continued, "In 874 A.D. there were many small kingdoms and as many kings. One Norse king became strong enough to proclaim himself the supreme king of the country. Many of the other kings objected, but one of them did something about it.

"After boldly refusing his allegiance, he began making plans to leave the country. Systematically, he went 'Viking' to nearby lands, as going on plundering expeditions was called. He laid in wealth and supplies until he felt that he was sufficiently prepared to embark on his courageous voyage.

"He probably loaded his long boats in a secret fiord in his kingdom. They held his warriors, his royal family, the members of his court with their families, his household possessions, and livestock and grains. The armada slipped away.

"The king's first goal was to go Viking along the coast of Ireland in order to add more women for his voyage. He successfully loaded the vessel with many women to serve as slaves, including noble women and a few royal princesses.

"Then he set sail for a distant island that he called *Iceland*. The Irish foray accounts for the fact that there are brunette blue-eyed Icelanders as well as blonde blue-eyed people."

The driver's stories intrigued his passengers. They begged him to continue as they drove across the monotonous lava flows. He agreed. "Our ruling body was established in 938. It is similar to the Norse parliament, the *Althing*, and it has the same name. Our language is Old Norse. We can understand modern Norwegian, but present day Norwegians cannot understand our language."

"Let's read more about the *Althing* on this trip," James suggested. "I have a history of Iceland with me."

The passenger in front of them turned around to talk about fishing trips and ended up inviting them for dinner. "I'll make a reservation for ten p.m. No one eats any earlier," their new friend told them after they accepted his invitation.

"But when do people sleep?" Phoebe asked James.

"In the winter," her husband laughed.

Reykjavik appeared around a curve, a town of colorfully painted frame houses, red and green, blue, yellow, and pink.

Phoebe decided that the inhabitants must choose these cheerful colors to help get them through the long dark winters.

"Thermal hot springs provide heat and hot water at no cost for all homes," the driver told them.

Bright summer flowers surrounded the houses and provided a riot of color in the public gardens that they passed. Phoebe was sure that the many hours of daylight were responsible. "The other side of the long dark winters must be the short bright summers," she told James. "I hear that even at midnight, when the sun has completely set, it's still not dark. Why is that true when the sun has set?"

"Because it only sets a little below the horizon in the summer, here in Iceland. If we were at the North Pole in the summer, we would see that the sun doesn't set at all."

"Thanks. Now that that's settled, we can go on with the fishing trip."

In the small crowded lobby of the Saga Hotel where most of the fishermen were staying, everyone milled around for more than an hour, waiting for luggage. The MacLeans found the quiet of their small room very welcome.

Soon, however, the brilliant evening sun beckoned them outside for a walk. They passed two soccer games and located the Catholic church where they checked on early morning Masses, window-shopped the closed stores, and ended their tour at the harbor. When they started back in time for their dinner engagement, Phoebe said, "I'm ready for bed. How about you?"

"In due time," James replied, "Say in about three hours."

In the dining room, fishing conversation spilled over from one table to the next. Soon, the MacLeans had met many people who were going to the Grimsa Lodge with them.

In the middle of dinner, the manager of the hotel came to their table and introduced himself with such a grand flourish that Phoebe glanced around for trumpeters. He presented her with a corsage box. Curious, Phoebe opened the accompanying card.

It was a gift from an Icelandic friend, Thorstein Thorsteinsen, who was traveling in Europe with his family during the summer and would miss their visit. In the box, ceremoniously displayed on cotton, were two salmon flies that Thorstein had tied for her. Even corsages were different in Iceland. "What a great gift. Do you suppose you would let me try one just for a few casts?" James asked enviously.

The next morning when the MacLeans settled down in the Grimsa van, James showed his wife the map and book that the driver had lent to him. "It looks as though we are not driving through the grounds of the *Althing* on the way to the lodge. I was hopeful that we might when I heard the driver mention that he was taking a detour because his instructions were not to get us to the Grimsa Lodge until the other guests had packed up and were ready to leave. They return to Reykjavik, he said, in this same van. Perhaps we can see the *Althing* later."

"Read about it anyway, please."

James began, "This park is where our parliament, the *Althing*, used to meet every summer. On a high cliff, the judges sat and meted out appropriate justice—imprisonment for thefts, and death for murder. Murderers had to jump from a part of the high cliff into a deep arm of the sea.

"The judges also performed marriages. This was the annual gathering place for family celebrations. There were games, contests, and many romances flourished here and brought about future celebrations of marriages and christenings!"

"It sounds like pages from a saga," Phoebe said.

"You're right," James agreed. "Family events occurred here every summer. Then during the long winters, family bards composed and sang sagas about them, complete with the names of all the family members."

"No wonder every family knows its genealogy so well."

When the driver turned inland, he pointed out the Grimsa River. The road paralleled it and was lined with green fields of hay that had deep ditches cut on all four sides. "The ditches are cut to drain the fields," the driver explained.

"The hay looks ready to cut," James observed. "We can probably watch the harvesting from our beats on the river. How's that for a new angle to fishing?"

Phoebe smiled and returned to her window viewing. She saw water running in the ditches, and the cuts of the ditches were glistening wet. "How can the farmers ever harvest such wet hay? Ours couldn't."

"They have to wait 'til it's dry enough to harvest and to bale. Sometimes they need to wait a long time."

"But when it is dry enough, they can probably work all night," Phoebe pointed out.

"Our ranchers certainly don't have wet hay as one of their problems, since our summers are our dry season," James answered.

The guide's voice brought them back to the fishing trip. "When we turn onto the Grimsa Lodge land, you may be able to see the high roofline of the building. Ernie Schweibert, the fisherman-author, is also an architect. He drew the design for the lodge. I understand he can fish free here for the rest of his life."

James beckoned her to lean closer and whispered, "Thorstein Thornsteinsen told me that the Reykjavik Fishing Club almost went broke from the cost of building the lodge. Local farmers were happy when the club was forced to sell the lodge. They bought the lodge from the club. They are very proud of it."

As they approached the lodge from the entry road, Phoebe could see the dramatic effect that the geometrically angled red roofs gave to the structure. "It's certainly different," she murmured.

Grimsa Lodge was designed to be a legend; that was apparent from the moment when redheaded Siggi, the head guide, escorted them into the large living room and gestured to a window on his left. There, a large plate glass window framed a high waterfall with white water tumbling over craggy rocks. Phoebe saw a fisherman casting into the pool below. The guests followed his every movement, fascinated.

"Beat number one," she heard Siggi say.

"Count me out," Phoebe whispered to her husband. "'I don't want it, you can have it.' No beat number one for me."

Siggi continued his remarks after the exclamations of admiration ceased. He looked to Phoebe like her mental image of a red-headed Viking. He herded them through the dining room beyond the living room and then back to the entry hall. He gestured to the room on the left. "This is the room where you hang your waders, there on those wooden hooks. You use this bench to put them on and take them off.

"The large freezer is beyond this room. The farmers will buy at market prices any salmon you care to sell. They all try to keep a well-stocked freezer for the long winters. Or you can have your fish smoked in Reykjavik and delivered to you at the airport."

"Splendid," James said enthusiastically. "I can't wait to serve such a delicacy to special friends."

"Also, it will be great for presents," Phoebe added.

Siggi continued, "Lunch is in a half-hour. Then you will have time to unpack and rest before the evening beat starts at four p.m. Tea will be served before you leave for your beat.

"Now I'll assign your individual guides for the week and the number of your beat for the evening fishing. You can fish until ten p.m., but no later, farmers' rules. Supper is after you come in, right before bedtime, around eleven p.m. Breakfast is at seven a.m. The hours are the same at all the lodges."

"Same question, James," Phoebe commented, "When do people sleep?"

"Same answer, during the winter," he said, surveying the crowd of eager guides trying to guess which one of the smiling men was to be the MacLean guide.

Siggi the Red cut short James's guessing game. He walked to them, accompanied by an older bald-headed man, short and rotund. "This is Sigurd. He has his own print shop in Reykjavik and, in addition, is a fine fisherman. He will be your guide."

127

"You must be tired," Sigurd said kindly, after vigorous hand-shakes. Turning to Phoebe, he asked, "Would you rather rest than fish today?"

Her husband answered quickly, "She's never too tired to fish, right, Phoebe?"

"Almost right," she smiled, "unless we are assigned beat one. Whenever that happens, I automatically will become very tired."

James patted her arm. "Agreed. We're room three. Right after lunch, Phoebe, I'll bring up our rods."

"And my bags?" asked Phoebe.

"If you need them that soon," her husband responded. He was a man completely absorbed in his favorite sport, fishing. He didn't want anything to keep him from getting down to the business of it, even the wife he was fond of.

At luncheon, the MacLeans drifted toward a table where two other couples sat. Nearby was another table made up of men only. They were already busy swapping fishing stories.

The MacLeans joined the two couples. Phoebe heard the women talking together. "I'm not sure, if I were a man, that I would bring a wife along on a fishing trip," announced one of them.

"And all her equipment," added the other.

Phoebe found herself jumping into the conversation by saying, "It could only be for love!" Laughing, the couples exchanged introductions.

After a rest and some unpacking on Phoebe's part, the Mac-Leans dressed for fishing and returned to the dining room for a cup of tea and pastries. In the fishing room, they pulled on waders first and then socks and boots. They collected jackets, rain gear, and all of their fishing equipment.

Two of the men they had seen in the dining room had lockers adjoining theirs. They immediately stood up from the bench where they were layering heavy socks. In soft Southern accents, they introduced themselves. The younger man was Earl Bailey, the older, Crawley Williams, both Virginians and in a courtly manner, both friendly. "We are putting on everything we brought. If it gets much colder, I'm going to wear a sweater on my feet!" Crawley Williams said.

Finally, Phoebe and James joined the general exodus to the cars, their hands and arms filled with rods, fishing bags, and other things deemed necessary. Soon, six loaded automobiles wheeled down the road, spraying gravel at each curve as though the vehicles were horses, eager to get into the fray.

Sigurd's car was an eleven-year-old Saab that might once have been white. He hurried the car toward beat number four where they would fish until the ten p.m. curfew.

The MacLeans saw wheat fields of such an electric green that the color looked artificial. In several, farmers were harvesting the wet hay. The steady hum of the tractors punctuated the country quiet.

Sigurd turned into a side road below a wheat field. He parked the Saab and hopped out. "Here we are. Take everything you need. We hike to the end of this lane and then across the tundra to the bank of the river. We'll work our way down the bank to beat four."

Stumbling over the tundra hummocks in her bulky waders, Phoebe remembered other northern terrains where she used the same moonwalker gait to cross between or over the hummocks. Should she step on the tops or descend into the little valleys between? "It's like skiing moguls," she thought.

From the bank above the Grimsa River, the stream gleamed below them. "Do you need a hand going down?" Sigurd asked. "If you don't, I'll keep up with James and show him a few pools. Then I'll return for you."

"Good idea. James is eager to start. I'll progress carefully and stay in sight."

She opened her wading stick to use as a staff and proceeded cautiously, stopping periodically to watch the men. She saw James walk into the water and position himself. She could almost hear his sigh of satisfaction as he began to cast.

Before she finished the descent, Sigurd returned. "Now for you.

I'll position you well behind James. I'd like you to try a fly that I have just tied." He patted the pocket of his fishing jacket, as he offered her a strong, firm arm. They skimmed down the steep bank.

The river was chattering noisily when they arrived beside it. "Two good pools lie above here. We'll try them first," Sigurd decided and sat down with his fly box.

He set up her rod and carefully chose a fly, a large, colorful one, from his pocket. "This is the one I mentioned. It is similar to a Green Highlander. A Scotsman gave me one, which I have copied. He told me that in his country it's a favorite fly for salmon fishing."

"I hope I can do honor to it," Phoebe said, somewhat dubiously.

"I'll position you midstream so you can reach the other side of the pool and let the fly drift around through the good water below. Be very alert when the fly makes the turn. But first try some practice casts to get used to the heavy rod and fly. Fortunately, the footing is quite smooth here."

Obediently, Phoebe cast. Disappointment followed, more intense than usual. She knew the cause, the heavy nine-foot rod and number eight line. Didn't her arm remember that James had had her practice with exactly the same rig?

She shortened her cast, but the nine-foot rod still felt heavy. The number eight line didn't help either. She still felt as though she were trying to cast with a baseball bat.

Sigurd left to check on James. Phoebe continued to cast three times from the same spot and then move. She felt that her casting had improved a little, but the fish didn't recognize that fact.

When Sigurd returned to her, she explained, "My arm's pretty tired. Let me go back with you to James. I'll sit and watch for a while and rest my arm."

She followed Sigurd along the bank. She was completely under the spell of this remote island country. Even the distant whir of a farmer's tractor sounded like birdsong.

In sight of her husband, Phoebe settled on a hummock to enjoy watching his strong casting. He projected his line into waters that she could never reach. Added to his finesse was his patience. It paid off with a strike!

He set the hook firmly and fished as though this were the only fish in the world. To James right now, it was. The salmon stayed deep. No trout-like jumping from him. Either he was a heavy fish or one determined to stay free. But James was equally determined to land him.

Inch by inch, James worked the line onto the reel, keeping him close. Step by step, her husband moved toward the beach, never frightening the fish by reeling too suddenly, always letting him run when necessary.

He guided the fish into a pool near a sandy beach. The tired fish lay quiet, getting his breath. James commandeered the net from Sigurd and swooped it behind the fish, one-handed. But the fish was faster than the net.

He leapt from the pond into the current. But the fly held. Line taut, rod high, James kept the fish from making another run. Painstakingly, he maneuvered the fish back into the pool. Sigurd had the fisherman's respect for a contest and again thrust the net into James's free hand. Phoebe saw her husband scoop so deep that he had the salmon in the net before the salmon could gather his strength for another run.

James had done it all. "Superb!" Phoebe called.

Willingly, James handed the rod to Sigurd and bent to take out the fly. "He's fresh from the sea, Phoebe," he called. "He still has sea lice on his back."

Sigurd dropped on his knees, a large stone in his upraised hand. James shook his head "no" and bent over the fish to protect him. Sigurd understood, but his disbelief was a cultural wedge between the two men. "But what about your smoked fish to take home or selling the fish to the farmers?" he asked.

"There will be others that I'll save for those things, but not this first one." James stroked breath back into the fish. A reluctant Sigurd watched the fish swim away to spawn.

"Catch and Release is not practiced widely with salmon fishing by Icelanders because it works a hardship on local fishermen," James told Phoebe later. "Fish are much too important as a staple of the national diet to release willingly. Around lodges like the Grimsa, Catch and Release is being introduced, and eventually it will be accepted in other sections. My guess is that on this trip, we'll continue to have plenty of smoked salmon to take home."

"Now it's your turn, Phoebe," James said. "I'll skip the next pool so that the water in it will not be disturbed. You and Sigurd can start there."

Phoebe obediently returned to the part of the stream that James had indicated. Sigurd left but explained that he would return often. She made several casts, fairly good ones, before Sigurd rejoined her, "James wants you to use this kind of fly, a Silver Doctor. It's like the one that his salmon struck on."

Sigurd changed the fly in midstream and then helped her move down three paces before he left. She went to work with the new fly.

She angled her cast fairly straight across stream, only slightly down, to give the fly a better float. She let it swing well around. "It's only a game," she explained to the fish, "but it's deadly serious for you. No pun intended."

The fish struck the fly, breaking clear out of the water momentarily, shining in the evening light. A fish on the line always changed any temporary reservations that Phoebe might have about this sport. Such is the perversity of man, rather, of woman; she rapidly became a positive participant. She found that she wanted that fish, not for her husband, but for herself.

She drew on everything that James and friends and guides had taught her. "Rod high," she admonished herself, "reel in whenever the fish runs. Don't keep the line so taut that you might break the leader. Tire the fish out first. Only a tired fish submits to the indignity of being caught. After all, he is fighting for his life.

"Stop being philosophical and fish," she lectured herself, and just in time. Suddenly the salmon jumped as though he thought himself a rainbow trout, shaking the fly in his descent. "Taut line, taut line," she chanted through clenched teeth.

Twice she and the fish went through their minuet. Would the knot in the leader hold? She began to say a Hail Mary.

Sigurd arrived and asked, "Is he tiring?"

"I hope so." She had no time to talk. She felt like a Stone Age woman, engaged in primeval battle.

"Try to angle him toward the beach. It's time now." Sigurd instructed quietly. "You're doing well. Keep it up."

The fish sensed her maneuver toward the shore and revolted, thrashing spray. Drops of water in the spray hung momentarily like miniature rainbows in a shaft of late sun seen through a break of heavy, low clouds. By the time Phoebe had the fish under control, he had swum into midstream. She began again.

This time it didn't take her as long to bring him close to the beach. Her feet felt the pebbles of the shore. She backed up on the grass, reeling as fast as she could. The fish was now in the shallows. Sigurd was there with the net. "Don't kill him," she ordered quickly.

"Whatever you say. But he'd make a splendid smoked fish." Sigurd accepted the inevitable, but Phoebe saw that he was sad. "However," he continued, "if you don't keep that rod tip up, you won't have a choice."

She kept the tip elevated until Sigurd had netted her fish, but then she stated firmly, "James's next fish may be smoked, but not this first one of mine."

Obediently, Sigurd carefully released the fly with an expert twist of his pliers. Phoebe placed her rod beside the fish to measure him and then took a quick picture.

When James arrived, he congratulated her. Phoebe's comment was, "I feel as if I've been fishing for a week and this is only the first day!"

During cocktails before the late dinner, Phoebe found it more pleasant than she could have imagined when guests, whom she didn't as yet know, came to the table with comments about her nice salmon. She decided that the guides must have an instant communication system, because the two men from Virginia also had mentioned her salmon and James's three before the MacLeans had even pulled off their waders.

At dinner, their table mate, Elaine Alson from Harrison, New York, invited the MacLeans to her birthday party the following night. "This will be my seventh birthday celebration in Iceland," she told them.

Later, in their room, Phoebe asked her husband if he didn't think this might be a little beyond the call of wifely duty, to spend that many birthdays in Iceland.

"It's all one's point of view," said James. "By saying any more, I might be pushing my luck!"

The MacLeans fished two beats a day. The rest time between one and four was for the fish, not for the fishermen, and was ordered by the farmers. James brought in two or three fine salmon a day and ordered them to be smoked. Phoebe began to dream of serving smoked salmon at special parties.

She fished daily, but not for her life, coasting on her laurel, *singular*. She enjoyed watching James, his zest for the sport resulting in consistent success.

She took frequent breaks from her casting, enjoying time to get the feel of this beautiful rural country, as well as to dip into her current book, always ready in the pocket of her fishing jacket. She was rereading *A Tale of Two Cities* by Dickens on this trip.

But one midmorning, Sigurd interrupted her reading. "We'll just have time before we need to start back for lunch, to get to a pool where I have seen a fine salmon."

"Agreed," Phoebe said diplomatically.

Sigurd nodded, pleased with her response, and instructed her to leapfrog around the pool where James was fishing, in order not to disturb him. She hurried to keep up with Sigurd's hastening strides. She began to feel the excitement of his determination.

Beyond a straight stretch of river, Sigurd stopped before a large quiet pool. "This is a good resting place, in my opinion, for a large fish. I want you to use a Thunder and Lightning fly."

Phoebe surveyed the water. Willows cast shadows near the far bank. At the bottom of the pool, the river tumbled gently on its way. She found that the footing looked manageable. She carefully glanced behind her and picked a spot clear of brambles. These could snag her line if she let it drop too low. She reminded herself of the weight of the heavy rod and line. She hoped that the muscles of her casting arm remembered also.

Temporarily, she withdrew from the beauty surrounding her and turned to the business of the day, casting to cover the water. She brought the rod upright and only slightly back, and waited 'til the line straightened out above and behind her before she cast.

Nothing sensational. Again, Phoebe made her three casts and moved, three more casts and another move.

Perhaps, on the next move she could reach the shadows under the willows. A fish might be taking his midday siesta there. She hurried as fast as she could, in water almost up to her knees. She made her first cast, then her second. "Third cast, charm," she said out loud, and a fish struck!

"Pull the tip up and keep it up," instructed Sigurd at her elbow. "Rely on your strong line unless he runs. Reel whenever you can and walk toward the shore whenever possible." She nodded, responding to his excitement. This was a joint effort. She mustn't disappoint him.

She managed a few careful steps toward the beach, where Sigurd had retreated. But the fish must have felt that his freedom was being threatened. He ran so powerfully that her line zinged with the sound of a swarm of bees. There was no reeling in now, just a fight to keep the rod tip up.

"Watch your backing. I'm coming with you," Sigurd called.

When she glanced at the reel, she saw the beginning of the white backing line. She pushed her elbow deeper into her rib cage and dug her feet further into the riverbed. Then, gingerly, she was able to reel in some line on the spool. Encouraged, she continued.

"You've reeled in all the backing part. Now, move toward the shore whenever possible, so you won't have to release more line," Sigurd instructed.

She glanced behind her. How many steps to the beach? This was a lot harder than admiring the landscape or reading a book. She stopped for a breath and then continued. But the fish had a mind of his own. He ran.

Phoebe held the line firm for what seemed an endless time. Slowly, she began to reel in, but the fish stopped that. He ran again. She stole a look, backward. Her progress to the beach had been wiped out.

"You're doing fine," Sigurd said quietly. "We have plenty of time. The fish will soon tire."

"But so will I," Phoebe answered.

The duet continued, first the fish's turn, then Phoebe's. Were his runs getting shorter? Was her reeling in taking a little longer? "Bear to the left," said Sigurd, "where there's a deeper pool. I'll use the net as soon as you get the fish into the pool."

Thank goodness. Her fingers were so numb from fatigue that she couldn't grip the rod handle firmly enough to hold it upright. She braced her rod against her body and kept walking backward, until Sigurd called, "Now."

She stopped walking. All the water around the salmon and Phoebe seemed to be about two feet deep, no more. In a skillful sweep Sigurd got the net under the fish. With the salmon still in the net, he brought it to the shore and laid it gently on the grass. "A female, ready to spawn. Over seven pounds, I make it. She'll be good for smoking. Congratulations."

Phoebe stretched her tired back, her legs, and her fingers. "I'll remember her right here."

"Fine," Sigurd agreed. "Do you want to go tell James?" Phoebe nodded.

The next morning their beat was number one, the waterfall

hole. "Remember, I'm not fishing this hole, James," Phoebe reminded her husband. "I'll be your photographer, down below first and then through the big window in the lodge."

"All right, if you want it that way, but I'll miss you."

"You'll be too busy to miss me," Phoebe laughed. "It's just too public, fishing there, everyone sitting at the view windows, looking down."

"Perhaps you're right. The excitement for me is fishing that pool under the falls. That's worth the small embarrassment of having an audience," James explained, a big smile of anticipation on his face.

James and Sigurd stationed themselves on the grass beside the falls and below the lodge. Phoebe waited on the same side as the men, but well out of their way. She hoped to snap some pictures of James, casting into the pool under the falls. She decided to stay for some action down there, before returning to the lodge.

She didn't have long to wait. James had a strike! From her angle, it almost looked as though the fish took the fly in the middle of a jump. James had to play the fish from almost a standing position because there was very little room to move in. Phoebe stood poised, reading the language of his rod.

When she saw the guide move closer, net in hand, she maneuvered herself sideways and focused the camera. Through the viewer, she saw Sigurd net the fish. She snapped the picture.

He gave the salmon to James, who held him up momentarily. He was a beauty. Sigurd killed him, and James, all grins, prepared to fish again. Phoebe went up to the lodge.

There, she found quite an audience, all eyes focused on James. She knew her husband was too exhilarated to give a thought to spectators, but she barely suppressed a shudder, thinking about how she would have felt in a similar circumstance.

"What a great show," Elaine Alson called to Phoebe, motioning her to the chair beside her at the big window. Crawley Williams waved to her from his seat and made the victory sign.

Basking in her husband's triumph, Phoebe settled herself, camera in hand. James was now fishing a little closer to the falls. "Your birthday party last night was great," she told Elaine. "The arrival of the great architect, Schweibert, may have been a happenstance, but it certainly added interest for many of us who had read articles of his."

Elaine responded, "We have quite a collection of guests here now, haven't we? What do you think of Joe Hubert? I'm sure he considers himself as much a celebrity as Mr. Schweibert."

"Joe certainly has been acting the role. Imagine, bringing your own artist to paint illustrations for the book, right on the stream as you fish. Pretty top drawer. I heard at breakfast that there will be a watercolor of each beat," Phoebe answered.

"Even that won't justify Joe's charging a thousand dollars a copy for his limited edition. At least, I don't think it will justify our spending a thousand dollars," Elaine announced.

"If you were Prince Philip of England or the President of Iceland, Joe Hubert would give you one free," Phoebe laughed.

But just then James got a big strike. That ended the conversation.

She forgot all about taking pictures and watched her James anxiously. How safe was the footing? The evil eye of the whirlpool beneath the falls glared back at her.

James, following the fish, moved closer to the waterfall. The falls took on the menacing look of gleaming knives to Phoebe. "Too much imagination," she lectured herself.

Suddenly she heard someone draw in a breath. Elaine grabbed her arm and pointed, "Look!"

James had another fish on his line. His rod rode high. Sigurd was close behind him with the net. James's stance telegraphed that he was in control.

In a few minutes that felt like hours, Phoebe saw Sigurd lift the net with a salmon in it. He thrust the net into James's hand. Her husband held it upright for a moment. Phoebe hurriedly snapped a picture that she hoped caught the moment of triumph. The two men extricated the fish from the net. Phoebe was relieved that Sigurd's back hid the killing.

For Phoebe, this part always jarred with the picture of fishing that many armchair fishermen talked about, a halcyon setting in which a contemplative fisherman calmly catches and releases a cooperative fish.

Midfjardara

THE FOLLOWING YEAR, James and Phoebe MacLean returned to Iceland, this time to fish another river, the Midfjardara. They had invited James's brother-in-law, Bill Weber, to go with them. The Midfjardara was northeast of the Grimsa River, a fine salmon spawning stream that emptied into the Straits of Denmark, off the Bering Sea.

Fishing guests were flown by chartered plane from Reykjavik to the lodge. As the plane approached its destination, the copilot pointed out the lodge to the dozen or so guests on the plane.

After the dramatic appearance of Grimsa, Phoebe found her first view of the Midfjardara Lodge disappointing. "It's like a U-shaped, undistinguished-looking elementary school," she commented to her husband.

"It's the river that is important," James assured her, a statement that proved to be true for them. The MacLeans returned several times to fish the Midfjardara River.

As the plane landed, a driver pulled a van up to the cargo door of the plane as though he had done this many times before. Two men materialized from the small airport. First they unloaded luggage from the van and put it to one side. Then came the great shift. The men brought the luggage from the plane and stacked it into the *van*. That finished, the luggage from the *van* went into the *plane*.

"Organization charts must be posted, to pull this switch off so successfully," Bill laughed.

At the same time, a van from the lodge arrived. The driver unloaded his passengers from the van just as the pilot ushered out his current Reykjavik passengers. The travelers waited in two camps for a few minutes until fishing melded them together for the brief time before departure.

Names, information, anecdotes, the state of local fishing, numbers caught, and weather conditions were exchanged rapidly while the plane was being gassed up for the immediate return trip to Reykjavik.

When farewells were accomplished and the departing plane waved off, an Icelander stepped forward. "I am Gunnar, your head guide. We will now board the van and drive to the lodge. There, while your lunch is being prepared, I will introduce you to your guides and explain the schedule."

On the way to the lodge, Phoebe and James explained to Uncle Bill, as he was lovingly known in the MacLean family, that the countryside was more open than that around the Grimsa. The rolling grazing land was not unsimilar to ranches in Northern California.

"That was one efficient operation at the airport," James commented as they jostled along. "These farm boys don't waste any motions."

"I still think it was the charts," Bill insisted.

"They've obviously done this before," Phoebe agreed.

"But remember, the fishing season for foreigners only lasts six weeks. The first six weeks are for local fishermen. That's six times only per year for this kind of operation," figured James.

Phoebe chuckled at the way her husband's mind worked, one of the things about him that had always kept her intrigued. "Here's another thing for you to figure out. Why do the farmhouses stand out in the landscape, like houses in a child's play village?" Phoebe asked.

"The bright paint jobs?" Bill suggested, from the seat in front of the MacLeans.

"Or perhaps because there's no planting against the houses to soften the outline?" Phoebe wondered.

"Too cold for landscaping, only summer flowers," James decided. "But every farmhouse has its flowers."

Here also they saw that the fields had deep ditches cut around them for drainage. Their arrival at the lodge came almost too quickly.

The front door stood in the center section of this schoolhouse plan, with wings stretching at right angles on both sides. Gunnar hurried before them to the door, turned and called, "Welcome. We'll gather in the lounge to the right. There, I will assign you rooms. To the left is the rough tackle room where you will keep waders and get ready to fish. Come into the lounge."

Phoebe saw a room beyond the lounge on the right that must be the dining room. To the left she glimpsed a long hall with many doors—bedrooms?

In the lounge, a group of men stood around Gunnar. Phoebe spotted a pile of Icelandic sweaters on a sofa and, before Gunnar began to speak, made a mental note of them. "These are your guides," he said. "Please raise your hands when I call your name."

Bill and the MacLeans's names were called together. A tall pleasant-faced man came to them. His smile lit up his whole face, but it was the handsome Icelandic sweater that he was wearing that caught Phoebe's eye. "I'm John Arnam. I'll be your guide for the week. How may I help you?"

After they had greeted him with enthusiasm, James said, "We won't need help now, but I'm sure we'll have many questions later, all three of us."

"Then I'll see you later. Have a nice rest."

"Or a good duffel," added Uncle Bill.

Gunnar made an announcement that broke up the happy greetings. "Lunch as soon as you can make it. If you want a drink first, bring your own bottle. Then after lunch and a rest, you will meet here again for tea. The fishing hours are from seven a.m. to one, and four p.m. to ten. The river is rested between these two periods, farmers' orders."

"The same everywhere," James mentioned.

Phoebe spoke up quickly to John Arnam as James turned to go. "Please, I do have a question. I'm very interested in Icelandic sweaters. The ones on the sofa have already caught my eye."

"Perhaps I can help you. My wife knits beautifully. She made my sweater."

"It is very handsome. But I need two that are difficult sizes, one for our very tall son and one for his very small wife. And I haven't been able to find them," Phoebe told him.

"If you show me the kind you like," John said, motioning to the pile of sweaters, "it's possible that my wife could knit them while you are fishing here."

"Two sweaters in one week?" Phoebe asked incredulously.

"She and our children are visiting a cousin who lives nearby. I can phone her tonight, if you are interested."

"I'm very interested. I'll look the patterns over after lunch and we can talk sizes in the car on the way to fishing. I am thrilled because we have given sweaters to our other children, but we have never been able to find the right sizes for these two. Are you sure that it won't be too much work for your wife, in such a short time? She sounds incredible."

"She's a very special lady," said John, a proud husband.

Phoebe almost danced down the hallway to their room.

Lunch was at a table with two couples. One of them was the Alsons whom the MacLeans had known the year before at Grimsa Lodge. The other woman spoke up, "I'm Cindy. We are the Landers from New Haven, Connecticut."

"Hello," Phoebe said with a smile. "And Elaine Alson, I remember you so well. How wonderful that we will be together again. Cindy, we are Phoebe and James MacLean from the San

Francisco area. Elaine, our brother-in-law, Bill Weber, is with us this year. He is also from Pittsburgh."

Lunch with the two couples consisted of hearty soup, cold fish, and dozens of European cheeses, followed by fruit and tarts.

Afterward, the MacLeans hurried to their two bedrooms. They were like Pullman compartments on a train, side by side, long, and very compact. They reminded Phoebe of train trips taken in her childhood. Uncle Bill's bedroom was directly across the hall.

Phoebe and James decided to use one room for sleeping and the other for fishing equipment and heavy clothing. After they were through organizing, Phoebe decided to stretch out briefly, before tea.

James wakened her a little before four. She couldn't believe how long she had slept. James told her, "Put on everything for fishing, except your waders, and dress warmly. Then come have some tea. At last, we're closing in on the river!"

He sounded like an excited little boy. It was catching, so catching that she arrived for tea before James, who was busy rechecking the contents of his fishing bag. She quickly chose two designs from the sweaters for John Arnam to explain to his wife.

Elaine Alson was already having her tea and was dressed to go fishing. A man and a woman shuffling cards at a nearby table called to them, "Bridge?"

They both shook their heads. "No, fishing," Phoebe answered, turning down the invitation with a smile.

"I'd hate to come all this way to play bridge," Elaine confided. Phoebe was going to enjoy having Elaine, another supportive wife, along.

When Phoebe and James, full of hot tea and buns, arrived in the rough tackle room, they found John Arnam already there. He insisted on helping Phoebe pull on waders and heavy outer socks and shoes, always an ordeal at the beginning of every fishing outing.

She secured the suspenders on her waders and then cinched a

belt around her waist, the safety measure to keep water out of her waders in case she fell in, something she didn't intend to do in this cold water.

While John Arnam went to collect three thermoses of hot tea, James studied their beats on the big map on the lounge wall. This showed each hole and described it. Then, ladened like gnomes, they headed for John Arnam's car and soon joined the happy procession, heading for the river.

The neat farms they passed often had two or three houses grouped together, attached or standing one behind the other. Barns and open-sided equipment sheds stood nearby. "Why so many houses?" Phoebe asked John.

"My guess is," James surmised, "that the first probably is for the man and his wife, the second, for the eldest son, and the third, for the eldest son of the eldest son," James concluded, "very old European."

"Thus, the buildings show the outline for the family sagas, of course! The only catch is, what if the children didn't agree with this plan?" Phoebe conjectured.

"That's their problem, not ours. I'd rather fish!" James retorted.

"Me too," Phoebe agreed, "but I worry about the children who aren't the eldest and who aren't sons."

"The girls become old maid aunts who spin and weave, and the boys become bachelor uncles who move around among the farms and build other people's houses," Bill fantasized.

They passed farmers still harvesting their electric green fields. "Do you suppose when it isn't raining, they work all night in the summer to get the crops in?" Phoebe had brought this question up on other Icelandic trips.

John turned off the road onto an unplowed field. It was a relief to move away from the large pieces of farm equipment that had been slowing down their progress. John bumped the car across the field, where he made as much time among hummocks of tundra as he had on the main road.

They came to a high bluff overlooking the river. The men stepped out for a powwow. She saw John Arnam motion down the bluff to the left. The path looked faint and steep.

"Are you ready to go down?" James asked his wife.

"Not quite. Where will you fish, John? To the right, down that path?" Phoebe asked. "I'd just like to sit up here a minute to take in this beauty."

"You're correct. Our beat is the upper part of the river, Bill's is the lower. At lunchtime we may swap," James answered.

James continued, "It's fine, Phoebe, if you want to sit here for a while. I'll carry your rod down the bluff. At the bottom, I'll assemble it and put a fly on it. I'll tie my bandana on the bush where I leave it. That way you won't need to hurry."

He was a kind husband indeed, but one who didn't want anything or anybody to delay his getting about his own fishing.

"Be careful coming down," he called back to her, after he started down the bank. "Fish close enough so we can see you. Good luck."

"I'll be right back up the bluff when I get the men settled," John told her.

Phoebe was content. Not only was she filled with the beauty of the countryside, but she had time to enjoy it.

Opposite her, across the river from her perch on the high bluff, she saw glowering dark clouds. Did they indicate rain or the approach of the long night? When a break in the clouds appeared, the setting sun shone in rays of brilliance against the darkness.

Just then a heavy pounding erupted like thunder across from her. In the glowing light of the sunset, she saw a herd of fifteen or twenty ponies galloping at full speed, manes and tails flying, following a wild-eyed lead horse straight to the edge of the bank.

She squeezed her eyes shut to block out the catastrophe that she felt was inevitable. When a clatter of stones and dirt rained down the opposite bluff, she forced her eyes open.

She saw the animal, undoubtedly a stallion, legs splayed, brace to a stop one stride away from the edge of the cliff. Behind him, the mares and foals reared also and stomped themselves to a precarious standstill.

In a matter of minutes, the horses were again quietly grazing as though nothing out of the ordinary had happened. Phoebe sat quietly for a moment to let the pounding of her heart subside. The horses became part of the quiet beauty of the evening. She couldn't risk moving for fear of startling the stallion and his mares.

Suddenly, the stallion lifted his head, ears laid back, straining to a magic call. The mares stopped their grazing and waited. The stallion pivoted and in a streaming gallop led his mares away across the field and out of her life. The evening settled back again into its quiet beauty.

John had not returned. She collected her gear and cautiously made her way down the bluff, not wanting anything to disturb the drama of the horses in her mind.

Back in the fishing world, she found her rod where James had left it, a Black Doctor fly tied on the tippet. She hiked to a location well away from James's spot, but within view of him.

She chose a place with no bushes to snag her line. Then she maneuvered her way a few paces into the water and began to make practice casts.

It was hard to wield the heavy rod, particularly when she tried to keep the weighted line upright over her shoulder, without letting it drop too far down behind her. She knew that that would ruin the forward part of the cast, even if she could manage to keep the unwieldy line from getting snagged on some bushes.

"It's like patting your tummy and rubbing your head," she said out loud. But doggedly she kept practicing.

John Arnam appeared. He had been hopscotching between the men. "How are the others doing?" she asked.

"James has had two fine salmon. We're taking them back to be smoked. I'm returning to Bill now. But first let's see how you are doing. I'm sorry it took me so long to return to you. How have you been doing?"

"For a while, I watched some amazing wild ponies. What beauties! Then I came down the path. Since then, I have been practicing with this heavy tackle. The weight makes it difficult for me. Did you see the ponies?"

"Not now, but many times before. They aren't wild, but they do roam free. The farmers raise them for meat."

"For meat? You don't mean they *eat* these lovely creatures?"

"Yes, they bring in good money. Now may I help you catch a salmon? Walk down the shore a bit to the point where the stream narrows. The fish like to rest against that far bank."

At first, in spite of her practice, Phoebe was too conscious of his educated scrutiny to do well. But, finally, her pride made her settle down and try harder.

She moved and cast, then cast again, until her arm began to ache. "I'm almost ready to call it quits, for the first night," she called to John on the bank. He held up one finger, for one more cast, gesturing toward the far side of the river.

She moved deeper into the stream, as far as she dared, and continued to cast. Finally, she reached her objective, a cast near the other side. A salmon struck the fly immediately and surfaced once.

All weariness forgotten, she set the hook. She had to pull with both hands to elevate the tip of the heavy rod. "How can I possibly reel in and get the salmon to the beach?" she called.

The answer came from John. "One step at a time," he said and began moving toward her.

If she'd had any extra breath, she would have called, "How can I get ready to bring the salmon in when he isn't ready yet?" She didn't have that breath, so she just kept reeling and walking backward.

The fish didn't run or jump. He too just hung in there. "If this is the battle of the ages," she thought, "why does the fish just lie there? I'd like some action from him before I reach the beach."

Instantly, her wish was granted. The salmon ran so far upstream that she began to worry as she followed him, about whether he was pulling out the backing. Soon she was too busy reeling and retrieving to think about her backing or any other problem. All she could concentrate on was keeping the rod tip up. She didn't have time to remember to be careful or to pray. John Arnam stayed right beside her.

As soon as she felt sand underfoot, she planted her legs wide, the better to keep the rod braced. She kept reeling. Her only reliance now was on the line. But she figured without John. He paralleled the line out to the limit of his hip boots, ready to help, net in upraised hand.

She tried to direct the line closer to him, while reeling and walking. Time stood still. So did John, until she saw him swoop the net under the water and bring it up with the fish in it.

"Keep reeling," John ordered.

She couldn't believe his instructions. "Hers not to do or die, hers just to reel the fly!" she muttered.

John with the netted fish and she with a taut line reached the beach together. He laid the fish, still in the net, on the ground. He killed the fish with a rock, with never a protest from Phoebe's lips. She was too tired to speak.

"I'll leave the fish here with you," he said, tucking it under some bushes. "Don't move 'til I come back."

She couldn't have moved if she had tried.

They got home about ten-thirty, with four fish, James's two, one from Bill, and hers. They pulled off waders, cleaned up sketchily, and sat right down for dinner, drinks in hand.

She slipped into her bedroom while everyone was still reliving the night's fishing. Her wristwatch said midnight as she burrowed blissfully under the covers, sinking as deep into the thin mattress as she could.

Elaine Alson told Phoebe a day or so later that she'd be having her birthday soon, her eighth time in Iceland. "We may make it at teatime," she mentioned. "Dinner is so late."

"You have it whenever you want. You're the birthday girl,"

Phoebe suggested. "How long will it ever take us to get oriented to such short sleeping hours? Of course, the long fishing hours are the real problem."

"Our men don't call that a problem!" Elaine laughed.

Phoebe's group was not on the river at seven a.m. each morning, but they were out as soon as the men could expedite Phoebe. The day when they were assigned the bridge beat on the Vestura River (in English, the West River), Phoebe made a superhuman effort. They were on the road among the early departees for the bridge. James beamed his appreciation to her for the extra fifteen minutes that this gave them. With his every smile, Phoebe stiffened her resolve to be prompt.

John Arnam either had to drive behind a succession of farm and road repair vehicles, which made for slow moving, or go around them. "The farmers certainly use the long daylight hours of summer to full advantage, while we foreigners are fishing," James commented. "This way, we are all helping their GNP."

"They must have the same problem that we do, finding time to sleep," Phoebe mentioned.

"Remember what all tourists need to learn, that winter is the time when Icelanders and their guests sleep," Bill reminded her.

John Arnam put Bill above the bridge and the MacLeans below. James and Phoebe tacked down the steep road embankment. Rather, he tacked. She slid.

Phoebe realized immediately that the best-looking pools in the river were too close to the bridge for any easy casting on her part. Even if she tried, she'd be in James's way. If she reclimbed the difficult bank to fish on the grassier side near Bill, she might create a noisy disturbance for both of them. She decided to watch and read.

She saw that James would have a big casting problem. He had to miss both the bank before him and the bridge beside him, and incidentally, his wife. Phoebe shifted a little farther away in order to diminish at least one of his problems.

Over and over her husband aimed for the one small open space available. His patience in trying to place the fly exactly where he wanted it was impressive. Her book remained unopened in her lap. She hoped the fish would wait for James's perfect cast.

He did. James got a good strike. Quickly, Phoebe returned the book to her backpack and settled down to serious watching.

She saw the fish run. James followed him on the few big stones that were visible above the water on his side of the bridge. Would the stones stay solid enough for James to reel in from such a precarious perch?

The fish must have been as confused as Phoebe was. She saw James's line go suddenly limp. Had the fish gotten off?

No, he had reversed himself and was swimming toward the bridge and her husband. James continued reeling in the limp line. Phoebe watched James finally get the rod tip upright. But the angle of the line showed that the fish had reversed himself again. He was swimming hard for the part of the stream on the far side of the bridge opposite from where they were.

What could James do next? Phoebe was sure that he couldn't attempt to cross the river as it flowed under the bridge. However, he told Phoebe later, that from where the fish led him, he had spotted an outcropping of pebbles under the surface of the water that formed a narrow peninsula to the opposite bank. Phoebe saw James make several huge jumps without falling. He made the opposite shore, still with the fish on his line.

She scrambled up the bank to the bridge. She dodged between two harvesters rumbling down the road and made the railing on the other side.

There was James midstream, rod high, fish still on, calmly bringing him to the right-hand shore where John Arnam and Bill were waiting, John ready with net raised.

James skillfully maneuvered the salmon to the net just as though there had not been a bridge to complicate his catch. His nonchalance was belied by the twitching of a small smile that Phoebe saw, playing around the corners of his lips.

At the lodge for lunch, John Arnam weighed the fish in at over nine pounds. James received congratulations with quiet pride as he downed a victory libation that was offered to him, even before he had gotten into dry clothes.

The day after James's experience at the bridge on the Vestura, the West River, the MacLeans and Bill were pleased to fish the Canyon beat on the Austura, the East River. James caught several fine salmon in the early morning. Bill, who had fished above them, had had big action, but only small fish.

During the evening period, they returned to the beat where Phoebe had seen the wild ponies. She fished a pool between the two men that John Arnam suggested for her.

When he returned to check on her and found that she had not had a strike, he proposed that she follow him a little farther upstream and cross over the river, in order to cast against the canyon wall that rose above that shore.

But it was after they fished through the canyon that they found a pool at the upper end, fed by the river as it flowed out of the canyon.

John Arnam stopped. "Here is a beautiful deep pool. There is a fish in there waiting to be caught before he swims on upstream."

"I'd be honored to try for it, but I can't promise the results," Phoebe answered, warmed by his smile. They were two conspirators, teamed against one salmon. She awaited instructions.

"We'll use a special fly for a special lady," John Arnam decided, "a Silver Doctor this time."

He tied on the fly and then pointed to a place in the stream. "I want you to start right here to get a full sweep of these prime waters."

Phoebe cast several times before she was reasonably satisfied with herself. "Watch that snag bobbing in the center of the current," John Arnam cautioned her.

She moved away from the snag, which made her casts go in the direction of the opposite shore. "I may as well try to reach it," she told herself, now close to the middle of the river.

"Shorten your cast," John called to her. "You can't reach the other side, and you don't need to try. The fish often follow the fly and lie much closer to you."

"But casting is the most fun, and making a long cast feels like progress, particularly if you haven't been catching fish," Phoebe explained.

"So, if the way to keep you from overcasting is to have you catch fish," John smiled, as he announced his conclusion, "then I need to guide you to more fish!" He moved into the stream and stood at her shoulder.

"Shorten your line," John told her again. "Cast in front of that submerged rock. Let the line swing. Retrieve slowly. Do it again . . . and again . . . Move down three paces and repeat," John Arnam instructed her.

She must have moved at least five times when she spotted another submerged rock. "There's a likely spot for a resting fish," she suggested.

"Try it" was the answer.

Once, twice, three, four times, she cast, becoming fond of this spot. Oh, bother, soon she would need to move.

"Once more," she was surprised to hear John say, violating what she now considered a casting rule, to move after three or four casts.

Phoebe tried to manipulate the fly to tease a fish that might strike from boredom or from recalling memories of prespawning hunger pangs. A fish struck the teasing fly. "Eureka!" John Arnam exclaimed. "Now go to work."

But it was a short success. The salmon shook the fly out of his mouth smartly and swam away. "Keep at it," John said tersely.

In her effort to do as he instructed, she came dangerously close to the snag that ruled over the middle part of the stream. It had been drawing her line like a magnet ever since she started fishing there.

The snag finally won, gobbling down her fly. But she jerked quickly enough and the fly flew free. Score, thus far—a draw.

She moved her stance and cast wide of the snag, and therefore, closer to the opposite bank. Avoiding John Arnam's eye, she continued, but each cast was short of the mark.

Finally, glaring balefully at the huge dangling fly that was so hard for her to handle, she made a mighty cast and saw the fly land, not in the water below the bank, but on the bank. Undaunted, she gave several steady jerks and the fly dropped off into the water. Instantly she had a strike.

It felt like a big fish. With a superhuman effort, she managed to get her rod tip upright. But then she realized that the fish was swimming straight for the snag. She could only follow, pulling hard to deflect him and reeling in steadily. Sick with fright that the leader would break from the pressure, she maneuvered him above the snag.

"Fine so far," said John Arnam at her elbow, "but don't let the fish run too much upstream, in case he heads for the left branch of the stream. You would need to ford the stream to follow him there. I'm not sure you could manage that."

Phoebe knew she couldn't. Cramps were running up and down her tired arms like the cords of a Venetian blind. But with the snag below her and the divided river above, she had no time to panic. She hung on to her fish, tighter than she knew was safe, in an effort to check his runs. Every time he rested between runs, she reeled in as hard as she could. Whenever she had enough time between runs, she'd take a backward step to the shore.

She didn't know whether to laugh or cry when she heard James's voice from the beach. Could she handle an audience? She was on a never-ending treadmill, trying not to lose the fish.

From the corner of her eye, she saw that John Arnam had moved into shallow water near the beach, waiting with net upraised. She staggered toward him, rod still taut, trying to bring the salmon close to him.

Finally, she reached the safety of beach stones under her feet. Now she could concentrate on manipulating the salmon. At last, she guided him into the shallow water by John.

Suddenly, she saw a spasm of movement from the fish, strong enough to create waves. Phoebe felt her line go limp. She reeled in. The line was empty. It dangled free. No fish!

Phoebe leaped toward the shallow pool where she had guided him and barely avoided bumping into John. Amazingly, she could see the fish lying quiet, breathing hard, probably as startled as she was. Then, he shook himself and pointed his body, arrow straight, toward the deep water.

But in that split second, John threw himself bodily on top of the fish, and pinned him down in the pool. He worked his hands around the slippery body and got a firm grip on it. Gently he lifted the dazed fish and tossed him high on the grass, where James took over, dropping on all fours above the fish.

John Arnam stood up and calmly began to wring water from his dripping sweater. He announced, "This is called the Lady Hole. This lady caught a salmon at the Lady Hole."

Then, glancing at the very quiet, very manhandled fish, he continued, "From the looks of him, he is all ready to be smoked. You have yourself a fine fish, Phoebe."

James embraced his wife, keeping a wary eye on the fish until John Arnam rose from killing him. Then both MacLeans simultaneously gave John such huge bear hugs that their arms met around his ample waist.

Uncle Bill still had only caught one fish large enough to qualify as a salmon. "Call me the Grilse King of Iceland," he mourned as the end of the week approached. "I know how slight the difference in action between a five-and-a-half-pound grilse and a six-pound salmon can be. I don't mind for myself. After all, I've had more action than any four people put together with these grilse. They're real fighters. My worry is what my cronies at the club in Pittsburgh will say, when they hear that, officially, I have only caught one salmon. They sent me off to Iceland with a big bash of a party."

"It's just a technicality," Phoebe comforted.

"The week's not over," James stressed.

Their beat on the final day was below the junction of the Ves-tura and the Austura rivers in a marshy area on the way to the air-port. Beyond this was the mouth of the Midfjardara River that emptied into what eventually became the Greenland Sea.

"I'm sure Bill will catch a salmon down here that will delight his Pittsburgh friends," John Arnam promised as they started the long drive to this lowest beat. "I've brought along a picnic hamper with a lunch so huge that we will have enough for tea. We will observe the rest period down here."

"Between the two periods of fishing, while we let the the stream rest, we'll play gin rummy," James decided. "I've brought some liq-uid refreshment," he added, "of course, just for good luck."

Phoebe told Bill, "I bet you've been saving your big triumph for the last day, in order to beat James, hands down. We'll send you off for the second half with a high tea."

"And welcome you back with a drink!" James concluded.

No one caught any counters during the morning hours. John Arnam suggested a beach near the ocean for the rest period. "Let's lunch there even if the weather at the beach may force us to take shelter in the car," he told them.

"Great idea!" they all agreed.

As they started the drive to the ocean, they noticed that the farmhouses became more windswept and the roads narrower the closer they came to the mouth of the Midfjardara River. At the beach, John made a driftwood fire. The drizzle held off and the fire dispelled the cold. John emptied the carton that held food-stuffs, and after lunch they played a token game of gin rummy. Soon Iceland became another one of a chain of fishing arcas where they had played gin rummy with Uncle Bill.

Four sets of eyes were watching the time during the game. When John Arnam propped a small kettle on a driftwood fire and gave them mugs of hot tea, they knew that it was time to pack up and return to the river.

Warm and refreshed, they began their fishing again. Phoebe started out between the men. Bill stayed closer to the mouth. "I want to catch a salmon with sea lice on it, the proof that she has just come in from the ocean to spawn."

"Think of what a long journey lies ahead for the fish!" Phoebe mused.

"And the difficulties that they will need to surmount," James added. Phoebe flashed him an appreciative smile. She did like this man of hers. *Liking* was a major ingredient of *loving*.

Phoebe found that she had drifted away from the men, but she still had them within sight, if not within sound. The evening was turning a monotonous grey. Even a brilliant sunset would have trouble breaking through this soupy thickness. It began to turn colder.

She was enjoying casting, hoping to surprise a newcomer not yet wary of the vicious two-legged creatures marauding these riverbanks. With every cast, she tried to keep a constant distance from James, but she was getting too close.

Phoebe put some more distance between them and found herself along a marshy bank where casting would be simple and easy, for a change, and where it would be warmer than standing in the river.

She cast several times and then turned sideways on the bank to edge to a new position for one more series of casts before returning to the cold water. She felt a sickening sensation under her feet. The bank was giving away under her weight. Her feet groped unsuccessfully for a firm footing. There wasn't any.

She tried to twist backward, hoping to drop to her knees and crawl to firmer ground, but instead the sliding bank carried her slowly forward with it. She continued to try to keep her balance by twisting backward and groping futilely for a handhold. There was nothing solid, just slippery dirt.

In front of her, a large chunk of bank gave way. As though in slow motion she felt herself falling forward. She was just able to jerk her rod upright before she fell on her knees into the water.

The muck broke her fall! She felt it oozing around her, but by digging in her toes, she found solid ground. It must be the gravelly river bottom. She wasn't going to die an icy death, after all, like the poor sailors in the hymn.

She took a big breath and pushed with her free hand against the river bottom, but she couldn't budge. She thrust the butt of her rod as hard as she could with the hand that held it, trying not to think of what was happening to the reel. She was able to struggle upright. What a place she had chosen to cast!

The muck sucked harder at her legs than she could push against it. But she knew now that there was a solid bottom underneath. Continuing to use the rod in the mud for balance, she propelled one leg forward, and with a push, the other. She found a rhythm and slowly worked her feet out of the mire toward a solid-looking bank.

She crawled up on all fours and didn't stop until she was safely back on solid ground. She sat up thankfully, laid the caked rod aside, and reached in a pocket to see if she could find her bandana handkerchief.

She wiped the mud from her face with the soaked handkerchief and began to feel as though she still belonged to the human race. She scanned the river for the men until she located them. Bill was in front, and the other two were watching him intently. He must have a strike! No one had seen her fall.

She was beginning to shake all over, only partly from the cold. She made her way to the car, squishing with every step. She found some dry socks that belonged to someone and her own loafers. She pulled off her soaked jacket and slipped on a mackintosh that must have been John Arnam's. She dug out her own dry rain gear that she had left in the car.

She raided the picnic hamper and found some raisins. Then she poured a cup of hot tea. After the first long sip, she decided that she was ready for reentry into her own life.

Now that she was safe, she was glad that no one knew what had happened. She wanted only to get to Bill. He needed all his support team.

John Arnam must have been keeping an eye out for her. When

he saw her, he motioned for her to hurry. In her loafers instead of waders, she practically skimmed over the rainy ground.

No doubt about it, Bill had a fish on his line. He was bringing all his skill and knowledge to land it. Phoebe glanced at her watch, eight-thirty. There might not be another chance for Bill to catch a salmon, if he lost this one, before their long trip back to the lodge.

James came over to her briefly. "It's a big salmon, a counter, if Bill can bring it in. Just so he doesn't get too tense. I think a fish can sense that," he said, turning to hurry toward Bill. Phoebe touched him briefly as he passed, as an assurance to herself that she was really back near him.

She found a stunted tree to lean against and went into her supporting routine, prayers, fingers crossed, tongue in left cheek. She strained to see the fish in the grey light.

She felt that Bill seemed confident, not tense. If she were a more experienced fisherman, she might be able to read the fish and the fishermen more accurately. As it was, she decided to rely on prayers.

Bill reeled steadily. Had his adversary tired himself out before she arrived? She thought, as she frequently did, of the nursery song that said, "You never can tell about fish."

Something had happened that was concerning the men. She saw John Arnam hasten to Bill and momentarily put both hands over the case of Bill's reel. She couldn't see what he was doing. Then he nodded, satisfied, and withdrew.

Bill continued his steady reeling and careful backward walk to the shore. She found out later that the cover of the reel had come so loose that Bill could have lost the whole reel at any moment, even after John Arnam tightened it on as hard as he could. Were the threads on the screws worn?

Phoebe started to shake uncontrollably with the damp chilliness, just as she had done in the river. She couldn't leave to seek warmth. "Now, Bill," she whispered and hurried closer.

Bill began to reel faster, backing up into the water in front of the marshy bank. Phoebe could glimpse his fish in the shallow water. He was big and mean-looking.

The salmon began to pull his head from side to side, thrashing his whole body. He was defying his fate. John Arnam stood at the edge of the water. He looked poised to jump in. Phoebe knew, from her own experience with him when he was guiding for her, that he would do that, if it became necessary.

Just then Bill got his line taut enough to maneuver the fish right in against the bank. He held him there until John Arnam arrived with his net. In a beautiful sweeping motion, John swooped the salmon into the net and eased him onto the grass.

Everyone finally breathed again. "I did it!" Bill almost shouted. "Now I can go home to Pittsburgh, respectable!" He beamed at the salmon like a long lost friend.

"Bill," James said solemnly, "I want to see him hanging on your wall the next time I come to visit."

"Me too," Phoebe added.

Bill stood up and reached a hand over to John Arnam. "And you too, Arnam. I want you to come see my fish, mounted."

"God willing," John said, holding up the fish with reverence. "It will be difficult to get him home in good enough condition to mount."

"At least, let's try. What will he weigh?" Bill asked. "Not that it matters. He is a salmon, and he is mine!"

"He'll go over ten pounds. And, look, he's so fresh that he still has sea lice on him," John Arnam pointed out.

"Let's get to the car where I have Scotch for a toast," James said. "Phoebe, you look cold."

"I am. I had to raid the car to get warm," she told him. And that veiled reference was all she ever said about falling in the muddy water just before the moment of Bill's triumph.

Deildara and Ormarsa

IN 1981, JAMES MACLEAN applied too late to get accommodations either at Grimsa or Midfjardara lodges. Before he could review other alternatives, he had a letter from Frontiers International, the premier booking agency for lodges and rivers in Iceland, announcing that two salmon fly-fishing rivers, the Deildara and the Ormarsa, had recently been opened to foreign fly-fishermen for the coming summer. Before this, only commercial fishing companies had operated there.

James found the area of the Deildara and Ormarsa rivers on a map of *Island*, the Icelandic spelling for the country. It was so far north that it almost touched the area around the Arctic Circle. "That will be a new experience," James told his wife, "regardless of how the fishing is. Let's give it a try. What do you say?"

"Let's investigate it, at least. That's far enough ahead that I have nothing on my calendar in July," Phoebe replied.

"Good gal. Spoken like a wife who knows that fishing is the most important thing on anyone's calendar!"

"Don't push your luck too far," Phoebe MacLean responded.

At the Saga Hotel in Reykjavik the next July, Phoebe and James met the four men who would be fishing these two Northern streams with them. They heard that there would also be another couple, a husband and wife who had arrived earlier and were sightseeing around the island. They would be at the airport the following morning.

The chartered two-motor plane leaving for Rauforhofm, the airport that served the Deildara and Ormarsa rivers, was waiting for them the next morning. "It holds ten people, just the right size for our group," James pointed out to Phoebe.

"It's too small for safety," she retorted. Intellectually, she accepted the principle of flight, but not emotionally. However, when she began to look around for the other woman, she forgot to remember to be concerned. Imagine, another woman on a fishing trip in this remote place.

At the Reykjavik airport, each guest formed an island in a sea of gear as they waited to board the small plane. A porter picked up Phoebe's duffel bag and suitcase. He gestured for her to take her rods and hand luggage on board herself.

The pilot remained at the controls during the loading, busy revving up the motors. She didn't have time to glimpse the other woman as she scrambled to fit herself and her gear into one of the seats in the two rows of single seats. Then, during take-off, she was too busy concentrating on her efforts to help the pilot get the plane airborne to look for the other woman.

It was not until they were in flight that Phoebe spotted her across the aisle and forward two seats. The woman was so surrounded by her bundles that all Phoebe could see of her was light brown hair and clear skin. She was talking brightly across the aisle to a man, probably her husband. Intermittently, the woman peered out the small window.

"She and her husband seem to be amicable, and she likes to talk," she said to James across the aisle.

"Who?"

"The other woman, of course." Satisfied with her observation, Phoebe turned to take in the view from her own window.

The day was grey and the countryside looked equally grey. "I miss the flowers we have seen in the other places," Phoebe commented above the noise of the motors.

"These are fishermen, not farmers with wives who have time to garden," James decided. "The women are busy running the farms while their husbands are gone."

Phoebe interspersed, "It's always been a wonder to me that with all the women have to do they manage to garden. Think how much time it must take them, for instance, to hang and rehang the washing in this constant rainy weather."

"I bet they just let the clothes hang," James decided and picked up his fishing magazine. Conversation completed.

At the end of the short flight to Rauforhofm, the pilot circled the town in order to get the plane in position for landing. They saw that the town was right on the sea. Fishing wharves and packing sheds lined the water. A small street led past the only two-story building in town. A few stores clustered around the wharves, and simple framed houses straggled behind them. "I don't see anything that resembles a lodge," was Phoebe's comment.

"You'll just have to wait and see. Consider it a surprise. You know how much you like surprises!"

James's remarks were a surprise in themselves to Phoebe. Was he trying to be conversational or was he trying to get her mind off a possible disappointment? Either way, she appreciated his concern and responded with a smile.

When they landed, everyone was promptly directed to a van. Again Phoebe looked for the other woman, but again she found that she was too far away to speak to. Phoebe waved and the woman waved back. The luggage was being loaded into a second van. Soon their driver took off.

The road ran along the sea that was dotted with fishing boats, some close to the shore, others further out. "I hope they leave a few salmon for us," James muttered from his reading of the map. "This bay must be a part of the Greenland Sea," he said.

The van pulled up in front of the only two-story building and let them out. Steep steps rose up on one outside wall of the building. The downstairs first floor looked like a store, converted to an office. A pleasant man stood waving to them at the bottom of the steps and led them up the stairs.

"Welcome to Rauforhofm, the fishing capital of the Northland. Come this way to the hotel."

"Perhaps he thinks we are tourists, not fishermen," Phoebe commented. James motioned her to be silent.

The stairs led to an open room, with several long linoleum-covered tables on both sides. Phoebe saw a hall straight beyond, with doors standing open at angles like spokes of a fan, to show the bedrooms. At the tables to the right, some workmen were eating a late lunch. They didn't look like fishermen. "Definitely a hotel, not a lodge," Phoebe said to James.

The man who led them upstairs gestured toward a drink dispenser machine and a pitcher of juice. "I'm Svenn. Make yourselves at home. I'll be back soon with room keys and the names of your guides. The sons of local families are acting as guides this summer, during their holidays from the university."

James mentioned to Phoebe, "The farmers are getting smart about the money they shell out for salaries to guides. They are keeping it in the families. I hope the kids know something about fishing these rivers."

Phoebe stacked her things near her duffel bag and moved toward the other woman, hand outstretched. "I'm Phoebe MacLean from San Francisco. I was so pleased to learn that there would be another woman on this trip. You must be Mrs. Ward."

"Yes, I am Jane Ward from Los Angeles. What a kind welcome." She clasped Phoebe's hand firmly. "It will be so nice to get to know you. What do you do when you aren't on a fishing trip?"

Before Phoebe could answer, a young fellow traveler came up and interrupted. "Excuse me, but my friend and I have been talking about you," he said to Jane Ward. "Aren't you Jane Wyman, the movie star? I'm sure I saw you on TV the other night. You were terrific."

"Yes, I am Jane Wyman. And I bet you were watching *The Yearling*. That's the one that keeps popping up on the late show. Thank you for the compliment." She turned directly back to Phoebe, terminating the conversation without being rude to the young man. Years of practice, no doubt. "Now to get back to us. Do you fish?"

"Oh, yes. I can't imagine James *not* teaching his wife to fly-fish. I think it's an outlet for his enthusiasm, like pouring over catalogues. Some men tie flies. James teaches me."

"Do you enjoy it?"

"Very much. I get too carried away with practice casting. A wise guide once told me that you don't catch fish with the fly in the air!"

Jane Ward laughed. "I get carried away with bird watching. I concentrate on birds, instead of fish, though I do go out almost every day with Edgar when he is fishing."

"Husbands do enjoy a built-in audience, don't they? I'm sure that they think my fishing or your birding are only sidelines to our real career of watching them."

"Oh, we're going to have a lot to talk about, and I love good conversation. Don't you?"

"Ask my James! Let's make sure we sit together at dinner tonight."

"Fine. We'll start right where we have left off now because here comes our leader, hopefully, with the room keys. You'd better watch out, my new friend. I'll turn you into a bird watcher too."

Phoebe waved and walked over to James and their island of luggage. When keys were given out, she claimed theirs and left to find their room, while James waited to see which of the very young guides would be theirs. "Tea at three-thirty," she heard someone mention before she left.

She located the bath and shower rooms down the hall and unpacked just enough to be ready for fishing after tea. She stretched out on the bed for just a moment and fell asleep.

James wakened her in time for tea. "The guide's a nice kid, but I'm sure that I know more about fishing than he does. How was Mrs. Ward?"

"Very interesting. It's going to be fun to have her here. She's a movie star. Do you remember *The Yearling* by Marjorie Kinnan Rawlings? She played the mother in the movie made from that book, as well as other roles in movies. Her movie name is Jane Wyman."

"I remember, vaguely."

"The more I talk to her, the more I recall her in 'The Yearling' role. She's going to be an interesting addition to the trip."

At tea, the MacLeans talked to the other four men and met Edgar Ward. "He's also fished at the Grimsa and at Midfjardara," James told her later. "Recently, he's been investigating bonefishing in tropical waters. I'll be interested to hear of that."

"Here we go again," Phoebe thought to herself. "I wonder how soon before I'll hear that James is talking about a bonefishing trip!"

The beats on the Deildara River covered only four miles, but Svenn said that, within that distance, there were seventeen small productive pools. "I'd settle for seven larger ones," James announced.

"Oh ye of little faith in statistics," Phoebe amended.

Their college guide, Christian, was a psychology major, whose course didn't include studying a river. He drove the MacLeans to their beat.

James chose a riffle just before the river widened into what looked like deeper but somewhat sluggish water. "Let's try here," he suggested to the guide, who obviously appreciated not having to make a fishing decision.

Phoebe watched her husband cast to the riffle, constantly in a different spot, first with a Green Highlander, then with a Black Doctor. Finally, he changed to a Thunder and Lightning, hoping that that might intrigue a resting salmon. But the salmon continued to rest.

Later, when James stopped to assess the stream, he found Phoebe sitting nearby. "I don't like the looks of that lower water," he said. "I'm going back to the top and try this pool again. The pool will rest while I walk back. If you come with me, stay well away from the river so you won't disturb the water. But why aren't you fishing?"

"I'm waiting for you to find me the perfect pool."

"You know you can't wait for someone to do that for you. You also know that you can't catch a fish sitting on the bank."

"So you've told me. O.K., O.K.," she said, getting up.

"Perhaps next trip, you'd rather stay home," he said in annoyance.

"Remember, you said that, not me."

"Phoebe, I'm sorry. You know I didn't mean it. You're a better fisherman than I am."

165

"You always say that in order to keep me coming on these trips and to show what a good teacher you are. All right, I'll choose my own pools and do my own fishing. I bet I can bring in a bigger salmon than you can, even on this slow river. If I do, will you promise not to heckle me about not fishing?"

"It's a deal. Now let's stop talking and fish." James turned up-stream abruptly.

Phoebe went downstream, skirting the riffle widely. James was right. The water looked very slow. But maybe a resting fish might like slow water. "If I were tired from fighting my way up from the ocean, I might want quiet water for a rest."

She fished well into the evening without a nibble. The salmon were either too tired or too bored to strike. She had tried all but two of the flies in her box.

Reluctantly, she decided to return to her husband to check his assortment of flies. She found him in the midst of a battle, tense with excitement.

No sign of young Christian, but she spotted James's net close to where he was fighting the fish. She picked it up and held it ready but kept clear of the action.

Twice, James reeled the fish in so near to him that Phoebe felt sure he would be able to bring him up to the beach, but twice the line twanged out again, and the fish swam farther away. Over and over, James repeated the process.

Phoebe's nerves were as taut as her husband's line. When James finally managed to get the fish in shallow water beside the beach, she saw him shortening his line.

Phoebe hurried to him, the handle of the net held toward him. James grabbed it and, keeping his rod high and tight in his left hand, scooped the fish into the net. From habit, Phoebe reached for James's camera in the back pocket of his fishing jacket and snapped a picture of him holding up the salmon.

She noticed the guide strolling toward them. He arrived in time to see James place the fish on the grass, hold him firm with one hand, and with the other, remove the fly with an expert twist.

166

Then James found a rock and killed the fish. The guide watched with interest, but without a trace of guilt for not helping.

James stood up with his prize, full of happy grins. "I bet he's close to seven pounds, an excellent size for smoking, if the farmers have arrangements here to do that," James said. "Remind me to inquire. Now, tell me how you are doing."

"Well, lots of good practice. I'm off again. Come find me when it's time to leave. I only came back to check some of your flies."

"Get any you want from my bag. I'll send the guide to stay with you, after he puts the salmon in his car."

Fortified with new flies and much resolution, Phoebe tried to think of what a weary fish might like to see float by. And where?

She chose a spot opposite a large rock as the most likely place. She began to cast her Blue Charm fly into the shadow of the rock where water coursed around it on both sides.

"Not tempted yet?" she asked the fish. "No hurry. I'll give you lots of chances."

She did, over and over. She knew she had to move soon or alert every fish in the river of her presence. Where had the fish, whom she had hoped were there, gone?

Upstream on the same side were several low shrubs that shadowed the water slightly. She favored shadowy places when she was trying to think like a fish. If food, brought by the current, floated past, it was like curb service for the waiting fish. She certainly appreciated food brought to her occasionally.

As silently as possible, she moved far enough out into the stream so that she could cast into the shadow of the willows. She sent several rather accurate casts into the shadow, hoping her retrieve was gentle enough not to frighten any fish who might be waiting. She saw a dark head emerge for one flash. The fish swallowed the fly and took off, just as she had hoped it would.

Holding the line high with one hand, Phoebe released her wading staff from the back of her fishing vest. She let it dangle, in order to use both hands to get the fish firmly on the reel, but it took too long. He was already swimming strongly away with her line.

She gripped the wading stick to help her move after the fish. She stopped periodically to get more line on the reel and to try to slow down the progress of the fish. She could have used the help of a good guide right now.

But her efforts did not pay off. One huge jerk shuddered down the rod and into her arm, followed by a limp deadness. No more straining rod, no strong tugging at the line. Her fish, her contest fish, had torn off the hook and was gone!

She reeled in, shaking what was left of the line in frustration and disappointment. She limped back to shore and dangled the empty line in front of young Christian, who had surfaced. She told him, "Along with the fly, that fish took my tippet. It broke right off the leader. I've never tied on a tippet without help."

Christian scrutinized the dangling line. "I've never tied a knot on a fishing line either, but I know how to tie some nautical knots that my father taught me when I helped on his boat during vacations."

"Let's give it a try," she said. Christian had just become a valuable friend to her.

Phoebe settled on a rock and began to rummage through her pockets. In her fishing jacket, she found a new tippet. "Thank goodness. I'll show you what I remember from watching James, and I'll get out a new fly. But we don't have much time left before the end of the fishing hours. "

"You have tomorrow and tomorrow," said Christian. Had he taken a course in Shakespeare at college?

"But I need to catch a fish tonight!"

Both heads bent over the problem. Never had such a knot been concocted, to fasten tippet to leader. Phoebe tied on the fly, jerking it hard to test it, and stood up. "Stay close to me with the net, Christian, just in case. I'm moving to a new spot. Follow me, please."

Leaving both the riffle and the shadow of the shrubbery behind, Phoebe surveyed a new territory, wishing for some sunshine in this twilight of grey. She was amused to realize that she was looking for a security blanket of warm sun rays.

Christian came up to her. "Are you starting?"

"Yes. Two things that would make for perfect fishing, to get a strike and to have our knots hold."

The river made a slight bend. Ahead, they saw a lone tree and a lean-to shed. In the tree, a solitary bird sang a monotonous three-note song.

"When I was little, I used to come here with my oldest brother," said Christian. "He kept a fishing pole he had made in that shed. While he fished, I built bridges in a little stream that flowed into the river beside this shed. I never liked fishing, but maybe now I will."

"Show me the stream where you built your bridges. Fish like to feed where a stream flows into a river. If we catch a fish there, I bet you'll begin to like fishing. We'll see what happens."

Christian led her to the stream, which was barely a rivulet. "Keep back from the water so that if a fish is lying near, he won't see you before he sees my fly," Phoebe told him. "And pray that he likes the looks of my fly. They say that fish don't feed going up to spawn, but I think they strike sometimes, just to keep in practice or because they're bored."

"I didn't know there was so much to fishing," Christian said. "But what if there isn't a fish here?"

"That's what you never know. That's the challenging part." How did she get herself into these fixes? Now she had to catch a fish because she had thrown James a gauntlet, and she had practically promised Christian to catch a fish in his little stream. She should take up knitting instead!

She moved carefully to the streamside. Not a stone, not a bush to give a shadow for cover, just grey sluggish water, a miserable place to mount a combat. Perhaps bright sun would have made the fishing harder. She was caught on the horns of a dilemma, until she noticed a few shrubs near the mouth of the riverlet.

Cautiously she stationed herself above the riverlet and the scant shrub cover. "I'll cast upstream with a wet fly. Anything goes in an emergency. The fly will float past the fish twice, once down and once back."

Her first two casts were wobbly. Her third was better. "Not bad," she told herself, "unconventional, but adequate to the situation." She was pleased.

Suddenly, her pleasant thinking was interrupted. She had a vicious strike. War had been declared!

She reeled in until her rod was dangerously bent by the weight of the fish. She'd have to move after him. To her relief, she heard Christian right behind her. "The wading stick is hanging from the center back of my fishing jacket. Please pull the end out to extend it."

He did, so hard he almost jerked her down, and thrust it toward her. She propped the rod against her stomach and held it there with one hand, in order to grab the stick. She planted it cautiously and began a series of backward moves, stopping, securing her feet, and reeling in when she could, always angling closer to the shore. Would the knot last? Would her arms hold?

Finally, she felt the crunch of pebbles under her feet. She kept reeling. The line was now short enough so that she could dimly see the shape of the fish. "Christian, get ready with the net. Scoop under the tail and scoop deep."

She stopped in order for Christian to get the net under the thrashing fish. He netted him firmly, keeping the rim of the net above the water so the fish couldn't swim out.

With the rod still attached to the fish in the net, she told Christian to keep up with her. Phoebe moved farther up the beach where she felt safe enough to tell Christian to ease the fish out of the net and hold him down with both hands.

To Phoebe, the fish looked huge. "Christian, I'm going to measure him on my rod," she told him, "before the bad killing part comes. First, I'll twist the fly from the mouth, and then you need to kill him. O.K?"

"Sure, I've killed lots of salmon on Dad's boat."

"For me, will you kill this one gently, please?"

"Kill is kill."

She whispered a 'sorry' to the fish as she held him down while Christian went for a stone.

She heard a yoo-hoo. It was James. "Time to go. We'll soon be late. How'd you do?"

She covered her ears against the smash of the hit and squeezed her eyes shut. When she opened them, she saw her husband leaning over the fish, tape measure in hand.

"Phoebe, he's a beauty. We'll weigh him at the hotel. You take the prize so far, and, sweetheart, I'm sorry I was brusque with you. Have you forgiven me?"

"Well, not entirely," she said, "but maybe soon."

"The sooner the better. I only wanted you not to waste such great fishing opportunities. And look what you did when I made you mad enough to go out and fish."

"Don't try it again. It may boomerang on you! How did you do?"

"One more, but nothing like this one of yours. Come on, champ, let's go home."

"Thank you, Christian," Phoebe said. "Tomorrow, would you like to learn how to tie on flies? James, our guide was wonderful. I couldn't have brought the fish in without the nautical knot that he learned to tie at sea or without his expert handling of the net."

The red flush on Christian's neck and face lit their way back to the car. The salmon weighed almost seven pounds.

At breakfast the next morning, Jane Ward was full of news. "I have been chatting with a young woman from the kitchen, named Helga. She's the tall, pretty blonde, who brings porridge at breakfast. I told her that I had read about the eider ducks in Iceland and asked her if she knew anything about them."

"Oh, yes," she told me. "My grandmother raises them on her farm, above the Arctic Circle."

"'Could a friend of mine and I go see them?'" I asked.

"What did she say?" Phoebe questioned eagerly. "I'd love to go."

"Helga said that if her grandmother told her that it was all right, she'd drive us there on her next day off."

"You're wonderful to invite me. I'll tell James today. He scolded me last night about not fishing every minute, and it made me mad. I went out and caught a fish that was bigger than any of his, so far. So, now I have lots of brownie points in the bank."

James got up from the other end of the table where he and Edgar were discussing different kind of rods. "Time to go, Phoebe. Christian will be here in twenty minutes. You'll never get another seven-pound salmon sitting here. Did she tell you, Jane, that hers was the biggest salmon brought in, bigger than either of my two?" He turned toward their room.

Phoebe stood up to follow, but Jane put a hand on her arm. "I also found out what the workmen at the other tables are doing. They're with the telephone company and are extending lines to some of the farmhouses. You can learn a lot when you start a conversation."

"You're so right. Well, here I go to converse with a stream. Do keep me posted about eider ducks."

James and Christian decided to try the Ormarsa River. The head guide never seemed to be much in evidence, so the fishermen, among themselves, decided where they would fish. The Ormarsa flowed into the Deildara.

When the MacLeans arrived at the Ormarsa, they agreed the word "trickle" might describe it better than "river." They chose a stretch of water with an abandoned weir above it. A filmy rain began to fall steadily.

James thought that at one time the weir might have been used to divert the flow of part of the stream. "It couldn't have been for irrigation. There's definitely no need for that in this country."

With rod in hand, James took his stance above the weir and cast below it with a tube fly. He fished there all morning. Phoebe thought that he should have moved on. But his decision turned out to be right. He caught a nice salmon.

Phoebe had done nothing except change flies. She was beginning to tie on another one when Christian came up and knelt beside her. "Would you like to watch how I do it?" she asked him. "Then you can tie on the next fly, whenever I need to put on a new one." He nodded enthusiastically.

"That's a handsome sweater you are wearing."

"My mother knit it. She has nothing to do when my father is out fishing. Would you like her to make you one before you leave?"

Phoebe doubted his statement about his mother's having nothing to do, but she couldn't pass up an offer like that. She pointed to his sweater and placed her order immediately. "I'd like one with the same design as yours, but a cardigan in white wool, in my size. If she can knit one that fast, I'll write her a letter of congratulations before we leave."

"Fine. She'd like the letter as much as the money. I'll translate it for her."

Phoebe fished conscientiously and changed flies regularly. Christian was having a lot of practice. He was an eager learner and was soon tying flies like an old hand. If Phoebe didn't change flies often enough, he showed his disappointment. So she began to choose to change flies often in order to give Christian more practice. But the fish were not interested in anything she presented. Probably no fish were there.

When the MacLeans arrived at the hotel, Jane Ward was watching for them. "I've just been in the kitchen. Helga's grandmother has invited us to come to the farm anytime, and tomorrow is Helga's day off! Ask James if you can go tomorrow."

"How great. Of course, I can go, but I'll be diplomatic and ask him. Just let me know what time. I wouldn't miss an adventure like this for the world!"

The next morning as soon as the fishermen left, Helga appeared with a thermos of tea. "Are your shoes sturdy and are you dressed warmly? It could be cold. I can leave as soon as you are ready."

"If it weren't cold, I'd be disappointed," Phoebe said with a laugh. "After all, it is the North Pole." She felt like a schoolgirl, cutting classes.

"Not quite," Jane corrected with a grin, "the Arctic Circle. Let's go!"

They practically skipped to the car. Jane sat in front, binoculars in hand. She rotated them widely to take in every movement along the roadside. Twice when they passed small clumps of stunted bushes rising from the empty land, she asked Helga to stop the car.

Jane stepped out on the road with her binoculars. When she moved toward the bushes, she flushed a bird that took off in low flight. Another bird raced across the road. Each time Jane riffled through her bird book and located the species.

The farther they drove, the more isolated the farmhouses became. They missed hearing the hum of tractors. Phoebe thought the farms looked somewhat deserted, perhaps because they were so near the Arctic Circle. She mentioned this to Helga.

"Oh no. It's just that the men don't have time to maintain the farms well as they are always out fishing. My grandfather worked as a fisherman all his life, and he died a fisherman."

"That's pretty hard on the women, having all the farm work to keep up and doing their own housework and laundry work as well."

"That's the reason why so many young women try to find jobs in town or abroad. Here's my grandmother's house, coming up on the right."

The two-story house, white with red trim around the windows, loomed large and square, dominating the landscape. A strong wind flattened the bright flowers planted in two round beds on either side of the front door, but between gusts the flower heads seemed to pop up, a signal that they were ready for the next onslaught of wind. Even the flowers were stalwart.

Helga pulled the car to the rear of the house where laundry danced on a clothesline. The grandmother came down the back steps, arms wrapped in her flowered apron for warmth. A grey handknit sweater covered her shoulders, which were so bent that her head rode between them like a turtle's. Her eyes snapped with interest, as her mouth beamed a smile of welcome.

Helga ran to her grandmother and hugged her. When she finished talking with her, she straightened up, towering over the bent little lady. "This is my grandmother, Hellgerda. She doesn't speak English. She has asked me to tell you how glad she is to see you. She wants you to come in for some coffee."

"She doesn't need to speak our language. Tell her that we can feel her hospitality," Jane said with a smile.

Hellgerda waved them through the permanent storm anteroom to the back door that opened right into the kitchen. The wood-burning cook range gave out cheerful heat. Hellgerda helped them off with their wraps, and Helga hung them on pegs that ran along the wall by the storm room.

Hellgerda motioned them to sit at the table in the center of the kitchen. It was set with heavy white cups and was ladened with plates piled high with different kinds of cakes. A big blue and white marbled enamel coffeepot, steaming and fragrant, sat on the range.

Helga poured the coffee and her grandmother heaped cakes on their plates. Now it was their turn to show their American friendliness, by eating everything!

Smiles and gestures accompanied Helga's translations as they ate. Finally, filled with cakes, they followed their hostess into the parlor. She motioned them to sit down on the horsehair straight-backed chairs grouped around a center table that held a bouquet of dried flowers, under a glass dome.

Helga and her grandmother had an animated conversation, at the end of which the granddaughter shook her head firmly. She explained to her new friends that she told her grandmother how eager we were to see the eider duck barn.

"Granny Gerda, as we call her, says to tell you how sorry she is that she can't show you the barn herself, but she's afraid of falling," Helga explained. "She has invited you to return to the house for dinner. However, I had to tell her that I have to get back in time to help serve dinner at the hotel."

Jane whispered to Phoebe, "I couldn't eat another thing, but I'm sad that we can't stay longer."

"I too," Phoebe agreed. "One kind little old lady, who, I bet, isn't yet sixty, has given us a sense of identity with the entire Arctic Circle."

Their 'thank-yous' and 'good-byes' went on for some time before they departed for the eider duck barn.

"If eider ducks waddle, then I feel like one," Phoebe commented.

Finally, they were once again near the line of flapping clothes. They saw the grandmother standing nearby, waving her apron in an affectionate farewell. "We'll walk down this path to the barn," Helga said and led off.

"I'm sorry Grandmother doesn't feel like walking with us, but it's understandable. She will soon be fifty-nine."

Jane whispered to Phoebe, "She looks eighty."

"And in this culture, fifty-nine is old. We wouldn't be too spry, if we had led her life," Phoebe replied.

The high dark barn was large and as snug against the wind as a house. They saw row after row of elevated shelves that held wooden slatted boxes, but no eider ducks. "Where are they?" Jane asked.

"They have returned to the wild until next mating season. They fly south for the winter months, and then they return in the early spring to the same place where they were fed and cared for the previous year.

"Grandmother thinks some of her ducks have been coming back here for years. They like to return to a big barn like this, because their eggs are safe here from marauders, and when they hatch, the babies are safe also.

"My grandfather dug a lake for the babies. They take to the water right after they hatch. They don't get their adult plumage until they are in their third year."

"Do they stay here all that time?" Phoebe asked.

"Oh, no, only until they can fly. Then the mother takes them off to ice-free waters, because their food is marine food."

"I remember reading that," Jane added. "They eat sea urchins, mollusks, and small fish that have just been spawned."

"You probably know that the mothers leave the young birds and fly north to breed," Helga said. "In the lands where the eider ducks leave their young, the birds from several families band together in colonies for protection, until the mothers return."

"Helga, this is fascinating, much more so than reading about eider ducks in a book," Jane commented.

"Those slats don't look very comfortable for little ducklings that have just hatched," Phoebe observed.

Helga took over again. "You're seeing the nests without the mother's soft feathers. The eider duck plucks the down from her breast to make the nests of earth and twigs comfortable for the babies."

"Poor mamma duck," Phoebe said.

Helga continued, "The feathers are the reason the farmers build these barns for the eider ducks. The down brings in good money, which helps the economy and the farmers."

"Call it a more sophisticated source of egg money!" Jane chuckled.

Helga continued her story while they were in the warm barn. "The government permits the farmers to remove the feathers from the slats twice and replace them with empty ones. Notice that the slats are on tracks for easier removal."

They walked down the long rows. Helga continued, "When the duck finds the nest bare, with, naturally, her eggs gone also, she hastens to lay more eggs and pluck more down from her breast for the new nest. In the wild, the duck lays her eggs on the bare ground that she softens with her down. So these slats don't feel hard to her."

"Your English is excellent. You explain everything very well," Phoebe mentioned.

"Three years working in New York City helped. But to get back to the eider ducks, if the government permitted the farmers to steal the eggs and the nest of feathers more than twice, the poor mother would continue to pluck feathers for her new eggs until she was dead."

Helga picked up a handful from one box and ran the combination of twigs, feathers, and dirt through her fingers, careful not to spill any on the ground. "Grandmother hasn't cleaned these nests yet. Sometimes it takes all summer to finish. It's a slow job, separating the feathers from the dirt and twigs. Members of the family come and help her when they can. There are factories that do the job with a series of screens, but that costs too much money for many farmers and their wives."

"Now I understand why eiderdown is so expensive," Phoebe said thoughtfully.

Eventually, they walked from the dim barn back into the cold sun and the wind. In the foreground, they saw the big pond and beyond that the open sea. And beyond that? The North Pole?

Helga gestured to the pond. "If you're fortunate enough to see the eider ducks bring the ducklings here to swim for the first time, it is something that you never forget. It is considered very lucky. Once, when I was a child visiting Grandmother, I saw that year's ducklings take their first swim."

Helga continued as they walked toward the car. "The next season when it's still very cold, the same eider ducks return to lay their eggs here. I've seen that too."

"Like salmon returning to their birthplace to spawn," Phoebe said. She couldn't wait to report all this to James. She found that she wasn't angry with him anymore. It was a good feeling, comfortable like an eiderdown quilt.

Thoughtfully, they turned back to the car and climbed in. As they were leaving, they saw the grandmother bringing in the wash. She put the basket down and took some clothespins out of her mouth. They heard her call and watched her wave good-bye to them with her apron. Phoebe snapped a picture from the back car window.

The MacLeans did not return to fish the Deildara and Ormarsa rivers again. Indirectly, they heard that sports fishing on those rivers was discontinued after that one year, too few fish resulting in too few fishermen. James's three fish were the highest number caught.

Whenever Phoebe saw the snapshot in their Iceland photograph album of Grandmother Hellgerda waving good-bye to them, she felt herself transported back to the farm in the Arctic Circle. They learned very little of its geography that day, but they learned a great deal more from Helga's remarkable little grandmother.

At the airport near Reykjavik, the MacLeans joined other departing sportsmen, whiling away the time of the inevitable delays by sharing fishing experiences. One fish story followed the other. Solid information about lodges and streams was also exchanged and filed for future use.

There was some constructive criticism voiced as well. The netting of salmon, both near the mouth of the spawning rivers and in commercial offshore fishing, came in for much discussion.

"Strict policing has to be enforced," one visitor declared.

"But some of the poachers are Icelanders," James mentioned. "Some of these men feel that the salmon belong to them. I must say that I feel somewhat sympathetic toward them."

"But the Icelandic government voted on these restrictions for the good of their citizens," said the first fisherman.

"That's why it is a matter for the government to police."

A new voice spoke up, "The real problem is that Iceland needs to push for the finalization of the treaty with Denmark that sets up firm boundaries for commercial fishing. That treaty has been hanging fire for years. The salmon are netted before they can return to the streams to spawn."

"I'm sorry," one man announced, "I can't continue to wait for these matters to be ironed out. I'm thinking about taking my fishing time and my vacation money elsewhere next year, perhaps Alaska."

James turned away thoughtfully to go to collect their smoked salmon. Phoebe was sure that they would be having some serious discussions along these lines on the long flight home.

The evening was clear and the take-off smooth. Iceland spread beneath them like a page from a huge atlas, a brief green footprint on the map of their lives. "I'll miss this country, if we don't return," Phoebe told her husband.

"We will return," he answered, "but maybe not immediately. Shall we do some reading about Alaska this winter? What do you think?"

Phoebe managed a farewell glance below her before the plane was enveloped in a white cumulus cloud. Then, she turned toward James and agreed with only a little reluctance, "A very good idea."

ALASKA

Brooks River

PHOEBE MACLEAN felt the excitement of return. She gazed intently through the window of the Falcon plane and recognized familiar Alaskan terrain under thin wisps of fog. Her husband James and two friends, Francis Drake and his son, Frank, made up the fishing party of four. They were flying from San Francisco up the Canadian coast to Alaska. Occasionally the clouds broke to reveal fingers of fiords reaching out from snowy mountain ranges that held majestic glaciers.

They stopped at Ketchikan for the usual gas stop. As soon as the travelers stepped from the plane, the sharp cold winds took charge and pushed them like clumsy dancers into the small waiting room. Phoebe was fascinated by the frontier appearance of the men, their garb, their stance, their weathered faces. She had just begun a conversation with one of the men when her husband and the pilot came up to her and told her that it was time to return to the plane.

As Phoebe and James hurried through the frigid wind to the plane, her husband teased, "Sorry to break into your encounter, but maybe it was a good thing. I might have saved you from discovering that your Alaskan type was an executive from Cincinnati." Phoebe made a face at him.

Unperturbed, James continued, "Here come the Drakes. Young Drake has been buying Ketchikan postcards to send back to New York State to his wife and children."

183

"Francis's son seems to have inherited many of his father's winning ways, James," she answered. "I'm glad you've included him on this trip. How about getting back to the gin rummy game while we're still ahead?"

"Fine, but a word of caution, Phoebe. One of Frank's 'winning ways' inherited from his father is his ability to win at gin rummy," he answered. "On guard, partner!"

In the plane, their longtime friend, Francis, pointed a finger at James. "You've got to keep a sharper eye on that wife of yours. You almost lost her to Ketchikan's 'Call of the Wild'. We need her skills for the game and her charm to introduce Frank to Enchanted Lake and the Seilers."

Frank shuffled the cards. "This is great, and we haven't even started fishing yet. I feel a small charge of guilt, being away from my wife and teenage sons. But the boys will have their own time later. I've waited years to see Alaska, and imagine, tonight we'll be in Anchorage."

The farther north they flew, the better the weather became. The players' commitment to the gin rummy game suffered as the scenery unfolded. "First things first," Francis finally announced and folded up his cards. That surprised Phoebe because he was a dedicated gin rummy player and the MacLeans were a little ahead in the score.

"Keep a sharp lookout on the right side of the plane," James said. "With the weather clearing, we may be able to spot the Malaspina Glacier. Sometimes you can see streaks of red from the small side glaciers. Perhaps it is algae in the snow from debris collected many years ago as the glaciers moved slowly to the sea." He stood up. "I'll ask our chief pilot, Vic, to keep a watch for the Malaspina and let us know when he spots it."

When James returned from a brief conversation with Vic, he continued, "Phoebe, you may not remember, but we couldn't see the glacier the first time we came to the Seilers. Frank, watch closely. I want to see it this time."

"I do too. I've been reading about it," Francis added. "It covers an area half as large as New England."

Vic opened the door briefly from the cockpit. "The glacier will be on your right in a few miles. We'll fly a little lower in order to get a closer view."

"Thanks, Vic. Frank, Vic is a fine fly fisherman himself. During the week that we stay with the Seilers, the plane will be based at King Salmon, mainly a commercial fishing village. No fly-fishing there. The pilots will be fishing for large salmon from a boat, using heavy tackle."

Frank nodded, his eyes never leaving the window. Lin, Vic's co-pilot, appeared. "Malaspina Glacier coming up on the right."

Spreading from a wall of high white mountains was the biggest snowfield Phoebe had ever seen. The glacier spread from the distant mountains and descended to the sea. Debris from side glaciers formed reddish brown vertical streaks along the white of the main Malaspina Glacier.

Occasionally, the friends caught glimpses of blue in deep glacial cracks. "It looks like a huge white canvas dabbed with colored paint," Phoebe said, immediately sorry that her words had broken the intense concentration of her companions.

When they passed the glacier, the Drakes settled back in their seats, absorbed by the overwhelming beauty of the Malaspina Glacier. But James kept his eyes fixed on the land below him. "This is the best viewing weather that we've ever had, flying along this coast."

He continued, "We should soon see Prince William Sound. At the upper end of this sound is Valdez, the southern terminal of the Alaskan pipeline that brings oil south from Prudhoe Bay to the head of the sound. We can't see Valdez from here, but we might be able to spot Cordova, a fishing town on the coast. Phoebe, do you remember the night we spent there with Helene and Andrew Holcomb when we stopped to examine the Alaskan pipeline?"

"How could I ever forget it?"

"What happened?" Frank asked eagerly.

"We arrived at the hotel with reservations and a letter of confirmation in hand, only to be told that there were no rooms available."

"What did you do then?" Francis asked, as interested as his son.

Phoebe interrupted her husband. "First, James ranted and Andrew raved, but to no avail. Our unlikely savior was the lady taxi driver, who was big, tough, and resourceful."

Firmly, James picked up his narrative again. "She motioned us back into her cab, the only taxi in town since the one paved street was barely two miles long. She drove us to the one other hotel in town, and led us in."

Phoebe restrained herself from interrupting. James hurried on, "There was no reservation desk, just a long ornate bar with a burly bartender behind it who greeted the taxi driver like an old friend. He looked us over, up and down, and then punched open the cash register at the bar. He demanded our names and ten dollars for each of the two rooms. When he received the money, he slammed the drawer of the cash register shut and turned to serve a beer to a customer while we waited."

"And then?" Francis urged.

"Finally, when he finished, he waved us up a wide stairway that rose between the bar on the left and what looked like a gambling room on the right that was filled with a rowdy crowd of people."

"Gambling is legal?" Frank asked.

"The taxi driver told us that it was, explaining that the only thing the sheriff required was that the doors stay open so that his men could get in quickly when trouble broke out. She grabbed a couple of heavy bags and started up the stairs, calling us to follow."

"We struggled up the steep stairs and stopped at the top to rest our arms," James continued. "Suddenly, a door flew open and out stepped a girl in a fancy red dress, with lots of black lace on it."

Phoebe burst in again, "And she didn't even bother to close the door behind her. James, tell what we saw."

"Our wives were really shocked because on the bed in the room behind her was a man stretched out, stark naked!"

Phoebe continued, "But the main thing I remember was the beckoning, flirtatious way she eyed you men. She took no notice of Helene and me."

"It was so noisy all night on our floor that we didn't get much sleep," James continued. "In fact, the noise was so overwhelming that, one time, we dressed and went outside for a quiet walk in the fresh air. On the street we ran into the lady taxi driver, who stopped to chat. She explained what the problem was. The fishing fleet was in town!"

James went on, "Boy, were those fishermen big beer drinkers! You should have seen the broken bottles. As soon as they emptied a bottle, they went outside and broke it in the street. No wonder it was too noisy to sleep."

"James, remember how still the streets were by the time we drove to the airport early the next morning?"

"And what you said they looked like—a glistening glacier of brown glass?"

"How clever of me," Phoebe laughed.

"I thought so," said her husband.

Surprised to realize that he meant it, she felt warm with pleasure as she turned back to their guests.

"That's a rousing Alaska tale," Francis pronounced with enthusiasm.

James's face reddened. "I'm afraid I got carried away by my Alaskan 'tale', as you call it. I've almost talked you past a glimpse of Cordova. Now you'll need to take a fast look because we're about to make our approach to Anchorage. There I hope we can see the bay whose banks slid into the water during the last earthquake. Many houses were lost at that time."

"Can we see Mt. McKinley from here?" Frank asked.

"Probably not, but if it's clear tomorrow morning when we fly out, it's possible that we can."

From the moment they stepped off the plane, Phoebe could feel young Frank's identification with fishing and the frontier part of the country. In his mind's eye, he blocked out any modern surroundings as he concentrated on old frontier times.

At their contemporary hotel full of tourists, Frank saw only the fishermen who were cautiously turning their fish over to bellboys for freezing. During dinner on the rooftop, they became overwhelmed by the enormity of this country that surrounded them. Mountains, bays, and lakes stretched from one horizon to the other, lit by the brilliance of the eleven o'clock sun.

"Want to take a walk around town before we turn in?" James asked. "It always strikes me as odd that Anchorage has one of the best bookstores that I have seen, anywhere."

"The long winter nights are probably responsible, don't you think?" Francis mentioned. "A walk sounds fine."

The Drakes found two paintings in an art gallery to take home. Phoebe bought an Eskimo soapstone carving of a dancer with arms held high. The proprietor explained that the carving was realistic of the way Eskimos danced, because the igloos were too crowded for them to dance any other way. James, meanwhile, browsed in the bookstore.

It was past midnight when the fishermen returned to the hotel. The light was still as bright as though it were noon. Gratefully, the MacLeans pulled shut the heavy curtains that hung across the hotel windows.

The next morning, James instructed everyone to dress in fishing clothes and to keep waders, fishing vests, long underwear, and rods handy in the plane.

"My hope is that when we meet Ed Seiler in King Salmon, he will tell us that he can drop us off for some fishing while he ferries the luggage to the lodge. There's not enough room both for bags and guests in his one-motor Cessna. Wait 'til you see how he carries the rods."

"I'm ready," said Frank.

They joined the long line of small planes waiting to take off.

188

"These are used the way cars are at home," Phoebe told Frank. "Since there are so few roads in Alaska, the sky is the highway."

Vic stuck his head out from the cockpit. "Folks," he announced. "I'm going to fly as far north as my flight plan permits. I hope we can show you Mt. McKinley."

Like children peering into a candy shop, the fishermen watched for the mountain. Frank was the first to spot its stately white-capped top that floated midway between earth and heaven, like a gigantic ice cream cone.

"Now, next is King Salmon," said James. "It is on the part of Alaska where the Aleutian peninsula and the mainland come together."

After miles of emptiness, the town of King Salmon appeared. The plane flew over a collection of shacks and small houses that edged the airfield. These were built between the airfield and the wide Naknek River off Bristol Bay that at this time of year was filled with boats.

"There's Ed in his old van, waiting in front of the building that houses the post office and the air patrol station," James pointed out. "He keeps a van in King Salmon, the only place around here where there are roads. It even has a few paved streets."

James continued, "The other big building is a warehouse that holds the general store. We'll pick up our fishing licenses there at the office while Ed fills Josephina's shopping list. He only comes here to pick up and deliver guests, to get mail and groceries, and to gas up. Staples are flown in twice a summer from Anchorage."

"Where is Ed from?" Frank asked.

"From New Jersey, but when he was growing up, he spent his summers in the Maine woods."

"And Josephina?"

"From Puerto Rico. Ed met her in New York during a summer vacation from college. He is an engineer. She was a music student."

The pilots brought the plane in skillfully. James was right behind the copilot when he opened the door. Ed, wearing a navy mackintosh and a visored fishing cap, hurried toward them, hand outstretched. "Hi, MacLean. Glad to have you and Phoebe back. Francis, welcome. How have you been?"

"Splendid. This is my son, Frank. How's Josephina?"

"Couldn't be better. She's eager to see you. After we put the luggage in the van, you can pick up the licenses at the store." He patted his pocket. "I'll grocery shop from her list while you get your fishing licenses."

"How's fishing?"

"Fine. While I was waiting for you, I heard that the first salmon of the season are running at Brooks River. They're taking them on wet flies."

Ed turned to the pilot. "Vic, glad to have you back. The commercial fishermen are pulling some big salmon out of the Naknek River. You and your copilot will have good fishing. Things are all set up for you two at the motel and for the plane at the airfield."

As Phoebe surveyed the gear being loaded into Ed's van, she was convinced that even homesteaders couldn't have had this much stuff. In the store, Ed turned to the grocery section to begin his shopping while the others filed into the dark office to get their fishing licenses. Two moose heads mounted on the wall watched the store owner peck out their licenses on an ancient typewriter.

After Phoebe had hers in hand, she gravitated to the shelves that held, in addition to groceries, a few items of clothing and small gifts, the only source in town for such things.

Back in the van, the group bumped along the river road to the dock where Ed's maroon and white Cessna was moored. "How would you like to fish at Brooks River while I take the bags to Enchanted Lake?" Ed asked.

"We had been hoping that you'd suggest something like that," James answered quickly. "We're already prepared!"

"Fine. We'll leave your bags in the van. I'll load them in the plane when I return for gas and the groceries. Then I'll fly to Enchanted Lake with the luggage before I return for you. In the plane I have some lunch for you, fixed by Josephina. Dress warmly."

Ed unlocked the shed where he kept his oil drums and other gear and waved Phoebe in first. Oddly enough, it was in the dim shed among the oil drums that Phoebe felt strongly the pleasure of return. She pulled on her long underwear, missing the presence of another woman to pal and laugh with.

Oh, well, with only enough room on the plane and at Enchanted Lake for four guests, it wasn't possible. She'd been the only woman on fishing trips before.

Ed instructed them to set up their rods but not to put flies on them. They watched with admiration as Ed carefully slipped the rods into the special carrying cases he had designed and built to hang under the body of the Cessna.

Phoebe took her accustomed place in the third seat, sharing it, as usual, with the huge green picnic hamper. James insisted that Francis ride in the copilot's seat. He and Frank sat in the middle seat.

Below them, the dun-colored countryside rolled by, pockmarked by small round lakes. In the unpressurized plane, Ed had to fly at a low altitude. Their view of the terrain was an intimate one. The yellow water lilies in the lakes were the only sign of color.

On one small lake, Phoebe spotted a pair of statuesque white swans swimming sedately across their own private domain. She knew from what Ed had told her on an earlier trip that swans mated for life and that they returned to the same lake every year. "Just like us on both scores," Phoebe thought.

"Naknek Lake," she heard Ed point out to Francis. "Brooks River flows into it from Brooks Lake, a distance of only two miles. You'll fish where it flows into Naknek Lake."

Ed taxied near a spit of gravel below the forest rangers' cabins. A few other cabins clustered around them. "Wein Airline uses those other cabins. It flies tourists from Anchorage here in a charter plane several mornings a week. The rangers take them in an antiquated bus on a very short stretch of the only paved road around here, to see Katmai Volcano."

Ed continued, "It's the one that blew its top in 1912 and spewed pumice over much of the Valley of Ten Thousand Smokes. The tourists spend the night in those cabins and then Wein Airline flies them back to Anchorage the next morning."

The men waded to shore with the fishing stuff. James came back to help Phoebe while Ed unloaded the rods and the lunch hamper. "The trip may take me three hours, what with my unloading at the lodge. Good luck. I'll beach the plane on the other side of the river when I return for you. Before I leave, I'll ask a ranger to bring you over in their boat when he hears the plane fly in. Watch out for grizzlies," he said in a matter-of-fact way and took off.

Grizzlies! The fishermen stood thoughtfully, watching the plane leave. James broke the silence by saying, "Ed forgot to leave the plastic sacks for us to put the fish in, if we want to take some back to the lodge."

"Or back home. I remember he has a big freezer. Oh, well, we probably won't catch any," Francis said.

"I don't care about plastic sacks. All I want is to see a grizzly," his son responded.

James led them up the river toward the bend. He positioned the Drakes upstream and Phoebe below them. "Keep in sight of each other," James told them. "I'll fish down the river from you, Phoebe."

Soon both the Drakes were casting. Phoebe found herself stationed in the middle between them and James. She had a perfect view of James. But catching her own salmon kept her too busy to watch anyone else. She glanced occasionally at the Drakes, who were as preoccupied as she was. She saw that they had kept several salmon to take to the lodge. She had a couple herself.

She looked from the Drakes to James and was rewarded by instant action from him. His rod bent forcefully. He had a strike.

Rod held high, her husband played the fish until he tired him out. He brought him to a pool near the beach and netted him. It was a beautiful salmon. It looked huge to Phoebe compared with the size of the trout that they usually caught in these waters, eight pounds at least.

Her contemplation of the taste of broiled salmon was abruptly interrupted when she remembered that James had no plastic sacks either. She watched with interest to see what he would do. He found a stone and killed the salmon, placing it on the beach near him.

Then he turned back to the river to continue his fishing. Phoebe decided it was time for her to follow suit. Pulling out some line, she walked toward the river. She took a last glance toward James and almost dropped her rod in the water.

Horrified, she saw a grizzly sow and two small cubs lumber over the spit behind him and come right to the place where her husband had laid the fish. James seemed oblivious to what was going on below him.

Phoebe called to him as she hurried out of the water. Only the Drakes heard her. They reeled in their lines and ran to her. James finally saw the bears, reeled in his line, and moved quickly up the beach away from them.

They all saw the sow pick the fish up in her mouth and disappear over the spit, followed closely by the cubs. James told them later that he could hear growlings, probably the sow keeping the cubs away while she devoured the fish. The bears didn't come back.

James began to fish again as though nothing had happened. The Drakes returned to their own fishing.

Phoebe was too frustrated with James's casual behavior to concentrate on her own fishing. Her eyes darted from James to the Drakes. She watched as Francis and Frank each caught two nice salmon in quick succession. She saw them carefully place their fish close enough so they could keep a sharp eye on them. Phoebe waved congratulations. Frank responded with a triumphant grin. They all continued to fish until lunchtime, after which they returned to their places. No bears appeared, but they watched somewhat apprehensively.

After lunch, she turned toward James once more before she began her fishing, just in time to see him with a salmon on his line. Faintly she heard him say, "I'll fix that bear if she comes back."

She watched him bring the fish in, kill it, and dig a hole with a stick as deep as he could. He buried the fish, patting sand and gravel over him firmly. Then, undaunted, he returned to his fishing.

As though this were the cue that she had been waiting for, the sow reemerged from over the spit, alone this time. She systematically used her radar, located the buried fish, uncovered it, picked it up, and carried it back over the spit to eat.

This time James was keeping such a sharp lookout that he saw when the bear dug up his fish and disappeared with it over the spit. James must have decided that caution was the better part of valor.

He motioned to Phoebe and the Drakes to follow him and loped up the beach. On the way, he came to the ranger, working on the outboard motorboat, and explained about the bears. "I'll row you to the other side to get away from the grizzlies. Ed's meeting you over there anyway when he returns."

The ranger had the motor started by the time the others arrived. He took them across the river.

"That bear will have a field day with the salmon we left behind," Frank mourned.

They had good fishing on the other side, without the bear worries. Phoebe was pleased to see that the Drakes had caught a couple of salmon to replace the ones that they had left behind.

The sound of Ed's plane overhead was welcome. He began taxiing the plane up the river. Everybody moved toward the plane promptly, but their progress was interrupted by Frank, who yelled, "Bears coming!"

The fishermen saw that the three bears were swimming across the river. Ed took in the situation immediately. He nosed the plane into the sand and kept the engine revving.

The bears came out of the water and lumbered up the beach at a gait that was incredibly fast. They were heading toward their source of supply. Phoebe felt that she was seeing, in real life, an old movie serial, *The Perils of Pauline*.

From the plane, Ed shouted to his passengers, "Jump in fast and close the doors! James, hold on to this rope until I give you the signal to push the plane off."

When they were all in, James shoved to help Ed get the plane turned downstream. Then he swung on the pontoons, jumped in, and slammed his door.

But Phoebe saw Frank hanging out his open door. "I'll stop those bears," he shouted and threw two salmon, one after the other, toward the animals.

Frank finally slammed his door and Ed began his takeoff, but before they were airborne, his passengers saw the sow standing upright, wolfing down a salmon as the hungry cubs watched. It was right at the spot where James had jumped into the plane.

"Well, I'll be!" said Francis. "Frank, don't you ever throw a fish of mine away again to a grizzly bear, hear?"

"But, Dad, I was saving lives!"

James turned to Phoebe. "Doesn't it seem to you, Toots, that we have already had more than our usual share of adventures?"

"Amen," Phoebe agreed.

"What's coming next?" Frank asked eagerly. "What else to add to my Alaskan saga for my sons?"

"I'll tell you what," came his father's emphatic answer. "I vote for an uncomplicated dinner tonight and an early sleep."

"The lake below us is Nonvianuk," Ed explained, just as though nothing extraordinary had happened. Soon we will come to our own lake. We call it Enchanted Lake."

"And there it is, coming up, lovely Enchanted Lake!" Phoebe called. "I see Josephina at the dock waving to us. Who is that with her?"

"That's Tom Spain," Ed answered. "He and his wife Ellen are graduate biology students from the University of Alaska. They are helping us this summer."

Ed circled the small lake, losing altitude in order to land the plane and taxi it to the dock. He stepped out and tossed a rope to Tom, who caught it and moored the plane. "Disembark, one at a time," Ed instructed them.

Phoebe addressed the picnic hamper as she waited her turn. "It's a privilege to return, don't you agree?"

Josephina embraced each of them as they stepped off the dock. "Ellen Spain and I have dinner ready, but there's time for a drink in the cottage and a shower, if you desire."

She continued, "Francis, it's lovely to have another Drake on this trip. Do you want to ride up the road in the jeep with the luggage?"

"Let's all walk up," James suggested. "Arriving by foot is the best way."

"Fine. I'll see you at dinner. Phoebe, I have many questions to ask you about the family and your winter."

James pointed out the laundry, the toolshed, the boat house, and then led them up the steep jeep road that wound to the top of the small hill on which Enchanted Lodge was built.

He explained, "Ed brought materials up this road when he was building the house. Twice, he stayed on the site until late in the autumn when Nonvianuk Lake froze over."

He paused to let his friends catch their breath. "Ed had supplies delivered commercially by Alaska Airlines to Kulik. Then, piece by piece, he snaked his materials in a homemade sled over the frozen lake to this road that he had made."

By the time they arrived at the guest house below the lodge, Tom Spain and Ed were unloading their bags. Frank Drake let out a sigh of contentment. "I feel as familiar with Enchanted Lake as though I had been coming here for years, and I haven't even seen the lodge yet!"

Ed stopped for a moment to say, "Phoebe, you and James decide where the Drakes shall be. There is ice on the table of the entry. I'll see you at the lodge whenever you're ready, or we'll buzz the bell if dinner is ready first."

"Thanks, Ed," Phoebe answered.

"Francis, why don't you and Frank take the right hand room. It has the best view," James suggested.

He continued. "When you've showered and dressed, come to this room and pour yourselves a drink. We can leave rods and tackle in this center room."

"Looks great," Frank said, "just the way Dad described it."

"And this is the same room I stayed in before," his father added.

After a shower and a drink, the four walked up the hill to the lodge. From the windows on either side of the front room, they saw a breathtaking panorama of snow-capped mountains. A fire crackled in the stone fireplace. On the opposite wall, an aquarium was already stocked with native trout and water plants. It bubbled hospitably. The table was set for dinner and soft classical music was playing.

Josephina presided graciously over an excellent dinner, but no one lingered long afterwards. Ed pushed back his chair and took charge. "I always listen to the weather report first thing in the morning. The weather in our country rules our flying, which rules our fishing," he explained.

"That's why I never decide where we will fish until the morning. Breakfast is at eight. We hope you sleep well. Let us know if you need anything. Good night," said Ed and left the room.

Josephina walked to the door with them. "Phoebe and James, I'm going to listen to the Mozart record that you sent us. I adore Von Karajan. Since I don't fish with you, I can listen later in the evening."

James responded quickly, "You can't fool us, Josephina. We know how busy you are from early morning on, manning the shortwave radio and preparing the dinner for the return of hungry fishermen!"

Josephina gave him a hug. "Good night. You and Phoebe are lovely friends."

At the guest house, the MacLeans explained to the Drakes how to use the top of the cupboards and the space under the beds to store things. "I forgot to explain before dinner the intricacies of the

Sears-Roebuck portable shower, but you've undoubtedly already mastered that yourselves," James told them.

Later, James knocked on the Drakes' door. Francis opened it. "Leave your windows open so that you can listen to the lapping of the lake and hear the wind in the pine trees. One last thing, our alarm clock in the morning is the sound the generator makes when Ed turns it on. Lights go off at ten p.m. when he turns the generator off. Good night, again."

Moraine River

THE NEXT MORNING the guests sat overlong at breakfast while Josephina reminisced about the Seilers's courtship after they had met at a concert in New York City. She had come from Puerto Rico to study voice. "When I married the handsome young engineer just out of college, I didn't expect to spend most of my married life in Alaska," she said in her lilting soft Spanish accent.

She launched into an account of their harsh early years in King Salmon after World War II. They had run a small cafe to try to make enough money to build a house on this homestead property.

Ed interrupted her with the latest weather report. "Clear until late afternoon. I think we can fish Moraine River today before the afternoon clouds come in."

Frank Drake spoke emphatically, "We will go fishing only, Josephina, if you promise to continue your story at dinner."

"And Ed," his father added, "if you will tell Frank more about the way you built this beautiful hilltop home."

Ed nodded and left for the lakeside to check the plane for departure. Josephina hurried to the kitchen to finish organizing the lunch. The Drakes and the MacLeans returned to the guest house. Minding one of Ed's numerous notes of instructions, they perched outside the cottage on the stoop to pull on their waders.

Phoebe reviewed the contents of her goody bag before they walked to the plane. On the way, small wildflowers peeping at her from the roadside delayed her arrival. "Hurry," James told her, "Remember, C deck boards first."

Phoebe's seat, with the picnic hamper as her companion, was too isolated for her to join in the camaraderie of the men as they started their flight. Instead, she recalled Alaskan stories told by the Seilers, indulging in a few Alaskan daydreams of her own. One that kept recurring was finding herself alone in the bush. How would she cope?

Ed started his take-off at the far end of the small lake to gain enough speed and elevation to clear the treetops at the other end. Soon, they were flying over Nonvianuk. She pressed her nose dangerously close to the window in spite of one of Ed's warning signs, "Do Not Touch Windows."

The quiet immensity of these northern lakes, encircled by fir trees stunted by winter cold, made her realize that this summertime fishing was only a brief distraction, a small interlude before the long cold that waited dangerously close.

Beyond Nonvianuk, Ed veered hard to the north, and flew over a wide plateau, at the base of which ran a river. "Moraine River," Ed called above the noise of the engine. "We'll take a look."

Abruptly, he flew low straight upstream, watching out his side window. He must have seen something because he banked hard left. The passengers banked left with him. Swiftly, he returned to the center of the stream and banked right. The passengers banked right. "It's like a tennis tournament," Phoebe explained to the picnic hamper, anchoring herself for the next bank. "Fish spotting," she told the interested hamper.

"Lots of fish," Ed decided. "We'll land on the lake as close to the river as I can anchor, and we'll walk across the plateau to the bend of the river where we spotted the fish."

"Can't you do fish spotting once more?" young Frank asked. "I'm just getting the hang of seeing the dark shadows that are the trout."

"No. I'm starting my descent."

They flew back over the plateau. Phoebe just had time to notice that it looked like a rough traverse in waders, when Ed brought the plane down and gently splashed through the shallow water until he stopped near a small tree.

James swung on to the pontoons and Ed handed him a rope. James jumped to land and anchored the plane securely to the small tree that Ed indicated. Then Ed dug his anchor into the dirt for more security.

Francis and Frank climbed out first, followed by Ed who unloaded rods from his underslung carrier and passed them to the men on shore. Finally he motioned to Phoebe, gave her a hand down to the shallow water, and followed with the picnic hamper. Soon the caravan started across the plateau. Ed took the lead with the picnic hamper on his back.

Phoebe kept falling behind because of the enchanting wildflowers. She was continually surprised that it was late August that brought springtime to these far Northern slopes. She stumbled along behind the men as fast as she could propel herself in the awkward waders.

At a bluff above the river, Ed stopped. "Francis, see the dark shapes we spotted in that deep pool? They are the ones we spotted from the airplane. They are trout following the salmon, returning to spawn in this river where they were born. See that crooked tree up the beach on the right? You will fish below that.

"Phoebe and I will go there by the tree with the lunch. She'll fish nearby. James, you will go above her, and I've told the Drakes to go below. We'll meet at the tree for a one o'clock lunch. Frank, I'll come to you shortly."

"O.K. dear?" James asked Phoebe, calling over his back without stopping as he hurried to his assigned spot.

The men started out with their rods, happy to have their marching orders. Phoebe followed Ed down the steep bluff, tacking from side to side like a sailboat.

Again, she wished for another woman. She knew the men felt slowed down by one lone female whose presence might possibly detain their immediate immersion into their fishing. Why did men always have to sound more macho than she knew they were? And why did it always make her determined to prove something by fishing well?

Ed told her to walk slowly along the river while he went ahead to stash the picnic hamper near the crooked lunch tree. Shortly after he left, she came upon James sitting on a hummock tying on a fly. "What are you going to use?" she ventured.

"Ed said to start out with this one that looks like a salmon egg. Then I'll probably change to a dry fly. Are you going to wait for Ed?" he asked, standing up.

"Not if you'll lend me one of your salmon egg flies," she responded.

Nobly, with only a small show of reluctance, he sat down again and reached for her rod. After tying on the fly and giving her two others, he stood up and started off. "Good luck," he called. "Wish me well."

She waved him off. Ed hadn't returned. She decided to begin fishing. She was on her own. No philosophizing now, just a fish to soothe her feelings and prove something, but what?

She watched her husband's retreating back. Several hundred yards above her, he stopped to read the waters before entering the stream. She could see neither the Drakes nor Ed.

Phoebe walked into the water just far enough to be able to practice cast without snagging the line on the bushes behind her, and yet not so far out that she had to worry about footing. With each cast, she felt soothed by a return of confidence. She took out her wading stick, snapped it open, and let it dangle, ready when she might need it. She waded deeper.

Three times she cast from this position, keeping the line high behind her, then letting the line drift a little past the end of the lower arc. As she retrieved slowly, she kept giving encouraging twitches to the line. Nothing happened. Grasping her stick firmly, she progressed three paces, feeling for a safe footing, using her toes like fingers in a glove.

After a total of twenty-four casts, three at each location, she stopped to rest and look around. Across the stream was a cutback perhaps twelve feet high, topped by tundra. With three more moves she figured she might be able to cast to it. She flexed her toes against the freezing cold and began to cast again with new resolve. She started to feel the water line on her waders creep toward her knees.

From a spot above her, she heard an excited exclamation. She saw that it was James, with his rod bent deep over the stream. She stopped to watch.

He began carefully to work the rod tip vertical. She was surprised to hear Ed call to her from the shore. She hadn't known that he was behind her. "Phoebe, if you're all right, I'll go see if I can help James. Don't go much deeper."

It was obvious that Ed wanted to be where the action was. "Are you all right alone?" he added.

"Yes, thank you. Take a picture and congratulate him for me."

She decided that she could chance a few more casts before the water became too deep. She cast toward the cutback. To her annoyance, every cast was short. She realized that she could only safely move one more time.

The water was creeping up. Carefully, with a firm grip on her wading stick, she inched three more short steps and stopped. She glanced again toward James. He seemed to be in control of the situation, but he hadn't been able to bring the fish any closer to the shore. She decided, however, that he looked like a man fulfilled in his sport and that he didn't miss wifely support at all.

Suddenly her own rod almost jumped out of her hand. She no longer had time for James's problems. She had a big fish of her own, a strike in water so cold that she could scarcely move, much less bring in a fish!

Quickly, lecturing to herself like a Dutch uncle, she said, "Get your feet set first, then work the rod tip up, firmly but gently. And, Mr. Fish," she breathed as she began to apply as much pressure in order to elevate the rod tip as the line would stand, "please be patient. I'm bigger than you and my fly has a small hook on it, but you can see me, and I can't see you.

"You don't know that I am going to release you, so that makes you fight harder. I'm out almost beyond my depth and freezing, but I'm fighting too."

An ancient, honorable combat had begun. She had recently read that there were accounts of just such fishing encounters in early Chinese writings.

After securing her feet, she reeled until the fish ran and she needed to give him slack. She found a safe position and began to work to get him back on the reel. The big danger came whenever the trout jumped. She was so busy admiring his beauty that she had to caution herself to keep a firm grip.

By taking one careful step at a time, she edged toward the shore. But there were so many things to do simultaneously! It was like rubbing your tummy and patting your head. How much farther? Wasn't it time for the fish to tire?

Ed's voice came to her across the water. "Try to walk toward the right. There's a small beach in the pebbles. You're doing great."

A flood of adrenaline coursed through her weary arms and legs at the sound of his voice. She nodded gratefully, relieved of the need to be completely self-sufficient. Ed was near. But after a quick glance, she realized that he was still closer to James and his fish than to hers. He was advising her by sound only. She was still battling the fish pretty much alone.

The fish made a long run. No time for sentiment. Her line screamed out. Frantically, she reeled in, but before she could get him firmly on the reel, he gave a magnificent jump. Frightened as she was of losing him, she tingled with the magic of the moment.

She reeled, and he gathered his strength. He broke from the

water a second time and danced upright for a moment before he leapt. She was thankful that she was going to release such a noble creature, but first she had to catch him.

While the fish was recuperating from his jumps, Phoebe managed to get him back on the reel, which shortened her line. She glanced toward Ed, who motioned her to work her way to the beach. She made each backward step carefully, anchoring her feet well before the next step and when possible, reeling in, rod tip up. Her progress was crab-like, but finally she felt pebbles instead of rounded boulders underfoot.

When the fish sensed that he was in water that was dangerously shallow, he gathered his strength and made one more brave run into the current. Phoebe worked him in to shallow water firmly but gently.

From there, she continued to back up until she felt grass. She shortened the line and swung the fish up over the grass safely away from the river. She dropped down over the fish and covered him with both hands.

She anchored the fish and the leader between her knees and managed to reach the rod with one hand. She placed the reel end by the tail of the fish and mentally noted where it reached on the shaft. She shoved the rod out of the way.

Now for the pliers. She groped for them in her jacket pocket and forced the mouth of the fish open. She found the fly in the cheek of the fish and gave what she hoped was a quick twist. The fish jerked in pain, but the fly came out clean.

Phoebe managed to get both hands around the fish and carry him to the water, facing him upstream. Keeping a firm hold around his stomach with one hand, she began to stroke his back with the other. He was so still. Resting? Dead?

At last, a quiver ran through him. She could see his sides moving. Finally, he shook himself all over. Phoebe released her grip and the fish darted off, disappearing immediately into the camouflage of his underwater world.

Phoebe stood up, stretching taut muscles, and reentered her own world. She saw Ed watching. He made the thumb and forefinger sign for "well done." She returned the sign and gathered up her rod. James was still playing his fish. He must be exhausted.

She took a farewell glance at the scene of her private triumph. She had had a strike, alone, fought the trout, alone, and released him successfully. Now, fulfilled, she returned to being a wife.

When she reached the men, Ed was in shallow water, net in hand. He pointed to his watch. "This is a huge trout. James has been playing him for over twenty minutes. I hope the fly and the leader hold. I'm going out to him now. But, first, congratulations on your fish. I'm proud of you. How long was it?"

"I don't know. I released him. But I know where he measured on my rod. He was a brave fish. He won his freedom."

Phoebe settled contentedly on a hummock until she felt warmer. Ed had entrusted James's camera to her, so she stayed ready for action.

James must have decided that his only chance was to try to bring the fish in quickly before the fly worked out of its mouth. But the fish was still so strong that James couldn't keep the rod tip up. She knew that he was caught between danger and necessity. What strength this was taking! Phoebe felt her own arms ache, just watching. She moved farther away to leave plenty of room in case her husband managed to back up the beach for the landing.

Ed followed closely in the water with the net. When James's feet reached the shore, he tried to lift the fish out of the water. It was too strong and too big. All James could do was to back up until the fish was in shallow water. He held him taut. Ed netted him and, with a struggle, lifted the fish up.

The head of the fish hung over one side of the net, and his tail, over the other. Phoebe realized that was why James had had such a struggle.

"James, get close to the fish," she directed, "while I take a picture. What a fish! What a fisherman!" Phoebe snapped a picture.

James knelt beside Ed to hold the fish while Ed released the fly. Phoebe heard Ed say, "He must weigh over ten pounds at least, the biggest so far this season. Congratulations."

Then the men cut off her view. Perhaps it was just as well because she heard a thud and then James's protests.

"I had to do it, James. The fly was too deep," she heard Ed tell James.

But when James held the fish proudly for more pictures, she decided privately that it might work out well that this fish was not released. Maybe Ed could find a taxidermist. This was truly an Alaskan specimen trout.

James and Phoebe left Ed with the fish and went to find the Drakes. James's smile conveyed his sense of accomplishment.

Lunchtime had come and gone. On the way to the Drakes, they passed the picnic hamper and picked up a few sandwiches to eat as they walked. James asked all about her fish. When she told him, she knew that her face also radiated joy. She did hope that the Drakes had had good fishing.

About a quarter of a mile upstream, they found the Drakes, fishing within speaking distance, well out in the river. The MacLeans sat on the bank and watched, admiring the father's casts and noting the quiet kind way he occasionally called a suggestion to his son.

Young Frank was casting almost too conscientiously, too eager to finish one cast so that he could begin another. "He doesn't let the fly work long enough for the fish to strike it," she mentioned, from her own prolonged apprenticeship.

They saw Francis move downstream where the river narrowed. He gestured to his son to follow and to cast across to a bank where, he indicated by holding his hands apart, he had spotted a good-sized fish. Young Frank nodded and began following his father's suggestion. "Walk out a little and cast more quietly. Leave the fly in the water a little longer," they heard Francis say.

Frank obeyed eagerly. His casts were carefully correct. He had learned well. The MacLeans watched as proudly as though he were their son. Phoebe crossed her fingers, the trusted good-luck device. She made up her mind, if necessary, to stick her tongue in her left cheek. That was the sure-fire omen. But there was no need for that.

Frank had a strong strike. Phoebe felt herself pulling her own rod upright to help him elevate his tip. It was a joy to see the pride on Francis's face as he moved out of the river to give his son more room. He spotted the MacLeans and waved.

With each jump, the trout arched silver against the low Alaskan hills. She knew that the memory of this fish would stay with Frank long after the vacation was over. Twice, three times, the trout jumped. Three times Frank brought him back on the reel, rod tip up, letting him run enough to relieve the pressure.

Then he began to bring him to the beach. It was always amazing to Phoebe how often places to land a fish materialized when needed. Frank brought the fish in expertly. She could see the victory smile begin to cross his face, when abruptly the fish interrupted this successful progression to the shore. He shook the hook powerfully, but it held. The trout changed the direction that Frank was trying to keep him in and headed out to deeper water.

Frank pursued his prize, reeling as he followed. The fish was heading for the opposite bank where he had been caught! "Steady, son. You have all the time in the world. Don't rush him," called his father.

He didn't. Phoebe began to feel the growl of hunger pangs, in spite of the pilfered sandwich. Fortunately for Frank and for them all, she noticed that Ed had brought the picnic hamper with him.

The fish seemed to have strengthened, not weakened, on this spurt to freedom. He fought heroically all the way in. Ed picked up the net and stood ready for action. At the first opportunity, he scooped the net successfully under the trout. After removing the fly, Ed handed the fish to the proud young fisherman, who accepted the congratulations gracefully as the cameras clicked.

The fish measured over twenty-two inches on Francis's tape. "Shall we release him, Frank?" Ed asked.

"Oh, no. He's my first Alaskan fish. I want to save him for my sons. Can you arrange that, Ed, please? You do everything else so well."

"We'll see about that. But now if we don't eat lunch soon, it will be time to leave to hike back to the airplane. I want to take off before the afternoon wind rises," Ed answered.

"This calls for a victory drink of Crown Royal first," James decided. "It will make afternoon fishing better. How long can we fish after lunch, Ed?"

"About another hour," was the reply.

That night at dinner, Josephina was gaily dressed, dark eyes snapping with interest as they recounted the day. Francis and James had four fish each to report. Frank had caught another besides his fabulous jumper. An old hand at this game now, he proudly announced, "Two."

Phoebe hugged to herself the triumph of the fish that she had caught alone. Putting on a splendid performance, as she told herself later, she reported laconically, "One nice trout who fought bravely, released."

Gibraltar

"TODAY'S FISHING WILL be at Gibraltar," Ed announced at breakfast one morning. This would be a new place for Frank, but for his father and the MacLeans it would be a cherished return.

They flew smoothly over a part of the immense face of Southern Alaska until they came to Gibraltar Lake. Ed circled, winging the plane from side to side, fish-spotting the outlet that was their destination.

The motion brought her out of her private musings about how each day on a fishing trip created its own unique experience. She pivoted her head from side to side as Ed banked. "Looks good," her husband turned to say to her, peering deep into the water.

Ed reversed and flew to the upper part of the mouth of the Gibraltar River, found a good mooring place, and landed. The men jumped in the water and helped Ed push the nose of the plane forward at a right angle to the shore. Ed tethered the plane firmly.

Ahead of them from the mouth of the river to a gentle bend, the river stretched smooth and inviting. "What's beyond the curve?" Francis asked.

"More river, all fine for dry fly-fishing until you reach a riffle that pours over some rocks to form a small waterfall," Ed answered. "For some reason, the fish don't lie below that. You Drakes start fishing here near the plane and progress down to that riffle, arriving about one o'clock, in time for lunch. Phoebe, please wait here. You and James will go with me in a few minutes."

The men checked the contents of their fishing jackets. When the Drakes turned into the river, James asked, "Where do I go, Ed?"

"Come with Phoebe and me. I'll show you a place around the bend where the river is shallow enough to cross. You can fish from the other side. Phoebe, you'll fish near the lunch spot. Now, let's hike across the tundra away from the river. It's better walking there. We'll return to the river where I want James to cross."

Phoebe, rod in hand, started after the men, feeling a little like a squaw, always ten paces behind. But when she began to walk through whole fields of wildflowers, she forgot her slight annoyance. The name of the flower, which she hadn't thought of in two years, now popped into the computer of her mind, Farewell to Summer. Its blossoms were like forget-me-nots. Soon, she saw that there were both blue and pink flowers on the same stem. The pink color, she decided, must occur during the fading process. But it certainly gave an enchanting effect.

Once Ed stopped to give her a hand through a small creek and to point out the path by the river. Then he hurried on. The two-colored forget-me-nots claimed too much of her attention to hurry. By the time she arrived at the picnic site, Ed was already in the middle of the stream with James.

Phoebe chose a Deer-haired Yellow dry fly and tied it on her line. A small thought crossed her mind as she glanced at the lunch, that an "elevens" might taste good about now. But she resisted and entered the stream. Behind her she noticed that there was a good pebble beach, not very large, but adequate for landing a fish.

The footing was relatively free from large stones. She kept her wading stick that dangled from the back of her fishing jacket, ready for her reach. She began casting upstream. She took care to retrieve the fly each time before it began to drag. She continued to cast and move, covering each area in three casts. While she felt for a good place to station her feet, she both read the waters and took in the beauty that surrounded her.

She had just established herself in a new position and made her first cast, a good one, when she had a strike! The thrill made her muscles tingle and sharpened her mind. Her fish felt strong, but so did she.

She let the trout run but was able to keep him on the reel. When possible, she took a backward step to the beach. She glanced quickly toward James, who was busy fishing, but Ed, who was behind him, gave a wave. She had an audience. Good.

Whenever the trout jumped, she gave him his head. She could see the rainbow color running horizontally across the silver, the reason for the name. Several more times he ran upstream, then exploded into a series of spectacular jumps. She was in no hurry and neither was he. She reeled him in between the jumps and his runs.

Finally, authoritatively, she brought the rainbow to the small beach. Ed was there in the shallow water and netted the fish. "Shall I release him for you? It's a beautiful trout."

"No, could we freeze him to take home?" she surprised herself by this request.

"I can freeze him at the lodge, but that wouldn't last until you get home. The problem will be finding dry ice for the fish at Anchorage."

"I will try to solve that Anchorage problem," Phoebe answered. "How much will he weigh?"

"Almost three and a half pounds. A nice fish. James has released two about that size. They gave him a good fight. Remember, Phoebe, only one fish per fisherman is allowed on Gibraltar. It's in the process of being designated as a trophy river. Next, probably all fishing here will be Catch and Release."

After Ed killed the fish, he put him in the back pocket of his fishing jacket. "Right after lunch, I need to fly home for a short time. I'll take your fish with me then. Now, I'll go check on the Drakes."

Three plus pounds of Alaskan trout, Phoebe thought, moving to watch her husband before returning to her own fishing. This could be the menu for the birthday dinner they were having the night after they got home. What an elegant celebration for a daughter and her brother-in-law who had the same birthdays. On that date he would be in town on a business trip. But would one fish, even a large one, be enough? Maybe she'd better try to catch another one and ask James to let it be counted as his.

She rose to her feet, full of resolve and purpose. But just then she saw James get a strong strike. Instead, she settled down to watch her husband.

It looked as though James had been casting to a large rock that protruded above the water about two-thirds of the way across the river, a likely spot for a good fish. "It's the principle of 'territorial imperative,'" Phoebe decided. "Any fish in a good spot like that had lived there a long time and would be a big fish. This could be a first-class battle."

Just then James took a false step and his feet tangled with a boulder. Phoebe held her breath for a moment, but he managed to gain his footing again, with his fish still on and with the tip of the rod straight upright.

Phoebe saw, however, that the water mark on his waders was rising. He couldn't go much deeper. Either he had to reel in a little or hold the fish taut until he could work his way into shallower water. James couldn't see that Ed was near, but she could. She relaxed. She would both learn and enjoy.

James had to work hard between the runs and the jumps to earn each backward step. Trout were truly the acrobats of the streams. Phoebe was sure that she, the spectator, was appreciating the trout's antics right now more than James was.

Over and over he reeled in, and over and over the fish swam out and jumped. It was almost time to worry about whether the hook would hold.

The trout must have swum toward James, for suddenly she saw her husband reeling in rapidly. But it was too good to last. The fish began a long run upstream, and James was forced to release that hard-earned line from the reel. He started the process all over again.

She couldn't get on with her own fishing while James was playing the principal role in this drama unfolding before her. She would have to put aside temporarily the fact that she needed another fish for the birthday dinner. She glanced at her watch, past one o'clock, lunchtime. She heard her name spoken behind her. It was the Drakes.

"That looks like a good fish of James's. Has he been playing him long?" Francis asked.

"At least fifteen minutes or so, long enough to put quite a strain on his fly," she answered, glad to have two more recruits for the support team.

"We've been standing here over five minutes. That makes it twenty minutes," Frank, the self-appointed timekeeper, announced and added, "Hurry up, fish. I have to get back to this sport myself. What a great morning! I've taken and released three trout, Alaskan trout. The only thing I'm not sure I approve of is releasing them."

His father gestured pointedly to the stream, and Frank stopped talking. They all returned to their roles as conscientious spectators. Phoebe realized that James found it harder this time to retrieve his fish. "Why hasn't the silly fish tired?" she asked.

"He doesn't know he'll be released," was Frank's logical conclusion.

James took perhaps five steps backward before the next explosion ended in another run. But James won a little in that exchange. Ed materialized and gestured to them to move back up the slope. He approached the shallow water. She saw soon that her husband had the fish only a couple of yards from Ed's net. "Hang in there, James," she whispered, her own need to fish dismissed.

James did, and, with his rod bent almost double, he brought his fish within a couple of feet of Ed, who scooped the net into the water but couldn't reach the fish.

The duet continued, but this time James was able to get more line wound on his reel. "Now," he called to Ed.

Ed bent and without any flurry that might disturb the water to alarm the fish, brought the net under him and made a clean lift. When the net cleared the water, they saw that the fish was so large that he filled the net.

"Boy, that's something. A fish almost too big for the net!" Frank exclaimed.

James's smile made Phoebe thankful that she had come on this trip, lone woman or not. She reached in the back pocket of his jacket for the camera. Ed already had the fish free from the fly and handed him to James to hold for a quick photograph.

"Put him back in the water quickly, Ed, please," James asked Ed. "He deserves a second chance."

"Ed said he heard that there's a taxidermist who's just moved to King Salmon. Want to try him? That might look fine on your wall, MacLean," Francis mentioned, playing the devil's advocate.

Phoebe could see that her husband was tempted. But resolutely he shook his head no.

At lunch, they toasted Frank with some Crown Royal that Francis Drake brought out of his fishing kit.

After lunch, the men disappeared on the inner trail, the better to approach with caution the new stretches of river they wanted to fish. Ed hurried to the plane for his necessary trip to the lodge. Phoebe could scarcely conceal her impatience for them all to be off. Like a homing pigeon, she returned to the place in the river where she had caught her fish.

She felt comfortable with the footing and with her casting. Each cast was exhilarating. When a fish struck, she wasn't even surprised, just pleased. She played him with all the expertise she could command and brought him in like an old pro. He was almost as large as the first one. She steeled herself to remove the fly and accomplish the killing.

This taken care of, she propped her rod against a shrub to mark the location. Then she carried the fish to the lunch spot. She wrapped him in the rain jacket that she always kept in the back pocket of her fishing vest and found heavy stones to use to weigh it down.

Impressed by her own efficiency, she hurried back to the stream. One more fish would make the dinner party a howling success, if she could control her conscience and ask Francis Drake to claim it.

On the way to retrieve her rod, she decided that it would be better to change to new waters. Other fish might remember what had happened to their playmates. Moving cautiously back from the stream, she walked to the next cove, where she found another small beach and welcoming waters.

Like an old trooper, she entered the fray. She cast well and moved conscientiously, but the fish didn't seem to appreciate her expertise. She began to talk rather pointedly to her Guardian Angel of Fishing, wondering at the same time what her name was. People did like to be called by name. She must try to find out when she got home.

Her words with her fishing Guardian Angel must have done the trick. She had just moved and finished bracing her feet when a fish struck. She quickly set the hook and pulled her rod tip high, higher, trying to stifle her conscience and her sympathy for her adversary. "I do need you," she apologized. "Two fish, counting the one Ed has already taken to the lodge, really won't serve my gang at home for a double birthday."

Then she went to work, reeling when she could, admiring his leaps, reeling again, and cautiously working her way to the beach. Where was it? How much farther?

What a relief to feel gravel under her waders. The fish ran twice more, but not so strenuously that she needed to follow him. Gradually, she worked him close to the shore. Walking far enough above the beach, she was able to ease the trout safely onto the stones.

Carefully, she tossed her rod to the side and dropped down by the fish. Securing him against her leg with one hand, she groped with the other and found a rock that she felt would be heavy enough to kill him. Just then a shaft of sun highlighted the beautiful rainbow colors of the trout. It saddened her to see how handsome he was and to think how dead he would be in a minute.

She raised the stone for the blow and then with sudden resolution tossed it away and managed to lift the fish with both hands. She hurried to the stream with him and lowered the limp fish into the water. She held him with one hand, while with the other, she stroked breath back into him.

She needed to stroke him longer than usual to get him ready to swim away to his own life. "I might have interrupted a chain of creation. Who am I to do that?" she said to herself.

The fish began a wriggle that moved through his whole body and then at last he swam away. Her feeling of elation made her forget temporarily the birthday dinner the night after their return. She'd solve that problem later.

Now she'd concentrate on how proud James would be of her. For the first time, she began to appreciate his insistence on Catch and Release.

She'd still have to own up to Ed about her second fish. At least, now there was not a third one that needed an explanation.

She felt a tiny twinge of regret, like a small black cloud in a summer sky, over not having enough trout for dinner. Oh well, she'd change the menu and serve trout as an hors d'oeuvre. She shook her head hard to allow the good feeling to reenter.

She found herself quite near the lunch spot. She checked on her second fish, wrapped in her rain jacket, and moved it farther into the shade. No point in advertising her save until it was necessary. Then she went back to retrieve her rod that she had tossed aside while she was taking care of the fish.

She picked up the rod with the line lying loose around it. She decided that the easiest way to straighten out her line was to walk into the water and cast it a few times.

She did this and turned to make her way to the shore, rod over one shoulder. She reeled in slowly as she walked. There was a strong tug. What was that? A floating branch, she hoped. She faced around and reeled in fast. Then she flipped the line as hard as she could to dislodge the snag. Something on the end of the line jumped. Heavenly days, it was a fish!

She jerked as hard as she could, hoping to break off the fly. Everything held, including the fish. She glanced around the stream. Thank goodness, no one was in sight.

She kept flipping and jerking the line, but she couldn't get rid of the trout. She reeled in a little and pulled the line fast from side to side in an attempt to break off the fly. No such luck. She felt tears on her checks, but all she could do was sniff and lick them off. The only thing left to do was reel in fast and hope the tippet, with the fish on it, would break off.

Nothing that she hoped for happened. She swung the fish on the beach and hastened to find the pliers to release the fly, in order to return the uncooperative fish to the water quickly.

But when she pried open his mouth, she discovered that the fly was embedded deep in his throat. Blood was running from the side of his mouth. There was only one thing to do. She found a rock and bashed the fish on his head to put him out of his misery.

Like a thief in the night, she picked up the fish and rod and crept to the picnic spot. She stuck the fish under the rain jacket with the other one and fearfully sat down to wait.

James, in high spirits, arrived first. When the Drakes returned, the three of them began to swap animated accounts of every catch, all, of course, released. They had had thrilling fishing. "Alaska fish are willing fish," Francis summed it up.

"That's the kind I like," his son agreed.

Ed arrived to tell them that they needed to leave quickly because the wind was rising. They knew well that a strong wind was the bane of small planes. Even so, Phoebe lingered before gathering up her belongings.

Ed came over to her kindly. "Tired, Phoebe? You'll be back at the lodge before you know it."

"Ed," she stammered, even more uncomfortable because every-one was still there. "I need to talk with you. I have kept three fish. I didn't mean to catch the last one. I had made a final cast to straighten out my line. I started walking to the shore before I reeled in my line completely, and a fish struck.

"When I tried to remove the fly quickly in order to release him, I found that it was lodged so deep in his throat that the fish was bleeding hard. Blood was running out the side of his mouth. I had to kill him. I'm sick about it."

Ed's face blanched. He looked stricken. "Phoebe, I explained that this is practically a trophy river. Didn't you remember that? Even one fish per person is frowned on. We now have three fish. What if the warden comes by? He often comes up this river from King Salmon by boat. It would be very embarrassing to have him question us."

"We are four fishermen," Phoebe insisted in a small voice. "James, I was just catching enough for a double birthday dinner the night after we return. Will you and Ed claim one each for me? Then, even if Francis and Frank have saved a trout, we will still be legal."

Ed's rueful smile came with great effort. "Barely, and it's not sportsmanlike."

Frank broke the silence. "Here's to Ed, pilot, guide, and now, practically a lawbreaker!"

Ed picked up the fish without comment.

James took Phoebe's rod from her and gave her a loving shake. "I'll keep her out of the river, Ed, but let's go fast, just in case someone like a warden comes by."

Agate Beach

AT BREAKFAST ONE MORNING, the four fishermen lingered with their hosts over a delicately poached trout that Francis, with permission, had brought in the day before. The morning was clear with little wind. "This might be a perfect afternoon for Agate Beach," Ed suggested. "I've had word on the shortwave radio of a complication over this same business that I need to attend to briefly in King Salmon. I could drop you and the lunch supplies some place nearby this morning. I'll return for you in the afternoon, and we'll fly to Agate Beach."

"Some place like Brooks River?" Frank asked eagerly.

"No, a river named Alagnek that flows out of Nonvianuk Lake not far from Enchanted Lake. The MacLeans fished it last time they were here."

"Sounds great," young Frank agreed, "particularly Agate Beach. Dad has told me a lot about it, but can't you throw in a few bears?" he added.

James shook his head. "Afraid not. The plans sound fine. Let's get suited up. Dress warmly. As I recall, there's a cold wind that comes in from Nonvianuk."

"No problem. I put on everything I brought, daily," Frank laughed.

"I've known other fishermen who have done that," Phoebe commented.

When they were all aboard, Tom Spain released the tie rope and pushed them off. Ed taxied to the far end of the small lake to get maximum distance for the lift-off. During their taxiing up and down the lake to get in position for take-off, he told them, "Watch for the loons. The pair that returns here every year has just arrived. The mother is building her nest now. There she is, flying low by the shore."

As they lifted off the lake, Phoebe could see Josephina on the hill by the lodge, standing by the flagpole, waving them off.

Almost immediately they were over Nonvianuk Lake. A few minutes later, Ed banked left and started his descent to taxi up the Alagnek River far enough to reach some reeds that he could use to secure the plane.

They saw a float plane near the opposite shore and two men casting spinners. Ed snorted, "Probably from King Salmon. We'll have to fish this side. Too damned many fishermen."

Phoebe in her solitary perch on C deck had a private chuckle. These two men were the first people they'd seen since the bear episode at Brooks River the first day they were here.

After the plane was secured, the fishermen removed the gear and carried it with them to the mouth of the river. Phoebe tucked the current book and her journal in the back pocket of her fishing jacket—alternatives for fishing if the water became too cold for her.

Phoebe was pleased to recall that this was one of the few Alaskan rivers she knew that had a sandy bottom instead of the usual boulders. Her remembered pleasure was short-lived when Ed cautioned, "Don't let the smooth footing lure you too far out. There is an undercurrent that can be difficult to handle."

So much for complacency.

By the time Phoebe pulled on her half-fingered fishing gloves and wound a scarf around her chin and mouth for warmth, each man was in his chosen fishing spot, silhouetted against the bright sky and hills. She studied James and then Francis as they fished, absorbing their form and style to remember for future use.

She noticed that Ed was taking some time to fish upstream before he flew to King Salmon. He was using a double-haul to reach the center of the stream. She watched, fascinated. Quickly she waded into shallow water and attempted to copy his double-haul casting movements, the first time she had tried this. She continued her attempts after Ed flew off. It was almost lunch time before she began to fish, going deeper into the stream.

Even then it was hard to concentrate on her own fishing. The three men were having a sensational morning, one of them constantly with his rod bent by a strike. Often they would release the fish without returning to shore. No wonder Alaska had a reputation for ready fishing.

She savored the smooth footing, but her enjoyment was somewhat spoiled as she remembered Ed's warning about the strong current. It kept her from having "ready" fishing of her own. She had to remind herself that she wasn't quite as strong as these other fishermen, even though she frequently felt as proficient. Or perhaps it was the delay resulting from her fishing alone. She couldn't release a fish she caught or check a fly in mid-stream. That cut into her fishing time.

She glanced at her watch and quickened the pace of her fishing. Since moving was easier with this good footing, she found herself farther out. She was puzzled that her casting was more difficult than usual, until she realized that only her arms were free for the casting movement. Usually the whole body helped to accomplish a good cast.

She mastered this new difficulty by keeping each cast higher. She found her line sailing out farther than usual. Perhaps it was being deep in the river that had improved her casting. This was fun.

When a fish struck, her line zinged out as though the fish were heading for Nonvianuk Lake. Settling down to the serious business of keeping him on the reel, she took a little time to relish how easy the backward walk to the shore on smooth sand would be.

She was so far out that this pleasant walk took a long time. She beached the fish, removed the fly, and returned him to the water quietly.

Phoebe continued this enjoyable fishing. She caught and released two more trout before she noticed that the others had left the stream and gathered at the picnic spot. James hailed her to come in.

"I'm making a fire to heat water in the billy that Ed left. A cup of tea will warm us up while we wait for Ed," he told her.

Phoebe hadn't realized how cold she was until she cradled her hands around her mug of hot tea.

When Ed arrived and told them that they should leave for Agate Beach, Phoebe had no regrets about not returning for an afternoon of fishing in the cold water. They were all filled with anticipation for Agate Beach.

Ed flew back to Nonvianuk and crossed the lake to Agate Beach that was in a cove directly opposite Enchanted Lake. He told them that the University of Alaska had been sending student geologists to Agate Beach regularly during the summer.

"I hope they aren't there now, and I hope they haven't depleted the supply of agates," Francis said, expressing everybody's sentiments.

Ed planned to pull the plane right up on Agate Beach, but the wind was not right. "We'll need to fly to the other side of this narrow peninsula in order to get enough shelter for the plane, in case the wind rises. You'll have to hike over to Agate Beach," he explained. "Josephina provided me with some plastic sacks for you to use."

It took some time to anchor the plane and then to clamber over the rough terrain of the spiny ridge that separated the two sides of the peninsula. "We'll only have an hour to hunt," Ed warned them. "The wind is shifting."

"Imagine, a whole hour at Agate Beach!" Frank exalted. He was the first one out of the plane and on the sand.

Each wave that broke against the beach brought in new sand containing agates from veins in mountains that had existed long before the lakes. The fishermen-miners scattered to scratch in the sand like a bunch of chickens, using anything available—sticks, shells, fishing knives.

Phoebe's hunting was constantly interrupted by someone's call to come admire a new treasure. When she wasn't busy doing this, she collected a few beauties herself, planning what she would do with them as she dug.

Too soon Ed called them to hike back to the plane. Reluctantly, clutching their plastic sacks filled with treasures, they followed him.

"My best agate goes to Josephina for remembering to send these sacks," Frank announced, hefting his sack with satisfaction. "I didn't know what a good agate finder I would be!"

The wind was higher when they arrived at the plane which was bobbing like a cork. Ed looked worried as he studied the situation. Finally, he said to James, "I don't think I can lift off safely with a full load. I may have to make two flights."

"It's your judgement to make, Ed. I'll wait. After all, a plane up here is your lifeline."

"I'll stay with James," Phoebe told him.

Ed nodded and explained the problem to the Drakes. "Let us stay," Francis insisted.

"No, but thanks," Ed said with a skipper's authority. "I want you two to board right now." The Drakes obeyed without question.

Phoebe stood close to James as they watched their friends take off, the plane shuddering in the wind. She crossed her fingers and prayed silently.

"How does it feel to be Mrs. Robinson Crusoe?" James asked, taking her hand.

"It makes the country seem big and empty, doesn't it? How long will it take Ed to return?"

"An hour at least."

She shook her watch. Was the second-hand stuck? James took her by the shoulders and propelled her to the biggest of the small shrubs on the bank. He hollowed out a place for them in the sand. They snuggled down in this somewhat sheltered spot.

Agate hunting had lost its appeal, at least for the time being. Phoebe decided humbly that her James would always be the top person on her list of whom she would choose to be marooned with.

Phoebe was determined not to worry about the cold, but she found that her teeth were beginning to chatter. The only movement was the wind. Time stood still. All the things that could happen to Ed, or to them, ran through her mind like a film on fast forward.

Suddenly, she felt James pull away from her. He was sitting up stiffly. He cupped his ears to listen. "Phoebe, do you hear something?"

She nodded her head affirmatively. As one body, they moved together to the beach, straining their ears and eyes in the cold dim twilight. "He's coming!" James shouted and hugged her happily. Close together, they waited.

Ed pulled up as smoothly as a taxi on a city street. James grabbed the rope that Ed tossed to him with one hand, and with the other he helped Phoebe climb on the pontoons and into the plane.

James closed the door behind them and Ed took off. "Josephina says no hurry about getting to dinner," Ed assured them and headed the plane for home.

"Fine. We'll have hot showers and a cold drink first. I don't know which will feel better," James answered.

"Both will be best," Phoebe stated and added, "This country is all yours, Ed. It's too big for me!"

"It will magically become the right size for you again by daylight," Ed predicted.

At dinner, Phoebe wore the polished agate that Francis had sent her from his first trip to Agate Beach. Ed's contributions were some hair-raising tales about adventures he had had when he and his plane on several occasions had been stuck in the bush overnight.

Frank Drake pushed himself away from the table as soon as he could politely do so. "Excuse me, but I have to go admire my agates, and, Josephina, I'm going to choose the prettiest one for you. It will be at your place tomorrow at breakfast."

"And I will ask my husband to make it into a pendant like Phoebe's. It will be a pleasure to receive it from such a good friend as you, Frank. *Muchas Gracias*."

Lower Brooks River

THE NEXT MORNING at breakfast, Ed told them reluctantly that again he had to fly to King Salmon. "The same tiresome piece of business as yesterday, but I can finish it right after lunch."

He continued, "Here are two suggestions I've figured out. I can drop you and your lunch at the opposite end of Brooks River from where you fished before. That's on Brooks Lake. I can land the plane there easily and you can fish the upper river. I can join you for the afternoon fishing," he explained. "Or if you'd rather, you can stay here and fish Enchanted Lake."

"I've never fished that part of Brooks River. I'd like that," James decided.

"I'd rather fish Enchanted Lake since I've never fished your lake either, Ed," Francis decided. "I've had enough of bears!"

"I'll go along with Dad," Frank said. "Bears are exciting, but even though the MacLeans invited me to Enchanted Lake, Dad paid to bring me out."

"Fine. Tom Spain can take you fishing around the lake in the rowboat. And Josephina can give you lunch here at the lodge," Ed said and added, "James, I've heard again about the taxidermist who has just come to town. I'll ask some friends about his work. He may be the answer for your big fish and Frank's first Alaskan trout."

On the flight to Brooks Lake, James insisted that Phoebe sit in the copilot's seat. "We'll fly to Naknek Lake," Ed pointed out, "and then right up to Brooks Lake."

Phoebe felt enveloped by sky above and lake below as though she were a double mirror between them. At the mouth of the river she spotted several grizzlies, but very few fishermen.

"Either the salmon run is over or the ranger is keeping fishermen away because of the bears," James surmised.

Ed nodded. "The latter, probably." He began to bank left and right, to spot fish. Phoebe found that she could spot fish much better from the copilot's seat. She memorized a couple of holes eagerly and hoped that she could recognize them when she was on the stream. James could have all the rest of the river.

Ed brought the helicopter down smoothly beside the lake near the beginning of the river. He idled the motor long enough for the MacLeans to climb out on the pontoons and drop into shallow water. From the sandy beach they waved Ed off, and with their lunches stowed in jacket pockets, they began to fish.

The footing was much rougher than it appeared from the air. Phoebe kept in sight of James in case she needed help. But with her trusty wading stick, she managed alone. She had three good strikes but, somewhat to her relief, each fish managed to escape.

She managed to find the first hole that she had spotted from the air. She settled down to prepare for serious fishing. She located boulders that were above the water to serve for stepping stones. She'd have to take her chance on the ones beneath the surface. She planned where she would cast and how and where to bring in a fish. Now all she needed was to maintain her balance and to get a strike.

When a fish from the pool finally struck, he led her determinedly upstream to a spot beyond the boulders that she had decided were safe stepping stones. She managed to keep the rod tip up, with the line firm but not too tight, and to keep her footing and balance while both hands were involved with rod and reel. She needed a third hand badly, to hold the wading stick along this rough stream. She thought again that people who pictured fishing as an easy, contemplative sport should try it sometime!

The fish finally outsmarted her. He swam into territory that had no stepping stones above water and none showing below the water! All she could do was to hold onto the fish as firmly as she dared. Very shortly, he broke off the tippet and swam away with the fly still attached.

Oh, well. She'd look for the other pool that she had spotted. She had marked it by a small waterfall. She found it around the next curve of the river. Water above some rocks tumbled into the pool. On one side, a ledge provided a comfortable place to sit. She would try to cast from there. If she couldn't, at least she could dap from her perch.

But first she had to tie on a new tippet. James arrived before she started the process. "Let's eat our sandwiches first and then I'll give you a hand. How have you done?"

"I'm still trying to catch my first. And you?"

"I landed and released two fighting ones and lost a third. He fought better than I did. I'm hungry."

While they ate their sandwiches and fruit, they heard the music of the wind in the pine trees; at least Phoebe found it music. James kept worrying about whether the wind was getting too strong.

James tied on the tippet and the dry fly that she had chosen, a Royal Wulff. When he stood up to go, he told her, "Try to stay near here. It's a good spot you've found, but watch these rocks. I'll keep you within sight. If you need me, call or wave. I can't be too careful with a good fishing pal like you."

She watched him fondly, touched by his concern. He was often so engrossed in his own fishing that he gave her the impression that he had completely forgotten that she was there. Refreshed, she returned to her own private pool. But her fishing wasn't as carefree as she had hoped it would be. What would happen if Ed couldn't land the plane in this wind?

"Don't get morbid," she preached to herself. "There's James within hailing distance. When you have a stalwart, loving husband, what do you have to worry about, even in this enormous country. Shape up, Phoebe. Go catch a fish!"

The lecture helped, even though she had a little trouble erasing the thought that very little of this country was even charted. A big fish struck.

She reeled in, trying to contain him in the pool. But he ran and gave a jump that brought him out of the pool into the current of the stream.

"Think like a mountain goat," she told herself, "but a careful one." She followed the fish into the stream, jumping from stepping stone to boulder. "Don't take me too far, Mr. Fish. I want to stay near James. I may need his help."

But on the fish went, a strong and spectacular jumper. They both rested between jumps. On his next run, she saw no possible footing. "James," she called, even though she now had the fish more securely on the reel, "I can't see any stones to jump to. I can't follow my fish!"

James heard her and started toward her, instructing as he leaped from boulder to boulder. "You have no choice but to make your stand. Reel in gently but steadily. The fish has forced you to put your trust in your rod, the tippet, and the leader. You either bring him in or you lose him."

James's words reassured her. No decisions to make, just pray, she told herself. She flashed a smile to James.

And she didn't lose the fish! She backed up, step by step, guided by James's instructions, and brought him to the beach. James released him for her.

His pride in her made this a special moment. She leaned against him, spent emotionally and physically. He hugged her close, in spite of the two rods he was holding. It was lovely. She vowed to call for help more often when James was near.

The wind was definitely strengthening. The music in the trees was now a Wagnerian overture. James glanced at his watch. "Ed's late. I wonder why?"

"Are you worried about the plane?"

James nodded. "Let's start walking toward Brooks Lake where Ed dropped us off."

They followed the shore or walked in the water when necessary. Not far from the mouth of the river they were surprised to meet Ed carrying the sleeping bag that he always stored behind Phoebe's seat on the plane. Because of the noise of the wind, they hadn't heard the plane fly in.

"The wind's too high to take off," Ed told them. "It was almost too rough for me to land. I've lashed the plane to a couple of small trees. I hope it holds. How about a slight change in plans? Let's head back to the outlet of the river on Lake Naknek and find a ranger." He motioned down a faint path.

Silently they filed along, Phoebe thankful for the long Arctic twilight. Eventually, the path led them to a jeep road that made walking easier.

Faintly at first, then louder, they heard the noise of a truck. It was coming toward them. "Hi! Need a lift?" called a cheerful voice. It was a ranger in a four-wheel drive jeep. "I heard the plane come in but didn't hear it leave. Too much wind to take off, Seiler?"

Ed nodded.

"No problem. The wind usually dies down enough by morning to permit a safe take-off. I can put you up tonight in an empty cabin because there are no Katmai tourists right now. Jump in."

Gratefully, they bumped along in the ranger's jeep to the station. In the cabin, he said, "I've finished my supper, but I'll rummage some food for you. But first I'll light the fire and the pot-bellied cook stove. Pull off your waders, at least."

"I'm good at rummaging for food. I'll help," Phoebe offered.

"I've got some Scotch," Ed added.

After spaghetti and Scotch, they felt better. "I'd love to know about the Drakes' day at Enchanted Lake," Phoebe wondered out loud.

"My shortwave radio seems to be out. It usually is," said Ranger Burt. "Ed, you bunk here with me. "I'll show the MacLeans their

cabin and the wash house and toilets. They are in a separate building in the middle of the camp. Always keep your cabin door
locked. Grizzlies sometimes wander around at night."

It was cold in the cabin. They each had one thin blanket to pull
up over the stringy mattress pad. They slept with all of their
clothes on. Phoebe contemplated pulling her waders back on for
warmth. She kept her hand around the flashlight the ranger had
given her, in case of emergency, and dropped into a troubled sleep.

A sound awakened her. She turned the flashlight on her watch.
It was two a.m. She circled the room with the beam. She saw James
standing by the front door that he had just slammed shut. That
must have been the sound that woke her up. How glad she was
that she hadn't needed to go out in the dark also.

Suddenly, there was a loud knocking at the door. The pounding
continued furiously. In the beam of her flashlight, she saw that
James was facing the door. "Phoebe, is that you?" he called and
pulled the door open. She heard him gasp and slam the door with
all his might, yelling, "Go away, get out! Scram!"

The knocking stopped. James leaned against the door in relief.

"What happened? Who was it?" Phoebe called.

"A bear, a huge grizzly. He must have followed me back from
the wash house. I thought it was you. I hope I scared him away. He
was standing upright, pounding on the door!"

They didn't sleep much the rest of the night and were awake
and eager to leave the cabin when the ranger arrived to call them
to breakfast. The morning was so still that the smoke from the
ranger's fire rose, a vertical white column in the blue sky.

The ranger drove them to the end of the jeep road and led them
along a better and easier trail to the lake. There, they found that
the plane had weathered the wind in good shape and was waiting
to take them back to their friends at Enchanted Lake.

Ed all but embraced his plane, his good friend and lifeline in the
wilderness. James sat in the copilot's seat, Phoebe, behind him.
While Ed prepared for take off, the MacLeans thanked the ranger
for taking such good care of his unexpected guests. "It was a plea-

sure. That's one of our many duties," he answered. "Write your congressman and tell him how well you fared!" he added and waved them off.

"James," Phoebe mentioned to her husband when they were airborne, "I keep finding how many things there are on a fishing trip besides fishing."

"Right you are. But the important thing is the fishing, first things first," he answered.

Then, turning to Ed, he asked in a voice filled with happy anticipation, "Where do we fish today?"

Before Ed could answer, something made James look back at Phoebe. After one glance, he hastily added, "Of course, I mean after we check on the Drakes and get ourselves cleaned up and have a bite to eat."

She gave him a tentative smile of agreement. Then she turned to the picnic hamper and murmured confidentially, "On fishing trips, I'm definitely an afterthought, but a cherished one."

NEW ZEALAND

Mataura River

THE MATAURA RIVER meanders through sheep farms on the South Island of New Zealand. It has many faces, all beautiful, and some of the finest brown trout fishing in the world. Fly fishermen who have been there daydream about returning, and the wives who accompany them, whether or not they fish, bask in the gentleness of the country and of its people.

One March, four couples from San Francisco and their four New Zealand guides explored several faces of the Mataura River on their biannual New Zealand fishing trip. The weather there also wears many faces, not all beneficial to fishing.

Daily, the group read the colors of the weather on the palette of the sky, painted masterfully by wind, rain, and clouds above the vivid green fields. These were dotted with thousands of sheep, like white paint splattered on a green canvas.

Because of the beauty that surrounded her, Phoebe MacLean frequently had difficulty keeping her mind on fishing. But not so the men. Each morning they stood with Peter Cullen, their head guide, next to the two jeeps packed with fishing gear and wives, reading the sky to learn its weather secrets.

Harry Rae, Peter's righthand man, was a superb fisherman from Scotland. He was now a New Zealand citizen with a New Zealand wife and six children. When Harry arrived with the lunch, that was the signal for the jeeps to pull off from Croyden Lodge to go fishing. But they only got as far as the first bridge that crossed the Mataura River.

There the men jumped out and hastened to the railing to peer over. Was the water too high? Was it too colored by silt from rains farther up the river? If so, what part of the river should they attempt?

The four women often rode together in one jeep. They lived in widely scattered parts of San Francisco's Bay Area and cherished their visiting times together on fishing trips.

Three of the four couples fished together often, the MacLeans, Andrew and Helene Holcomb, and Ben Sergeant and Susan. This year another good friend and fishing pal and his wife were with them, Robert and Elizabeth Armstrong.

Each man fished differently. Andrew was usually off first because his fishing bag was so well organized. If he came in for lunch, he arrived late and ate fast. An active fish was more important to him than food. He fished only with dry flies and caught trophy trout in waters where everyone else was using wet flies.

Phoebe knew that Andrew's prowess in dry fly-fishing came from his wide experience and great ability. But privately, she thought that he also drew on his strong business judgement. The fish didn't have a chance.

James was slower getting ready to fish because he usually had to duffel for a lost article. Also, he liked to be sure that Phoebe went fishing, and he stuck around to make sure that this happened.

When James, with or without help from his guide, found an ideal spot to fish, he stayed longer than he knew he should, changing flies often from his cherished collection. This perseverance regularly paid off with a winning fish.

Ben equalled his competent friends both in fishing and in business ability. Phoebe often thought he should have been a courtroom lawyer instead of a corporation lawyer. She felt sure that his curly-headed good looks would have been an additional asset to his legal ability in court. Ben found fish that weren't there, and he was an uncanny stalker.

Ben's wife Susan was petite, musical, and witty. Through following her husband's various pursuits, she had added athletic experiences. Not only did she go on fishing and hiking trips, but she would soon find herself involved in bird-shooting, another of Ben's sports.

Robert Armstrong was a perfectionist. He wore numerous hats and wore them well, in sports as varied as field dog trials, shooting, and golf. When he donned his fishing hat, good friends, beware! He often marched home with the money.

Elizabeth, an excellent gardener, often opened her home for benefits, for which she made the flower arrangements with flowers from her own garden. She was a splendid cook and, in addition to these talents, she loved fishing and was very excited whenever Robert donned his fishing hat and took her with him.

Sometimes Phoebe worried about James's tough competition, but never for long. A single glance at her husband on a fishing stream flooded her with a sense of joy for his dedication and fulfillment. Add to that the number of fish he caught and released, why worry?

The men always set up their betting the first day of the trip. Then over an aperitif every evening, they did their reckonings. Lawyer Ben stated that he was the logical choice for scorekeeper. Accounts of each Catch and Release were recited and recorded by him, not without many challenges. "Shouldn't I win occasionally for keeping the records?" Ben asked periodically. Often he did win, but not for that reason.

The guides who usually accompanied them were New Zealand businessmen and farmers, knowledgeable about the sport that they loved. They guided mainly for visitors from other countries, many of whom became their good friends.

Some years before, Andrew, James, and Ben were on a construction inspection trip near Invercargill, New Zealand. They asked the manager on the job, Neville Long, a close San Francisco friend and fellow fisherman, to inquire about a guide to take them fly-fishing sometime on the renowned Mataura River. Neville agreed to try.

He asked Peter Cullen, the owner of a sporting goods store in Gore, to help him. "I don't know anyone who guides," he told Neville, "but I know lots of good fishermen. I was born and brought up on the Mataura River. "I know it like the palm of my hand. I've never guided anyone myself, but I wouldn't mind giving it a try. I'd rather fish than eat."

"You're on," said Neville, and Peter had been 'on' ever since.

Peter's wife Heather, a schoolteacher, supported her husband's new profession wholeheartedly. When his friends whom he enlisted to guide with him lived too far away to commute, she fed and housed them in their home. It always sounded to Phoebe like a rousing house party, kindness of Heather. Before long she was also preparing a good part of the excellent daily streamside lunches.

Peter's brother Blair from Invercargill, a retired nurseryman and an outstanding rugby player who now ran the local rugby club, and Harry Rae, who owned a sheep farm at Cattle Flat, were the regular guides. But Peter had no trouble getting other friends or relatives to guide when necessary, such as his son-in-law, Martin.

Invercargill was the southernmost town in New Zealand and the one closest to the Antarctic Circle. But Christ Church, farther north, had a better harbor. Therefore, it became the port of supplies for the Antarctic. Townspeople of Invercargill, except Chamber of Commerce types, were just as happy not to have their town chosen, mainly because their famous Bluff Island oyster beds might have been disturbed.

Peter and Blair's parents had reared a large family near Gore, mainly sons. Most of the brothers became farmers in that area. Peter frequently requested permission from his brothers and farmer friends to fish the part of the Mataura River that ran through their paddocks, as the farmers called their fenced fields. Opening and closing a half dozen gates, coming and going, was not a chore for the visiting fishermen.

That morning the four men and the guides finally finished reading the river and made the decision where to fish. They reversed the two jeeps and headed south for the farm of Peter's brother, Frank.

Peter was driving the women. When he told them where they were going, Susan said, "I remember it. That's where you have your Fishing Club House."

"And watercress grows in a small stream nearby," added Helene. "Once we picked watercress, along with green peas, from your brother's garden, to make a streamside salad."

"Could we make a quick stop by the store for some tomatoes?" Phoebe asked. "Then we could have another one of our famous streamside salads. Perhaps we might even ask permission to pick watercress and peas again, if we find some."

"Of course. I'll ask Frank," Peter agreed and signaled to the other car to stop at the market.

They passed open boxes of fruits and vegetables in the small store. "What a marvelous fresh smell," Helene exclaimed. "It's like walking in an orchard in the summer."

"It's the smell of fruit picked when it's ripe," Peter explained.

"How right you are, Peter," Phoebe said. "I've smelled it around our apricot tree on a warm day in summer. Look at this beauty!" She picked up an apricot and felt it gently before placing it in a brown paper bag.

Her friends were doing the same thing with other fruit. The men wandered in to see what the delay was and began the same process. Phoebe saw James happily tasting and bagging local cherries.

"I'd better not forget to buy the tomatoes we came in for," Helene laughed. She was the salad maker, *par excellence*.

They returned to the jeeps and continued down the Invercargill road. At the small cheese town of Edam, they turned left and went through the first gate of brother Frank's farm.

Three gates later, Peter stopped in front of a neat farm house with a yard filled with flowers and children's wheel toys. He hurried into the house.

"Permission granted for fishing and peas," he called when he came back. "The vegetables are near the next gate, and Bob's wife says the peas are 'right'. We may see Frank there too."

At the next gate, when Ben, the current gate-opener, jumped out, so did the salad seekers. "The watercress is in the creek right here!" caroled Helene.

The others headed for the nearby pea patch while the men talked fishing with Peter's brother. When they continued, Peter remained close to the fence because the field was planted in corn. The Mataura River bordered it.

Through the heavy willows growing between the fence and the river, they caught tantalizing glimpses of the water, glistening in the sun.

The next field was unplanted. The jeeps bumped across it down to the river and stopped behind a small cabin with a porch on the river side.

Each man took out his fishing equipment and began to suit up before the guides could unload the folding chairs that were always in the trucks. Peter opened the cabin door, the women right behind him. He turned on the water valve and lighted a small heater, checked the kerosene lamp and put matches nearby. Then he hurried outside to the men.

Phoebe followed him in order to speak to her husband. "James, I want to look around the cabin first. Then I'll come fishing," she told him and rejoined her friends.

"Why, Peter," Helene called from the door, "you've glassed in the porch."

"Keeps the house warmer on a cold day," he answered, setting up a rod. "This is now a proper club house."

Inside were two bunk beds built against opposite walls. A pot-bellied stove was set against another wall and on the fourth sat a linoleum-covered table. There were three framed type-written pages hanging above it. One listed the four members; they were three Cullen brothers and a Mainland dentist friend. The other was the charter, and the third, the club rules.

"I'm going fishing shortly," Phoebe told her friends when they had finished the inspection.

Helene fished out two decks of cards from her backpack. "How about a game of Spite and Malice, Susan? I heard the men decide to fish until two p.m. before coming in for lunch." Helene's enthusiasm for this two-handed game was infectious.

"Fine," Susan agreed.

"And I'll challenge the loser when I return," Phoebe said.

From the riverbank, she saw Andrew already some distance downstream, knee-deep in the water, casting his dry fly up the river. Blair Cullen was hastening to catch up with him. Upstream, Ben was just disappearing around a bend of the river, Harry with him. Elizabeth and Robert were not in sight.

In front of the cabin, James and Peter were fishing on a pebbly point of land that split the river. It looked as though there were some good pools on both sides.

Phoebe stood watching quietly. Peter happened to turn. When he saw her, he started toward the cabin. She hurried back to locate her gear.

"We've been keeping our eyes open for you," Peter said. "Elizabeth insisted on going off immediately with her husband. She was only half ready."

Phoebe quickly pulled on her waders, oversocks, and her wading shoes. Last, she adjusted her suspenders and fastened a belt around her middle, the latter the usual safety precaution in case she fell in the water.

Peter had her rod ready. "Let's walk in the paddock to a bend in the river well ahead of Ben. It is not too deep. You can fish there alone and cast to the opposite shore. I'll return to you after I guide a bit with James. Ben can leapfrog you."

"Fine. I want to get back in time to work on the salad."

"Of course. I need to return also. I'll come for you in plenty of time. Ready? Let's go!"

Walking through the field was much faster than walking in the river. Peter gave her a hand through the fence and a strong arm down the bank. He settled her in the spot he had chosen and stayed a little while to watch, pointing out the best water.

Then he took off. "Good luck," he said and strode rapidly but quietly through the shallow water.

She relished this solitary moment on a beautiful river in faraway New Zealand. Green hills dotted with sheep surrounded her while blue skies punctuated with popcorn white clouds arched above her. Only one thing marred the perfection of this moment, a suspicion that the brown trout she was soon to challenge would be smarter than she was.

Before she moved into the prime waters, Phoebe began by casting a few times. Her movements were so awkward that she concluded that her muscles hadn't absorbed enough from the recent practice sessions that she and James had had on their front lawn.

She moved out farther but not yet into prime waters. Over and over, she practiced getting her Deer-haired Yellow fly into a good float, but each cast continued to disappoint her. She moved into the prime waters anyway.

"Now cut down on your false casts and keep that fly in the water," she instructed herself tersely, in the manner of a guide or a husband, as she took her stance. "Take three steps, anchor your feet, back cast with a firm wrist in a high arc. Don't permit the line above your shoulder to drop past one o'clock."

The hardest part for her, the impossible part, was sending the line shooting with gentle force onto the water and have it land quietly without any wiggles in it. Only when she was asleep and dreaming did her line shoot across the water ramrod straight.

She kept on trying, moving regularly, lost to time.

Peter's voice carried to her across the water, but closer to her than she had thought. "Time to go. How did you do?" She shook her head to indicate, nothing. How long had she been fishing? She took one final cast before reeling in. The line went straight! Now she felt good inside and couldn't wait to return to the river in the afternoon. But at the moment, it was salad time.

Peter told her on the walk back that James had caught and released a nice brown and one scrappy rainbow. "He'll return in time for lunch."

At the cabin, the Spite and Malice game was wild and the slapping action too furious for conversation. The individual piles that each player tried to get rid of were diminished but equal.

Phoebe went out on the porch, shucked the sweet firm garden peas and washed the watercress in a bucket of water that Peter brought her. She'd leave the salad dressing to Helene. Meanwhile, outside, Peter set up the folding table and began to unpack the hampers. Phoebe washed the fruit chosen from the small store and found a tray to mound it on.

Ben and James wandered in, followed by the Armstrongs. Even Andrew arrived. Elizabeth was radiant. "I remembered! I could cast, not well yet, but a fish struck and I had him on for a few seconds. I love it!" She ran to the cabin door, boots still on, to share her news.

Phoebe was amused at the usual sparring the men went through, each trying to avoid disclosing any fishing facts. Finally, about the time the women arrived from the cabin, the men began to reveal the sizes and numbers of the morning's Catch and Release.

Andrew's fish was a half-inch longer than those of the others. "Did you measure carefully?" Ben queried. "Did you see it?" he asked Blair. Blair had.

Robert had caught and released three, the most so far. Now they knew the goals they needed to fish against that afternoon.

The salad was pronounced the success of the picnic. After lunch, Elizabeth, Robert, and guide Martin, Peter's son-in-law, were off first, the result of Elizabeth's urging. Ben left soon afterwards. Andrew headed downstream, Blair calling after him that he and Helene would follow as soon as his K.P. detail was finished.

Harry and James were assigned to fish as a team that afternoon. "Come join Harry and me whenever you're ready," James told Phoebe, heading for the spot where she had fished earlier.

"After the card game, I will. Leave one for me," she told her husband, feeling a proprietary interest in those waters.

Soon, Helene and Blair started toward the river. Susan and Phoebe settled down to a good, long game, finally won by Susan. "I had lots of practice during the first game when Helene beat me," she laughed. "Now for a walk."

Phoebe returned eagerly to the river.

Harry came to meet her. "We've been expecting you," he said with a smile. "I have a good place saved for you farther upstream."

"How did my husband do in my spot?"

"Very well, two browns slightly down the river from where you started. With the ones he rose this morning, that must be four. Would you like to catch up with him?"

"I'd settle for one." Phoebe laughed. "How's your pretty wife, Bernie, as busy as ever with her horses and the the family?"

"Yes, she is. One of her pacers has already won two ribbons this season. As to the children, they are growing like weeds. Because of the distance from Cattle Flat, Sandy, the eldest, has had to be a boarder at upper school in Gore during the week. We miss him," Harry said sadly. At the roll of Harry's deep "brrr," Phoebe felt herself cross the ocean to Scotland and return.

"I hope we can see some of them when we fish at Cattle Flat later in the week," Phoebe told him, "at least your young twin sons."

"Those boys have become fine fishermen," Harry continued. "They slip away to the river every afternoon after chores, and sometimes before, just as Sandy used to do. The girls don't get home until supper time," he finished.

"Enough about me and mine," Harry stated positively. "Let's get on with your fishing. A good pool lies over there against the willows."

Her morning of practice paid off. Phoebe's confidence in her casting gave a smoothness to the rhythm. She loved this motion for itself and enjoyed creating it, often with little thought of its goal.

Gently, Harry interrupted her casting. "On the next move, let your fly swing around a bit longer. I'll tell you when it drags. Sometimes a fish will strike just before the retrieve."

Conscientiously, Phoebe followed his instructions until she had fished far enough to see James. She realized that she hadn't even glanced once at the beautiful cloud formations.

Perhaps she should soon think about leapfrogging her husband in order not to bother him by fishing too close. With relief, she realized that she could leave that decision to Harry.

She cast again. At this moment, she wouldn't want to be any place else in the world. A fish struck! Perfect timing.

Steadily she pulled her rod tip sky high, a little worried that she hadn't done it fast enough. She felt a strong determined tug on the end of the line. Joy flooded through her. The hook was set! Now her primary purpose was to keep the fish on the fly.

"Forceful gentleness," she instructed herself. She could spoil it all in a second by being too casual.

"There's a small beach behind you," she heard Harry say. "Try to angle back toward it, but do nothing suddenly. Browns spook easily, as you know." Harry's quiet instruction guided her steadily to the shore.

Once she stumbled over a rounded rock. Her pressure on the line slackened for a moment, but she felt Harry's hand on her elbow steadying her. She scarcely missed a turn on the reel. She managed to get the line tight and back on the reel before the fish had a chance to take off.

When she had the fish in water shallow enough to see him, she noticed how he blended into the colors of the stones, a perfect camouflage, everything dappled together. She etched the moment in her memory, confident that if her steady pull didn't falter as she reveled in this beauty, she could bring the fish to Harry and to the net.

"He's well hooked," Harry reassured her. "Keep walking backward. You can land him yourself, and it will be right under your husband's admiring glance."

Oh happiness! She looked over at James. He made the victory sign.

Phoebe drew the beautiful brown trout past the net and close to the shore. She flipped him onto the grass and dropped down to anchor him.

Harry took the fly out and measured the brown. Together they took him to the river, pointed his head upstream, and Phoebe watched Harry stroke him until he was ready to swim away. Who says you can't go home again? At least, some fish can.

Fulfilled, Phoebe walked back up the shore, settled herself behind James, and alternated between watching her husband and reveling in the scenery, only occasionally dipping into the book that she took from the back pocket of her fishing jacket. "I'll go check on the card game in a little while," she told herself, "because now I have caught my fish!"

James moved several times, Phoebe following from the shore. A sense of expectancy moved with them.

An explosion rewarded them. She riveted her eyes to the end of her husband's line. It was a stupendous strike, worth waiting for. Phoebe felt as proud as if it were hers.

With a strong jerk, James set the hook. However, the fish bent the rod double. Inch by inch, James began to elevate the rod tip. At last he pulled the rod vertical. Now the battle began in earnest, two opponents in this struggle, both worthy, but with irreconcilable goals. Phoebe scrambled up the bank to give her husband more room.

Twice, the heavy brown leaped like a rainbow. Twice, James let the fish run and began to reel in all over again. Phoebe's arms ached as if she were the one with the rod. This was harder than catching her own fish. She forgot all about the Spite and Malice game.

On the next reeling in, James's line came so quickly that it looked as though nothing were on the end. Had she missed seeing the fish make a long run? The alternative was that the fish was gone, had gotten off the hook.

But suddenly James elevated the rod as though a fish had just struck and began to reel in fast. What was going on? James began to scuttle backward faster than Phoebe could walk forward. She retreated even farther up the bank. James kept coming in fast, Harry paralleling him, net in hand.

They reached shallow water. What a trio. Phoebe saw Harry give a mighty sweep, skimming the shallow water with the net. Using both hands, he dipped the net under the fish and hoisted the heavy net as high as he could.

Phoebe saw a huge brown. She ran down to see the finale. She needed to get close enough to her husband to share his success, after what that fish had put him through. James's reaction was the joy of victory. His excited laugh was infectious.

When Harry pinned the fish in the grass, they saw that he had an underslung jaw and was huge and ugly. Harry began to work unsuccessfully to release the fly. Blood started to trickle from the crooked mouth of the fish. "If his mouth is too injured, he won't live if we release him," Harry told James, who nodded that he understood.

Harry killed the fish and began slowly to measure him. There was no need to hurry the measurement of a dead fish.

This worthy opponent, she thought to herself, wouldn't be one of the lucky ones to make it home. The tape measure showed him to be close to twenty-two inches.

"If I hadn't witnessed it, I wouldn't believe it," she told James. "If you aren't worn out, I am. I'm going in."

"Don't mention the size of the fish, dear, please. I'll tell everyone later. I think I'll fish a little longer," said her husband, with a smile that he couldn't erase. She left a happy man, two happy men, on the river as she returned to the cabin.

She found Susan just back from a walk. "Helene is still out fishing. How did you and James do?" she asked.

"I caught one that Harry measured before he released him. He was about eighteen inches. James caught a nice one just before I came in."

"How large?"

"I really don't know. Shall we play a game if there is time?"

"Sure," Susan answered.

Phoebe turned away to hide her smile. She was becoming as clever as the men at being devious.

Helene and Blair Cullen came into view from the porch. Watching Helene cast was always a pleasure for Phoebe. In her opinion, Helene was one of the most graceful casters that she had ever seen. In addition, she was accurate in her casting, either to a fish or to a mark in a flycasting pool.

Blair and Helene arrived with two lovely small rainbows. "It was fun catching these beauties," Helene said as she dropped down on an outside chair to pull off her boots. "I couldn't resist saving them for breakfast fish. As guilty as it makes me feel, I can almost taste them."

The women sipped welcome lemonade served by Blair as they waited for the men. A cold wind came up. They bundled in sweaters, realizing that it would soon be too late for dinner at the lodge by the time the others arrived.

Finally, the men wandered in separately, all but Robert with Elizabeth.

Blair passed beer to the men as they pushed off boots and waders and pulled on warm jackets. Andrew started the questioning. "Scorekeeper, let's have it. How did you do?"

"Not bad. How about you?" Ben cadged. "We need to wait for Robert."

"MacLean, let's hear from you in the meantime," Andrew pursued.

"I elect to follow you three."

"Sounds suspicious," Andrew told him. "All right, I caught two this afternoon, one a fairly nice one, perhaps twenty-one inches," Andrew stated. "Now you, Sergeant?"

Robert's head appeared above the bank before Ben could answer. He had a very tired Elizabeth in tow. She dropped down near the gals as he hurried to join the men.

Ben answered, "That beats my twenty inches. James, you and Robert better give Andrew a run for his money. You first, Armstrong."

"Well, I tell you, fishing all day with a wife is a different story and very time-consuming," Robert drawled. "However, Elizabeth would score high in persistence if the women had a contest."

"Man, I've heard everything now. Trying to win through his wife's fishing. Come on. Tell us about your own." Ben's stern tone was spoiled by a twinkle in his eye.

Robert saluted and stated, "Some scrappy browns, two almost twenty inches."

"James?"

Phoebe saw Harry, smiling broadly, pull James's fish out from behind a bush and place it on the ground. The men moved in, forming a tight silent circle around the fish, tape measures in hand.

"Perhaps this is the winner," James's modesty was so phony that it was funny. "The fly was so difficult to get out that the fish was bleeding too much to release. We had to kill him."

"I make it a little less than twenty-two," said Ben, measuring the fish.

Andrew moved in. "I'll measure also, just to keep the score-keeper honest."

Andrew straightened up, nodding and smiling. "Congratulations, MacLean. I guess we'd better concede to you on length. Now how about the number of fish caught?"

The women listened with interest. Through the noisy congratulations that followed, they gathered that Andrew with five was ahead in that category.

Ben held up his hand for silence. "I may win something yet. Number of fish taken from the same hole? I had three. Try to beat that!"

"I can! Four! I win it!" Robert chuckled.

"Well, I'll be. If I weren't so indispensable, I'd resign as the scorekeeper," Ben concluded.

Susan turned to Phoebe. "Congratulations to you, Mrs. Mac-Lean, for James's biggest fish," she said. Phoebe acknowledged the accolades as though she were the wife of an Olympic champion!

They all helped load the vans as Peter closed up the cabin. On the trip home to Gore, Helene said, "Elizabeth, if you've caught your breath, tell us about your fishing. I can't wait any longer."

"It was memorable. The first time Robert invited me to go on a fishing trip, we went with Phoebe and James to Montana, and I borrowed your waders, Phoebe, remember? They were huge for me."

She continued, "This time I had my own. What a difference. Robert was wonderful. He kept telling me where to move and how to cast. I had my second strike in one day and had the fish on for three and a half minutes by my watch. Next time I'll land him. I'm not sure, though, about releasing him!"

Tired but fulfilled, the fishermen drove home through darkness to a quick change and a good dinner at the lodge. The manager had arranged to have some dinner saved for them.

He stopped by to tell them that Alastair Watson and his wife Jo had been calling all day from Queenstown. "They want to talk about joining you wherever you will be fishing tomorrow, if that's possible."

"That will be great," Ben said emphatically.

Andrew suggested, "James, if we can fish the upper stretches of the Mataura River, perhaps we can drive part way to meet them. How about phoning Peter?"

"And ask Heather if we could have one of her very super picnics for the Watsons," Susan suggested.

James telephoned Peter who agreed to arrange with Alastair about a meeting place on the upper Mataura.

This friendship with the Watsons started years ago during the time that the San Francisco men were making periodic inspection trips to the big South Island hydro job. Alastair's father was then the mayor of Invercargill. Phoebe still remembered that Alastair's mother was always addressed as Lady Mayor.

Alastair had visited the MacLeans on his "Grand Tour," taken after he finished reading law at his university. His father, the mayor, told the MacLeans that he also had taken a grand tour after he had finished reading his law, twenty-five years before. Neal Watson asked James, "May Alastair visit you this next summer? I'm sure he'd enjoy being with your large family." So Alastair had visited the MacLeans on his grand tour, and they had been friends ever since.

The next morning they all stopped by the greengrocer again for fruits and streamside salad to add to the picnic packed by Heather. Peter told them that he was bringing his portable grill. "I seldom use this since we now encourage Catch and Release, but this one time, you catch the fish and I will cook them," he announced.

"Fair enough," James said, "I'm sure I speak for everyone else."

Peter explained, "We'll have an hour and a half drive and at least that long again to fish for our lunch before the Watsons arrive at the rendezvous spot."

The part of the Mataura that the guides had selected was perfect, spreading shade trees and gin-clear water. The brilliant sunny day would make fishing hard, but it would be fine for a picnic.

Blair and Andrew started off quickly, telling Helene to follow when she was ready. Peter decided that he would set up tables and chairs before he left. "Ben, I'll find you when I'm through. How about you, Susan? Will you join your husband and me?"

"I'll stay in camp to watch for the Watsons and carry the word when they arrive. Wasn't it Patrick Henry who did that?"

"I'm not sure," Peter said. "Our history in New Zealand is different. Instead, you'd better carry word to me about who has caught some fish!"

"Come with me, Phoebe," Harry told her. "James has already left. I fished here earlier this season. I know where there are a couple of nice browns waiting for your fly."

Phoebe had time to admire the incredibly white and puffy cumulus clouds before she started to fish at the spot where Harry had brought her.

They seldom saw this kind of cloud in California, too dry. She had to store this beauty in her mind to remember later at home.

"I've put on a new fly that Sandy tied. He hasn't even named it yet. Cast up and slightly across toward the willows. Then let the fly float very gently down as close to the bank as you can get it. Browns can slurp a fly so quietly that the only way you know to set the hook is to be aware of any small twitch at the end of the line or to notice a slight difference in the surface of the water."

"It's hard to see in moving water."

"All fishing is hard. The only people who think it isn't are the ones who have never tried it."

"Wise Harry. Well, here I go for the Watsons' picnic fish."

Phoebe cast conscientiously. Sandy's fly floated well. She worked hard to keep her eye on it throughout the float. When she thought that she detected some slurping action, she set the hook purposefully. But it was always a false alarm.

Each time she moved to another area, she promised herself that she would return to the first pool when the river water had quieted down a bit. Phoebe had pangs of guilt about her intentions for a fish if she caught him. But their guests were invited for a fish picnic.

After she fished in several other pools, she glanced at her watch, eleven forty-five! What if the Watsons came before one o'clock? She moved back to the pool where she had started. Harry returned and waded toward her. "Let's change to another fly."

She hated to part with Sandy's fly. "Have you heard if anyone has caught a fish?" she asked Harry.

"I haven't heard," he answered. "Let's go."

Phoebe cast three times. She knew that she would need to move again soon. She'd only have time left for a couple more moves. This smart fish that Harry told her about was giving her an inferiority complex. "I need to find a dumb fish," she prayed to her

250

Guardian Angel in charge of fishing. "And please, I need him now!"

On the next cast, the fish didn't slurp. He exploded. Nobody was going to call him dumb! Phoebe set the hook as firmly as she dared. Then steadily she began to pull the rod tip upright. But the fish managed to get his head and swim strongly away. This lowered the tip and kept it there. Firmly, trying not to panic, she worked to get some line back on her reel as she edged the rod up.

"Easy. Take plenty of time to play him," she heard Harry's voice nearby.

"I don't have plenty of time," she called back.

"You don't want to lose him."

That steadied her. Quickly glancing over her shoulder, she saw that by walking straight backward, she could reach a grassy beach.

Whenever there was a bit of slack, she reeled in carefully. When the fish tugged, she gave him a small amount of line, continuing to reel as soon as she could.

"Good work. Keep it up. I have the net ready."

The fish was in water shallow enough that they could see him, a very respectable brown, beautiful in a subdued way, not flashy like his rainbow relatives. He seemed to be well hooked.

Phoebe kept walking backward until she felt grass under her feet. She reeled in more line and lifted the fish, to his surprise, right onto the grass. She didn't want to give a chance to an accident to happen. Harry dropped over the fish and enclosed him in his large hands.

She let out enough line to place the rod safely to one side. She turned herself away from the killing, glad she didn't have to perform that part of supplying a picnic fish. If this were the only fish that had been caught, they could use it as an canape. It was one o'clock!

Harry must have had the same thought. Fastening the brown on a forked stick to carry back, he said as Phoebe reeled in her line, "If the others don't have fish, I'll borrow your rod, if I may, and slip back here to try for another one."

"Of course you may use it."

When they reached the picnic site, Helene and Susan were helping to empty the two hampers. They asked, "How'd you do?"

"One, middle-sized," Helene answered.

"Congratulations. I hope you're as happy about yours as I am about mine."

Helene laughed joyously, "We women know how to produce when necessary! I have one also."

"If the men bring in some fish, we'll be set," Susan added.

Elizabeth arrived. "I'm glad to hear that. My rainbow is only appetizer size, but no way was I going to throw him back. He's my very own fish!"

Each man brought in a fish, both browns and rainbows. Peter rolled up his sleeves and went to work. When the Watsons arrived a quarter of an hour later, the fish, poaching in water and white wine, gave off a beautiful aroma. The salad was finished, and the men were sampling the wine and the beer that they had opened.

During the happy confusion of greeting fond friends, Phoebe noticed Harry slipping in. "How'd you do?," she asked him privately.

"When I saw that there were plenty of fish and after we finished the jobs, I couldn't resist your offer to let me try your rod. It is a joy to use. I caught a fish to take home to Bernie."

After the picnic, everyone sat and talked. They touched on family news and events, recent trips, and the state of the economy of New Zealand and the United States, all interspersed with amazing fishing stories.

Reluctantly, Jo and Alastair began their departure. "With both girls in boarding school at Christ Church, young Thomas needs a hand with chores," Alastair told them. "I want to get home before dark."

Jo added, "When Thomas goes to his father's boarding school at Christ Church next year, I shudder to think how busy we'll be then."

"You mean how busy I'll be," Alastair interrupted. "We bought a house in Christ Church where Jo can stay when she visits the three children and where we both can stay when we attend their school functions."

"It's much cheaper than a hotel!" Jo laughed. Also, it will give the children a place to go on weekends. Heidi is old enough to run it. Alastair can lease or sell the house when they all are graduated," Jo explained.

"I dare say, I'll probably arrange my chores to get there occasionally," Alastair told them. "I do hope we can see you again while you are here. What about fishing for rainbow trout in the Greenstone River? I might be able to get a good friend of mine, a helicopter pilot, to fly us in."

Peter interrupted, "We already have a couple of firm commitments, including fishing beyond Harry's place at Cattle Flat and an overnight at a small lodge I've recently heard about, at Rotoua, that is, if they can accommodate a group of our size."

"Why don't we talk it over with Peter and phone you?" Andrew suggested. "The Greenstone sounds very tempting. I've read about fishing for rainbows in that river. I'm sure the others have also."

"Regardless of fishing plans, could you join us later for our biannual dinner with our guides and their wives at Croyden Lodge?" Helene asked. "We don't know yet what night it will be."

"Let us know and we'll give it a try," Alastair said and firmly pulled Jo away from one more fond embrace.

The Gore party stood waving as the car disappeared down the dirt road. Watching their good friends leave threatened to dampen their high spirits. Peter came to the rescue. "How would you like to fish for an hour or so on the way back to Gore? It's a place that I'll surprise you with. Our drive to Gore isn't as far as the Watsons' to Queenstown."

The fishermen approved of Peter's suggeston. They hurried to get ready to leave. "And we can play Spite and Malice anywhere!" Helene reminded her friends. "I carry the cards with me."

Peter brought them to a farm, new to them, owned by a cousin of his. He stopped first at the farmhouse to chat and ask permission.

The cousin came out and waved them down the farm road. After passing through a few more gates, they came to a beautiful stretch of the Mataura River, bordered on both sides by very thick willows.

Helene had the cards out before the men turned off the motors. Harry unpacked the card table first and set it up for the women. After Phoebe surveyed the thick willows, she announced, "Count me in for cards. We'll have four players, enough for partners."

An hour later, with four fish caught and released and a doubles game completed, the guides loaded everyone in the cars for the drive home.

For two days, the group fished near Gore. After several phone calls between Gore and Queenstown, the men concluded the arrangements for fishing the Greenstone River. Peter and Harry would each drive a jeep to Queenstown where everyone would stay in a motel. Blair would have a few days off to spend in Invercargill with his wife, Joy.

Early the following morning, Alastair would have two helicopters waiting to fly them into the Greenstone River, one piloted by his friend. Harry and Peter were the only guides to accompany them.

D-Day dawned bright as a button. The men rode together with Peter. The four excited wives settled happily into Harry's jeep. For the first two hours the drive was through familiar territory. When the road veered west away from the Mataura River, Elizabeth announced, "Suddenly I feel as though we were deserting a cherished friend, the Mataura. It makes me sad."

"It's only for two days," Helene pointed out. "The river will wait."

"But will the fish? I have a lot of lost time to make up for," Elizabeth insisted.

Harry spoke up to change the subject. "Two mountain ranges, one on each side of the road, are poised to captivate you. The one on the right is called The Remarkables. The long mountain lake between the two ranges is called Wakatipu. It reflects the ranges as though two lovely ladies were admiring themselves in a mirror."

"Bravo, Harry. Thanks," Elizabeth told him. "Now I'm eager to proceed."

"You speak of the beauty ahead of us like a poet!" Susan told him. "I can see the beginning of the mountains, that blue smudge on the far horizon."

As the jeeps approached the mountains, late afternoon colors of lavender, blue, and rose began to play over the mountains, draping them in pastel finery. The Remarkables wore their twilight garments with proud dignity.

Queenstown hugged the shore at the end of the lake that elbowed west like a boomerang. Alastair met them at The Lofts, the motel where they were staying. He had recently built this as an investment. The building was set back into the hill so that each split-level apartment had a panoramic view of the lake.

"Freshen up and make yourselves at home. These apartments are built for families, two bedrooms downstairs and two in the loft, but tonight you will each have a whole unit," Alastair told them.

"Ice and Scotch and cokes in the pantry. Peter and I have arranged for two other guests to join us for dinner at a new, rather outstanding, Chinese restaurant. My father, Neal, and his second wife have recently moved to Queenstown."

"That's a most welcome surprise indeed," Andrew said. "It will be a pleasure for all of us to see Neal Watson again."

Ben said, "I love to reminisce about early jobs. You've provided us with a real treat!"

James and Robert agreed. The gals waved and scattered to turn fishing clothes into dinner clothes in their usual way, with scarves. It was a very fulfilling evening.

The next morning, both helicopters were revved up when they arrived. "Keep clear," Alastair's friend, Bill, the pilot, ordered. "Alastair will tell you where to sit. It looks to be a fine day for a trip. Heads down to the waist when you board."

Alastair assigned the Holcombs, the MacLeans, and Harry to Bill's helicopter and explained, "With the pull-out seats in the back, there will be room for five passengers and the pilot in each helicopter. That should do it. Bill will stay in with us and the other pilot will return in the late afternoon for the trip back."

"It reminds me of the game of getting the missionaries and the cannibals across the river without a cannibal and a missionary ever being left alone together," Helene decided.

"Who's who?" Andrew asked.

"I'm not giving hints," she laughed.

When Bill lifted his helicopter straight up, they saw Queenstown lying below them like a fairy village, with The Remarkables silently awaiting their return. Ahead of them and slightly to the west, the Greenstone beckoned.

On the short flight, James pointed out to Phoebe where the Greenstone River flowed into Lake Wakatipu from the southwest. The helicopters turned and followed the river.

She saw many large stones lining the riverbanks. She was sure that they also made up the river bottom. From the air they looked like pebbles, but Phoebe knew that actually they would be at least tea-cup size. They probably would be rounded and slippery from the action of water on them over the centuries.

Dome-shaped mountains appeared at intervals. "They look rougher than those in Yosemite," Phoebe told James.

"And darker, probably sandstone that has been discolored by weather and rain. The Yosemite granite is so hard that it doesn't get stained and retains its lighter grey color."

"Thanks," Phoebe smiled. "It's great having a resident geologist."

Native tussock covered the ground, amber-colored because it had never been touched by a plow or overgrazed by domestic animals. Its color was as tawny as autumn leaves in sunlight.

Bill's helicopter landed like a butterfly, but a noisy one. Helene and Phoebe stepped out, crouching to keep well below the whirling blades. Alastair and their husbands joined them after carrying out the gear in the same crouched position. Bill moved the helicopter away from the river.

They stood, united in their temporary isolation, as they waited for the other helicopter to bring the remaining five. "My friend Bill is a remarkable pilot and a kindly gentleman," Alastair told them as they waited. "A few years ago, he was given the highest honor that New Zealand awards in peacetime. It is for an act of heroism that saves a person in dire peril."

"Tell us about it, please," Helene said, settling down on a hummock.

The others moved closer to Alastair. He began, "A German couple unwisely attempted to cross on rocks behind a high falls, not realizing the force of the veil of falling water.

"They were swept down below the falls, but fortunately, miraculously, they landed on a small ledge to one side. There was no access by foot to the ledge. Bill, with his helicopter, was called to the emergency by a forest warden, whom some horrified spectators notified.

"The helicopter hovered slowly back and forth across the ledge as Bill assessed the problem. He left and returned with two strong ropes dangling from the helicopter. He passed back and forth as near the ledge as he could manage. The onlookers were breathless."

Alastair continued, "On the third pass the husband caught a rope. Bill dropped him on the meadow below as gently as a mother cat would a kitten. He returned to continue his flights past the ledge. On the sixth pass, the wife managed to catch one of the ropes. He brought her down also to safety."

"Boy, would I have grabbed that rope," Phoebe declared solemnly, "if James had already swung away from me to safety."

"Bravo for Bill! I won't worry about anything else on this trip," Helene announced.

The other helicopter arrived and was unloaded. The men hastened to set up the rods. Bill flew James, Andrew, Harry and Alastair to some pools that Alastair knew. They disappeared into the challenging beauty of the remote trout stream that they had all read about. As soon as Elizabeth was ready, Robert and Ben Sergeant took off with her in the opposite direction.

"I'll follow you after I've worked with the three women, here," Peter told them.

"No fishing for me," Susan said. "I'm hiking along the shore."

Peter established Helene downstream from the landing spot and told her to fish back up to Phoebe and him. He turned to Phoebe. "I'll fish with you until Helene arrives."

In spite of Peter's many constant instructions, Phoebe felt that he gave them with a mind so preoccupied with his responsibility for the whole fishing trip, understandably so, that she and her fishing were only a secondary concern, merely a duty. "Give the fishing, not the clouds, your concentration," he told her brusquely.

In quiet defiance, she sneaked a glance at the loveliness of the setting. Was it because of this that she had a good strike? Her surprise slowed her reaction. "Set the hook fast," Peter told her. She did.

"Not that strong," Peter called. Then he all but shouted, "Watch it! The fish has gone. He's broken off the tippet!"

After Peter replaced the tippet and fly, Phoebe, still in disgrace, began casting all over again. She skipped the traditional three pace moves and fished doggedly until a welcome helicopter sound engulfed her. She hoped it was Bill, returning.

She was overjoyed that it was. She started for the shore immediately. James and Alastair emerged, rods in hand to reassemble. "We're off to some special pools that I want to show James before we leave," Alastair explained to Phoebe when she joined them.

James, busy connecting the sections of his rod, indicated a boulder beside him. "Sit here with me a minute. Isn't this a fantastic place? We fished briefly with Elizabeth on the way back. This helicopter fishing is astounding."

He continued, as he tested the rod, "Elizabeth is eager to share some fishing news with you gals. Well, I've finished. Wish me well. I'm off with Alastair."

Harry moved clear of the machine as Bill lifted it away. He came over to Phoebe. "Would you like to do some fishing until everyone gathers?" he asked.

Before she could give a resounding 'yes', Peter interrupted them to talk plans. When Harry returned to her, she told him quickly, "I'd love to go fishing, but first, how did James do?"

"Very well. He caught and released two fine rainbows. He telegraphs his joy in fishing. It is a pleasure to watch him, even when he doesn't have a fish on his line."

Phoebe laughed, "And when he has a strike, I can always tell, even when I can't see his line. It's body language! Now it's my turn."

Just then Elizabeth wandered in alone. She was tired but triumphant. When she saw Harry and Phoebe, she stopped in her tracks and waved her arms for attention. Helene and Susan were within sight of her. They gathered around Elizabeth immediately.

Elizabeth began, "Wait 'til you hear what Harry did for me. He helped me catch a beautiful fish. Can you believe it, I caught and released a rainbow trout on the Greenstone, that is, with his help."

She ran to Harry and, throwing her arms as high as she could, she gave him a big hug. Harry's face turned as red as his hair. He fled downstream, pulling Phoebe after him, but keeping well away from the stream at the same time.

When he finally stopped, he began to examine her rod and fly. "Let's get on with your fishing, Phoebe," he told her. "Just before Elizabeth arrived, I saw a shadow swim by close to the bank while I was talking to Peter. Let's fish up to that spot in case there's still a fish there. We'll float our fly by him so cleverly that he will think it's real. The Deer-haired Yellow fly you have on should be fine. But if it works and you bring in a trout, promise me that there will be no hugs." She nodded.

When Phoebe entered the water and made her first cast, she was sure her purr of joy was audible. After three casts in each location and three cautious moves among the treacherous rounded stones, Phoebe had a strike. "You did that beautifully," Harry spoke quietly from her elbow. "Now steady, but gentle, on the reeling."

His firm grip was on her elbow when she moved over the slippery stones. This meant that she could keep both hands on her rod instead of one on her wading staff. She heard encouraging calls from her friends, waiting together for the take-off time. She mustn't let them down.

The rainbow began to jump, each time followed by a strong run toward midstream. She was sure if anyone were reading her body language, it would spell "concern" as well as "joy". Twice she got the trout back on the reel. Across the water, she could hear plainly a conversation that her friends were having with James. They asked him about his fishing. His response floated over the water to her.

"Two nice ones," he answered. "I hope Phoebe lands a fish soon because I need to go with Alastair. He wants to show me one more pool before we leave. He saw some big rainbows here on his last trip. Cheer Phoebe on for me and tell her that we'll be back in time for the take-offs."

Any size fish would suit me, Phoebe thought, just so I land it. She brought her full attention back to her own fishing.

Over and over, each cast in a different position, she covered the water in the pool. "One last cast before we move," Harry told her.

And a willing New Zealand fish struck.

"Begin to angle to the shore as soon as you get your rod up and the fish secure on the reel," Harry told her. He continued, "I'll deal with the rocks, you deal with the fish."

He made this fishing carefree fun. Step by step, Phoebe moved closer to the beach until she had the fish on the edge of a pool where the water was shallow. His tawny beauty rivaled the color of the native grasses.

Harry gave her time to admire her fish, definitely a beautiful rainbow, before he scooped the fish into the net. He photographed Phoebe with the rainbow trout and then rapidly measured him. "He's a good eighteen inches and fat, a fine 'incident fish', as the New Zealanders say."

Harry placed the fish in the water and began to stroke breath and strength back into him. Phoebe thrilled to be part of returning the trout to freedom. She could barely restrain herself from giving Harry an Elizabethan hug.

Phoebe returned to the beach where her loyal supporters waited. After she thanked them, she said, "Now, I'm going upstream a little way to watch James and Alastair. Want to come?"

"Of course," Susan said. "Every fisherman needs a wife as audience, that is, if she can find him. Elizabeth is looking for hers right now."

"I've given up on mine," Helene said, jumping up to join them.

They found James filled with the pleasure of fishing the famous Greenstone River. Alastair stood near him. The three wives approached cautiously and stayed well behind the two men.

They watched James bring in an unusually active rainbow. Then they slipped away, not wanting to overdo sharing the pleasure that he might prefer to enjoy somewhat privately. Back at the landing area, they found Elizaabeth.

The four women lay in the grass and let the twilight blue of lengthening shadows wash over them. They were almost dozing when the sound of a returning helicopter aroused them.

It was Bill, coming in from his roundup. He had picked up Ben and Robert. Bill dropped the men and moved the helicopter a little apart.

"Peter suggested to me earlier that we drive home right from the airport. Our stuff is already checked in lockers there," Ben explained to the women. "He thinks that tomorrow is the best day to go to Cattle Flat. That fits into the schedule better than later. We've been talking this over in the helicopter."

"Suits me," Robert told the women.

"Here go the missionaries and the cannibals again," Phoebe mentioned.

Susan commented, "It's a moonlight night and I remember seeing an all-night cafe at the airport."

"What are we waiting for?" Helene asked.

"The reckoning, and for a few more people to come," Ben answered.

James and Alastair arrived, two friends who lived miles apart, talking rapidly to span the distance. "All accounted for now but two," Ben said. "Let's start the reckoning while we wait for the other helicopter. Andrew will arrive any minute."

The others agreed. Peter and Harry moved closer.

"Robert, give me your results, please," Ben requested. The women were all ears.

Robert stood up, center stage. "Four choice rainbows, all over twenty-two inches. Try to beat that."

Ben gave a happy laugh. "Nothing personal, I assure you. The larger of my two was twenty-three and three-quarter inches. I measured him twice. That's got to be the winner. However, I think you'll win for the most, Robert, with your four."

"Sadly I concede on the length. I'll pin my hopes on the most. Congratulations, Ben." Robert, like Miss Muffet, sat down on a tuffet.

"Not so fast, Ben," James announced. "I hate to do this to such a good friend, but move over. The rainbow I caught with Alastair less than a half-hour ago was twenty-five inches! Sorry, old man."

Just then they heard a voice, Andrew's. He walked over and stood in front of his friends, running his eyes over each face. "Have you started the reckoning without me?"

"We've just heard that we're driving back to Gore tonight directly from the Queenstown airport, because tomorrow we go to Cattle Flat," Robert explained. "We've just begun."

"Who has the biggest?" Andrew asked.

"Hold on, Holcomb. We're not in that much rush," Ben drawled. "This is a historic reckoning on the banks of the beautiful Greenstone. Sorry you almost missed it. Robert's largest was over twenty-two inches. I topped it by an inch. James, carry on. It's your turn."

"I don't like to count my chickens before they're hatched, but I feel pretty safe with my twenty-five inch rainbow on Alastair's stretch of the Greenstone," James said smugly.

"Well, my children," said Andrew, "thank you for the very

helpful rundown." He waved to Bill, the pilot. "Come over quickly. This is too good for you to miss."

Bill joined the reckoning session. Andrew continued, "Bill flew me up to a falls that has a deep pool below it."

"He should know about falls," Ben commented.

"He does," Andrew agreed. "I had a strike on my first cast. It was so strong that I almost lost my rod. I played that fish for a good twenty minutes. I'm sure that he is the champion deep-water-diving rainbow of the Greenstone."

"I know he is," Alastair broke in. "Bill flew me in there last summer. I've seen that fish, but I've never gotten him to rise to a fly. That's a triumph, Andrew."

"I saw him closely for the first time today," Bill said. "It was worth the trip in. He's an ugly monster."

"How close did you see him, Bill?" James asked.

"Ask Andrew. It's his story."

"I caught him," Andrew said, with the dignity that the occasion called for, "and released him."

"How long?" Ben asked, pen poised. "Apply the knife quickly, Holcomb, so it won't hurt so much."

"I don't know about the rest of you," Andrew laughed, "but I'm having a great time! Bill and I measured him carefully before we returned him to the pool. He was twenty- six inches long."

"Well, I'll be," James broke the stunned silence. "What a fish. I wish I had seen him. As the runner-up, may I be the first to offer congratulations."

Ben cut through the hubbub. "It looks as though James and I, in spite of our two superb fish, are giving the party today, since Robert wins for the most fish, unless you can top four, Andrew." Andrew shook his head.

Peter raised his hand. "I want to be the first to thank Alastair and his friend Bill for arranging this admirable day for us. In case Andrew didn't hear the news, Harry has arranged for us to fish at Cattle Flat tomorrow. We'll drive back tonight, right from the air-port. Let's go!"

Reluctantly they left the beauty of the Greenstone, still tawny in the sunset, to fly to the Queenstown airport. They packed up and bid good-bye to Bill.

Jo had come to the airport to meet them. She joined the Greenstone group for a bite of supper, and then the Watsons waved their friends off to Gore in silvery moonlight.

"What are the round dark humps all over the road?" Helene asked Harry.

"The ones you can't avoid hitting," Susan added.

"They are hedgehogs, imported at one time to solve some problem or other. Now they have become a public nuisance and a traffic hazard," Harry explained. "It was probably a bureaucratic decision."

That's the last thing Phoebe remembered about the drive home until they arrived at Croyden Lodge in Gore. She found that everyone in the car, except Harry, had also dozed all the way home.

Cattle Flat

THE NEXT MORNING the picnic hampers included enough food for two meals. "Because if we stop by Harry's farm on the way home, we'll miss even a late dinner at the lodge," Peter explained. There were now three full vans, including Blair Cullen's. He and his van came from Invercargill the night before because he and the van they were both needed for the Cattle Flat trip.

James and Phoebe rode with Harry. They made a quick stop at his farm to invite Bernie to come for lunch on the river. "We hope the twins will be home from school when we return on the way to Gore," Phoebe mentioned.

From the Raes' farm, they left the metal road, the name in New Zealand for a hard surface. On the right, the Mataura River beckoned.

On the left was the mountain range that the local farmers drove their cattle up for summer grazing. The autumn roundups to muster the animals down to the farms for the winter were exciting events. Bernie always rode with her husband and older children as one of the regular hands.

For the first few miles, small vacation fishing cabins dotted the lower slopes bordering the river. Soon their progress slowed to a rough crawl because of the large mountain boulders, too big for tractors to push off, that filled the road. Eventually, they left the road and made their way across the bush to a heavy grove of trees by the river. "Here we are," Peter announced.

Harry made a suggestion, "Instead of fishing here this afternoon, let's take Blair's and my van, with the lunch and the ladies, farther upstream. The men can drop off here and fish up to the lunch spot. Then we can return here for the late afternoon fishing that Sandy and the twins say is particularly good at that time. We can have our supper right here."

"Good suggestion," Peter agreed. "I'll leave some food and drinks with tables and some chairs in case the ladies want to come back here earlier in the afternoon."

The men fished the river near the lunch spot until Harry told them about a falls a couple of miles upstream with several good pools around it. "The trail to it is very rough," he cautioned.

The men immediately decided to go investigate. "I'll come for a while," Andrew told them, "but I'm returning mid- afternoon to a pool I spotted before lunch."

"No card game can compete with Cattle Flat today," Helene announced after the men had left. "Blair, can you handle a fishing harem, if I come along too?"

Blair doffed his fishing hat and swept it to the ground. Phoebe could almost see the plumes. "My pleasure, fair ladies! Fish upstream within sight until I finish my lunch chores, and then we'll go slay some brown trout dragons."

Susan announced, to everyone's surprise, that she had decided to open her own personal fishing season this afternoon. She busied herself laying out her equipment.

Helene found a rounded boulder only a few feet from shore with no bushes behind it to snag her line. The only danger was a friendly cow grazing behind her. She tried making shooing sounds before she manipulated her way to the boulder, but to no avail. "Now I'm pretending she isn't there," Helene told Phoebe, fishing above her.

Phoebe wanted to wade and cast in midstream over water with no bushes around, but she decided to be sensible and wait for Blair. In the meantime, Susan began to practice-cast in the field before she approached the water. The tundra behind her had been grazed smooth by the cattle. Her friends were impressed with her casting.

Blair arrived. "Any time you want to change flies, ladies, let me know. I've brought extras. I know a smooth beach a little farther up the river where I fished once with Harry. It is wide enough for three or four ladies to cast at once. There's an easy path to it above the bushes. Let me know when you might want to go there."

"I'd like to wade out a little way and fish here first," Phoebe answered, "but I didn't want to do it until you arrived."

"And I want to continue my flirtation with a trout who is lurking behind some stones out there," Helene said from her perch on the big rock.

Susan called, "I have lots of practicing to do in this field first."

Blair waded out with Phoebe and checked the footing.

Then, net in hand, he returned to Helene. And just in time. She had a beautiful strike. "The fish was so frustrated by my fly that he struck it to get even. Silly fish," Helene said, rod upright, trying to reel in enough line to keep him from getting into midstream. "Blair, if you could give me a hand to get off this rock, I'd feel less precarious and have a better chance of bringing my fish in."

When Helene was safely off the rock, she began a careful battle with her fish from the bank. Phoebe moved out of the river so she wouldn't be in the way if the fish chose to run in that direction. "Susan, let's retreat a little downstream," she suggested.

They watched Helene bring the fish into shallow water. Blair netted it and helped her hold the fish up for her friends to view.

"Too big for a breakfast fish," they heard her say, "I'll mark the length on my rod. Then will you release him, Blair?"

After the fish swam away, the women decided to take Blair's suggestion about fishing farther above. He led them upstream to a wide gravel spit of beach. Helene spotted another large boulder rising above the water near the shore, but Blair advised against it.

Helene reluctantly agreed. "It was fun, casting from a rock. I'm sorry you think it's too dangerous to try again,"

"Susan, how about continuing your practice, but over the water?" Phoebe suggested. "It's just the same, and there isn't a bush behind us, just pebbles."

Susan brought a dancer's grace to her casting, and a little of the actress also. "If we didn't have to catch a fish, this would be fun!" she told Phoebe.

To their delight, Andrew appeared on the shore. "Pardon me, ladies, I'm just passing by. Too crowded up above." He stopped to watch Susan.

"Crowded!" Elizabeth laughed. "Four fishermen in ten miles of river! Cattle Flat and New Zealand are spoiling us forever."

Andrew smiled and turned back to Susan. "You're doing splendidly," he told her. "Mind if I show you one thing?"

"Delighted to be instructed by a master!" Susan said, reeling in her line as he came to her.

Andrew pulled out some line. "Excuse me," he said and placed his hands over hers. "It's good that you are keeping your upper back cast high enough to avoid any bushes that might be behind you. Now remember this about the forward cast. When you stop at one o'clock, no lower, the line behind you straightens out. When you project it forward, it should lie on the water, like this."

A few minutes later, after several very successful solo casts from Susan, a fast learner, Andrew turned to go. "If you would spend a little more time in the river, Susan, you'd give us all a run for our money. And maybe we should all spend more time studying dancing!" He turned to continue toward the pool he had mentioned earlier.

"Andrew," Phoebe called to him, "before you go, would you watch me make a few casts across the stream? I can't seem to direct my fly well enough to get it where I think there might be a fish. You do it so beautifully."

"I don't know about that," Andrew answered, "but sure. See that tuft of native grass on the far bank? Let's walk out to where you think you can reach the water below that."

"Please, you show me first," Phoebe asked. She saw Susan and Helene coming closer to watch.

"All right. For me, I've figured out that lining my feet up the way I do in golf helps with the direction. And that way I can cast a little to the side. You get your body out of the way of your casting."

Andrew dropped his fly directly in front of the tuft. She saw that he purposely did not let the fly float very long in case a fish were waiting, but raised it directly off the water. He even knew how not to catch a fish!

"Now let's move down a bit so you can cast over new water," he told Phoebe.

They did. Phoebe cast mentally as she positioned herself. She'd like to repay Andrew's generosity by showing that she had been a good pupil.

Twice she fell short of her mark. But the third cast felt good from the start. She watched her fly drop gently on the water above the tuft and stay upright as it floated by.

She felt a pull. She had a strike. The timing was right.

"Good gal, now take your time," said Andrew, pleased.

Would she! She worked the rod tip upright and exerted more strength than she thought she possessed in order to keep it there. She reeled in when the fish swam toward her and gave him slack when he ran.

"Angle a little more upstream. Watch out for some big boulders behind you. That's a nice fish you have on your line."

Phoebe flushed with pleasure, but the fish interrupted her special moment. He made a strong run that ended in a jump. Phoebe saw that he was a good-sized brown. She was sure that he was one of the handsomest fish she had ever seen. She worked him in closer to the shore.

In moments of elation Phoebe had often thought of the old adage, "Pride cometh before a fall." At that moment, she felt something clamp her right foot like a vice. She tried to wiggle her foot free. Her foot was jammed.

She dug her left foot deep and reached for her wading stick. She planted the stick firmly and gave a strong jerk to try to extricate her other foot without losing her balance. It didn't work. She began to fall backward. She felt herself collapsing into the cold shallow water.

She kept wiggling her whole leg to get her foot free, but nothing happened. She managed to keep the rod tip upright and peered into the water. She could see that her leg was wedged between two boulders.

Just then she felt the fish gather himself to try to jump again or to streak away. All she could do was brace her good leg on the bottom, reel in, and pray.

Andrew hurried to her side. "Here, I'll pull you up. I can steady you while you finish reeling the fish in."

"No, thank you. I'll play him right here. I'm a little shaky."

James arrived. "Are you all right?" he asked anxiously. "I was passing by and saw you go down."

"Fine," she said, but she couldn't keep the quaver from her voice.

"Let me give you a hand up," James persisted.

"Not yet. I need to sit a minute." She turned her attention to the fish. He was almost upon them when he must have spotted all the legs. He began to thrash, churning the water white.

Blair materialized and managed to dip his net into the foaming water. He scooped up the agitated fish. James took Phoebe's rod from her limp hands and handed it to Blair.

James slid his hand under the water and down the outside of her thin waders. "There's a big lump just above the knee, sweetheart. You'll have to let us lift you up. We need to get you to help fast."

"James," Andrew suggested, "Blair and I can make an Indian seat and carry her to that big log on the beach. You can walk behind to steady her back."

James and Andrew put their hands under her armpits and pulled. She couldn't seem to help. She was a dead weight. When they managed to get her legs parallel under her, the pain hit her with such force that she lost her breath.

"Are you all right?" Andrew asked. Blair had returned from handling the fish and took James's place. James moved behind to support her back. Phoebe had no strength to answer.

She felt herself separated from them by a wall of pain so strong that her eyeballs saw fiery red. The pain shook her back and forth like an explosion.

For a second, James's soothing voice penetrated the searing pain. But when the men made an Indian seat for her and carried her to the shore, her leg dangling, nothing could reach her through the jabbing pain.

At the old log, they eased her down. Her back rested against little Susan who slipped in to support her. Then, gently, they lifted her dangling legs to a horizontal position on the tree trunk. The pain receded to a dull ache.

Slowly she felt almost human again until she spotted the unnatural bulge on her right leg. "Dear God," she whispered, "please make me Victorian enough to faint." But she didn't.

She saw the others approaching. "Someone reach down under the waders to my jeans pocket for my lipstick. If I can't faint, I'll need my red badge of courage."

Everyone stood around talking about how sorry they were that this had happened, as though she weren't there. Harry came over, looming large and comforting above her. "Phoebe," he told her, "all the men except James will come with me to go help Peter clear the brush in order for him to bring his four-wheel drive to pick you up. James will stay with you."

She flashed him a grateful smile. Harry continued. "You women make your way down with Blair to the other vans as fast as you can. He will follow Andrew and me to my home to phone for a doctor. Andrew will locate someone to get in touch with the hospital in Invercargill. Then Blair will drive you women back to Gore."

James eased into Susan's place, supporting Phoebe. Blair rolled down her waders gently. "This will make it easier for you when they move you into Peter's van. Good luck."

The gals told her good-bye. "We'll try to keep the missionaries and the cannibals straightened out," Helene whispered as they hurried after Blair.

"This isn't a very convenient place, sweetheart, where you chose to hurt a leg," James said, trying to be conversational as they watched the exodus.

"You can say that again."

They listened to the quietness around them. The river murmured its apology and birds sang to reassure them that the beauty was undisturbed.

Phoebe tried to sit up, but it hurt to move. A slow tear made its way down one cheek. "I'm so ashamed to be taking good fishing time away from everyone."

"We'll fish more later," James assured her. "Now is the time to get your leg checked out. "Do you hurt much?"

"Not if I don't move. But, darn it, I want to move. I want to fish. I hate to be still."

She made a gesture to sit up. "I wish I had thrown the fish and my lovely rod away, even though I planned to ask you if we could give it to Harry at the end of the trip. He told me he thought it was an outstanding rod."

"It is. That's a splendid idea. But we'll take care of your leg first."

Finally, they heard engine noises and voices. They saw Ben and Robert in front of Peter's four-wheel drive, hacking with big knives, like machetes, through gorse and brush. Peter inched along behind them right up to the log. He hopped out and opened the back door.

"Your chariot, Madam," he said.

"And your steeds," Ben said, "who need water and maybe something stronger. Are you all right?"

In a few minutes they picked her up and gently laid her in the middle seat of the jeep, working her legs up on the seat. Peter held a flask of whiskey to her lips. She sipped some willingly. James sat beside her to brace her against the bumps on the one-hundred mile trip to the hospital in Invercargill.

Peter told the MacLeans later that he consistently exceeded the speed limit all the way to Invercargill. "I kept hoping that some sheriff would arrest me and give us a police escort, siren blowing, to the hospital. But no such luck."

At the hospital, Phoebe roused enough to become aware that some orderlies moved her into a room where there was a collage of people, many clad in white. Later when she roused again, James and a kindly-faced mature nurse in white were the only ones she saw in the room.

"I'm hungry," Phoebe said.

"We don't serve food in Emergency," said a soft voice. "I'm the nurse in charge of the Emergency room."

"But I'm hungry. I know my husband is too. We haven't eaten since an early lunch."

"I'll see what I can do. Most people aren't hungry in here," she said and hurried away.

Phoebe raised up on her elbows. She seemed to be in a high bed with one leg elevated over the foot of the bed by what looked like pulleys strung over a high rack. "What's this?"

"You're in traction."

"Why?"

"You've broken your femur in five places. That's the large bone in your upper leg. Mr. Willson, who took care of your leg, told me it was fortunate that it was above the knee."

"I thought that long ride was to get me to a doctor."

James told her, reassuringly. "I asked about that too. Mr. Willson is a specialist and the head of the Orthopedic Department at this hospital."

"Then why isn't he called 'doctor'?" Phoebe asked as she lay back in the bed.

"They follow the British system here. When a medical man becomes a specialist, the term 'doctor' is dropped because that term used to include barbers also. He is then called simply 'Mr.'"

Just then the nurse returned with two small rather anemic tomato sandwiches that might have graced a tea party. Phoebe and James wolfed them down gratefully.

"Sweet," James explained. "They have arranged a room for me in the hospital. The others have gone back to Gore."

"Is that all right with you?" Phoebe asked, reaching for James's hand.

"The important thing is to be near you."

"How long will I need to be here?"

"We'll talk about that tomorrow."

"Like Scarlett O'Hara in *Gone With the Wind*," she said with a faint smile.

Two orderlies arrived. "They're looking for a patient," she whispered.

"No, for a patient in traction," her husband corrected.

The nice nurse came over to her. "We have a private room for you on the orthopedic floor. The nurse on duty there will get you settled for the night. Perhaps she can arrange for your husband to have breakfast with you in the morning."

"Thank you for the sandwiches. You've been very kind to us," Phoebe told her.

"I'll check on you tomorrow when I come back on duty. Ask your husband to tell you where his room is! You can get the nurse to call him there at any time. After I got rid of all the men who arrived with you, I found you to be a very good patient. Good luck tonight."

James went with her to the third floor. The orderlies pushed open double doors and wheeled her into a room with a window.

At last she could sink into her exhaustion instead of fighting it. "Where is your room?" she asked James faintly.

His face turned red. "It's in the student nurses's dormitory. I'll see you in the morning." He kissed her and fled.

The next morning, a young student nurse rolled her up and washed her face. She handed her a comb. "It's mine, but I just washed it. Your husband is waiting outside. He sent this in."

She handed Phoebe her own lipstick. "He's eager to come in. I'll get coffee for you two while you wait for breakfast."

Phoebe smiled and quickly put on some lipstick before James arrived. "How are you, pretty?" he asked, coming to the bed to kiss her.

"Much better. Whatever they gave me last night really knocked me out. How was life in the dormitory?"

"Fine. No one came near me, except the matron this morning, who asked if I wanted breakfast. I told her no thank you, that I had a date for breakfast."

The student nurse returned with two mugs of coffee. "My name is Eleanor. I'm working with your RN on this ward. I'm looking forward to learning about your country."

As nurse Eleanor left, the breakfasts arrived. "Now, James, my first question. How long do I have to stay in this friendly country? You promised last night to tell me."

"Phoebe, I really don't know. When I asked the doctor, he said until the bone has knit strong enough for you to travel. I guess being in traction helps it to knit."

"Oh bother. An answer like a Greek oracle. Couldn't we go home for the knitting?"

"Can you see getting this contraption on a commercial plane? The military has a corner on ambulance planes. If I were a general, I could commandeer one. You married the wrong guy, I'm afraid."

"No, I didn't. I'm so thankful that you are you, but Mr. Willson will have a lot of questions from me to answer. Have the others gone fishing? If so, what are you doing here?"

"Because this is my errand day. I want you to make a list of the things you need from the lodge. I'll telephone Helene, and the gals will collect them during the time that Blair drives me to Gore. May I have a dinner date tonight with my sweetheart?"

"You sure may. I'd die if you didn't." For a moment, she almost choked on self-pity. "Watch it," she told herself and began writing down what she needed.

"Tomorrow will be errand day in Invercargill. You start working on that list while I'm gone."

He kissed her good-bye, list in hand, and just in time. The RN bustled in, followed by the student nurse holding a businesslike tray of equipment.

The nurses had barely finished with her when the doctor arrived. He began by checking the pulleys and weights around her leg. "I feel like a trussed chicken," Phoebe told him.

"I'm sure you do. We couldn't find a solid enough piece of bone in your leg to use as an anchor to put it in a cast. Traction was the only solution."

"How long will this process take?"

"It depends on how fast you can make bone."

"I've never had to make bone before. How can I hasten the process?"

"By lying still and doing your therapy."

"Therapy?" she almost gasped.

"It begins gradually with the good leg. Fly-fishermen don't usually break bones this badly. The therapist and I will work together on the exercises. You must be very dedicated to fly-fishing."

"I'm very dedicated to my husband!"

"I'll see you tomorrow," said Mr. Willson and left before she could ask another question.

Next in the procession of specialists was the young therapist. "I am Betsy. When I was five, I lived in Carmel, California!" Her words rushed out in her eagerness to explain. "My father went to the Naval language school there. I hope to return to America someday as a therapist. Will you tell me a great deal about your country?"

It wasn't until Phoebe assured her that she would, that Betsy began to explain about the flexing exercises.

Lunch was a hot lamb meal. This turned out to be the fare twice a day.

During lunch, a man burst into the room, hand thrust out. "I'm Dr. Jamison. My wife is secretary to the manager of the aluminium project on which your husband's company is doing the engineering."

He examined the traction equipment as he spoke. "Andrew Holcomb called the manager last night about your accident. My wife was asked to phone the top orthopedic specialist in town, as well as the emergency room of the hospital. I was here at the hospital last night. Tomorrow I may have a surprise for you."

He left as abruptly as he had arrived. Phoebe wondered how many other people were in the emergency room last night?

Dr. Jamison came daily, always unannounced, even at inconvenient moments such as during bedpan operations. She never found out what kind of doctor he was because he never stayed long enough to be questioned. His departures reminded Phoebe of the Cheshire Cat. His grin left last.

She tried to rest before James's return. But no such luck. Suddenly, her room was filled again with people, two nurses, two orderlies, and two women from the business office. One of them announced breathlessly, "International telephone call!"

A young intern materialized and freed the traction frame from its tetherings under the bed. An orderly pushed open the double doors and another maneuvered the bed and Phoebe into the wide outer hall. He pushed the bed up to a wall telephone. Someone thrust a receiver in her hand.

"Mother," came the voice of Jamie, their elder son and eldest child, calling from Pittsburgh. "What have you done to yourself? Daddy's secretary phoned us. Are you all right?"

"I'm fine, really. Don't worry. Kind people are giving me good care. My leg is in traction. I've just been rolled, in the bed, to a wall phone in the hall." As much as she loved this son, she must be brief. It was his call, his 'nickel', as they said in the family.

"But Mother, what happened?"

"I broke my femur in five places, bringing in a fish! The doctor says I'll be here until the bone knits enough for me to fly home."

"How did you manage that?"

"Two boulders caught my leg. Give your doctor wife Pam my love and ask her how long it takes bones to knit."

"Poor Mother, bad luck. We'll write often."

"Or phone. Use our credit card number. I know you have it. I'd like you to phone the other children, will you? I love you so much. Thank you for calling. Don't worry. I'm fine and Daddy is right here with me. Good-bye." Purposely she hung up quickly.

She dried her eyes. She didn't want others to see the American lady acting like a crybaby. She looked around. She needn't have worried. She was alone, marooned on the island of her bed in the big hall.

She must have dozed. Suddenly something swished by her to the tune of wild yelling. Wide awake, she jerked up. Two wheelchairs careened past her bed in a race!

Nurses popped out from many doors, followed by the floor office supervisor who bravely planted herself in the middle of the return course.

"Enough of that!" she called. "You're not on your motorcycles. Apologize to this American lady. You could have hit her. Nurses, get these young men back to their rooms."

Two sheepish teenagers sedately rolled their wheel chairs to her bed and apologized. "Who won?" Phoebe whispered before she was wheeled to her room and strung up again.

When James returned, Phoebe met each of her possessions joyously. "Well done, my smart errand boy."

"Wait. I'm not through."

He reached in the pocket of his jacket and pulled out a plastic flask. "Have a Scotch, Mrs. MacLean?"

"Happy to, Mr. MacLean. An illegal drink will taste even better than a legal one."

James poured the drinks. "Cheers. Now tell me about your day."

"The biggest news is that Jamie phoned. They unattached me and wheeled me into the hall to a wall phone. He's fine and will relay the news to the other children about my landing in the hospital. He had a call from your secretary, probably contacted through Andrew's office."

"Not from mine. I haven't had time for anything but my sweetheart. Now close your eyes for another surprise."

James pulled a small radio out of another jacket pocket. "And something else comes tomorrow."

"James, how could you do all this?"

"Blair took me to downtown Invercargill on the way back. What's coming tomorrow is a TV, the only one in Invercargill for rent. It's yours for a month."

"A month! What do you mean, a month?"

"The storekeeper said that I can return it early," James hastened to add.

"Let's hope so. How sweet of you. Now you absolutely *need* to go fishing tomorrow because I may be too busy with the TV to visit with you!"

"O.K., I will. It just so happens that Peter has arranged to fish near his brother's farm again, tomorrow. It's the one halfway to Invercargill. Blair and I will meet the others there around noon. Then Peter will drive Helene, Susan, and Elizabeth here to visit you. They've been very worried about you."

"It will be wonderful to see them. But the main thing I'm happy about is that you are going fishing."

Phoebe continued. "I'm beginning to understand your scheme, sir. It's to keep me so busy with people and activities that I'll lie here and grow bone like crazy. I'll do a better job if you go fishing regularly, remember that."

"Good gal, good sport. When I come back from cleaning up for dinner with you, let's start a big gin rummy tournament. Blair will take me to pick up the TV tomorrow morning before we leave for fishing. O.K.?" The day progressed according to plan.

That night after James had left, Phoebe met her night nurse, a man. After her first shock, she found his care very comfortable. He was sturdy, strong, and gentle. On one of his days off, he brought his wife and three children to visit her.

When Blair dropped her friends off to see her, it was a real shot in the arm. Helene brought her a New Zealand sheepskin rug to lie on, Elizabeth brought her an exciting new book, and Susan came not only with fragrant soap and matching powder but with shampoo. "I hope you're not laying in supplies for me for the rest of the year," Phoebe told them, "because I intend to heal this leg sooner than that!"

"You've given us a wonderful excuse to go shopping," Helene told Phoebe. "Gore will never be the same. Anthony and I need to leave for a business trip to Australia before we fly home. We have found a good book store in Invercargill and have arranged time to shop there for you on the day we leave."

"Also, I may go home early," Susan confessed. "Your accident hasn't endeared fishing to me."

"Excuses will get you nowhere, my dear. You are a natural caster. We'll have a practice again before long," Phoebe insisted.

Peter walked in. "Time to go, ladies. Phoebe, everyone from Croydon Lodge sends you love and greetings. I'll see you often."

"We'll be back in a day or so," Helene promised.

"Me, too," Susan added.

"I may be back sooner than that if I hear from my North Island cousins," Elizabeth finished by saying. "I'll let you know."

On the doctor's next visit, Phoebe again asked the question that he had been evading. "On an average, how long does it take to grow enough bone for a patient to go home?"

"It's hard to tell."

"Just give me an average."

"All right. You force me. About a month. Now, are you happier?"

"No, I'm in shock. Then?"

"Probably ten days in your own hospital. I'll be in touch with your orthopedic man before that."

"Thanks, Mr. Willson, for leveling with me. It's easier to know. It sounds as if I'll have time to start writing a book."

"Fine. Put me in it!"

The mornings continued to belong to the hospital people and to therapy. The afternoons were filled with callers from the aluminium clients and company people who were working on that job, some of whom Phoebe had known from visiting them with James, on other jobs around the world.

These friends, as well as the guides and their wives, even the Raes from Cattle Flat and the Watsons from Queenstown, kept Phoebe's afternoons busy. The student nurses were shifted regularly among the various floors.

Phoebe's second student nurse was a local girl named Meredith, whose sister was to be married soon. Meredith agonized to Phoebe over everything connected with the wedding. A few years later, by correspondence, Phoebe again agonized with Meredith over another wedding, Meredith's own, to a London Bobby whom she met when she was nursing in England.

"Want any advice about your next wedding, James?" Phoebe asked her husband one night.

"Not for a little while, I hope," he responded. "Ask a silly question, get a silly answer."

When a woman holding a basin and a bucket arrived shortly after breakfast one morning, Phoebe was puzzled. She didn't think anything else could surprise her in this place. She was wrong.

"It's time for your shampoo," said the woman, arranging articles from a bucket on the bedside table.

"I have my own shampoo," Phoebe hastened to say.

A nurse came in and rolled the bed up so high that Phoebe's nose could almost touch her trussed leg. Then the two women curled her mattress and the wire coils that it rested on into a roll underneath Phoebe's back and secured it.

Next they rolled her down until she was suspended over a basin teetering on the wooden slats that the coils and mattress rested on.

Obviously the routine was familiar to the woman. Since Phoebe couldn't see what was going on, it took her several shampoos and many questions to figure out the operation.

"Curl your back and your head over the mattress," the woman ordered. "Nurse, water!"

Obediently, Phoebe did a back-bend and her weekly shampoo began. This became a weekly event.

One young wife, whose husband worked for the engineering company, was originally from Western Texas. She frequently came alone to visit Phoebe. "I love to talk with older women. They can answer my questions and give me such good advice," she confided to Phoebe.

"Particularly a captive older woman," Phoebe thought. She could feel herself aging during each visit.

"James," Phoebe said to him one evening after such a visit, "do you know that you are married to an older woman?"

"I thought," James said gallantly, "that I was married to a child bride."

On one of his visits Harry Rae from Cattle Flat told her, "A few years ago, some clients of ours asked if their son could work for us one summer. He did, and now they have sent us money to come to Los Angeles in April for the boy's wedding."

Bernadette Rae, nicknamed Bernie, continued with excitement, "If you hurry and get well enough to go home by then, we'll visit you in the Bay Area afterwards."

"I'll make it," Phoebe promised. "I'll hurry."

Late one afternoon, Phoebe could feel a lonesome attack coming on because Ben, James, and Robert, the three remaining fishermen, had gone up to Rotoua, on the North Island, to fish for a few days. Elizabeth had been the last gal left, besides Phoebe, but now she had gone to visit her cousins in Australia. Afterwards, she planned to meet Robert in Auckland for their flight home.

Phoebe had insisted that James go. But now alone, marooned on her high bed, she felt depressed. By accident, she found the New Zealand Australia cricket match on her television, a tournament that continued for several days. Word spread like wildfire that the American lady had the cricket match on her TV. From then on, people jammed the room. She had no more time to be lonely.

The wheel chair racers were always the first to arrive and the last to go. Everyone tried to explain the game to her, without success, until the shyest person she had ever met, the hospital chaplain, tried his hand at it.

She saw his eyes for the first time, peeping out from beneath his bushy Celtic eyebrows and forelock. Usually, during his official visits, he hung his head so low that they weren't visible.

He followed every play avidly, and he answered every question so articulately that she began to understand the game a little in spite of herself. Later, when the match was over, the chaplain's head dropped down again to his chest, but Phoebe was sure that from then on, she occasionally detected a twinkle in his eyes as they peeked out at her.

The Watsons arrived one Saturday after a long drive from Queenstown. With them were two of their three children, Christiana and Thomas, handsome preteenagers. Heidi, the eldest, now had a weekend job.

Alastair and Jo piled numerous knobby packages on Phoebe's bed as the children examined the mechanics of the traction. "Wouldn't a cast have been simpler?" Thomas asked.

"I agree!" Phoebe said, "but I'm told that the weights do a better job of pulling shattered bones together."

Soon, the children, with parental permission, left to explore the hospital. Immediately, Alastair beckoned to James and handed him a bottle of Scotch. "Will you prepare drinks, please, in these plastic glasses. The nurse in charge assured me that she will look the other way. I'll return in a minute with a surprise."

He returned carrying a tray covered with a towel. He put the tray down and raised his glass. "Will everyone join me in a toast to the opening day of the Invercargill Bluff Oyster Season, the best oysters in the world!" He whisked off the towel and displayed four bowls of oysters.

"I consider myself an oyster connoisseur," James announced, "and I like to practice my chosen profession as often as possible."

Phoebe raised her glass: "To the Watsons for their party celebrating the opening of the Bluff Oyster Season and to the perfect time that I chose for breaking my leg."

They feasted bountifully on oysters, which registered a resounding top count of *ten* on James's oyster scale. Not a nurse interrupted. "I brought some oysters to them," Alastair confessed.

Jo picked up a package that she had kept in her lap during the oyster party. As she held it out to Phoebe, Alastair interrupted her. "I didn't approve of Jo's bringing this to you," he explained, "because it can't be replaced. But she won me over by saying that this is the time when you need special gifts."

Jo thrust the package to Phoebe. "Well, open it before there are too many explanations," she told her. "You may not be the least bit interested."

It was a book written by Jo's father about his part in the early days of New Zealand aviation. She read the title, *Ski Plane Adventure* by Henry Wigley and saw that it was autographed and addressed to "Dear Jo."

"Jo, it's marvelous of you to want to share this with me, but I understand Alastair's reservation. My life is pretty public here, and I'm not always the master of it. But I'm more touched than I can tell you."

"It's out of print," Alastair explained. "After World War II, Jo's grandfather, Rodolph Wigley, a veteran of the British Army in World War I, bought a surplus Jennie airplane from the New Zealand government for a few pounds, a project designed to encourage aviation locally. He told his son, Jo's father, who had flown in World War II, "Get some practice flying this and we'll start a family airline company."

"What an assignment. Did he?" Phoebe asked.

"Yes. That was the beginning of Cooke Airlines," Jo answered and continued. "For several generations, the Wigley family first had operated a wagon business and later a bus business. But this was a completely new development."

Jo stopped a minute. "Am I boring you or tiring you?"

"Not at all. I am fascinated," Phoebe insisted.

"We were brought up as children on the tales that Father told us about how he managed to get some practice flying the machine. He taught some of his young adventurous friends enough about flying so that they could navigate for him. Most of them were sheep farmers, so they let him use their paddocks for take-offs and landings."

"Please continue, Jo," James said. "Here we are, savoring Bluff oysters as we are hearing about history in the making."

Jo smiled and complied. "Father said that they were constantly crashing into sheep fences. They'd patch the plane with bailing wire and tape and go up again".

Jo continued, "As Alastair explained, that was the beginning of Cooke Airlines. Father wrote it all down in this book. I hope reading it will help pass the time more quickly, Phoebe."

Alastair added, "A few years ago Jo's father was knighted by the Queen of England for his contributions to aviation in New Zealand."

Phoebe and James pored over the book. Then Phoebe handed the book to Jo. "The pictures alone are treasures. But, Jo, Alastair is right. I cannot keep it. Let me read it some other time on another fishing trip, but I'll never forget your wanting to lend it to me in the hospital."

But Jo wouldn't take no for an answer. "I'll make you a proposition. I will be returning to Invercargill in a week to meet my mother, flying in from Christ Church for a business appointment.

I'll pick the book up before we drive home. Mother has already mentioned that she wanted to see you. She'll be with us for a week."

"Is that all right with you, Alastair?" Phoebe asked as Jo laid the book back beside Phoebe again. Alastair nodded.

"Then I'll guard it with my life and read it with enormous pleasure!"

Even before the Watsons were out the door, Phoebe had an exciting idea. It was to try to find a copy of the book to take home, perhaps for a birthday present for James or a Christmas gift for Jamie, or both. But how?

She spent a great deal of time at the wall phone in the hall calling bookstores, both local and throughout New Zealand, mainly ones that searched for books out of print. The orderlies were now so well trained from her international phone calls that they were extremely efficient getting her to the hall phone.

But before her efforts were successful, the head nurse dealt a blow to the project. "This is delaying your recovery," she told Phoebe. "You may not be able to fly home as soon as you hope to, if you keep up this constant moving back and forth, in and out of traction, to use the phone."

Phoebe decided she needed help!

The young Texas wife who liked "older women" came by that afternoon. Again, she begged Phoebe to tell her what she could do to help.

The solution to her problem stood before her! "Lillabeth, I now know how you can help me, but it's a secret. I'm trying to buy a book that is no longer stocked by regular bookstores, a surprise birthday present for my husband," Phoebe explained. "You could help me locate a store that has a copy."

"But what if I can't find it for you?" Lillabeth asked.

"I'm sure you can, and keep in mind that we'll be doing this together. You have a telephone at home, and the head nurse doesn't want me to get disconnected from traction to use the phone in the hall anymore. She says it's not good for my leg."

Phoebe fished out her wallet from the bedside table and handed Lillabeth her international telephone credit card.

"Ask your husband if you can use this on your phone. Tell him that you will keep a list of the calls and how much they cost. But ask him to promise to keep it all a secret, please."

"Oh, I love surprises. I'll do it!"

"I'll make a list of places to call both in New Zealand and in Australia. I hope we find the book before I go broke! Leave me your phone number, please. I'll make you my Vice-president in Charge of Surprises!"

Lillabeth left, smiling happily.

They soon exhausted all sources both on the South Island and the North Island of New Zealand. They then began on Australia.

One morning, before visiting hours, Lillabeth burst into Phoebe's room. Bravely she pushed past two nurses and the therapist. "I couldn't wait to tell you that I've found a copy! It's in Melbourne, Australia!" She tossed Phoebe a piece of paper with a number on it and Phoebe's credit card, and hurried out.

Phoebe waited impatiently for the nurses and Betsy to leave. She rang for the head nurse and buttonholed her. "This is an emergency. Please will you call an orderly to take me to the hall phone as soon as possible."

In the hall, she phoned the Melbourne bookstore. The shopkeeper told her that he had not one copy, but *two*. She ordered them both!

That night she told her husband all about her success in getting a copy of the book. "Won't that be a splendid Christmas gift for our flyer son, Jamie?" She refrained from any mention of the second copy that was for him. "I'm afraid the days will drag, now that my search is over," she admitted.

"No, they won't," James told her, taking her hand. "I've also been doing some phoning. How would you like to have a visitor this week?"

"I've been having visitors constantly."

286

"I mean a family member, such as Meg, our daughter from Oregon."

"Oh James, I can't believe anything that wonderful could happen! You're a sweetheart to want to do this for me, but she could never leave all four children."

Suddenly, Phoebe gasped and grabbed James's arm. "Has something happened in the family? Is there an emergency? Do you need to leave? Is that why she's coming?"

"No. Everything is all right, thank God. It's business."

"You mean you are going on a business trip?" It was the age-old construction question, new each time a wife asked it.

James's face had the affirmative answer spread all over it. He began to pace the small room.

"It's the periodic Board of Review in Saudi Arabia the first of next week. Oh, Phoebe, I've tried every way to change the date, but there are too many other people involved, including the Saudi clients."

Phoebe was speechless. James broke the silence that engulfed them. "Sweetheart, Meg will be with you the whole time. It's all arranged. She will stay in my room in the nurses's dormitory and take you home on the plane."

"You mean you won't get back here?" Anger choked off her wail. "And who, Mr. Fix-it, will stay with her children? The doctor hasn't even told me when I can leave!"

"Her mother-in-law, Sarah Sutherland, for as long as necessary. She told Meg that she'd love to keep house once again for her eldest son."

"And his four children!" Phoebe sat up as straight as possible. "I'm very fond of Sarah, and it's an incredible offer, but it's beyond the call of duty. I can't let her do it. I'll go home alone."

In spite of the traction machinery, James managed to scoop her into his arms. "The doctor won't let you, dear. Meg and Harris asked his mother together. I had nothing to do with it. They worked it all out and called me with the offer."

Phoebe lay back, stunned. "If you need to go, Meg will carry on well, I know, but darn it, I'd rather have you!"

"I'd rather not go. You know that. Tomorrow, I'll tell you all about the plans, but you've had enough right now. Let's play gin rummy tonight, and we'll double the stakes."

"Suits me," the tremor in Phoebe's voice betrayed her. "On guard. I'm going to wallop the daylights out of you." And she did.

James was right. Meg's arrival two days later was a big shot in the arm. He had a few good days with them before he had to leave. Phoebe would be the last of the Mohicans of the fishing party.

Proudly, she introduced Meg to all her New Zealand friends. James helped his daughter move into the dormitory room. He was given a small room nearby to use until his departure.

James spread out maps to show his women how much more direct his route to Saudi was from New Zealand. "That's why I have more time to be with you two," he explained. "Ben, however, is flying to Saudi by way of San Francisco in order to bring the papers necessary for the meetings there."

Phoebe was sure that James and Meg had nightly planning sessions to ensure a smooth transition. The morning that they gave James a tearful good-bye, Meg pulled out a duffel bag that she had hidden under Phoebe's bed.

"These are presents for everyone who has helped you, the people in the hospital, the guides whom I feel I know well, your doctor, and our good friends, the Watsons. Do you realize that I haven't been back to New Zealand since the year after our wedding, when we were having a delayed honeymoon? We stayed with Jo and Alastair at the beginning of our trip."

"You are a darling to do this," Phoebe said. "When did you ever find time to shop for gifts?"

"I began the minute Daddy phoned me. I had been planning to send you some presents to give away when you left, but after his phone call, I didn't have to mail them."

"Now I understand. The reason you came was to save air express postage!"

Phoebe peeked inside the bag. She saw note pads, picture frames, address books, and some good-looking ties. There was also pretty tissue paper in different colors and assorted ribbons.

"Mamma, this may cut into your writing time because every day now, we'll need to wrap the gifts to be ready when the doctor tells us that you can go home. Keeping the things a surprise will be the hardest part."

"We can try. Do you have *two* duffel bags, one for the finished, one for unfinished? You can take the finished ones back to your room nightly. Life on my bed, as you know, is pretty public. Your tactics are the same as your father's, to keep me so busy that I'll be so contented that I will grow bone fast!"

James telephoned almost every day from Saudi. The connection was much clearer than the Saudi calls were to California. Phoebe suspected that he also talked regularly to the doctor. "If I stay long enough, the hospital may have to install room phones in order to keep employees's work hours under control," Phoebe told Meg.

One New Zealand specialty that Phoebe had heard much about was called Pavlova. It was a yellow cake made with such heavy whipping cream that the plate holding it could be turned upside down. This was the sign of a superb Pavlova.

Bernie Rae sent word that the next time she was coming to the hospital with Harry, to meet Meg, she was bringing a Pavlova. But Blair's wife, who worked in the hospital, beat her to it. Phoebe had two Pavlovas!

A few days later when Peter and Heather came to meet Meg, Peter arrived bearing a rainbow trout from the Mataura River. "I'm going to cook it right here for Mother!" Meg told him.

"How can you manage that?" Peter asked.

"The head orthopedic nurse and I have become good friends. I'll ask her if I can use the nurses's floor kitchen," was Meg's answer. "All she can say is 'no.'"

"You'd better let the hospital kitchen cook it for you," Heather advised.

"Not on your life," Meg said. "A beautiful fish like this deserves one person's complete attention, mine. And I know just how Mother likes it."

And she did. After the Cullens left, Meg scooted between the nurses's kitchen and Phoebe's room all afternoon. When she began to scrounge around in Phoebe's bedside table for paper napkins, her mother knew this must mean that the fish was nearly ready.

Soon after, Meg came in bearing the fish centered on the back of a tray and decorated with sprigs of flowers from Phoebe's bouquets. Phoebe's afternoon nurse followed her with two plates and napkins.

Meg handed the tray to the nurse and served their plate with a towel folded over her arm, like a maitre d'. "Now please take the rest back to the nurses's station, as a gift from Mother."

The fish was delicious, moist but firm. There was a pleasant taste that Phoebe couldn't quite identify. "Meg, you cooked it superbly. I'm sure some way you managed to poach it, but what did you use as the liquid?" she asked.

"Daddy's Scotch!"

During Mr. Willson's next call, he gave Phoebe some welcome news. "I think that your leg is ready for me to examine it in the theatre as soon as an opening is available. My colleagues and I will then decide if we can put a traveling cast on your leg."

"Does that mean I can go home?" Phoebe practically shouted with joy.

"Not so fast. First, it will be necessary for you to have enough therapy so you can function with the cast," he said. "I'll get the therapist to prepare the exercise list soon. "After therapy, we'll discuss when you can fly home. The rest depends on you."

"Does that mean I've grown enough bone?"

"Only enough to tolerate a traveling cast."

"One more question, please, before you leave. What is the theatre? It sounds as though I were going on the stage."

"Sorry. I should have explained. It's the operating room." Mission accomplished, Mr. Willson departed.

"Mom, you've reached the first step of departure. You've done it!" Meg exclaimed. "Daddy's going to be so proud of you! Let's try to finish wrapping the presents before you go to the theatre because after that the therapy with the cast begins."

"Glory be, Meg," Phoebe answered, "It's time to think about tickets home."

"That's under control. The hospital office here and Daddy's secretary at home have been working on the schedules. Your job is to concentrate on the therapy."

The therapist's list came the next day.

Exercises with cast

Balance
Sitting
Getting up from a chair
Crutches
Bathroom

"We'll start on this as soon as the cast is dry," Betsy, the therapist, told Phoebe.

When the doctor announced that the theatre was free the next day, Meg decided to accept Blair's offer to drive her to Queenstown to stay overnight with the Watsons.

"Are you sure you'll be all right, Mother? We've almost finished the wrapping. I'll complete what's left in my room tonight. Blair's wife may drive up with us if she can get the time off. They'll stay overnight with a Queenstown cousin."

"I'm delighted that you will see the Watsons' home and garden, Meg. You'll be fascinated with everything. For instance, the front lawn doubles as the croquet court. The heads of their English mallets are at least sixteen inches long. Isn't it funny the things that stick in your mind?"

The shampoo lady interrupted their conversation. Phoebe told her with pleasure, "This may be my last shampoo here."

The next morning Phoebe went off to the operating room in high spirits, sent off as gaily by Meg and the nurses as though she were going to a party.

She was wheeled into a circle of spotlights surrounded by seats set up like an amphitheater, probably the reason for the room's name. Students were poised to observe, notebooks and pencils ready.

"I feel like Exhibit A," Phoebe murmured, but the many people in masks and gowns were too busy fastening things to her arms and taking her blood pressure and temperature, to listen to her.

An attendant, needle poised, said, "This will hurt for a minute." Phoebe could feel herself drifting into sleep.

She woke up back in her own room, slightly annoyed that she had missed all the action in the theatre. "It's just like our operating room," she told Meredith, the student nurse. She saw that it was now dark outside.

"I'm hungry," she told her. That was the same thing she had said to the emergency room nurse when she and James arrived from Cattle Flat those many long weeks ago. She missed James and Meg badly for a moment.

"I'll see if I can make you a cup of soup," Meredith said, "but I'll have to ask the head nurse first. Our main orders are not to let you move while the cast is drying."

"May I peek at it?"

"I don't see why not."

Like a couple of conspirators, Meredith lifted the covers and they looked in. The white cast was huge, like Moby Dick. Wasn't that the name of the great white whale in Melville's novel about the sea?

After the welcome cup of soup, she was given a sleeping pill by the night nurse. She knew it was to keep her quiet enough so that Moby Dick would dry as fast as possible. She was only the instrument to complete the task.

Phoebe could scarcely wait for Betsy, the therapist, to arrive the next morning. When she arrived, Phoebe's first question was, "May I sit in a chair?"

"Of course. I've ordered one brought in." Betsy was pleased

when she felt the cast. "It's drying nicely. I'll ask the doctor how soon we can get you up on crutches."

Two orderlies arrived immediately with a reclining chair that had a footstool attached to it. They placed it near the window and moved a bedside cupboard beside it. Two nurses swung Phoebe over the side of the bed, while the therapist held Moby Dick. The orderlies lifted Phoebe into the chair.

Meredith stayed to rearrange things for her. Phoebe could now look straight into the hallway. "Oh, it's been so long, Meredith, and now things are happening so fast. Meg will return any minute."

She heard her before she saw her. She was talking to a nurse. Meg's bubbly enthusiasm made everyone within hearing distance smile, including her mother.

She burst into the room. Dropping packages and her purse on the floor, she pulled up a chair by Phoebe. "May I have the first autograph?" she asked, patting the cast.

"With pleasure. An honor. Use my pen. I may have it gilded. This whale of a cast is named Moby Dick."

"Of course. That's logical." Meg autographed Moby Dick with a flourish. "The Watsons send love. I'll tell you all about the visit when we have time. Oh, are we going to be busy! How long can you sit up?"

"Until I need to use the bedpan! Here comes the doctor."

"So, you're starting the steps for your departure," Mr. Willson said and felt along the cast. "You can begin practicing with crutches tomorrow." He began to give instructions to the nurse.

Turning back to Phoebe, he commented, "Now, you needn't look quite so happy. We'll miss you and your daughter and the regular phone calls from your husband. Your hasty departure prevented my wife and me from having you and your daughter for tea."

"It hasn't been exactly hasty. Thank you for your invitation to tea. May I postpone it for a couple of years until we return here for our next fishing trip?"

"Of course. We'll look forward to that. Now, Meg, if I were you, I'd make plane reservations for the middle of next week. I know there's a Wednesday flight from here to Auckland that connects with a Pan Am flight to the States. I'll stop in tomorrow to see how you are doing with crutches."

"Mother," Meg said, burrowing into her travel purse when the doctor left, "here are gift cards that Jo and I shopped for. You make some of them out while I go unpack and run an errand for Alastair Watson." She dipped into the bag again and came up with a small lapboard and a colored flow pen.

Phoebe's gift card notes were constantly interrupted by orthopedic floor visitors who spotted her sitting up in a chair. The first ones were the racing motor cyclists, followed by the chaplain.

The next morning, Phoebe with Meg sitting beside her, began giving out the presents that Meg had brought. She was kept busy adding New Zealand addresses to her notebook.

"From America!" was the constant exclamation when her friends received the gifts. Dear, dear Meg.

Phoebe stayed surprised at how difficult the simplest act became with Moby Dick. Standing and balancing, even with a helping hand, became a triumphant accomplishment.

Cautiously, Phoebe began to try the crutches alone, but she was still awkward, in spite of all her practice. Moby Dick was so much heavier than American casts! Finally, with help, she was able to wobble up and down the hallway, returning calls from friends.

The only exercise that wasn't successful was manipulating the bathroom. Moby Dick was just too big. Even in the largest one on the hall, the nurse needed to add to its depth by putting a screen around it.

Meg checked on the dimensions of an airplane "biffy" and relayed this to the doctor. He decided the only solution was a catheter for the trip home. "What next?" Phoebe groaned.

Soon, Phoebe and Meg were so ready to leave that the hours until Wednesday dragged like tortoises in a race. Phoebe commented one morning, "Pretty soon friends will start saying, 'Still here?'"

But Wednesday finally came. Phoebe in a wheel chair, was loaded into a hospital van that had rear swinging doors. A crowd of hospital well-wishers clustered around her. "There would have been more," said the Emergency head nurse, "but some of your friends on the staff had to stay to run the hospital!"

They drove off amid cheers of the staff. The driver got into the spirit and gave a small bang on the siren. At the airport, faithful Blair Cullen and his wife joined a group from the aluminium office to wave Phoebe off. She was placed on a hoist and lifted aboard the Air New Zealand plane ahead of the other passengers. From this unusual position, Phoebe found it hard to get too sentimental about the departure.

Inside the plane, she and Moby Dick were placed across two seats. Phoebe blessed the nurse who had pressed some hospital pillows into Meg's arms as the van took off.

The forklift operation was repeated in reverse in Auckland. Then they lived through four exhausting hours, waiting for the Pan Am plane. Its wheel chair was narrow enough that the stewardess rolled Phoebe down the aisle to a first class seat in the front.

Meg used a small collapsible footstool that she had bought to extend the footrest for Moby Dick. During the long miles to Hawaii and then on to the Mainland, Phoebe yearned again in vain to be able to indulge in a Victorian faint.

As they were about to start the final approach to San Francisco, a Pan Am attendant came to tell them that Phoebe was to be met by an ambulance.

"By whose orders?" Phoebe roused herself to ask.

The attendant read from his paper, "Dr. Petersen."

"Bless him," Phoebe murmured, too weary to express the enthusiasm she felt.

The ambulance drove directly to the plane to pick up Phoebe. In the ambulance, she whispered to Meg, seated beside her, "We made it."

Soon, through the narrow side windows, Phoebe caught glimpses to the west of the black outline of the Peninsula hills. On the other side, lights of cars that were being driven on the correct side of the road passed them. She was home!

Phoebe was taken directly to her hospital room where she and Meg found family members surrounding the bed. Emily, Phoebe's Woodside daughter, her husband, and their three children smiled in welcome. Behind them Phoebe saw their son Jamie, from Pittsburgh, looming tall and loving.

She stretched out both hands to them all and beckoned to Meg to move closer. "My jewels," she whispered.

A nurse bustled in. So much for sentiment. She was pushing in a contraption that she explained was a portable X-ray machine. What next?

Dr. Petersen followed behind. His fairy-godfather smile indicated his pleasure at having combined a family reunion with a medical examination. "Your husband is phoning here from Saudi Arabia in a few minutes. We'll take X-rays of your broken leg before he calls. I have already reserved the operating room for changing the cast."

Meg handed him the X-rays from New Zealand.

The technician adjusted the X-ray machine over Phoebe's leg while Dr. Petersen studied the New Zealand X-rays. He indicated where he wanted the new pictures shot. Then he ordered everyone out of the room while the X-rays were being taken.

Dr. Petersen left with the operator and the machine. "I'll have a look at these after they are developed and be right back."

The phone rang. Meg ran in from the hall, followed by the rest of the family. She picked up the phone. "Daddy, we're all with Mother in her hospital room. Yes, we made it, with lots of good help. Dr. Petersen is looking at the X- rays right now. He took new ones in this room. Here's Mother."

"James, we made it!. I'm out of traction and I'm home, well, almost. Dr. Petersen had an ambulance waiting for me at the airport. Did it feel good!" Phoebe stopped because the doctor walked in, X-rays in both hands, and reached for the phone.

"Meg," Dr. Petersen instructed, "hold the phone so that your father can hear what I am going to say. Mrs. MacLean, your leg is progressing well, but I'm not going to change the cast. I had hoped to put on a lighter one, the kind that we use, but I don't want to disturb the excellent alignment of the traveling cast."

"How long will the traveling cast need to stay on?" Phoebe heard James ask.

"Several months at least. Before she leaves the hospital, our therapy department will give her exercises to help her handle the heavy New Zealand cast before we let her go home. How long in the hospital? Perhaps ten days. You're welcome. I'm glad you can hear us. Yes, we'll keep a close eye on her. Here is your wife."

"Hi, love. I hear that I'm stuck with this huge cast for several months. I call it Moby Dick. Four months sounds like forever. With the month in traction in New Zealand, that makes one third of a year! Oh, James, I think I've run out of gas. Talk to the others. Good night, dear, come home soon."

James told her, "I'll be home in ten days."

"Not until then? I may beat you home," she managed to say and handed the phone to Jamie.

A nurse came in. "I'll have to ask everyone to leave now," she announced firmly.

"But Mom," said Bo, Emily's young son. "You promised that Grand-Phoebe could open the box from New Zealand that just arrived for her. We brought it down with us because you promised."

The urgency in his voice roused Phoebe. "Nurse," she asked, "please, may they stay just five more minutes. I've been gone from them for a long time. Thanks."

"Are you sure you can last for another moment, Mom?" Emily asked. "The children have been so curious."

Phoebe nodded. The children plunked a heavy brown parcel on top of her. "Come help me," she said.

Thirty strong young fingers attacked the wrappings and tore them open. Emily rescued the name of the sender, "Peter Cullen," from the growing mound of brown paper.

The children exposed a handsome piece of varnished wood. In

the middle of the plank, a clever taxidermist had mounted a fish, a brown trout. He was arched as if ready to jump. Underneath was a small brass plaque.

"Is he real?" asked a child.

"Is he yours?" asked another.

"Read the plaque, Emily, please," Phoebe told their daughter, "before I fall asleep and miss the surprise."

Emily read,

THE INCIDENT BROWN TROUT

ALSO A COUNTER

LANDED FROM THE MATAURA RIVER

CATTLE FLAT, NEW ZEALAND

BY

PHOEBE MACLEAN

MARCH 23, 1982

EPILOGUE

EACH FISHING TRIP is a tapestry that weaves its own story. Two years after the 'incident trout' trip, the MacLeans joined the Holcombs and the Sergeants to fish again in New Zealand.

These biannual trips have continued, as have other fishing trips. The most recent New Zealand one was in the spring of 1990, which is early autumn there. Peter Cullen, his brother Blair, and Harry Rae guided for them. There are plans in the making for a trip in February, 1992.

Sometime the Mataura is high and colored from rains upstream. Sometime the fishing is superb, sometime it is slow. The wind may blow, the rains may come, but mostly, the sun in the blue sky laced with white clouds perseveres.

The patterns of clouds in the sky and of sheep in the paddocks are constantly the same and yet constantly different. "Shouldn't we occasionally try another New Zealand fishing stream?" Phoebe once suggested.

"But why change?" asked her satisfied, logical husband.

On second thought, Phoebe agreed.

DESIGN AND COMPOSITION: *Wilsted & Taylor*

TEXT TYPEFACE: *Granjon*

DISPLAY TYPEFACE: *Nicholas Cochin Black*

PRINTING AND BINDING: *Malloy Lithographing, Inc.*